Praise for the book

This is a 40-year journey from secular to Hindutva.

You need to cross a certain mental Lakshman Rekha in order to call yourself a Sanghi, given the negative associations the label attracts in 'secular' media. But Rahul Roushan has never been afraid to put himself out on a limb in his voyage of self-discovery and pursuit of political incorrectness.

He has repeatedly been in the line of 'secular' fire for calling out their hypocrisies, first in *Faking News*, a satirical portal, and later in OpIndia.com, the digital platform he was instrumental in founding. In this book, Roushan mixes the personal with the political to document both the nation's and his own journey away from Nehruvian secularism to Hindutva.

It encompasses 30 tumultuous years of the Republic, starting with the first stirrings of change in Hindu society after the Mandal agitation and the movement to build a Ram Temple in Ayodhya, and culminating in the rise of Narendra Modi as Bharat's prime minister.

Today, many Hindus no longer see Hindutva as a communal slur, just as Rahul no longer sees the term Sanghi as a handicap, even though he has no illusions about the RSS's strengths and shortcomings. Many Indians have become covert or partial Sanghis; that is, they are in the process of rediscovering their Indic roots.

This book is a must-read for anyone who wants to understand changing India, and emerging Hindutva.

—**R. Jagannathan (Jaggi)**, senior journalist and
Editorial Director, *Swarajya* magazine

Years ago when I came across *Faking News*, I was struck by the sheer ingenuity and audacity of the person behind this digital spoof show, which took the mickey out of the mainstream media for its predictable, biased and often silly coverage of politics and personalities in India. Curiosity made me seek him out.

That first meeting was revelatory. I had expected a brash young man with an in-your-face attitude. Rahul turned out to be soft-spoken, polite, more of a listener than a speaker and had a beguiling smile. I have closely followed his work since then, especially his tireless efforts to create an alternative, Right-of-Centre platform for news and views.

The story he tells in this book helps readers understand the amazing rise of Narendra Modi, first as CM of Gujarat and now as PM of India, and why he is so crazily popular among the masses.

It explains why and how pink champagne Nehruvian socialism died, taking down along with it the Indian faux liberal elite's over-vaulting sense of entitlement. It offers a post-mortem report on the causes that led to the unmourned demise of pseudo-secularism and the loud clamour in its wake for the recognition of Hindu rights.

SANGHI
WHO NEVER WENT TO A
SHAKHA

RAHUL ROUSHAN

RUPA

First published by
Rupa Publications India Pvt. Ltd 2021
7/16, Ansari Road, Daryaganj
New Delhi 110002

Sales Centres:
Allahabad Bengaluru Chennai
Hyderabad Jaipur Kathmandu
Kolkata Mumbai

ISBN: 978-93-90547-66-1

Tenth impression 2022

15 14 13 12 11 10

The moral right of the author has been asserted.

Printed at Repro India Limited, India

To Shaili,
for supporting me, for tolerating me

Contents

Contents

Foreword

There are explicit dangers in writing the foreword of a book by a 'woke' turned 'Sanghi' like Rahul Roushan as there are no assurances that he would not turn his blazing guns at you on a subject he is most passionate about—Bharat. Recognizing the hazards, I still brave the same.

From 'making news' as the creator of *Faking News* to becoming news by establishing OpIndia as one of the most celebrated online news portals, Rahul's journey as a man of independent thought has come a full circle.

This book analyses events that have impacted Rahul over the years while contextualizing the political and ideological shifts. Rahul goes back into his own past to understand the paradox of why and how the prejudices and biases against anything and everything connected to the word 'Hindu' proudly existed in a deeply religious nation during the Congressi Raj. True to his nature, he does not shy away from admitting to his own such biases.

This book also contains dissent, disagreements and, at times, his negation of certain issues that people presume Rahul holds dear, given his ideology.

From his days at IIM Ahmedabad to him feeling offended at being called a 'Sanghi', Rahul's embrace of the Sanghi label post BJP's 2014 victory and its reasons mirror the change that millions of Indians have undertaken.

His exasperation with the Sangh Parivar for always downplaying their social and public welfare activities has made way for a calm understanding of why the Sangh operates the way it does and how it has dedicated itself to 'Vyakti nirman' and 'Samajik samrasta'.

While one would believe that this book is autobiographical in nature and exalts Rahul's life journey, to me this is a story of the coming of age of an average Indian who dared to break the shackles of a Nehruvian past and contribute to creating a New India.

Smriti Irani
1 December 2020

Introduction

It was sometime in 2012—when the anti-corruption movement led by Anna Hazare had inspired a section of the urban Indian youth to find a renewed interest in the state of affairs and politics of the nation—when I was first called a 'Sanghi' by someone.

Those were times when Facebook and Twitter were fast emerging as the new tools of building the political narrative. Riding on this new wave of social media, and with active help even from the mainstream media, Anna had momentarily changed the landscape of national politics. At that time, I was better known as *Faking News*—the Indian news satire website I had founded and later sold off to Network18—opining on politics and society through humour and satire, and sometimes in all seriousness as well.

My ideological leanings were not really a secret in those days. Although I was not vocal about my beliefs, those who understood ideological nuances knew very well that I was anything but Left-leaning, especially when it came to economic and political matters.

For various reasons, but primarily due to their pretentious intellectual snobbery, I didn't like the leftists, and that reflected in my writings to an extent. Actually, earlier in 2010, I, as Pagal Patrakar—the pseudonym I used for myself while writing for *Faking News*—had written an open letter to Arundhati Roy, which was more of a rant to be honest, but which went viral, earning me some new fans—obviously, 'Right wing' fans.

That was also the first time when I got hate messages from random strangers in the virtual world. Those abusing me were committed leftists, who fanatically believed that any form of art, including satire, must conform to their worldview to qualify as being a legitimate form of art. They saw me 'misusing' my art and the platform to 'hurt the cause'.

Somehow the leftists had acquired the rights to decide how the website that I built from my own money should be run. Only later I would realize that my website was just a small fish; leftists believe they have a right to decide how even Google or Facebook should be run, and that these big tech companies would even surrender to their whims and fancies!

Anyway, back then I was taken aback by both my newly gained haters and fans. The condescending and patronizing messages from the leftists, if not downright abusive and insulting, made me dislike them even more. But I continued to identify myself as 'libertarian' rather than 'Right wing' in terms of my ideological leanings for years to come.

Being libertarian meant being fiscally conservative and socially liberal. However, the 'socially liberal' part of it, in my case, didn't mean that I identified or pledged myself to be radically at odds with tradition or culture. I was just tired of this 'liberal' habit of linking every vice in the Indian society to some aspect of the Hindu culture and religion. As a satire writer, I found it more challenging and satisfying to explore new narratives and not use the same old template—blame Hindus and Hinduism—to offer a critique.

My soft corner for Hinduism was not the result of being born in any deeply religious family. In fact, my father gave me (and my brother) a perfect 'secular' upbringing. He bought us books in Hindi on Islamic philosophy, and a statue of Jesus Christ adorned our living room when we were growing up. We celebrated Hindu festivals and took part in puja-aarti only to the extent an average Hindu household would.

My affinity towards Hinduism wasn't borne out of any affiliation to a common interest group either. I have never been a member of organizations such as Ramakrishna Mission, ISKCON or the Art of Living. Neither was it an outcome of something as harmless as having tried some yogaasans suggested by Baba Ramdev (remember, this was pre-2014, when yoga was not hated as stemming out of 'Hindutva').

Affiliation to any political group was simply out of the question. I was no doubt interested in politics, but only as much as I was interested in cricket—a passionate follower and fan with no intention or skills of becoming a player.

So what made me feel like a Hindu?

It was just a strong sense of belonging, a sense of inheritance, a part of my identity handed over to me by my parents, a link that connected me to the larger society. I saw Hinduism in my roots. I saw it as a bond that I shared with others. I felt no need to attack it or declare it as the root cause of all problems which troubled me as an individual or us as a society—something that the Left loves to do, and something that unintelligently is adopted by those wanting to be identified as 'socially liberal' and 'progressive'.

Perhaps this reluctance to attack Hinduism, apart from my dislike for the likes of Arundhati Roy, is what made me appear 'Right wing' to many committed leftists. However, my self-image was that of a libertarian. I found the term Right wing a pejorative, thanks to how it was perceived in popular parlance—a term meant to denote a bunch of obscurantist killjoys.

I would block anyone who added me to any Twitter list that was named 'Right wingers' or 'RW handles' or something similar, so that I end up not being on that list. Names of lists to which a Twitter user is added by anyone are visible on that user's public profile. I didn't want that label on my profile. I wanted to be seen just as a witty funny guy who is politically aware. If not a leftist, then not a Right-winger either.

I was scared of labels. Much later I would realize that that is how the Left wins the narrative war. They control the labels, which are the crucial weapons in this war. It is they who decide who is an activist or a scholar or a liberal, and who is a goon or a troll or a fascist. You are expected to live a life yearning to earn the right kind of label from them, and by corollary, you are in constant fear of being stuck with the wrong label.

One label that I was very much scared of was—Sanghi.

So, I didn't take it kindly when sometime in 2012, on Twitter, I saw someone claiming that I was most likely a member of the Rashtriya Swayamsevak Sangh (RSS), executing some secret project under the garb of humour and satire through *Faking News*.

I could as well have found it funny, because during those days even the Anna movement was alleged to be sponsored by the RSS. Actually, at least on this criterion, I shouldn't have been called a Sanghi because I never went all out supporting the Anna movement. While I appreciated and even marvelled at the kind of public support the movement attracted, I had written satirical articles and made many comments on social media that questioned the idealism of the whole Jan Lokpal movement. I was largely unimpressed by it even before the movement got 'Kejriwalled.'

Let me come back to the Sanghi label before I digress again.

As a policy, I try not to get affected by random personal comments made on the internet. I had realized the importance of insulating oneself against unsolicited online feedback quite early. But this 'allegation' of me being a Sanghi was made by someone during a conversation with another Twitter account I used to regularly interact with; so, I happened to take note of it. That Twitter account also professed libertarian ideology and we would often agree on many issues.

After blocking the guy who called me Sanghi, even though I was tagged nowhere in the tweets, I sent a DM (direct message) to my libertarian Twitter buddy. I protested, saying that by interacting with someone who had called me a Sanghi, he had unwittingly become a party to my 'character assassination.'

At this point of time I don't really remember if that libertarian guy took any corrective actions, such as deleting his tweets or sending another reply to that random guy to calm my frayed tempers down, but I clearly remember that not so long back, being labelled a 'Sanghi' would upset and anger me, and that I would term it as 'character assassination.'

Today, I write a book where I have labelled myself with that term, happily.

This book is to recount the journey, which began much earlier than 2012, that subconsciously shaped my ideological preferences. It narrates various incidents from my life that would explain the reasons why I decided to be vocal about my ideological beliefs and not care about the label 'Sanghi' anymore. In fact, the bulk of the book is about why it took me so long to be comfortable with that label.

It is, however, not an autobiography. While it is my story, I believe it is also the story of millions of others, which can help explain why the socio-political landscape of India has changed.

I have tried to retell the story of my childhood, teenage and youth, with a new way of looking at things that I came to acquire only after I was in my mid-30s, which incidentally also coincides with the rise of Narendra Modi on the national stage.

With Modi returning to power with an even bigger majority in the

2019 Lok Sabha elections, there has been an ongoing debate regarding whether India has 'fundamentally changed'. The shade and spread of this debate are often ideological, with people wondering if the long established 'idea of India'—epitomized by Nehruvian secularism—has been replaced with Hindutva, a term popularly identified with politics and philosophies of the RSS. The new India appears to have embraced Hindutva; and incidentally Modi himself talks about making a 'New India'.

If India has indeed fundamentally changed, it means Indians have changed. People who might not have identified themselves with the RSS earlier are now supporting and voting for Modi, and by extension, people are no longer treating Hindutva as anathema. Ideally, the debate should be about this change, and about the circumstances and factors that made people change their beliefs or at least their attitude towards Hindutva politics.

Unfortunately, the debate in the established circles is still around Modi, or around the BJP and the RSS, not about the people. If at all the focus of the debate shifts towards people, it is only to berate and malign the people who have changed, instead of understanding what brought this change in them.

My story is about this change. It is the story about someone who had no idea about the RSS, who never found this organization highly appealing and who is still not a member of the RSS, but now he has no problem in being identified as a Sanghi.

This book is thus a memoir of a Sanghi who never went to any shakha.

Before I start telling my story, I want to make it clear that the dictionary meanings and standard definitions of the two words—secular and liberal—are very different from the way they are used and understood in India. In this book, I will be using them in a fashion they are employed in popular parlance, especially in political circles.

It doesn't mean that I am comfortable with these words being twisted to mean something else, but I'll stick to the popular or corrupted usage. Because if I don't, typography and syntax will be ugly, as I will need to put quotes on these terms to signal my discomfort every time I use them. So please imagine quotes on these terms at appropriate places!

Take, for example, secularism. Without getting into the history of how it was born, the term secularism primarily refers to the policy of separation of the church and state. It advocates that the state shouldn't care about or interfere in religious affairs; basically, religion is none of state's business.

However, the Indian state cares and interferes a lot in religious matters. The Constitution has various articles that take into account religious identities, and we have multitudes of laws that revolve around religious identities and even feelings. The goddess of justice in courts is supposed to be blind, but in reality, she is staring at religions all the time.

One may claim that while the Indian state is not blind to religions, it is also not biased. However, this doesn't happen in practice. There are multiple examples, such as rulings about animal sacrifice, where principles were applied differently when it came to Hinduism (as compared to how they were applied when dealing with Abrahamic faiths). Further, the Constitution of India gives special rights to religious minorities, allowing them to run and control their own educational and religious institutions and affairs while denying the same rights to Hindus. Temple money and properties virtually becomes public assets while Waqf properties are reserved only for Muslims. At the core of it, the secular state of India discriminates against Hindus by assuming that they can never be disadvantaged.

What can be more farcical than the fact that Hindus are denied minority status even in states where they are numerically weak? Everyone sings paeans to the 'federal structure' enshrined in the Constitution of India, which is invoked regularly to demand more and more decentralization of power and policies because different states of India are unique in their own ways. Local history, local economics, local customs, local language, local flora and fauna are all cited as reasons why some laws and policies can't be uniform, but one is required to turn a blind eye to local demography if minority status for Hindus is demanded in a few states where they indeed are in minority. Suddenly, the federal structure concept is junked and India becomes a monolith union, just to deny Hindus their rights. This is how 'secular' India is.

Let us leave aside legal or technical definition of secularism as a state policy, and come to its generic meaning. The dictionary definition of the word secular is 'not having any connection with religion'; in other words, it is 'irreligious'. But in India, every secular act or belief is connected with religion. Politicians wearing the Muslim skullcap or organizing Iftaar parties during Eid were your quintessential 'secular' acts until Narendra Modi changed the rules of the game.

Some have argued that Indian secularism is not about being irreligious or anti-religious, but it is a virtue of giving equal respect to all religions—a stupid impractical concept to begin with, because some religions simply don't believe in this business of mutual respect—but even that fanciful version has got corrupted over decades. Currently, being secular means giving respect to all religions except Hinduism.

Similarly, being liberal and the definition of liberalism have been corrupted in India. Ideally, a liberal person is one who supports individual freedom and bats for equal rights for everyone. He is also accommodative of dissenting views. But a liberal in India is willing to be liberal only with people who don't assertively identify themselves as Hindus.

If you identity yourself as a non-Hindu claiming to be resisting the 'Hindu majoritarianism' in any manner, even your slogans, such as 'Afzal hum sharminda hain, tere qaatil zinda hain'—which basically is a war cry for the murder of a judge who awarded capital punishment to the terrorist Afzal Guru (the way Jammu & Kashmir High Court Judge Neelkanth Ganjoo was murdered for having awarded capital punishment to the terrorist Maqbool Bhat)—is counted as free speech that should be allowed. But if you are a Hindu, even a greeting such as 'Jai Shri Ram' is termed a war cry that should be disallowed. Forget accommodating dissenting voices, the 'liberals' in India frequently throw labels—such as Sanghi, bigot, fascist—at dissenting voices to discredit and silence them.

Most of the guys claiming to be liberals in India are essentially leftists, who are ashamed to admit it or clueless people who have not yet understood how the leftist propaganda works. And those who are shameless call themselves Left-liberals, which is the most frequently used oxymoron in the entire world.

Since we are dealing with definitions here, let me also make it clear that the term 'leftists' has been used globally to refer to a range of people who could be socialists, communists or even anarchists. But here I am largely referring to the communists, who have camouflaged themselves into outfits such as student organizations and a motley of 'Rights groups,' and are also active in academia and media. The day the Left starts winning elections outside a few universities in India, all these guys will come out of the closet, rather come out of the bunker, and join the revolution where rivers of blood flow to colour the world in shades they love.

On the 'other side' of these terms, I should also make it clear that I have used the term 'Hindutva' in this book in the way it's perceived in popular parlance. Hindutva is supposed to be a political doctrine that was developed by Veer Savarkar in the early twentieth century. However, this is not true. Hindutva literally means Hindu-ness, or the essence of being Hindu. Primarily, it is a set of common identifiers among all the Hindus. The term as well as the philosophy behind it existed much before Savarkar popularized it in the twentieth century. It is important to note that Hindutva is not something that is distinct from Hinduism. It is veritably the definition of Hinduism.

Since many decades, the objective of the 'liberal' project has been to deny that something like 'Hinduism' even exists. There are theories arguing that Hindus didn't have any common identity until they came in contact with Abrahamic religions, which set foot in India in the form of invaders or preachers. Indigenous customs and communities of India are increasingly defined as distinct and 'non-Hindu' entities. In fact, most communities are encouraged to identify themselves as non-Hindu, with alternative and imaginary histories. The entire exercise reeks of attempts to ensure the Balkanization of India, even though it is dressed up as some scholarly pursuit.

Hindutva is the antithesis of such theories and contentions. It shows how a common identity was always there, since the ancient times. It explains how Hinduism is not any 'negative identity' that developed only after the Islamic invaders came to India. It defines the essence of being a Hindu. It defines Hindu-ness, and that is Hindutva, literally.

Hindutva is not really a 'political arm' of Hinduism, the way many believe the term to denote. However, I myself will use Hindutva with that connotation, that is, to refer to political awareness and political movements that were inspired from Hindutva. So you see, I'm at least being impartial in sticking to the corrupted usage of the terms on both sides of the ideological divide! On that note, yes, even the use of the term 'Right wing' will be loose and as understood in the common language.

And finally, when I mean Sanghi, unless otherwise explicitly mentioned that I am talking about members of the RSS, I would mostly be using this term to mean anyone who is seen or labelled as Sanghi by people who are 'secular' and 'liberal'.

I am sure that many events, many observations and many emotions in this book will strike a chord with millions who would have undergone similar journeys, especially the generation that was born and grew up in the 1980s and around.

Thanks for picking it up.

1

Pa-loo-ral and kaal-ph

A candid friendship

Yeh teri meri yaari, yeh dosti humaari,
Bhagwaan ko pasand hai, Allah ko hai pyaari

The above two lines are from a song from the Bollywood movie *Daata*, and it finds a special place in my memory when I try to recall incidents from my childhood. No, I am not exactly a fan of Mithun Chakraborty, who was the 'hero' in this movie, which released in 1989, neither is this song sung by Kumar Sanu, whom I loved to imitate in my boyhood.

The song stayed with me only due to its lyrics and picturization. *Daata* literally means 'the giver'—an agnostic term that can be used for god, especially in a literary way. The song was sung, on screen, by two characters in the movie who are friends, one a Hindu and the other a Muslim, played by Mithun Chakraborty and Suresh Oberoi, respectively. In the song, they are averring that their friendship is loved both by Allah and Bhagwaan—terms used for god in Islam and Hinduism, respectively. And it could well be a coincidence, but the playback singers are also a Hindu–Muslim duo—Suresh Wadkar and Mohammed Aziz. So secular!

The song reminds me of my school days, of my first school, of my first friends. It also reminds me why it is so easy to be a secular and not a Sanghi for a common Hindu, unless they are born in Sanghi families.

I was born in Patna, the capital city of Bihar, but grew up in a place called Bihar Sharif in Nalanda district of the state, where my father was employed as a professor of English literature in a government college.

Those were the Rajiv Gandhi and later V.P. Singh years. In fact, it's better to call them the Lalu (Lalu Prasad Yadav) years as we are talking of Bihar. These years revolved around the mid- and the late 1980s, which saw the Punjab militancy, Indira Gandhi's assassination, Rajiv Gandhi's unprecedented parliamentary majority and finally, the birth of the Mandal and mandir politics. I was too young when Indira Gandhi was assassinated, though I do blurrily recall having watched bits of her funeral procession on a colour TV, which one of our better-off relatives had. Yes, that was also the decade when colour TV came to India, and it was a status symbol to have one.

That brief encounter with a colour TV had happened in Patna in 1984, and around the same time my family moved to Bihar Sharif, a small suburban region some 80 km away from the capital city of Bihar, but a different universe altogether, as are usually the neighbourhoods of most cities in India. Shrilal Shukla in his novel *Raag Darbari* had put this so succinctly in Hindi—*Shahar ka kinaara. Usye chhodte hi Bharatiya dehaat ka mahasaagar shuru ho jaata tha* (the ocean of Indian villages begins as soon as you leave the borders of a city).

Bihar Sharif was not exactly a village though, in the sense that the main occupation of the residents was not farming. Most of them were small traders, daily wage labourers or people engaged in other small jobs, who dreamt of getting a government job. It was more of a small town.

Our family was comparatively well-off even though we didn't own a colour TV. We bought a Weston portable Black & White TV after settling in a rented house next to what was supposed to be a bypass or a highway, though it was just a 6-ft wide coal-tar-coated pathway flanked by a foot or two of kachcha road on both sides. One can only imagine what the lanes inside the town would be like.

Some months down the line, an LML Vespa scooter, which looked more stylish than the 'Hamara Bajaj' scooters, was also proudly owned by us to navigate those lanes. A few years further down the line, we even had a refrigerator, which fascinated me and all the kids in the neighbourhood, as it gave us small pieces of ice that we would otherwise see only during a hailstorm.

In the language of someone 'woke', who probably was living in an air-conditioned house and moving around in a Premier Padmini on the roads of Delhi while growing up in those years, I was enjoying a 'privileged' life.

My father could earn enough to buy a two-wheeler for his four-member nuclear family not because government college employees were paid well, but because in the evenings or early mornings, outside of his working hours, he offered private tuition classes to Bihari students who were perennially scared of English. Learning English was considered more important than acquiring any other knowledge or skill. My father was a professor of literature, but the students would understand literature only if they understood the language, so for all practical purposes he was just an 'English teacher.'

Biharis don't spend much; we like saving money and spend only on necessities. Spending on something like tourism could be seen as criminal waste of money by Biharis, at least in those times. But spending on education is seen both as a necessity as well as an investment—a mindset and emotion unfortunately exploited and abused by some Bihari students, who choose to remain students, living off their parents' money, even after getting into their 30s.

My father could earn extra money as people were willing to spend extra money on education. He also offered free tuitions to some students who came from families that were not so well-off. One such student, the son of a carpenter, taught me how to ride a bicycle while my father would teach him English. Perhaps that was his gurudakshina.

My father's tuition classes were so much in demand that he had to turn down many students, as our rented house couldn't accommodate all those batches. And he needed time for us too. But yes, he toiled hard to give us a privileged life, at least when compared to the neighbourhood we resided.

Behind the house where we lived, there was an empty piece of land, smaller than an acre, which was used for farming, while our immediate neighbouring buildings were either small kachcha houses or huts, occupied by a few carpenters. There were pucca buildings too, interspersing such small houses and huts.

Bihar Sharif had—and it continues to have—a significant Muslim population. There were many pockets that were entirely Muslim-dominated. The rented house we lived in was in an area that was not too distant from one such pocket.

I went to a school that was next to a mosque. It had many Muslim students too. It was a private school, though was ironically named 'Public School.'

Although I don't remember the curriculum, the Nursery class in my school clearly was not where you would get toys to play with or new games to learn. We were taught letters of the alphabet, some rhymes and basic arithmetic. Nursery was basically Class I, while the school offered education up to Class VII, which for some reason they named 'Standard IV.'

The only other thing I recall from Nursery class is a girl who terrorized me. It was a co-ed school and she sat next to me on the same bench. One day she tore my notebook and scratched my hands with her nails. I hope she is currently a feminist.

I so vividly remember the school, even now, that I can draw on a paper the map of the school. I still remember which classes were on the ground floor, in which corner was the room from where you could collect some balls or rings to play during the tiffin break and how the stairs went up to the first floor, where classes for Class V–VII were held. Kids studying on the first floor felt 'senior' to those on the ground floor, where they descended only during tiffin breaks, if required. They didn't need to, as there was a terrace on the first floor to have lunch or play during the breaks, but a bigger playground was downstairs.

I remember that this playground was L-shaped and it always appeared dry and brownish yellow. I can't recall any patches of green on it. The boundary wall of the mosque led to the L-shape of the ground. The playground of the school would become a parking area for trucks after school hours, and possibly that's why no grass grew there.

The school conducted morning prayers, where Saraswati Vandana was sung daily, and I don't recall any Muslim kid opting out of it. Around 10 years later, when I moved back to Patna to get enrolled in a high school, and when there was cable TV in India, I witnessed on TV how Saraswati Vandana created a controversy at an event headed by the then HRD Minister Murli Manohar Joshi during the Vajpayee government. It was termed a 'communal act' by the opposition and the intelligentsia.

A couple of Urdu prayers were also recited in our school. I especially remember *Lab pe aati hai dua ban ke tamanna meri*, which I later discovered was a poem written by Allama Iqbal, as a child's prayer to the Islamic god—the same Iqbal who gave intellectual support to the idea of two-nation theory and the creation of Pakistan. This prayer is a common prayer in the morning assemblies of schools in Pakistan, and I, too, grew up singing it.

I don't know if my school still exists, and if it does, whether the Saraswati Vandana is still sung in the morning assembly. I highly doubt it. Even if no Muslim families might have any issues with Saraswati Vandana—which I also doubt given how things have changed since those days—someone from the secular political camp and intelligentsia will ask the school to stop forcing Hindutva on children. Though I'm sure they'd allow Iqbal's prayer to continue, for Iqbal is secular.

Anything in Urdu is secular. Anything in Sanskrit is Hindutva.

But no Hindutva—as defined by those who instinctively hate the term—was forced upon us by the daily recital of Saraswati Vandana back then, else my favourite song from those years would not be about Allah and Bhagwan loving the friendship between a Hindu and a Muslim.

The *Yeh teri meri yaari* song was the anthem of my friendship. I used to sing it with a friend of mine, whom I had decided to make my best friend. He was a Muslim. I remember this song entirely because of him.

Those were the days when you used to have just one best friend and not BFFs. You could additionally have a pen friend too, if your parents were rich enough to spend money on buying a few international envelopes—the ones with striped red and blue borders—after you spot a newspaper ad of some pen-friends club. My parents were neither that rich nor did I feel the need to have a pen friend, as I was happy with my best friend.

Our friendship was rather short-lived as I had to leave Bihar Sharif to get enrolled in a high school in Patna. We must have been friends for barely two or three years, because the vague visions of only the first floor of the school come to my mind when I try to recall him; so our friendship must have started only after we were in the 'higher' classes, where for some weird reason, boys and girls were seated on different benches despite everyone being a pre-teen. But I was happy to sit among the boys, because sitting next to a girl wasn't really a happy experience earlier. My best friend sat next to me.

I still remember his name—Ragib Ahmed. We must have been around 9 or 10 years old then, a guess confirmed by the release year of the movie *Daata*. Funnily, I have not watched this movie till date.

Watching a movie in those times was an experience and challenge in itself. Challenge not just because I was a kid, but because we had to wait for weeks for a new movie to arrive in the local cinema halls of Bihar Sharif. Radio and audio cassettes would bring you songs from a newly released movie almost immediately, but the movie would take time to arrive as physical prints of the movies were limited. And if a movie was a hit, that is, if it was celebrating silver or golden jubilees in cinema halls, it meant that its prints were stuck in bigger cities like Patna. In small towns, sometimes one had to wait for months before a new movie came to a cinema hall. If one did not want to wait, one needed to buy a bus ticket to Patna.

This is one of the reasons why video cassettes of movies, mostly pirated and stuffed with random animated ads at the bottom of the screen, used to be in high demand in those days. There was no satellite TV then, and Doordarshan would play movies that were some three generations old. This made VCP (video cassette player) a vital part of an entertainment ecosystem, which was pretty diverse and deep, though a bit disorganized, before digital technologies disrupted the entire chain. Owning a VCP was as much a status symbol as owning a colour TV.

So, once a movie released and you were in a place like Bihar Sharif, you either had to board a bus to Patna or watch it via a video cassette, which was most probably illegally recorded in a cinema hall of Patna. If one didn't do either, they had to wait until the print arrived in local cinema halls. But who waits for so long, or as Ghalib said, *kaun jeeta hai teri zulf ke sar hone tak.*

There was, however, a third option if you didn't want to take a bus or hire a pirated VHS (video home system) cassette—read the movie! There used to be short books titled after Bollywood movies. These books were hardly 30–40 pages thick, if I recall correctly, with the story narrated as it appeared on screen. They were not screenplays though, but similar to short novels, with scenes and dialogues narrated in a very simple and summarized way. They also contained full lyrics of the songs in the movie.

I don't know who wrote and published those books, rather booklets, but I'm sure they were not part of any official merchandise. Such movie booklets were sold in book stalls outside the cinema halls, where they would also sell popular magazines, newspapers, 'special' magazines such as *Sachchi Kahaaniyas* and *Dafa 302*—containing real-life stories about sex and crime, respectively—and popular novels of Ved Prakash Sharma, along with Hindi translation of James Hadley Chase's novels.

Since I couldn't watch the movie, and couldn't have travelled to Patna alone as a 9-year old, I bought the *Daata* booklet. It had the movie poster as its cover page. Such booklets had colourful covers and back pages to attract the reader's attention, but it was completely boring—at least for a young boy—with black-and-white pages inside. But all I wanted was the story of the movie and lyrics of that song, which I thought was the anthem of my friendship with Ragib.

That was one of the first non-comic books I ever bought as a young boy, if not THE first book. Later my father, who to his horror saw me reading about a Mithun Chakraborty film, would take me to a proper book shop and buy me 'meaningful' books, such as the biographies of Subhash Chandra Bose and Bhagat Singh in non-fiction, *Akbar-Birbal* in fiction and *101 Rochak Tathya* (101 interesting facts) as infotainment.

I liked reading books, and I liked talking to my friend Ragib too; internet has ruined both the habits now. We used to sit next to each other in class. Ah, I recall I was not a backbencher before I shifted to the high school in Patna, where I became a backbencher because of late admission, and later by choice. We also visited each other's homes. I remember he didn't like his neighbour, who also happened to be from a Muslim family, because he lived in those Muslim pockets of Bihar Sharif. A girl from the same family studied in our class. I didn't like that girl simply because he did not like her.

The *Daata* song has a stanza that talks about how the (Hindu-Muslim) friendship of Mithun Chakraborty and Suresh Oberoi shines in the lamps lit during Diwali. I remember having asked my friend to visit my home on Diwali, but he couldn't. The next day in school, he claimed that though he didn't join me for the celebrations, he remembered me on Diwali. He said he had even shouted my name from his roof but I couldn't have heard as loud Diwali crackers were being burst in the city. He could well be joking about shouting my name, but I believed him.

There was no reason to disbelieve.

I was a child so well raised around the ideas of secularism that my Diwali had to have a Muslim element. Such ideas were propagated by the mass media, which shaped the thinking of people in those days.

People—both on the Left and Right side of the ideological divide— often claim that the *Ramayana* TV serial being aired on Doordarshan inadvertently neutralized the state-sponsored secularism, which is essentially about diluting, disregarding, disowning and finally disparaging your Hindu roots.

The rise of Hindutva politics is also often tied to the airing of *Ramayana*, which has apparently helped the BJP become a major political player on the national stage. It is believed that the proposal of the serial had to face resistance from some ideologically committed bureaucrats, who claimed that the public broadcaster of a secular state shouldn't air anything remotely religious (when it comes to Hinduism, the definition of secularism suddenly adopts its western form).

While I do find some merit in the argument that *Ramayana* played a part in the socio-political history of India, I think the claimed ideological or political effects of the serial are exaggerated. I am more inclined to believe that since the Left was dumbfounded by the success of Advani's Ram Rath Yatra, they somehow blamed it on a TV serial, just like the Left in the US blamed it on the social media, especially Facebook, after being dumbfounded by the victory of Donald Trump in 2016.[1]

In both the cases, the Right too gleefully accepted the respective hypotheses, for it made them feel good about having registered a victory and having outfoxed the Left in using tools of communication. While *Ramayana* as well as Facebook were undoubtedly catalysts in respective cases, they were not the reasons for the rise of an Advani or a Trump.

The Rath Yatra was undertaken by Advani in 1990 while the telecast of *Ramayana* was already over by 1988. Two years is a long time in Indian politics. If *Ramayana* would have caused an upsurge in Hindutva sentiments, then the BJP should have seen a huge jump in vote share in the ensuing 1989 Lok Sabha elections, which was closer to the serial being aired. It is a fact that the BJP jumped from two Lok Sabha seats in 1984 to 85 seats in the 1989 Lok Sabha elections, but the vote share that it got did not see any huge jump.

The BJP got a little over 11 per cent of national votes in 1989, and that too when it fought the elections in tactical alliance with V.P. Singh's Janata Dal, where both parties benefitted from each other's support base. This number is not a huge improvement if we consider the fact that other pro-Hindu parties, such as the Bharatiya Jan Sangh (the predecessor of BJP) and Akhil Bharatiya Ram Rajya Parishad, could together muster around 8-9 per cent vote share regularly in the Lok Sabha elections of the 1960s and 70s.[2]

Therefore, one can claim that 8-9 per cent of the Indian electorate were always Sanghis. The *Ramayana*—if it alone were making people Sanghi and warm up to the BJP—could impact a maximum of 3 per cent of the voting population, which is nowhere near the big political impact it is supposed to have created.

The BJP jumped to over 20 per cent vote share only in the 1991 Lok Sabha elections, by when Doordarshan had also aired *The Sword of Tipu Sultan*, glorifying the eighteenth-century Muslim ruler of Mysore as a great patriot who had respect and tolerance for Hindus, when in reality there are numerous instances of the sultan persecuting his Hindu subjects and destroying Hindu temples.[3] Basically, the vote swings, especially of the BJP, don't match the assumed impact of any TV serial.

While a weekly TV serial might have reminded a few of their Hindu identity—if at all one buys the ludicrous leftist theory that the popularity of Lord Ram was as a result of a TV serial, as if no one knew about Ramayana before it aired on TV—every other popular form of entertainment, including weekly TV serials, periodically kept reminding them that a good Hindu must live as a family and friend of a Muslim.

If you had Ramanand Sagar's *Ramayana*, you also had Sultan Ahmed's *Daata*.

Often, more than the parents, it is the education system and the mass media that raise children. This is especially true of Hindu families, as running educational institutions with the primary aim of protecting the religious identity is a constitutional right available only to non-Hindus in India. The education system and the mass media almost own the Hindu children and the youth. They still own them, though the grip has weakened a bit.

The academia and the media (news as well as entertainment) were and continue to remain crucial vehicles to propagate any ideology. This is the reason why the Left hates anyone in these two fields who 'goes astray' from the chosen line.

Recall how veteran journalist M.J. Akbar was relentlessly attacked and psychoanalysed following charges of sexual harassment against him—and I'm not passing any verdict on the veracity of charges against him—but compare how Tarun Tejpal did not face the same kind of public trial by the same lot despite being accused of rape, a more serious accusation. Basically, Akbar had gone astray by joining the BJP, so he was the bigger sinner. By virtue of being in the mass media, Akbar was supposed to be a soldier, but he betrayed the army. He had to face court martial.

You can similarly see how veteran actors, such as Anupam Kher or Paresh Rawal, are pounced upon even for a minor tweet here and there, while others in Bollywood have literally gotten away with murder and charges of helping terrorists. Again, Kher and Rawal, by virtue of being in the mass media, were supposed to be the soldiers of secularism but they betrayed the army by speaking up in BJP or Narendra Modi's support. They too became candidates for court martial.

Similar treatment is meted out to any professor or researcher if they dare to differ. They are maligned, ostracized, and every attempt is made to finish off their careers.

To give you a small but recent example, in December 2019, a statement in support of the Citizenship Amendment Act (CAA)—an act that enabled non-Muslim refugees living in India but originally hailing from the three neighbouring Islamic nations to seek Indian citizenship—was released and signed by hundreds of academicians and researchers across various universities and institutes. The statement, along with the names of signatories, was published on OpIndia, a website run by the company I currently head.

Within 24 hours of that statement being published, I was approached and requested by those who coordinated the campaign to collect these signatures—something that could happen only because Modi had returned to power and some people could feel a little secure in opining ideas that did not conform to the leftist worldview—to remove the link to a public document that contained the full names of all the signatories, because one of the signatories was hounded by his leftist colleagues and students to the extent of being threatened of physical assaults and fake sexual harassment charges. He finally gave up and asked his name to be removed from any publicly accessible document. We obliged.

And this happens on most campuses. Anyone who does not toe the leftist line has to face unbearable hostility. It is almost like being punished for blasphemy, and well, the Left indeed mirrors the Abrahamic faith system in many ways.

That is how much strong tribalism is in the leftist circles, who ironically talk about individual freedom and diversity. Soldiers must not go astray. And if they do, not only will they have to be disowned, but also taught a lesson. An exemplary punishment has to be given, so that no one dares to tread that path again. Thus, there are no rewards for anyone who is not a loyal soldier.

I am sure Ramanand Sagar, too, has not won any awards controlled by the 'progressive' artists, as his TV serial was supposed to have helped the BJP rise. The Padma Shri he won was given to him when the Vajpayee government was in power.

Back in the 1980s or 90s, not many in academia or media would dare to go astray, and thus, secularism was raising me well. Still, I don't disown or dislike this phase of my childhood. Neither do I disown or dislike that song or the movie. There were elements of mutual respect and acceptance (not mere 'tolerance') at least among us kids, and thus all those memories are sweet.

I remember that during one of the tiffin breaks, while we kids were playing some silly games, a Muslim boy caught hold of a big empty earthen pot, which was used to store drinking water for the students during summers, and raised it with both hands shouting 'Jai Shri Ram.' He was imitating the *Ramayana* TV serial scene where Lord Hanuman raises big boulders and throws them at Raavan's army. Today, forget Muslims, our intellectuals are busy teaching even Bengali Hindus that 'Jai Shri Ram' is not part of their culture and they shouldn't chant this phrase.

Even in retrospect, as a self-declared Sanghi, I won't like to change anything—not even Iqbal's poetry—when I recall my childhood. It is not merely nostalgia why I value them. These stories are personal, genuine, and there is an element of innocence in them, but the same can't be said when you move to stories on a communal* level.

A contrived friendship

There is another Hindu–Muslim friendship story that I remember from my childhood days in Bihar Sharif. It was narrated to our family by a local guide when we had visited a tomb called Badi Dargah, associated with a Sufi saint named Makhdoom Sharfuddin Ahmed Yahya Maneri, or just 'Makhdoom Baba' for us back then.

Barely a couple of kilometres away from this tomb, there was an akhara (wrestling campus) of a Hindu saint called Sant Maniram or Mani Baba. The akhara complex had a temple and a water tank too.

Even now, both these places witness annual events that have seen chief ministers and other dignitaries take part in the festivities. The Dargah hosts an annual Urs while there is a Langot Mela organized by the akhara every year.

We were told by that local guide that Makhdoom Baba and Mani Baba were very good friends. There was also a weird story he told us about how the Hindu and Muslim babas met. As far as I can remember the story, Mani Baba was resting on a wall of the akhara (don't ask me who perches on a wall to relax) when he was informed about Makhdoom Baba coming to meet him. Makhdoom Baba was supposed to be riding a tiger while on his way to the akhara.

Since Mani Baba couldn't have gone on foot to meet Makhdoom Baba (again don't ask me why, as I don't remember having asked the same to the guide), he ordered the wall to carry him towards his guest. He is supposed to have said 'Chal chal re diwar' (O wall, start walking)—a phrase that I actually found scribbled on a wall in the akhara—and the wall actually 'walked'. That's how both the saints met each other, apparently for the first time, and then became good friends for life.

I don't think that even as a child I might have believed this wall-and-tiger bit, but I did believe and trust that Makhdoom Baba and Mani

---

*used as opposite to personal, not as opposite to secular

Baba must have been good friends. I linked it to my own Hindu–Muslim friendship story, somewhere feeling proud that I was furthering the legacy of these two great saints of Bihar Sharif by having a Muslim friend.

But, now it appears that this story was made up by that guide. Not just the wall-and-tiger bit, the entire friendship part could be fiction, as the associated historical facts and timelines don't add up. I discovered it only recently when I thought of penning down my memoirs in the shape of this book.

So here is a little bit of history.

As mentioned earlier, Bihar Sharif is in the Nalanda district of Bihar, a place that is not unknown if you had not slept through history lessons in your school. The region has a rich Buddhist and Jain history. The famous Nalanda university—not the current avatar—was acknowledged to be a global centre of learning way back in the seventh century itself, at a time when Islam was yet to be founded.

The university as well as the Buddhist monasteries in Nalanda were ransacked and destroyed in the thirteenth century by Afghanistan-born Bakhtiyar Khalji, a Muslim military general of the Delhi Sultanate, who is also credited for having conquered Bengal and spreading the Islamic faith and rule in the entire region.

How the Muslim invaders wiped out the rich heritage and architecture of the Nalanda region, within a matter of days, has been a known and popular knowledge as well as a folklore for decades. The momentous and massive library of the university was burnt down by the invaders led by Bakhtiyar Khalji, wiping out bulk of history and knowledge literally overnight. The ruins and footprints of this destruction are visible even today. A place called Bakhtiyarpur, named after Bakhtiyar Khalji, is situated around 30 km away from Bihar Sharif and some 40 km away from the Nalanda ruins.

However, as secularism demands, of late there have been attempts to whitewash the destruction of Nalanda by Bakhtiyar Khalji.

Some historians have tried to argue that Nalanda had a 'complex history of destruction and reoccupation' even before Muslim invaders arrived in the region. Some downright shameless ones—incidentally the same ones who vociferously denied the existence of any Ram temple at Ayodhya, which was destroyed by Mughal invader Babur—have actually come up with the story that 'radical Hindus' put the university on fire.[4] Basically, the attempt is to tell people that, 'Look, even if we agree that Khalji reduced Nalanda to ashes, he is not the only villain. Hindus are villains too.'

There is a desperation to give a clean chit to Khalji, just as there was desperation to give clean chit to another Khalji—Alauddin Khalji—during the *Padmaavat* movie controversy that erupted in 2018.

There is essentially a desperation to make us believe that these horse-riding sword-wielding barbaric invaders were just having some wild fun beheading people, which was apparently pretty normal as per the standards prevailing in those times. Even Hindu rulers supposedly indulged in such deeds. All this is further used to directly or indirectly argue and conclude that the Muslim invaders didn't have any special hatred in their hearts that was based on their religious beliefs or considerations.

This magnanimously wise principle of judging someone from standards of their time, however, was denied to the women who committed 'jauhar' (self-immolation) to escape the sex slavery of Alauddin Khalji and his barbaric army. The women, the victims, were instead judged from modern feminist standards and branded 'regressive' for having reduced themselves to just vaginas (exact words used by a woke actress).[5] Rajput women shouldn't have died for their 'honour', which is such an archaic concept, our modern secular intellectual said, who earlier did not find beheadings by Alauddin Khalji archaic or horrific because one should not apply modern civil standards to the deeds conducted centuries ago.[6]

Tragically, ironically and nauseatingly, this whitewashing of Alauddin Khalji was done barely months after the world had seen fighters of the Islamic State (ISIS) forcibly take Yazidi women in Syria as sex slaves. Most of these women were later killed, but some survived to tell the horrid tales of their ordeal, where they lamented that death would have been better instead of going through that barbaric period of sex slavery. But someone making the same decision centuries ago was regressive, if our progressive secular commentators are to be believed.

Coming back to the original Khalji in the context of this book, once Nalanda was destroyed by Bakhtiyar Khalji, the region consequently came under the control of Muslim rulers, but only temporarily. The

Muslim rulers were driven away by local Bundela Rajputs, who regained control of the area and established their rule. The last Rajput king to have ruled over the area is believed to be one Raja Biththal.

Raja Biththal is credited for having established the akhara of Mani Baba to train youths in fighting. So, Mani Baba was, in all probability, giving physical and spiritual training to youths to save the region from being controlled by Muslim rulers again.

However, just because someone is fighting against Islamic aggression, doesn't mean that the same person can't have a Muslim friend on a personal level. The reason I suspect this Hindu–Muslim friendship story of Makhdoom Baba and Mani Baba to be made up is because Mani Baba is supposed to have taken samaadhi, that is, he left his physical body, around 1300 AD, whereas going by the timelines mentioned in various news reports and historical accounts, Makhdoom Baba settled in Bihar Sharif a few years after that. In all probability, they never met. Neither riding on a tiger nor sitting on a wall.

Now, local guides—most of them self-appointed with no formal training or even education—are not unknown to spread fiction in the name of history. However, later I would get to know that even some of our 'eminent historians' have written such fiction, all in the name of ensuring harmony and Hindu–Muslim unity in the society.

Take the case of the Khilafat Movement, for example. The fact that it was part of a pan-Islamic movement to defend the authority of the Ottoman Sultan as the Caliph of Islam was given less prominence; instead, it was presented as a nationalist movement backed by Mahatma Gandhi against the British. Our history textbooks had a picture of the Ali brothers—who championed the Khilafat movement in India—with one Sankaracharya, painting a picture as if the movement was all about Hindus and Muslims being united against the British rulers of India. These textbooks presented Gandhi and the then Congress' support for Khilafat movement as a joint struggle of Hindus and Muslims against the British rulers.

As a schoolboy, I thought the name Khilafat was derived from the Urdu word 'khilaaf', which means 'against'. The movement was *against* British rule in India, or so I thought, only to realize later that Khilafat was actually derived from the word Caliphate, which is the concept of one grand Islamic nation. The Ali brothers were essentially fighting for an Islamic state, where the Sankaracharya would not have the same rights as 'Maulana' Shaukat Ali, the elder of the Ali brothers.

And that's exactly what happened. Once the Ottoman Empire was dissolved and the Republic of Turkey was founded by modernist Mustafa Kemal Atatürk, many leaders of the Khilafat movement started working to create an Islamic state within India itself. Shaukat Ali himself campaigned for the Muslim League in the Muslim constituencies of Uttar Pradesh during the by-elections in 1937. He is reported to have introduced himself as Khadim-i-Kaaba (servant of the Kaaba), who would work towards making a 'Spain of India' (Spain had become part of the Umayyad Caliphate and come under Muslim rule in the eighth century). He also talked about a possible civil war between the Hindus and Muslims.[7]

What a great Hindu–Muslim friendship story!

To say that the Khilafat movement achieved Hindu–Muslim unity would be a damn lie, but that's what our history textbooks suggest, with images of the Ali brothers and a Sankaracharya sitting together, and with Gandhi's support for the movement.

Much later in my adult life, I realized that this 'lying for harmony' was almost an acceptable practice in the secular world. And, it was not limited to just re-writing or manipulating the story, narrating the episodes that took place centuries ago, but it also meant lying even about incidents that were happening right at that very moment. One of the major examples of such 'lying for harmony' in modern times is perhaps the admission by Sharad Pawar to have lied about the Mumbai bomb blasts of 1993.

Pawar was the chief minister of Maharashtra when Mumbai, then known as Bombay, was rocked by a series of bomb blasts in various parts of the city. Around 300 people died in the blasts, which took place at around a dozen places. Underworld don Dawood Ibrahim was revealed to be the mastermind of the blasts. Dawood fled India, and is currently believed to be hiding in Pakistan after being designated as a 'global terrorist.'

As the chief minister, Pawar had come up with an official statement and details about the blasts, naming the places and suspects for the terrorist act. Years later, on various public platforms, Pawar proudly claimed that he had lied and deliberately misled the public by inventing an extra bomb blast at a place called 'Masjid Bunder' in Mumbai, which was Muslim-dominated.

His logic for this lie, uttered in the capacity of a chief minister, was that he wanted to prove that Muslims were also victims. He believed that this lie will help in maintaining communal harmony in the city. However, it was not limited to just inventing a new blast. He also issued statements saying explosives used in the blasts resembled those normally used by 'Southern India terrorists', and thus tried to move the needle of suspicion towards the LTTE, the Tamil insurgent group of Sri Lanka. So, not only did he try to show that Muslims were also victims, he went on to say something that essentially shielded Islamic terrorists who had carried out the attacks. And these are his own words from a TV interview.[8]

To his credit, at least Pawar accepts that those were lies peddled for immediate gains, and he didn't perpetuate them as truth that would later become part of history textbooks—which is what normally happens in the secular-liberal scheme of things, where you start believing and living in your own web of lies. If Pawar wanted to turn his lies into truth, he would have pressurized the police to slap false cases against some people, plant witnesses and do everything to turn his fiction into a reality. God bless him that he had not become 'secular' to that extent.

In the same interview, Pawar claimed that Justice B.N. Srikrishna, who retired as a Supreme Court judge, praised him for his lies. Justice Srikrishna headed the commission investigating the Mumbai riots, which had taken place a year earlier. Pawar was seen as acting 'responsibly' in the secular-liberal framework by lying, and thus he deserved high praise.

This 'lying for harmony' is so common that I myself indulged in some of it in my first job in the news media. You will find that in the later chapters of this book, when I discuss 'responsible journalism', I would also invent a Hindu–Muslim harmony story. Keep reading.

Along with the academia, news media and politics, such inventions of imaginary incidents to ensure communal harmony are present in the entertainment media too. You may wonder why one should have any issues with imaginary incidents in the entertainment media, because fiction is supposed to be imaginary. However, I'm referring to manipulations in storytelling. Let me just give you an example.

People of my generation would remember a TV serial named

Chandrakanta, a fantasy series based on the eponymous novel by Devaki Nandan Khatri. The villain Kroor Singh with big bushy eyebrows saying 'yakoo' was a rage then.

While the serial was a hit, the producers and people at Doordarshan were grappling with an aspect that perhaps none of us bothered about. They realized that the original novel didn't have any positive character who had a Muslim name, while it had a few Muslim characters who were either villainous or comic. A popular form of entertainment was failing on secular parameters.

To 'correct' this bias in the original novel, a new character was introduced in the story for its televised avatar. A Muslim character named Janbaaz, played on screen by Mukesh Khanna, was introduced in the story who, if I remember correctly, helped the Hindu hero get his love interest. If I further remember correctly, the background sound of azaan—the Muslim call for daily prayers—was also heard when this character made its first appearance on screen.

I am not sure if there is any such precedence in the West, from where usually our secular-liberal and social justice warriors copy ideas for activism. It is like introducing a positive Jewish character in works such as *The Merchant of Venice* because all Jewish characters in Shakespeare's plays are villains. I don't think that has been done yet.

Such contrived attempts at 'creating harmony' risks killing even the natural process of building harmony and trust. You feel cheated, and then you start noticing even those things that you might have overlooked otherwise. For instance, now I realize that while Makhdoom Baba's dargah had a decent number of Hindu visitors, hardly anyone in skullcap was present in Mani Baba's akhara.

Slowly, you start to understand that the famed Hindu–Muslim friendship aspect of the Indian secular project is essentially a one-way street. Not just that, the relationship dynamics of this friendship is such that Muslims have all the rights to be exclusivist—to the extent of demanding separate electorates—and Hindus have to feel obliged to accommodate all those demands. Further, Hindus have to make sure that they don't indulge in something, not even complain about some aspects of the community's behaviour, which 'hurts sentiments' of the Muslims.

But not everyone realizes it. Not everyone becomes a 'bigot.' Because the stories are so well crafted and so often repeated in various forms that you start believing in the fiction you are being fed. But once you dig a little deeper, it is not a nice feeling to know that much of the history that you have been fed is either plain lie or clever half-truths or shameless whitewashing—whitewashing not just of Khaljis and Khilafat, but even of Sufis, who I thought didn't need any whitewashing.

For a long time, I believed that all Sufis were singing and dancing mystics, who believed in love and tolerance and never harmed a soul. I'm sure an overwhelming number of Hindus still believe the same. Many of us go to dargahs and pray for the fulfilment of our wishes. We love Sufi music, and find it all very charming. Makhdoom Baba was a Sufi too and his dargah was visited by many Hindus, such as our family.

There is another tomb in Bihar Sharif. Buried there is one Syed Ibrahim Mallick, also a Sufi saint. He was also a military general—something that many of us would find counterintuitive, as we are conditioned to believe that a Sufi is someone who sits mystically in some dargah and belts out pearls of wisdom or sings soulful ghazals, with no interest in politics or wars. But Sufis were warriors too. Syed Ibrahim Mallick, the 'Sufi saint', defeated and killed Raja Biththal, after which the area went back to Muslim rule.

The events of Raja Biththal being killed by a Sufi and Makhdoom Baba, another Sufi, settling in Bihar Sharif, happened close to each other. In all probability, the Sufi settlements happened as a result of Raja Biththal being killed and the area going under Muslim rule.

This was nowhere close to a Hindu–Muslim friendship story that I believed as a child. I could sense a stench of bloodshed buried under the aroma of agarbattis, which were lighted aplenty at the dargah.

I would later come to know that incidents of Sufis being warriors and launching military campaigns were not so rare, except of course in popular parlance and liberal narrative, where they are supposed to be detached from politics or orthodoxy and perennially engrossed in finer elements of human emotions and philosophy. Sufis have been part of many battles by virtue of aligning with one of the warring Sultans or on occasions even being one of the warring sides themselves. And this has happened not just in India, but in places such as Iran, Iraq, Syria, Central Asia and Northern Africa.[9]

Kashmir is one of the regions that is testament to the fact that Sufism doesn't mean mysticism and syncretism only. The brutal Islamization of Kashmir happened under the Shah Mir dynasty, especially during the reign of Sikandar Butshikan, whose second name literally means destroyer of (Hindu) idols. The dynasty, as well as Sikandar, patronized and facilitated the settlement of many Sufis in Kashmir, whose teachings also went on to influence state policies. These policies included destroying the temples of Hindus, ban on construction of temples, officially relegating Hindus to second-class citizens and forcibly converting them to Islam or killing them. Kashmir, which was once a place of Hindu rishis, soon became Islamized beyond recognition. The land of rishis was dead and 'Kashmiriyat' was born, all under the watchful eyes of the Sufis.

Apart from Kashmir, there is another story of violence and bloodshed involving Sufis, this time on the other geographical extreme of India, in Kerala in 1921. The incident is known as the Moplah massacre or the Malabar rebellion, where thousands of Hindus were killed or converted to Islam by armed gangs of Muslim 'rebels' who had sworn on the Holy Quran that they were ready to die for the Khilafat movement. A rebellion, ostensibly launched against the British, was practically a widespread massacre and subjugation of Hindus living in the Malabar area of Kerala. The leader overseeing this massacre was Ali Musliyar, who is often identified as a member of the Sufi order known as Qadiriyya.

Despite such historical context, the word Sufi continues to sound soothing and peaceful to our ears. Compare it with the word 'Brahmin' and what was done to it by people who controlled the narrative.

Like the Sufis, the Brahmins have also been at the forefront of society, contributing to music, philosophy and education, and have shaped the civilizational growth of India. But today, dare you say so! Brahmin as an adjective is only to be used to denote caste oppression, which should ruffle your feelings, while Sufi as an adjective is supposed to soothe your outraged senses.

I can take a bet that you would not feel even the slightest discomfort if a person in front of you said that he was a 'proud Sufi' but you would conjure up all kinds of monstrosity in a person who identifies himself as a 'proud Brahmin'. The supposed good deeds of the Sufis are meant to cancel all the bigotry and bloodshed by them, while no amount of good deeds by the Brahmins is enough to remove the albatross around their neck.

Secularism in India has remained so blatantly biased, with glaring double standards, that you have to be wilfully blind or blissfully ignorant to celebrate this charade. You don't have to go to an RSS shakha to realize it. I never went to one.

Of course, as a child, none of these issues bothered me. I was hardly aware of the facts to understand the ramifications. In fact, even as adults, most of us don't care, and I too was not any different from the rest, but various events over the years changed me, which I will recount in this book.

However, what we must take note is how these things affect us, right from childhood. You may not understand politics—as a child you simply can't—or you may choose not to understand or be interested in it, but it affects you. It affects your life. It affects your children. You can choose to be not interested in it, but you can't choose not to get affected by it.

When I hear people say, 'how does the future of Hindu civilization depend on politics?' I just want them to pause and think for a while. It affects in more than one way. Politics is not just electoral politics. From the outside, each political party could indeed appear similar as far as daily administration under their respective governments is concerned. Most of the time, you don't feel any palpable change as your points of contact with the government—the bureaucrats, the police, the tax guys, the government offices—remain the same, and their behaviour remains the same too, no matter who is in power. That is why one gets the feeling that all political parties are the same, and it is not a big deal who is in power.

But something else changes. Every political party is not the same when it comes to the environment they end up creating by the mere virtue of being in power. They trigger some changes directly, and some indirectly, some as a driving force, some as a catalyst, some intended, some unintended. You may think it doesn't affect your daily life, but it affects you daily. It affects your present. It affects your future. It even affects your past. Your history, your identity, your roots.

The first elections

In your childhood, you are, naturally, totally clueless about these ideological issues. Let alone children, many adults too are clueless about these topics. However, electoral politics is something that you are not totally clueless about, even if you choose to be entirely disinterested in it (but as I said, at your own risk). Elections are one big festival in India, and thus even as a child, you can't escape noticing it.

I still remember various flags of political parties adorning the houses and streets of Bihar Sharif. I guess this must be the time around the 1989 Lok Sabha elections and then the 1990 state assembly elections of Bihar. I was born in 1980, so technically the 1984 Lok Sabha and 1985 Bihar assembly elections took place when I was a child, but I was too young to have a clear memory of any flag or slogans associated with those elections.

As I had mentioned earlier, somehow, I vaguely remember having watched Indira Gandhi's funeral on TV after she was assassinated in 1984 by her Sikh bodyguards, but have no other memories that could be linked to Rajiv Gandhi's massive victory in the Lok Sabha elections afterwards. Maybe I was too young to note the flags or understand the slogans, which I would notice in the next elections.

However, I do have some memories linked to the anti-Sikh riots of 1984, which had marred Patna too. Remember, Patna has the Patna Sahib Gurudwara, which is one of the holiest shrines in Sikhism, and the city is the birthplace of Guru Gobind Singh, the 10th Guru of the Sikhs. Many Sikhs reside in the city, especially in and around Patna Sahib.

Fortunately, my memories are not linked to any violence or bloodshed during the riots, but I do remember that in one family gathering, adults talked about how even ordinary people had taken advantage of the total collapse of law and order during the riots. There were some big shops owned by the Sikhs in Patna, which were plundered, and middle-class families took away stuff from the shops. In that family gathering, a lady from the neighbourhood was accused of having amassed saaris for herself during the loot. Obviously, the Sikhs suffered far worse than just their businesses being looted, but this is one of the faint memories that I could retain from my childhood about this tragedy.

Many years later, I would read innumerable articles and reports about the 2002 post-Godhra riots of Gujarat—articles about how the moral compass of the middle class broke as they became participants in the pandemonium. The Gujarati society was painted as some special evil. These articles were written as if India had witnessed such moral bankruptcy of the middle class for the first time, and something was uniquely broken about the Gujarati society, often linking it to the religiosity of Gujaratis. And despite having heard similar stories about the 1984 riots, however faint they maybe in the memory, I would not be able to see how such articles were totally unfair against the Gujaratis, as I would be in my first job as a journalist then.

We will come to that later. For now, let's go back to my first memories of elections that saw V.P. Singh's ascent at the Centre and Lalu's rise in Bihar. I remember Janata Dal's green flags, with a white wheel at the centre, adorning our neighbourhood.

Our neighbourhood had many carpenters, by occupation as well as by caste (I assumed, though I never asked.). Carpenters are known as 'barhai' and they are classified as OBCs (Other Backward Classes) in Bihar. Janata Dal's promise of implementing caste-based reservations as suggested by the Mandal Commission was a big draw amongst them.

Our family belonged to a caste that is known as Bhumihar. It's technically Bhumihar-Brahmin, but not many Brahmins consider the caste as belonging to the Brahmin varna. That's another controversy and another story altogether, but Bhumihars, whether Brahmins by varna or not, are one of the four upper castes in Bihar, the other three being Brahmins, Rajputs and Kayasthas. Baniyas, who are listed as upper castes almost everywhere else, are classified as OBCs in Bihar.

Our family as well as our caste people were traditional and loyal supporters of the Congress party. The green flags of the Janata Dal discomforted our parents a bit. My younger brother and I didn't know much about politics, but those flags did lead us to ask questions to our parents, and that's when we brothers, not even 10-year olds then, became aware of something called caste.

We were aware of religion because of obvious differences, such as Arabic names of Muslim friends, and due to the fact that they went to mosques while we were supposed to go to temples, that they had dargahs and we had akharas, but caste was a complex thing to understand.

As caste became a talking point with green flags around, one of the first questions my younger brother had asked my father was: 'Bhaiya kaun jaat ka hai?' (What is the caste of my brother?) I wish the concept of caste, and more importantly the practice of it, was actually this fluid.

In the school, kids didn't appear to care about caste, and obviously about politics, though there was one boy who would speak in a loud and assertive way that the chakka (the wheel, symbol of Janata Dal) was going to win. His nostrils would flare up and lips would get stern, almost like Hanumanji of Ramanand Sagar's *Ramayana*, when he would make that claim. Had mobile phones and internet existed then, his video would have gone viral—a young kid with funny expressions belting out strong political opinions.

Right now, I find it difficult to imagine why we kids, barely 10-year olds then, would even talk about who would win the elections, but I do remember that particular guy and his assertion about Janata Dal's victory. Maybe, we kids ended up discussing elections one fine day after watching numerous party flags from the terrace of our school during the tiffin break.

There was still no cable TV or internet back then, so most of the electoral campaign happened in the form of putting up flags in the streets and atop homes, sticking posters and writing slogans on walls, and distributing pamphlets in the neighbourhood, and obviously, as advertisements and paid news in the newspapers.

Unlike this kid who was politically aware at quite a young age, I couldn't care less about who would win or lose. Though by then, I had discovered that my family supported Congress. The fact that the Congress party's flag resembled our national flag made me like it too. I even remember the name of the Congress candidate—Shakiluzzama— and that's the only name I can recall among all the names that I must have seen on various posters and pamphlets during my childhood.

But, I discovered later that my friend Ragib didn't like the Congress party. And with that I also discovered that perhaps I was the only one in the school who is totally clueless about political parties and leaders!

I have an explanation. Perhaps, most of the other kids lived in joint families—Ragib certainly did as I had gone to his home and met most of his family members—where they were frequently exposed to political talks and debates by adults in their homes. For sure, the kids were just repeating what they heard from their elders.

But in my case, I lived in a nuclear family, and there was no reason why mom and dad would talk about politics in the presence of my brother and me. In fact, I doubt they would have done that even in our absence. Maybe they do it now, after having been added to random WhatsApp groups by extended family members, where political forwards arrive along with good morning messages, random jokes and totally made-up stories and facts.

So, it seems that the Janata Dal-supporting kid and my Congress-hating best friend picked up these preferences from their family and community. Ragib also told me a story about how some young men in his locality forced Congress workers to retreat when they had gone there to canvass for votes. One angry man supposedly jumped on the campaign jeep to tear down one of the party flags. He then apparently cleaned his shoes with that flag to show his contempt for the party.

'But why so angry,' I wondered and asked, and Ragib said something about his people not being happy with the Congress for opening the locks at Ayodhya. I had no clue what locks he was referring to, though thanks to *Ramayana* I knew what Ayodhya was.

Evidently, Muslims had decided to junk Congress and vote for the Janata Dal because Rajiv Gandhi allowed some puja at Ayodhya by 'opening the locks' of the Babri Masjid. The Congress subsequently lost the Lok Sabha elections of 1989—it was only the second time that the grand old party lost power at the Centre in over four decades. They also lost the assembly elections of Bihar the following year. The Congress has not returned to power in Bihar since then. It's been over three decades now.

Lalu rose, thanks to the might of the Muslim–Yadav vote bank. Yadavs, a dominant backward caste or OBC, were obviously with Lalu as he was one among them, and Janata Dal had promised to implement the Mandal Commission's recommendations, which would bring reservations for the OBCs in jobs and education, but Muslims deserted the Congress because Rajiv Gandhi allowed Hindus to worship at Ayodhya.

The 1989 Lok Sabha and 1990 Bihar Vidhan Sabha elections were going to change the political landscape, both at the national and regional levels. A period of change and churn was coming for the society.

Around the same time, a period of change and churn in my personal life was waiting for me too, when we left Bihar Sharif sometime in early

1991, as my parents wanted a better education for us. I needed to be admitted to Class VIII in Patna.

My parents wanted us to study in a school that followed the CBSE or ICSE curriculum—the Public School followed the curriculum set by the State Board of Education—and which was 'English medium'. The English teacher at my school in Bihar Sharif was scared of my father, as my father had once complained to the principal about the horrible pronunciation of words he was imparting to the students. And he indeed was. He used to pronounce plural as 'pa-loo-ral' and calf as 'kaal-ph'. No, seriously.

My father was ready to travel almost daily from Patna to Bihar Sharif for his job, but his sons must get a better education. So one fine day, in the wee hours of the morning, all our household goods were packed and loaded on to a truck, and we boarded a bus to Patna.

2

The Congressi Hindu

Chacha Nehru's kids

Our first rented house in Patna was pretty underwhelming. There was a cow shed just next to it. The house owner was a senior college professor, who had built a nice big house for himself, but the rented part of it, where we lived, was disjointed from the main building. It was a series of four rooms with a tin shed; one of them became our living room, two became bedrooms and the remaining one was converted into a store room. Our house, the cow shed and the owner's big house were part of the same plot of land, and had a common boundary wall.

The privilege we enjoyed in Bihar Sharif, where our house, though rented and not owned by us, stood tall in the neighbourhood of carpenters, was gone. More loss of privilege was waiting as I was temporarily put in a government school while my father parleyed with various private schools to secure admission for me.

The government school building was huge. I discovered that the number of classes in a school could be independent of the number of classrooms, as every class had various sections, each with their own classroom.

Every classroom was noisy. Bathrooms were not only stinky but students had sketched all kinds of anatomical drawings that their imagination and experience could help them with. Some 'dirty words' and phrases I had overheard 'big boys' in Bihar Sharif use while talking to each other were also scribbled on the walls of the bathrooms, and sometimes on the classroom benches too.

I was in the company of teenagers, though not one yet. It was intimidating.

I went to the school just for a couple of days before giving up. My father didn't ask me to go there again as the very reason we had shifted to Patna was to get a better education, and government schools were not associated with it. Further, the government school was 'Hindi medium'.

I could get admission in a private English-medium school after much struggle. The schools won't accept that a boy should be given admission in Class VIII when he had passed 'Standard IV' in the last school he attended. After much deliberation on the curriculum that was followed by the Public School of Bihar Sharif, after taking note of my age and after making me take some admission tests, I was finally admitted in Class VII in a school called Gyan Niketan in Patna, which was affiliated to CBSE.

Gyan Niketan was run by a trust founded by Kishore Kunal, a former IPS officer with a keen interest in issues related to the Hindu society. He was appointed an Officer on Special Duty by the then Prime Minister V.P. Singh to mediate on the Ayodhya dispute in an effort to look for an amicable solution to the matter. This, of course, was before the Babri Masjid was demolished.

Kishore Kunal, or Acharya Kunal as he is also known as due to his Sanskrit knowledge and qualifications, was instrumental in renovating a Hanuman temple or Mahavir Mandir located just outside the Patna Junction railway station. It is said that the temple was frequented by petty criminals, some of whom even used it as a hiding place after stealing the belongings of passengers at the railway station. The temple was renovated in the early 1980s.

The renovated temple was not only cleaner, bigger and safer, it also went on to have a Dalit priest. That was a revolutionary step taken in a deeply casteist society, but there was no popular resistance to this move. Literally thousands of people, including people belonging to the upper castes, visited the temple daily and accepted prasad from a Dalit priest, bowing their heads to him as well as to the deity when they accepted it.

Kunal has since then replicated this model in many temples of Bihar, as he was later made the chairman of the Bihar State Board of Religious Trusts by Chief Minister Nitish Kumar.[10]

In his personal capacity, Kunal, who had earlier earned name and fame for being an upright and no-nonsense police officer, has been working to reform beliefs related to caste. He has also been working to improve management of temples, apart from spreading awareness about Hindu culture and contributing to various philanthropic causes.

The trust founded by him—Mahavir Mandir Trust—also runs a cancer hospital in Patna where the poor get free treatment. The money earned by the Hanuman temple from the sale of laddus partly subsidizes the operations of the hospital.

However, there were no active attempts made at Gyan Niketan, the school he founded, to endear the students towards an ideology or philosophy similar to his. I wish there were, so that later when some smart-alok (*sic.*) says, 'Why not build a school or hospital in Ayodhya?', I would slap the person back (figuratively) by retorting with, 'Yeah sure, just like Mahavir Mandir Trust is running a school and hospital in Patna after building a big Hanuman temple at its original place, Ayodhya too can have a school and hospital after a grand Ram Mandir is built at the Janmabhoomi.'

Incidentally, Kunal had prepared a map of the Ram Janmabhoomi after going through various ancient texts and historical documents. The map showed where Lord Ram was born and where the temple should be built. The map was presented in courts too, but it was torn by the lawyer representing the Muslim parties in the Ayodhya case in the Supreme Court in October 2019.[11]

After the Supreme Court awarded the Janmabhoomi to Ram Lalla, the Mahavir Mandir at Patna announced that it would contribute at least ₹10 crore towards the construction of a temple, apart from offering free food to the visitors.

One could be inclined to believe that a student going to a school founded by such a person would obviously turn out to be a Sanghi, but no, that was not the case at all. The school had to follow the secular curriculum prescribed by the secular state despite being run by a trust and a person whose aim was to protect and preserve Hindu traditions. The right of running educational institutions aimed at preserving one's religious traditions and faith is available only to non-Hindus, as per Article 30 of the Indian Constitution.

Being an upright police officer, trained to remain fiercely loyal to the state and the Constitution, Kunal would be the last person to go against the rules and laws enacted by the state. Back in 1983, he had resisted enormous political pressure while investigating the death of a young woman named Shwetnisha Rani, a typist employed at the Bihar Legislative Assembly, who was feared to be murdered by powerful people after being sexually exploited. The infamous incident is known as the 'Bobby sex scandal' of Bihar.

Kunal was then the SSP (Senior Superintendent of Police) of Patna. He had gotten the dead body of Bobby, that is, Shwetnisha Rani, exhumed to ascertain whether her death was unnatural. The truth of the Bobby sex scandal is believed to have been buried as the investigation was taken away from Kunal, apparently under political pressure, and handed over to the CBI. It is said that a lot many powerful politicians and people in the corridors of power would have been exposed if the truth came out.

Essentially, Kunal was wired to be disciplined and dedicated to his constitutional duties. If the Constitution did not allow him to propagate his beliefs on religion in a school he himself founded, he would not do it. That Kunal Sir—as we students at Gyan Niketan used to call him—had a keen interest in preserving and protecting Hindu culture and traditions, was something I would realize much later, by reading about him in the newspapers. I can't recall a single thing that he said or did at Gyan Niketan that could expose us to this other aspect of his personality, where he was pro-Hindu.

Therefore, despite studying in a school run by someone who, too, certainly would be termed a Sanghi by today's liberals, I did not receive any Sanghi education. The secular state made sure that Chacha Nehru's kids continued to be his only.

There were no special classes on Hindu religious epics, such as Bhagwad Gita, nor was there any temple on the school premises. In fact, there was a Hindi teacher who tried to impress us by saying that he can prove that all the villains in the Hindu classics—be it Raavan, Duryodhan, Kans or Mahishasur—were good men. This he said while teaching a chapter named *Mahabharat Ki Ek Saanjh*, which was part of the Hindi-language textbook that CBSE had prescribed for schools.

Mahabharat Ki Ek Saanjh is a one-act play that depicts a fictional conversation between Yudhishthir and Duryodhan, which takes place post the war that was lost by the Kauravas. Duryodhan lay vanquished, waiting for his impending death, when Yudhishthir pays him a visit.

A conversation takes place between the two. The discussion revolves around a web of arguments, where it is reasoned that Duryodhan was not pure evil and he or the Kauravas were not the only parties responsible for the war and the ruin it brought. I no longer remember the exact dialogues of the play, but I remember that it did a good job at bringing forth its point. I, too, was impressed, and that's why even today I remember the name of the chapter.

Now, I don't have any issues with such compositions. Such debates and discussions enrich the learnings from any literary work, including our epics. And who knows, maybe our Hindi teacher was being sarcastic when he said he wanted to paint all villains of Hindu religion as good men. Sarcasm is so easily lost even on adults, something that I learned later when I started writing satire. My limited point is about how even a school run by a Hindu trust could be a ground for propagating a thought process that encourages a person to deliberately invert a widely accepted Hindu belief.

As a rebel teenager, you are impressed by such ideas and thoughts. Your parents like Krishna, so you'd rather like Duryodhan or Kans to register your rebellious self. You feel that you've gained a unique insight—that villains can be heroes too—which the common person on the road doesn't have. You feel enlightened and 'intellectual', that is, more informed and evolved than a common person on the road. It is entirely possible that this early feeling is manipulated or internalized as learning, where you start believing that merely by going against widely held beliefs, especially religious beliefs, you become intellectual. Worse, you actually start believing in 'alternate histories' that are full of internal contradictions.

A secular education system will not look at these possibilities as a 'risk'. On the contrary, it will be a desirable outcome of education. And a secular constitution won't allow the school to do something to 'neutralize' this risk.

I was not exactly a rebel teenager, as I was fortunate to have parents who were quite supportive. If I must spot any issue during my teenage years, it could be some 'issues' that I had with my father, which I find non-issues now. There were a few dad-son issues during my boyhood and teenage years because my father was strict about studies. We brothers were slapped around liberally on various occasions for being too naughty and troublesome, so that could also be cited as an 'issue', though now we brothers only laugh about it. Nonetheless, there was a little rebel inside me, probably due to these reasons. Or maybe because, well, I was a teenager after all, who must think that he knows better than his father. The hormones.

The little rebel in me didn't exactly conclude that I must go against widely held religious beliefs to be an intellectual, but yes, I was not religious at all. I questioned religious beliefs quite frequently. I remember throwing away an 'ashtadhatu' ring that was given to me by my mother to bring me good luck. I saw it as superstition, so I threw it away in a heap of garbage. Though, I fetched it from there after a few minutes, realizing that I was being an unadulterated idiot. After all it was given to me by my mother. It was her faith. I didn't necessarily need to subscribe to that faith. But I could surely wear something on my finger for someone who had worn birthmarks for me.

The point is that my school was not even making me religious, forget making me a Sanghi. The only Hindu thing that I can recall my school doing was a one-time distribution of Bhagwad Gita to its students. I don't remember what had triggered the distribution, but I remember the incident because I liked the small pocket size of the book. It might as well have been a voluntary exercise offered by the school, with students being asked to pick a copy if they wanted, for there were no compulsory Gita classes or any subsequent class tests to check if we actually read and imbibed the teachings of Lord Krishna after picking up our copies.

Even now, almost as a routine, every year some school gets embroiled into a controversy—of 'thrusting' the Gita upon its students. I am sure that had some noise been made even back then, Kunal Sir would have been on the back foot. Not because he is not loyal to his religious beliefs, but because of his past as a disciplined police officer, where he will abide by what the laws and Constitution say, even if his personal beliefs say something else. Further, Gyan Niketan had employed teachers to teach Urdu to a few Muslim students who did not want to take Sanskrit as a third language, so there was no way he would have thrust the Gita on anyone.

The education system—both the curriculum as well as the laws that govern the sector—is designed very carefully to protect and propagate the Nehruvian brand of secularism. It was designed so since the time of the British itself and we will talk about that later in the book. No wonder even a cosmetic change or tinkering to the education system triggers cries of 'saffronization' of education. It is the fount from where everything else flows.

Thanks to the way the education system is designed, there was nothing that could endear me to any pro-Hindu ideology while I was growing up. The secular state was raising me well at school, despite it being run by someone who will be termed a Sanghi today, while at home I was being raised by my parents, who had nothing to do with the RSS. In fact, as I had mentioned earlier, my family was a traditional supporter of the Congress party. My father actually had brought us booklets on understanding Quran and other Islamic beliefs from the Patna Book Fair, and a statue of Jesus Christ was there too, at our home—total Amar, Akbar, Anthony.

However, both at the school and back home, things were not so bad that I would grow up to become a self-hating Hindu. At home, my mother followed all Hindu festivals and performed regular puja, and expected us brothers to not be totally aloof and away, while at the school, the secular education system had some elements that were a saving grace.

For example, Ramdhari Singh Dinkar's 'Krishna Ki Chetawani' from his masterpiece *Rashmirathi* must be one chapter from the school days that every person from my generation remembers. It is essentially *Mahabharata* in the form of poetry. The secular state was not teaching Gita, but it was teaching a chapter from the *Mahabharata*, where Krishna shows himself up as God.

If *Mahabharat Ki Ek Saanjh* could appear to be something that may cause an impressionable mind into believing that Hindu epics need to be read the opposite way, 'Krishna Ki Chetawani' was something that seemed to encourage one to read and enjoy them without applying any filters, except the filter of poetry.

As an aside, thank god Dinkar had a soft corner for Nehru, or else his writings would have not made it to the CBSE textbooks and we would have never read 'Krishna Ki Chetawani'.

Jokes apart, let me make it clear here that I'm talking about these two chapters entirely as independent compositions in a school textbook, without any context of the ideologies the respective authors might have believed in, or what literary criticism of either of these two works could throw up. I am only referring to the range of thoughts that could be triggered in a teenager with these two chapters in front of him.

And I have not even talked about the history textbooks, which are rife with whitewashing the atrocities committed by Muslim invaders. It was actually an official policy of the Marxist historians who dominated the committees and panels that wrote history textbooks. In 1989, the West Bengal Secondary Board of Education is reported to have ordered the deletion of all 'controversial' references to Muslim rule during the medieval period. The circular explicitly said that, 'Muslim rule should never attract any criticism. Destruction of temples by Muslim rulers and invaders should not be mentioned.'[12]

Such policies made sure that an average Hindu child grows up believing that everything was totally screwed up in India until the Mughals and then the British arrived, who, especially the Muslim rulers, didn't do anything spectacularly evil that had not already happened in India earlier.

In fact, history books try to suggest that these invasions were some sort of necessary evil. The religious conversions from Hinduism to Islam are argued to be voluntary and triggered due to Hinduism being an unjust religion, despite historical accounts written by Muslim chroniclers themselves,[13] documenting in detail how Hindus were slaughtered and forced to accept Islam by various Muslim rulers, including many who are supposed to be 'moderate' rulers. Not only such chapters from history have been whitewashed, they have been glorified, too. Medieval history is virtually only Mughal history, the way the school curriculum is designed, and it appears as if every great thing about India happened in that period only.

It's not just about Mughals or other Muslim rulers, but there are various other issues. Attempted propagation of some thoughts, such as belief in only one god or opposition to idol worship, are referred to as 'reforms' within the Hindu society, instead of presenting those as proof of multiplicity of thoughts within the wider Hindu society. Many such ideas are evidently influenced by Abrahamic faiths and referring to those as 'reforms' insinuate that any such Hindu belief, which is not in consonance with Abrahamic beliefs, is crude and outdated. Semantics matter, and surely the writers of history textbooks knew that.

Either through direct seeding or through employment of such semantics, we are further made to believe that India as a nation didn't exist before the Islamic invaders established the sultanate or the British imperialists established the Raj, despite various kings and kingdoms before the Mughals that foresaw India as one great nation that must be united.

I don't even want to go into all that is wrong in our history textbooks and how it makes sure that a Hindu, especially an upper caste male, grows up to become a guilt-ridden and self-loathing Hindu. Perhaps the only reason the history textbooks were not able to entirely destroy the Hindu society was because the education system itself was broken and ineffective. The focus in schools was not much on learning and developing a character, but on getting good marks and acquiring rote knowledge. We used to memorize entire paragraphs from 'guides'—I still remember the authors, Kundra & Bawa—and paste those as answers in social science papers to get passing marks. God bless Congress for keeping some things broken.

But the ecosystem that produced these textbooks also knew that the system was broken, so its efforts weren't limited to capturing young minds only through formal education. Apart from textbooks, the magazines or other books that a boy or girl could pick also had elements that would wean young minds away from their Hindu roots.

I remember a Hindi magazine called *Sarita* that used to arrive fairly regularly at our house. As a curious teenager, sometimes I'd pick it up and try to read a few pages. I distinctly remember many essays deriding Hindu beliefs and undermining the authority or even the utility of Hindu religious texts.

An essay I especially remember is one that ridiculed the *Upanishads*, positing the question whether these were religious texts or sex manuals—in fact that was the very title of that particular article. All such 'criticisms' for Hindus and Hinduism were dressed up as attempts to reform the society and to have an educated debate, while the idea clearly was to weaken the faith. Obviously, not once did I see any criticism of a non-Hindu faith or religious book in such magazines.

Sarita was published by Delhi Press, which also published a children's magazine named *Champak*. It didn't have such blatant agenda of course, but it did make sure to 'secularize' the children in its own way. *Champak* mostly contained fables, but not traditional stories. These new stories were carefully written to ensure that any iconography related to the Hindu religion was either absent or minimal.

It is the same Delhi Press that publishes *The Caravan* magazine, which had published the caste break-up of the CRPF men who were killed in Pulwama in February 2019.[14] Recently, in June 2020, there was a controversy where an Amazon customer had ordered a copy of the *Bhagwat Purana*, a Hindu text, published by an associate company of the Delhi Press, and the publisher sent a free book along with it as a 'special gift'. This free book argued why the *Bhagwat Purana* was irrelevant to our lives.[15] You can imagine what messages would be inherent in anything coming from a publisher with such a mindset.

There were many magazines published by the Delhi Press, which were fairly popular. It included family magazines such as *Sarita*, a women's magazine, *Grihshobha*, a children's magazine, *Champak,* and 'entertainment' magazines such as *Manohar Kahaaniyan*—all of which were decently popular, with loads of subtle propaganda.

However, not all was lost. There were Amar Chitra Kathas too, the illustrated books for children that didn't have such liberal agenda, although of late 'corrections' are being done there too, I hear. Then I remember a magazine called *Chandamama*, which published stories that were almost entirely full of Hindu iconography and themes.

In *Chandamama*, there were stories that drew inspiration from Hindu folklore as well as fictional stories around such themes. The illustrations were really good—a picturesque landscape that showed a young Krishna playing with his friends, with birds and animals around or stories that featured a majestic waterfall that was supposed to hide a treasure belonging to some great king. As a child, I wished to visit those times.

Also, while my father gave us a very secular upbringing—in Congressi style—he was not a communist who hated his ethnic identity. He saw that I liked reading books, and brought me books such as the *Panchatantra,*

Sinhaasan Battisi, Baital Pachisi—which was partly triggered by the popular show *Vikram aur Baital* on Doordarshan—and even simple *Mahabharata* tales. These books are still there at our house in Patna, partly moth-eaten.

In retrospect, I am so grateful to the publishers who came up with such magazines and books. My school might have been barred from imparting such education, but these magazines and books could, to an extent. Not that they made me a Sanghi, not at all, but they made sure that I was not entirely uprooted from my identity. Due to them, I could feel a sense of history and belonging as a Hindu—something the entire liberal education is designed to deny.

While Gyan Niketan didn't do anything special to endear students towards the personal ideology or beliefs of its founder Kishore Kunal, there was one entirely non-ideological and non-religious reason why some students of his school could actually be conscious of their Hindu identity. The reason was very secular (in a literary way)—school rivalry.

Gyan Niketan was affiliated to CBSE. It competed with another school of Patna to top the board results. That school was St. Michael's High School. As the name suggests, it was run by Christian missionaries. There were at least three other schools—all run by Christian missionaries—that were most sought after for admissions by parents. Gyan Niketan in that sense already stood out as Hindu, as there was no Saint, Convent or other such marker in the school's name.

What made this rivalry more 'personal' was the fact that St. Michael's was a co-ed school while Gyan Niketan was only for boys. Basically, there was an element of envy involved too. High-school boys at St. Michael's had the company of girls while we had to try too hard to make any friends from the opposite sex. The envy was really strong, so much so that once, when the then principal of St. Michael's had visited Gyan Niketan, some boys from my class decided to drop a table or at least a duster on him from the second floor—a perfect example of teenage stupidity. Fortunately, a teacher walked in just then and no such tragedy happened.

The principal of St. Michael's wore a white cassock—that full body frock that priests in churches wear—with a cross dangling from his neck. He represented our rival. He represented our envy. We had to be the opposite of him to keep the competitive spirit alive. He was a missionary who wanted to convert Hindus, so we must not be Hindus who were willing to throw away our identity—maybe this thought might have been there subconsciously, triggered not due to religion, but due to rivalry. Think *Jo Jita Wohi Sikandar*-type school rivalry, and not a Sikandar vs Porus civilizational rivalry.

Although being aware and assertive of your Hindu identity is enough to be labelled as a Sanghi, I was still an average Hindu, more likely to support the Congress than the BJP during my school days. I was aware but not really assertive of my identity. I remained an average Hindu, or should I say a 'Congressi Hindu', for many years to come.

The great Congressi trick

It was only in the year 2016 when I became vocal, primarily in the virtual world, about my ideological slants. I started aggressively countering the arguments of the lot that calls itself Left-liberal because there were just too many inconsistencies there—something that I'll discuss in the later chapters of the book.

My vocal opposition to this group translated into a vocal and partisan support to the Modi government and the BJP soon after. This eventually led to me being invited to a few gatherings of BJP supporters, where some of these 'born Sanghis' wondered how I could have ever associated myself with the Congress party if I realized and appreciated the fact that Hindus got a raw deal in this country. The Congress was an anti-Hindu party, how can any Hindu support it, they wondered.

The Congress is a very unique political party in this sense. One can reasonably argue how the party, or rather the various governments run by the party since Independence, have worked against the interests of any chosen social group, and yet the party can claim to represent and care for the interests of that very group.

While it was in power, it was accused of working against the interests of Dalits and tribal communities by taking away their lands and rights in the name of fighting Naxalism. One can argue that if these communities have remained poor and never enjoyed any meaningful share in power, the blame lies with the party that has ruled India for decades after Independence. Poverty and denial of share in the power structure are often offered as causes of growth in extremist and separatist movements in different part of the country. Yet the party claims that Dalits and tribals are its 'natural voters.'

Not only did successive Congress governments fight the armed Naxals with bullets, they also went after a group that was later popularly identified as 'Urban Naxals,' many of whom, except the privileged few like Arundhati Roy, were jailed under various charges, including sedition, by the union government led by Manmohan Singh. Yet, the same Congress decided to throw its political weight behind the same people when they were arrested under the Modi government under similar charges.

Similarly, the Congress has been accused by Muslim community leaders of not doing enough for the Muslims, both on economic and social fronts, due to which the community has lagged on both these counts even decades after Independence. But the Congress proudly claims to stand by the minorities and is identified with the policy of Muslim appeasement.

The same pattern is seen even if we analyse groups beyond religion and caste. The anti-Hindi agitation in various states, especially in the South, were all triggered during the Congress regimes due to the central government's policy of promoting Hindi, yet it is a party that proudly says it stands with the diversity of India and accuses the BJP of 'Hindi imposition.'

And finally, the Congress is accused of promoting crony capitalism, with many industrialists being its patrons or members, yet Rahul Gandhi accuses a government led by a 'chaiwala' of being the 'suit boot ki sarkar.'

It is worth a thesis to analyse how the Congress could manage this unique distinction. This is why when a controversy broke out ahead of the 2019 Lok Sabha elections that Congress had hired the services of Cambridge Analytica[16]—a political consultancy and data analytics company that had helped Donald Trump in his successful US presidential campaign in 2016—I felt that it was a pointless exercise by the oldest political party of India. Firms like Cambridge Analytica should actually be studying and consulting Congress veterans to draw lessons in strategic communication.

The biggest and unique strength of Cambridge Analytica was reported to be their targeted communication to various sub-groups, which triggered varied set of emotions and reactions among the respective sub-groups, sometimes in conflict with each other, but the sum total of this exercise benefited a particular party, which happened to be their client. Essentially, Cambridge Analytica was helping its client speak in different voices to different sets of groups, and yet not appearing incoherent or insincere to any of them. That's precisely what the Congress had been doing since decades!

The Congress never appeared incoherent and insincere to the common man, until as late as 2010, because its incoherence was dressed up as its virtue of believing in diversity, and voices questioning its sincerity were either discredited (by branding them fringe or facetious) or co-opted (by rewarding them in the well-oiled and entrenched ecosystem).

However, to be fair to the grand old party of India, its incoherence was originally indeed a reflection of its belief in diversity, for the pre-Independence Congress party was the big stage where people believing in various shades of different ideologies came together for the common cause of complete self-rule (Purna Swaraj) over British Raj. Leaders such as Bal Gangadhar Tilak, Lala Lajpat Rai, Madan Mohan Malaviya and others would easily qualify as 'Sanghis' as per the liberal definition, but all such leaders were leading and influential members of the Congress party in British India.

Once the British left, this incoherence should have been gotten rid of, even if it meant disbanding the Congress and breaking it into smaller political units with more refined and focused ideologies. Eventually the Congress did break, first in 1959, leading to the formation of the Swatantra Party by C. Rajagopalachari, where Congress leaders who didn't agree with the socialist policies of Jawaharlal Nehru decided to part ways, and later in 1969 when the party split with the expulsion of Indira Gandhi, who was seen turning the Congress into her personal fiefdom. She was also recklessly following policies that were even more socialist and populist than her father's.

However, these splits didn't really bring any coherence to the Congress party, because they were not exactly vertical splits on well-defined ideological grounds. The 1969 split, particularly, was more about Indira Gandhi's way of functioning where many of her decisions, especially her decision to not support her own party's official candidate for the presidential elections that year, made a section of the Congress party uncomfortable. She was expelled from the party as a result, but it ended up proving that she enjoyed majority support within the party.

The split was primarily a power tussle to gain control of the party. Incidentally, Nehru, too, was seen as a leader who wanted more and more control over the party, causing many leaders to leave the party, ranging from socialists such as Jay Prakash Narayan to classical liberals such as Rajagopalachari.

Further, on both these occasions of the Congress party splitting, the ideological articulation on the socio-cultural matters remained absent or rather unaddressed by either of the factions. At best, it was more of a Left-wing vs (comparatively) Right-wing divide over certain economic policies than any split on socio-cultural matters. And of course, it was primarily about the personalities of Nehru and Indira, respectively.

This lack of clarity or articulation on ideological issues, especially on socio-cultural matters, made sure that the Congress (or its factions) did not appear anti-Hindu to most Hindus for decades after Independence, even though such criticism had existed right since the time of Mahatma Gandhi, who was accused of harming Hindu interests by pursuing the policy of Muslim appeasement.

The Gandhian policy of Muslim appeasement was continued as a state policy by Nehru after the British left. But, at the same time, the party continued to showcase the legacy of the likes of Bal Gangadhar Tilak, Lala Lajpat Rai, Madan Mohan Malaviya, Sardar Patel and others as part of their history and ethos, and thus a common Hindu did not have compelling reasons to believe that the Congress was 'anti-Hindu', even though Nehru—the person who shaped modern Congress before his daughter chiselled it to perfection—was not a religious person and had no special love for his Hindu identity. 'I was born a Hindu, but I do not know how far I am justified in calling myself one or in speaking on behalf of Hindus,' Nehru had said back in 1929 itself.[17]

Even though Nehru had no special love for Hinduism, the Congress under him, even after Independence, was not overtly following policies that would go on to strip India of its Hindu identity and consciousness altogether. Perhaps, it was too early to do that. India had witnessed widespread communal riots around Partition and people were sensitive about religious issues, and Nehru would have lost popularity had he pushed overtly secular policies down the throat of ordinary Hindus.

Additionally, some attempts by Nehru in that direction, such as his opposition to rebuilding and restoration of the Somnath temple, were met with resistance within the party and government. The then President Dr Rajendra Prasad went ahead and inaugurated the restored temple despite Nehru asking him not to do so. 'I believe in my religion and cannot cut myself away from it,' Dr Prasad had told Nehru, justifying his decision to reopen the Somnath temple.[18]

Dr Rajendra Prasad was a Congressman too, and there were many other Congress leaders with a Hindu outlook, and one could not really term the Congress as an anti-Hindu party then. Someone had jokingly said that in those times there were more Sanghis in the Congress than in the (Bharatiya Jan) Sangh.

Except for the dislike of Nehru as a person, and a critique of his personal ideology and deeds, such as his handling of the Kashmir issue, perhaps there was not much one could say against the Congress party during those times to paint it as some anti-Hindu outfit. One can very well argue that the Congress under Nehru was, ironically, not exactly Nehruvian.

The Congress became somewhat of an active ally in de-Hinduizing India under Indira Gandhi, when she decided to turn leftward and adopt hardcore socialist and populist economic policies. Though socialist economic policies don't by themselves mean de-Hinduization of policy, it helped in that process unwittingly. Communists gained access and control in the corridors of powers primarily due to the shift in economic policies, but they used that access and control to influence government policies beyond economic matters.

Unlike Nehru, who was Left-leaning due to his 'intellectual' pursuits or ideological beliefs, Indira turned Left mostly due to realpolitik. Slogans like 'Garibi Hatao' helped her score political victories, and she could see that the socialist rhetoric worked like a charm. The Soviet Union influence is also believed to be one of the factors behind Indira turning Left. If one is to believe the papers leaked by the former KGB operative Vasili Mitrokhin, Indira Gandhi's government was highly compromised and controlled by the Soviets, who vowed to extend the sphere of influence of communism to the entire world. Many declassified files of the CIA suggest that such influence of the Soviets, that is, communists over India continued even in the Rajiv Gandhi era.[19]

These files claim that the Soviets were paying huge money to politicians belonging to the Congress and communist parties to shape domestic and international policies, which obviously were policies that not only furthered the interests of the USSR but also promoted their ideology, that is, communism and socialism. The Soviets were reportedly also paying many journalists to shape public opinion in favour of their country and ideology. So, this could well be one of the reasons why the leftists became deeply entrenched in the ecosystem under Indira Gandhi—because it was all well paid for.

I remember having read a book named *Russi Lok Kathaayein*, which translates to Russian folk tales. It was a children's book of fables that our father had bought for us brothers when we were 8–9 years old. Such books were part of the cultural exchange programs between USSR and India. The folk tales were good and the book had nice glossy pages, which we loved. I suspect USSR might have made it available at subsidized rates for Indian kids, else the quality of pages and printing would have made it a bit too costly for our father to afford.

There were many tales and signs of India–Soviet friendship in those years, even though India officially maintained a non-aligned status between the US and the USSR. Raj Kapoor was supposed to be a major hit in the Soviet Union, with his movies being dubbed in Russian and doing well—those were the Indira Gandhi years and I wasn't even born then. But during the Rajiv Gandhi era, I remember news reports and hazy TV visuals of Rajiv Gandhi being welcomed in Russia, where a young Russian woman made him eat bread and salt as a gesture of friendship. Rajiv later kissed the Russian girl as well. I was a bit too young to get excited or scandalized by the kiss, but I connected the visuals of Rajiv eating the bread and salt with the Hindi idiom—*Rajiv ne Russia ka namak khaya*, so now he will have to be loyal to the Russians?

As a boy, Russia or the USSR sounded like a really nice place to me, based on the popular stuff that I read in the newspapers or saw on TV; so, my Prime Minister eating the *namak* of Russia was okay. I remember reading up newspaper and magazine columns by many authors who would praise how things were far better in the USSR. As a young boy, I was somehow given to understand that not only a far higher standard of living existed in the USSR, which indeed was true, a perfect equality also existed there, so much so that everyone got the same salary, whether he was a professor or a janitor—something that was not really accurate, as I found out much later.

The broad point is that there indeed was Soviet influence on the narrative, not all of which can be termed illegitimate, but the use of money to push this narrative in favour of socialism can't be ruled out either.

Whatever be the reason—whether realpolitik where Indira Gandhi was being advised by a coterie to play around with populist and socialist rhetoric, or whether under the political and monetary influence of the Soviets—it is a fact that Indira Gandhi started pursuing leftist agenda that was not limited to economic matters only. It happened especially after the 1971 elections, where she managed to win a bigger majority of her own after having split the Congress party earlier. This was the election where she had given the slogan of 'Garibi Hatao'. Populism seated her in a position of strength within her own party and the Congress was secured as the private property of one family—something that will become the only 'ideology' of the party going forward.

After winning the 1971 elections, Indira made Nurul Hasan, a former professor of history at Aligarh Muslim University (AMU) with leftist leanings, the minister for Education, Social Welfare and Culture in her government. The Left couldn't have asked for a better deal. The leftists went on to have a mafia-like control over these three sectors, thanks to Indira Gandhi's Faustian bargain with them. Do remember that this was the period when Indira Gandhi turned even more autocratic, leading to the imposition of Emergency, when the words 'socialist' and 'secular' were added to the preamble of the Constitution of India.

In his tenure that lasted over 6 years, thanks to the Emergency extending it by one year, Hasan set up various institutes around culture, social sciences and history, which were stuffed with Left-leaning academics and activists, and which acted as vehicles to secularize and de-Hinduize much of India's history, education and sense of culture.

Even though Indira Gandhi lost the 1977 elections and many of her decisions were overturned by the Janata Party government, these institutions continued to flourish and the Left continued to call the shots in these matters, no matter who won the elections. These were the institutions that helped frame the policies and write the textbooks, which made sure that even a school run by a devout and assertive Hindu failed to impart those values to its pupils. These were the institutions that became the real establishment, while their benefactors as well as beneficiaries continued to pretend to be anti-establishment.

So, at least the Congress under Indira should have been identified as anti-Hindu given what was done? In hindsight, that may appear obvious, but for an average Hindu, these things were a bit too complex. One needed to have a decent education to understand and grasp what the Marxist thought process was doing to the Indians' sense of history and culture, whereas almost 60 per cent of the Indian population was illiterate during those times. The damages being inflicted were not obvious to the masses.

Further, there was hardly any representation of pro-Hindu voices in the media that could have talked about these issues. Voices like those of Arun Shourie were heard much later and they were few and far between in the mainstream media. There were 'non-mainstream' writers, such as Ram Swarup and Sita Ram Goel; however, they had a limited reach and some of their works were published much later.

But most importantly, Indira Gandhi did not do or say anything that could be construed as going against Hindu beliefs or sentiments in manner and matters that could be noticed and understood by the common man. On the contrary, she wore rudraksha beads, frequented temples and mathas—her puja at Sringeri in Karnataka before fighting the by-elections for the Lok Sabha in 1978 was a public spectacle—and had people like Dhirendra Brahmachari, a yoga guru, among those who were seen around her. Essentially, her public persona was very Hindu, something her grandchildren try to fall back upon even today when accused of being anti-Hindu.

One instance that could have painted Indira anti-Hindu was firing on sadhus and Hindu activists, who were demanding a ban on cow slaughter all over India, in 1966, when she was the prime minister. Many were killed when firing was ordered on protesters in Delhi.[20] The incident appears to have hurt Indira and Congress as Bharatiya Jan Sangh gained political strength in what is known as 'cow belt' in the subsequent elections.

However, it didn't paint the entire Congress party as anti-Hindu because the party had already supported and implemented a ban on cow slaughter in many states before and after this incident. Indira too had tried to arrest the damage by appointing committees to look into feasibility of a blanket ban on cow slaughter pan India. It appears that she took lessons from this incident and didn't publicly do or say anything in her subsequent terms as prime minister that could be construed as anti-Hindu by ordinary masses.

What further helped her was the fact that during later years, there was a lull period between the Bharatiya Jan Sangh merging itself into the Janata Party and the birth and rise of the Bharatiya Janata Party (BJP). So, a strong pro-Hindu political voice in the opposition was also missing. Thus, the Congress continued to look and sound like a Hindu party to an average Hindu, even though it helped a Hinduphobic ecosystem to flourish whenever it was in power, and it was in power almost all the time in those decades.

The Khalistani terrorists killing Hindus during the insurgency period in Punjab and later Indira Gandhi's assassination by them were used by the Congress party to play the Hindu card in the 1984 Lok Sabha elections, where it scored an unprecedented electoral majority. The Congress was then led by Rajiv Gandhi, who had a clean image and one could hardly point out anything about him that could be termed controversial, let alone anti-Hindu. And when he was in power, he opened the locks of Ayodhya and allowed the Hindus to perform a puja at the Ram Janmabhoomi—at least that is what Congressmen claim. Under these circumstances, how could an average Hindu perceive the Congress or even the Gandhi family as anti-Hindu?

In March 2020, during the nationwide lockdown due to the Covid-19 pandemic, the *Ramayana* TV serial was re-telecast on Doordarshan and it gained massive eyeballs again. Seeing the reaction, Congress leader and the former chief minister of Madhya Pradesh, Digvijay Singh, claimed that the original *Ramayana* series was produced after Rajiv Gandhi had personally requested Ramanand Sagar to produce a televised version of the epic. Now Digvijay Singh is hardly a Raja Harishchandra who only speaks the truth, but the point is that the Congress party made every effort to appear Hindu, even if the policies and people it promoted were working at the same time to undermine Hindu causes and interests.

Yes, the Shah Bano case was there too, where the Rajiv Gandhi government overturned a Supreme Court ruling to ensure that Muslim personal law prevails, but that was an example of Muslim appeasement rather than anti-Hinduism.

And even during Rajiv Gandhi's term, there were not many popular voices of dissent who could reach or appeal to an average Hindu. The BJP too used to accuse the Congress of Muslim appeasement and 'pseudo-secularism' rather than calling it anti-Hindu. By and large, there was no apparent reason for an ordinary Hindu to consider the Congress an anti-Hindu party.

Even Sonia Gandhi adopted the same tricks, and many local Congress leaders continued to be Hindu in outlook. Forget public posturing by Hindu Congress leaders, in 2006 a Muslim leader from the Congress party belonging to Madhya Pradesh had offered a reward for chopping off painter M.F. Husain's hands, as he had made nude paintings of Hindu goddesses.[21] All this while the Nehru–Gandhi family would receive paintings of their own family members drawn by Husain as gifts.

The average Congress leader regularly indulged in signalling to profess that the party did not approve of hurting the religious sentiments of Hindus, while the Congress leadership enabled and strengthened an ecosystem that increasingly hated everything Hindu—something an average Hindu, or should I say a 'Congressi Hindu', was not able to discern. An average Hindu used to be a Congressi Hindu for a very long time, I'd say even at the time of the 2014 electoral victory of Modi.

A Congressi Hindu is essentially someone who has a sense of belonging to the Hindu identity, but doesn't really understand the theological basis or political aspects of that identity. He is ever willing to accommodate and adjust the expanse of the identity, but not elaborate and construct the contours of that identity. He could be ready to wear the identity, but is not willing to defend it. And that's how they are different from a Sanghi, who focusses on the latter aspects.

In 2013, a year ahead of the general elections that were won by the BJP, Rahul Gandhi had said that if India was a computer, the Congress was its default operating system. He had actually said 'default program', but I'm assuming he meant default operating system because 'default program of a computer' doesn't make any sense. As usual his statement was mocked and made into memes and jokes, but he was entirely right. Thanks to decades of being in power, and thanks to the ecosystem that the Congress had nurtured and fed, the party indeed had become the default choice of Indians, especially ordinary Hindus.

Over the decades, the Congress went on to become a party that practically had no distinct and definite ideology, and its sole purpose was to survive and self-preserve; and that's exactly how the Congressi Hindus were like—with no well-defined or clear concept of their religious identity, and who were just happy to survive. In fact, the Congressi Hindu, or rather the average Indian Hindu, was worse than the Congress in terms of self-preservation. At least the Congress party tried to preserve its power, while the Congressi Hindu was entirely oblivious to even existentialist threats.

Let me clarify that while the Congress party didn't appear to have an ideology, the ecosystem had. They enjoyed a symbiotic relationship. The Congress never went all out against the ecosystem, while the ecosystem never went all out against the Congress. We will come to that later in the book when we talk about this ecosystem. For now, let's go back to the 1990s, when Sanghis like me were Congressis.

1990s—The decade of churn

The 1990s are widely accepted to be the decade when many fundamental things in India started changing—Hindutva became an electoral force to reckon with, the intermediary castes realized their political clout in the Hindi heartland, giving rise to powerful leaders like Lalu Prasad Yadav and Mulayam Singh Yadav, political instability at the Centre became a norm and India witnessed the economic liberalization, which gave the hope that pace of urbanization and wealth creation will go up and socialism may not remain the state dogma, only to find out later that a supposedly communist China did better than us on those two counts.

For Bihar, the 90s is synonymous with the meteoric rise of Lalu Prasad Yadav, who is credited to have created the MY (Muslim–Yadav) vote bank. The Yadavs were obviously his own caste people, who led the rise of the OBCs, or the intermediary castes, against the political hegemony of the upper castes, while Muslims rallied behind the Janata Dal after ditching the Congress due to the Rajiv Gandhi government opening the locks of Ayodhya. Additionally, the fact that many Muslim groups were enumerated as OBCs, who too would benefit from the recommendations of the Mandal Commission, made a large section of the Muslim community support the Janata Dal and Lalu Yadav. The Mandal Commission had recommended reservations in government jobs and educational institutes for the OBCs.

Apart from the lure of reservations that Lalu Yadav's Janata Dal promised, the intermediary castes realized that they did not need to play second fiddle to the upper castes to gain share or representation in the electoral power structure. Numerically they were stronger than the upper castes, and economically, while weaker, they were not so weak that they would live in perpetual fear of the next meal being uncertain.

In Bihar, especially, even Baniyas are listed among the backward castes, while almost everywhere else in the country they are supposed to be a forward caste. There was a widespread belief, and it was not entirely unfounded, that the four upper castes enjoyed disproportionate power and wealth in the society. These four castes were: Brahmins (also called Baabhan in local dialects), Bhumihars, Rajputs and Kayasthas (also termed as Lala).

During the 90s, a popular slogan by the Janata Dal was 'Bhura baal saaf karo' (get rid of the brown hair)—where 'bhura baal' didn't exactly mean brown hair, but was an acronym or proxy to mean the four upper castes: *Bhu*-mihar, *Ra*-jput, *Baa*-bhan and *L*-ala. Whether it meant a call for genocide or a call to get rid of them from the power structure is something that one can keep debating.

Due to the sheer caste arithmetic in Lalu Yadav's favour, his supporters as well as detractors believed that he will rule for a record duration in Bihar, breaking the record of communists in the neighbouring West Bengal, where they ruled for three decades, uninterrupted. Before Lalu's rise decimated the Congress in Bihar, the grand old party was as strong in the state as they were nationally. Most of the influential leaders and chief ministers in Bihar hailing from the Congress belonged to the upper castes, though there were a few exceptions.

One could wonder that if the other castes were not represented or rewarded well enough in the party, how come the Congress kept on winning elections and form governments in the state? Well, one of the reasons was the ability of the Congress to speak to various groups in different voices without appearing incoherent, something that I had mentioned earlier. So, while the Congress invariably had local feudal landlords under their patronage in almost every state, including Bihar, their elite central leadership could sweet-talk to appear egalitarian and non-casteist. This could help them garner some votes too, and appear as the 'natural home' for every section of the society.

However, the other reason was the fact that the political participation among the masses itself was low. Elders in my family would tell me that the lower castes, especially the Dalits, were not even aware of their democratic rights, especially in the villages. Either they just would not care to vote—while ballot papers would be stamped in their names—or they would be forcibly kept away from polling booths.

Booth capturing, which is also synonymous with Lalu Yadav, was originally practiced by the Congress in the state. And it was mostly the upper castes who captured booths for the Congress party. People in my own extended family used to brag about it, and once Congress leader Kirti Azad, the son of former Bihar Chief Minister Bhagvat Jha Azad, had blurted out the same, only to later deny his words.[22] Later, Lalu's men took this 'art' of booth capturing to a whole new level,[23] which was one of the reasons for their downfall, as it became one of the signifiers of the 'Jungle Raj'.[24]

A village elder would tell me that in the old days, the Yadavs would wield lathis on behalf of the Bhumihars and capture booths for the Congress for a few bucks, but soon they (Yadavs) realized that if they possessed the power of lathi, why should they wield it for the Bhumihars and settle for a few bucks, when the entire government treasury could be theirs.

Such factors and sentiments, too, contributed to the Janata Dal winning the 1990 assembly elections in Bihar and Lalu Yadav becoming the chief minister. While my family members, being traditional supporters of the Congress and belonging to the Bhumihar caste, hated the development, in some corner of their hearts, rather begrudgingly, they also hoped that maybe Lalu Yadav would remove the inefficiencies and corruption that the Congress had institutionalized, that maybe the new regime won't be as bad for them as they fear.

Anyway, the point I am trying to make is that in the 90s, it was all 'caste, caste and caste' for someone growing up in Bihar. The surrounding that I lived in was obsessed with caste, while the school that I went to had to follow secular Nehruvian pedagogy. There was no chance of becoming a Sanghi!

In fact, my name itself is testament to how caste reigned supreme in Bihar. I don't use my caste surname. While now I feel rather good about it, it was not really a decision that I took out of some principled stand. My parents decided to drop the caste surname from my name in the official records, so that I don't become a victim of 'reverse discrimination', which had become rampant during the 90s. You can find many Biharis with such 'double names' such as Rahul Roushan, Rakesh Ranjan, Amit Suman, et al., in my age group, and the reason for them being named so would mostly be the same—to hide their caste identity.

By the way, let me share another trivia about my name. While, primarily, I was given this 'double name' to hide the caste identity, there is another reason why I got a second name. My mother didn't want me to be named just Rahul. According to legends, Rahul was the name of Gautam Buddha's son, and Buddha, then Prince Siddhartha, had renounced the worldly life at the time of his son's birth. He is supposed to have left the palace without even taking his newly born son in his arms, lest paternal emotions overpower his spiritual resolve. My mother chose this second name, Roushan, due to this rather funny superstition of hers around the name Rahul.

Coming back to caste and post-Buddha Bihar, the exposure to casteist sentiments, especially among those of my own caste, meant that I did not need lectures by 'woke' people to understand how caste works and how someone's caste itself could indeed be a privilege or a handicap. It also meant that I could see how absurd or manipulative, or at best outdated and pedantic, some of their theories around caste oppression were.

For example, almost all the woke folks seem convinced that upper castes, especially Brahmins, exploit or ill-treat lower castes because some verses in *Manusmriti* apparently endorse such oppressive beliefs and actions. I don't want to get into what the verses say or even if such verses exist, but I do, for sure, know that such casteist and oppressive people existed, and I could see them in my extended family itself, in the ancestral village. Some of them couldn't change their attitude even after moving to cities.

All I know that not a single one of them ever mentioned anything about *Manusmriti*, or for that matter anything related to any religious scripture to me, while they surely told me how lower castes people deserve to do menial jobs only, and why I should be proud of my caste identity. In fact, hardly any of these deeply casteist people were religious. On the contrary, some of them cracked really obscene and sick jokes about Hindu gods and goddesses. Thankfully, I never had to spend much time in the company of these folks.

Whatever time I spent in the village, which was mostly during school holidays, as we weren't privileged enough to go to bigger cities or foreign countries for holidays, I never saw my grandmother, a deeply religious lady, insisting on any lower caste person to not enter the house or not touch this utensil or that.

But some of the young men of the extended family would take pride in a putative story that one of our patriarchs, some great-great-grandfather or someone, had beaten one lower caste guy black and blue just because he dared to cough loudly while passing by the main gate of our ancestral house.

These men didn't even have 5 per cent of the religiosity that my grandmother did. Some had 0 per cent, as I mentioned earlier. They just wanted to be bullies. And we see bullies all around us. We ourselves become one during school or college, either as individuals or as groups. Ragging becomes a tradition in college, and we just adopt it as a tradition, without any critical thinking. We don't read a book or attend some sermon to become a bully. It's an animal instinct. It's a herd mentality. It's an inherited mindset.

The feudal mindset is just there. It doesn't necessarily need any scriptural endorsement. One can keep analysing how it might have started and blame a verse here or there, but the fact is that after a few generations, feudalism becomes the default and independent mindset, almost like a mutant that is autonomous and unrecognizable from the original form. It becomes a religion in itself. Even if you remove the original religion, you won't be able to remove the mindset—and in Bihar you indeed had castes among Muslims, and these castes had their own separate mosques and graveyards.

But the leftists have a mission to equate Hinduism with feudal casteism. Their solution to get rid of casteism is to get rid of Hinduism—something that appears to be a farce to me, given what I had experienced and witnessed.

I won't say there was no element of caste feelings in me during my adolescence, but I absolutely didn't believe in caste supremacy. Fortunately, my parents did not give me an upbringing that could make me a caste supremacist. I remember a man from our village who had come to our house in Patna to deliver our share of rice and pulses that grew in our agricultural fields, where he worked. As he waited, he sat on the floor, presumably because he was from a lower caste and thus should be sitting 'lower' too. My parents asked him to take the chair and sit on it like any normal guest would. I remember his initial discomfort as well as the subsequent delight at being treated respectfully.

Later when I got married into a Gujarati Brahmin family, I came to know of at least two incidents of Brahmin–Dalit marriages that had taken place in the extended family of my wife. That was just one family, and like a typical Gujarati Brahmin family, they were religious, and many were Sanghis too. So, the BJP-voting communal Gujaratis were breaking caste barriers while the Congress-voting secular Biharis couldn't think beyond caste at all. Who were more likely to have read *Manusmriti*?

Anyway, these realizations dawned upon me later. During the 90s, popular sentiments in Bihar were around caste, though the BJP too had started making an impact, with Advani taking out the Ram Rath Yatra and the 'Sangh Parivar' taking the Ram Janmabhoomi movement to each village. Lalu Yadav got Advani arrested, bringing an abrupt end to the Rath Yatra as well as to the tenure of the union government headed by the Janata Dal, which was thitherto being supported by the BJP from outside. The then Prime Minister V.P. Singh had to resign, and the Congress backed a splinter group of the Janata Dal to form the next government headed by Chandra Shekhar.

Lalu Yadav ordering the arrest of Advani, and Mulayam Singh Yadav ordering the firing on kar sevaks in Ayodhya, where dozens—some claims put the number in hundreds—of ordinary Ram bhakts were killed, were the events that ignited Hindutva sentiments among a larger chunk of the masses. The talking point no longer remained 'Muslim appeasement'. Now, people could sense 'persecution of Hindus' with such actions—something that was not too obvious under the Congress governments, as I had mentioned earlier.

This is the reason why the BJP saw a huge jump in vote share in the ensuing 1991 Lok Sabha elections. They got over 20 per cent vote share, which was almost double of what the pro-Hindu parties would usually get in earlier elections. And I will repeat, BJP's rise as an electoral force was not due to sentiments triggered by the *Ramayana* TV serial—those sentiments were soft and spiritual—but due to sentiments triggered by the incidents like the firing on kar sevaks that took place in 1990. People were affronted and anguished. A sense of victimhood grew, even though the ecosystem wanted Hindus to believe that they can never be victims.

And that was not the first time when the (justified) feeling of victimhood had led to a surge in support for pro-Hindu political parties. If one looks at the performance of the Bharatiya Jan Sangh between 1962 and 1967—in both the Lok Sabha elections as well as in the assembly elections in the Hindi belt, which took place in the same years—one finds a significant jump in the vote share for the saffron party in those five years. In fact, 1967 was the best-ever performance by the Bharatiya Jan Sangh before it merged with the Janata Party.

What could have led to this sudden spurt of support for Sanghis? In all probability, it was the 1966 police firing at sadhus and other Hindu activists who were protesting outside the Parliament in Delhi to demand a blanket ban on cow slaughter. While the official records of those killed is very low, the popular claims of those killed range between few hundreds to even thousands. Whatever be the real numbers, the fact that it led to the feeling of 'Hindus under attack' among a segment of people, in all probability helped the Jan Sangh in the ensuing elections.

Firing on kar sevaks at Ayodhya similarly helped the BJP in the 1991 Lok Sabha elections. However, I can't claim that it changed me, as I was barely 10 years old then, and obviously the mainstream media—

Doordarshan and the newspapers—didn't talk much about it. It didn't even change my parents, as they were hopeful of Rajiv Gandhi returning to power in 1991.

For some weird reason, I remember my father muttering 'Zyada mat bol budbak, Rajiv Gandhi phir aa raha hai' ('Don't blabber too much idiot, Rajiv Gandhi is coming back.'), when a person was speaking about the Bofors scandal on Doordarshan's news bulletin sometime in 1990. No, it was not a high-pitched debate like we have on TV these days. It was simply a reporter talking to some common people.

We were accustomed to not hearing or listening to anything against the Gandhi family on TV. What common people used to say was also carefully handpicked and censored before being aired on TV, which is why that statement against Rajiv Gandhi by an ordinary man on TV elicited such reaction from my father. Such a statement could air as there was a non-Congress government in power then, led by the Janata Dal.

Rajiv Gandhi couldn't return to power though. He was assassinated on the night of 21 May during the 1991 Lok Sabha election campaign at Sriperumbudur in Tamil Nadu. We got the news the following morning as our family would sleep early.

I distinctly remember how the front page of the newspaper looked on that day. The top headline—about Rajiv's assassination—was in capital letters, in a font size that was bigger than the newspaper masthead itself—something I had seen for the first time. It was indeed that big a news. And it was devastating for us traditional Congress supporters. Even I, a young boy who was not too aware of politics, shed a tear. It felt like a personal loss.

There were fears that violence against the 'Madrasis' could begin just as Sikhs were attacked after Indira Gandhi's assassination. Fortunately, nothing like that happened, probably because South Indians, at least in Patna, were a handful and mostly in high-ranking positions. And of course, the Congress was not in power, neither in the state, nor at the Centre.

But there was anger, at least among the Congress supporters, and among the upper castes and definitely among the Bhumihars, who were the traditional supporters of the party. There were murmurs about how the Janata Dal supporters or Lalu's supporters—by default assumed as the backward castes—had celebrated the death of Rajiv Gandhi and distributed sweets, for they thought the Congress party itself was dead. As I write this in 2020, Lalu Yadav is a trusted ally of Rajiv Gandhi's widow Sonia Gandhi. How times change.

There were a few face-offs, some skirmishes, as Congress supporters took out impromptu rallies shouting 'Rajiv Gandhi amar rahein' ('Long live Rajiv Gandhi.') and passed by any Janata Dal office or group of workers (remember the assassination took place in the middle of the election campaign), but fortunately none of it resulted in anything similar to that of 1984. If riots were triggered around caste lines in Bihar, it would have perhaps been worse than 1984.

Caste wars, however, did take place in Bihar later in the 1990s, though it had nothing to do with Rajiv Gandhi's assassination, and were limited to some select pockets.

The Naxal influence had grown rapidly in many parts of Bihar. Landlords, many a times belonging to the Bhumihar caste, were targeted and killed by Naxal groups, and in response some Bhumihars formed a private militia named Ranvir Sena, which carried out multiple revenge attacks and massacres, often of people belonging to the most backward castes and the scheduled castes, accusing them of either being Naxalites or providing support to them.

The Ranvir Sena was not the first or the only caste-based private militia. Communist and Naxalite influence in Bihar has a long history, where they exploited the caste fault lines to push their ideology among the common masses. They simply replaced class with caste in their framework.

The mainstream communist movement, however, comprised upper caste members too. In fact, most communist leaders were from the upper castes only. The communist parties were a serious and powerful political force in Bihar, performing well in many elections. Begusarai in Bihar was once proudly proclaimed as 'Leningrad of the East' by the communists, who thought Bihar would soon go the communist way, like the neighbouring West Bengal.

When the Naxal movement started in West Bengal, it didn't take much time for it to reach Bihar. Armed insurgent groups were formed to bring a revolution in Bihar. Since most of the landless belonged to particular castes, these armed Naxal groups largely functioned as caste militias.[25]

The armed groups formed by the upper castes to take the Naxals on were obviously caste militias. Rajputs were one of the first ones to have their own 'sena' as soon as the Naxals formed armed groups in the 1970s, but the Ranvir Sena in the 1990s became the most dreaded and ruthless one, as it didn't spare even women and children.

These groups received overt and covert support from the mainstream political leadership as well, which comprised leaders from every political party, including the Janata Dal. There was an outfit of Kurmi caste landlords too. Kurmis were among the OBCs and supporters of the Janata Dal. Even the Muslim landlords had a sena—the Sunlight Sena, where Rajputs allied with them—all purportedly to fight against the Naxals, who would on occasions fight amongst themselves, killing each other to establish supremacy. Thousands of them lost their lives. The 1990s was truly a troubled decade, at least in Bihar.

In such a society, deeply divided along caste lines, where Muslims were also virtually a caste group with whom one set of Hindus would ally to fight and kill another set of Hindus, it was not easy for an ideology like Hindutva, which aimed for the unification of Hindus beyond caste lines, to flourish.

And some Muslims indeed were like one of the various castes in Bihar. They would observe the widely popular Chhath festival of Bihar, where Surya bhagwaan and Chhathi maiya are offered prayers and prasad. Many would take part in Holi and Diwali festivities, too. With an average 'modern' Hindu family's religiosity beginning and ending with the celebration of a few festivals, one could even argue that these Muslims were as much of a Hindu as they were!

But things had started changing in the 90s; in fact the seeds were sown in the 70s and 80s itself, with a more puritan form of Islam being promoted among Indian Muslims. The reversal of Shah Bano judgment in 1986, under pressure from the community, was one of the indicators of how things had changed. At least the clergy and Muslim leadership, except the lone dissenting voice of Arif Mohammad Khan, ended up proving that their religious identity and purity were non-negotiable.

Liberals love to exculpate the Muslim community of any blame and keep attributing any rise of radicalism and obscurantism to external factors. The demolition of the Babri Masjid in 1992 is often presented as the reason for a 'wave of self-radicalization' among Muslims. It is also cited as the reason why things started changing in the 90s.

When you point out what Islamic radicalism did to the Kashmiri Pandits in the late 80s and especially in the year 1990—incidents that took place before the Babri Masjid's demolition—they will bring geopolitics and sheepishly try to blame Pakistan, but not without censuring India and the Indian Army.

Further, the liberals love to invert the causes and effects. Just like they believe that sentiments around Lord Ram became popular due to a TV serial—while in reality it was the popularity of Lord Ram that made a TV serial, with a rather low-budget production quality, super successful—they are convinced that the BJP's rise radicalized the Muslims, while totally discounting the possibility that it could actually be the other way round.

They somehow can't put the primary blame on the ideology of Islamism, especially the Salafi and Wahhabi version of Sunni Islam, which had been growing for many years before 1992. The Babri Masjid demolition was not the fount of radicalization among Indian Muslims.

Saudi Arabia had started investing in the promotion of their version of Sunni Islam in the late 70s and 80s, and the Indian subcontinent was a part of that project. Many Muslims who went there to work in oil fields and later for other skilled jobs would return with 'purer' version of Islamic practices and beliefs. Bigger mosques and various madarsas in the suburban and even some rural areas were being built in many parts of India, including in Bihar, as the money trickled in.

Zakir Naik, one of the better-known personalities who promoted Salafi-Wahhabi version of Islam quite aggressively and successfully in India and in the neighbouring countries, had founded his organization in 1991, again before the Babri Masjid's demolition. Currently, he is a fugitive. The TV channel he used to propagate his beliefs—ironically named Peace TV—has been banned in India, Bangladesh and Sri Lanka, because he is wanted for inspiring terror attacks.

The quest to make Muslims understand their religion better and to inspire them to strictly follow the religious practices in their pristine form is an age-old one among the Muslim community. Outfits like Tablighi Jamaat work with similar objectives. They were founded much before India became independent. However, their influence did not spread as rapidly until the petro-dollars from the gulf countries became instrumental in taking the project to large masses.

In a research paper titled 'Stoking the Flames: Intra-Muslim Rivalries in India and the Saudi Connection' published in May 2007 in the journal *Comparative Studies of South Asia, Africa and the Middle East*, author Yoginder Sikand has written in detail about how many Islamic organizations and institutions received patronage and funds from the Arab states in the 1970s. He writes:

> The sort of Islam that the Saudis began aggressively promoting abroad, including in India, in the aftermath of the 1979 Iranian Revolution, had a number of characteristic features. It was extremely literalist; it was rigidly and narrowly defined, being concerned particularly with issues of 'correct' ritual and belief, rather than with wider social and political issues; it was viciously sectarian, branding dissenting groups, such as Shi'as and followers of the Sufis as 'enemies' of Islam; and, finally, it was explicitly and fiercely critical of ideologies and groups, Muslim as well as other, that were regarded as political threats to the Saudi regime.

The aforementioned research paper also talks about funds from Saudi Arabia and other Arab countries being used to set up mosques, madarsas, publishing houses and other such institutions to propagate the Salafi-Wahhabi version of Islam. An organization called Ahl-i Hadith is reported to have received most of the funds, while others, such as Jama'at-i Islami and the Deobandis too, are said to have benefited to some extent.

Essentially, things had started changing much before the Babri Masjid was pulled down. One cannot rule out that people started seeing merits in Hindutva politics after witnessing how Muslim society was becoming more and more assertive about their separate and 'purer' identity. Even if one may fail in spotting behavioural changes in the community, one would certainly notice the new mosques and madarsas that were being built.

I was too young to notice such changes, though in retrospect there are certain things that now I can claim were signs of how radicalism was growing among the Muslim community.

For example, at my high school in Patna, Muslim representation was not too high, but the school had arranged for an Urdu teacher for them, as the Muslim students did not want to study Sanskrit as the third language. This was in sharp contrast to the students at the middle school in Bihar Sharif, where Muslim students did not opt out of Saraswati Vandana.

Back in Bihar Sharif, I'd overhear adolescent Muslim boys wanting to be Imran Khan and Wasim Akram as they played cricket in the nearby playground. That in itself is not problematic, I must clarify. On YouTube, so many times I myself have indulged in binge watching Wasim Akram and Waqar Younis devastating batsmen with their swinging yorkers. It's a treat to watch them bowl that way, except against India of course.

That 'except against' was missing when I moved to Patna. I would hear crackers being burst in certain areas, especially in an area called Sabzibagh, if Pakistan beat India in a One Day International cricket match.

Still, as a teenaged Hindu boy in a Congress-supporting family, I found these issues to be 'minor', which shouldn't be fretted upon, and thus these observations did not push me towards Hindutva or Sanghi ideology. Your daily life was not impacted by these things, you felt, or rather, you didn't make an effort to ponder how these things can indeed impact your daily life, especially your tomorrow.

The shakha I never went to

I don't recall having seen any RSS gatherings in Bihar Sharif, where I spent my childhood. As young kids, my brother and I didn't venture out much, except when going to school or to the nearby playground in the evenings, so I might have missed seeing any shakha even if it was around.

But in Patna, where I spent my teenage years and completed my graduate studies, I did notice a shakha in a local park. There would be a bunch of men belonging to various age groups, with all of them wearing khaki-coloured 'half pants', who gathered for some physical activity. I would find grown-up men wearing half-pants funny, and would pause to observe them.

In their public gatherings, there was a discipline that you would usually see in schools during the morning assemblies—people standing in parallel queues and someone addressing them. As a teenager, you don't exactly value this school-like discipline and want to rebel against it; so, I can't really say that I was impressed by the sight of Sanghis attending their shakhas, but the sight surely aroused curiosity about who these people were.

That curiosity was mostly satisfied by the mass media. Those were the mid-90s, when private TV grew really fast in popularity and a new bunch of businessmen in the form of cable TV operators came into existence. Limited current affairs programmes were allowed on these private channels, before many 24-hour news channels came into existence towards the end of the decade.

Faced with competition, even Doordarshan came up with shows whose production quality and content type were 'non-sarkari.' Doordarshan also had made available their alternate channel, which was called DD2 and later DD Metro, on an all-India basis. Aaj Tak, currently the most popular 24-hour Hindi news channel, had started as a standalone news bulletin on DD Metro, while Rajat Sharma became a household name due to his hugely popular show *Aap Ki Adalat*, which used to air as a standalone program on Zee TV and was one of their flagship programs along with *Antakshari*.

And obviously, there were newspapers. In the media, the RSS, or rather the Sangh Parivar—a routinely used term to broadly club a motley of Hindu organizations together, which may or may not have an official relationship with the RSS—would be in news mostly for the wrong reasons—for opposing some event or person, for being blamed by the government for some trouble or for airing views that sounded ridiculous and irrational. Basically, they appeared to be a bunch of people from whom one should stay away.

A friend of mine in college—and college starts early in Bihar, where classes 11 and 12 are taught in colleges if you opt for the State Board of Higher Secondary Education, which I had done—used to go to a shakha. I was preparing for the IITs then, and the only non-college gatherings I used to attend were private tuitions to study maths and physics, so I was least interested in going to a shakha. My friend would tell me that it was not a bad experience to visit one. However, I didn't pay heed to his advice.

Once, when both of us were returning from college on our respective bicycles—and I had a 'modern' one with straight handlebar and cable brakes, which was good enough to give me a sense that I was driving a motorbike—he said that he needed to walk into the local RSS shakha to collect some reading materials. He asked me to accompany him inside, but I didn't go. Instead, I offered to stand outside the shakha and take care of the bicycles, and asked him to quickly go inside and fetch the books. This was the closet I got to a shakha in my teenage years, and while studying.

I think in my subconscious mind those media reports were playing their part. It must be 1996, by when the Babri Masjid had already been demolished and the RSS was briefly banned in its aftermath. There had been communal riots in some parts of the country, too, for which the BJP and the RSS were blamed. In Delhi, the Janata Dal was in power, supported by the Congress from outside to 'keep communal forces out of power.' Hindutva and the RSS were villains in the national narrative, and that could have prejudiced my mind.

It was also the time when my father had taken a long leave without pay from his not-so-well-paying government job, and taken up the job of teaching English language and linguistics at a university in Yemen, a Middle Eastern country. As a result, we were being supervised and raised only by our mother in those years. As the elder son, I was expected to not go astray by taking any 'illegitimate advantage' of this lack of paternal scrutiny. Going to the shakha would be going astray, I'd think.

While I didn't go inside that shakha, I accepted some of the booklets my friend gave me. Those were in Hindi, and they were not about imposing supremacy of the Hindu religion or glorifying our past and dreaming about a Hindu Rashtra—the only thing the RSS thinks about, if one looks at them from the lens of the liberal media.

In fact, some of those booklets were about economics, with a focus on Swadeshi. This was the time when WTO (World Trade Organization) was just formed and many in the RSS looked at it as a modern colonizing attempt by the Western countries. At least one of those booklets warned against WTO and advocated protectionist policies to be adopted by India. Not at all 'Right wing' you see.

However, back then, those bunch of booklets were hardly enough to make me think that the RSS could be different from how they are presented in the mainstream media. Honestly, I didn't even read them properly; the textbooks and the pressure to do well at the IIT entrance exam were at the top of my mind then, not any ideology or politics.

Additionally, I feel that the RSS never really cared about the way they were presented in the media, so those booklets were mostly meant for the already converted and not to impress someone like me. Perhaps, they thought it was not a battle—fighting the negative perception created by the media—where they should spend their energies upon.

There were a few Sanghis in the college too, or rather 'communal Hindus' as I would consider them, though they were not exactly my friends. They were batchmates whom I would hear debating on things that sounded all too aggressive and needless to me.

For example, once they debated on the issue of propagation of religion, which happens to be a fundamental right granted in the Constitution of India. It followed after Atal Bihari Vajpayee had called for a 'national debate on religious conversions', which was triggered by news of attacks on Christians. This was around 1999, when Vajpayee was rather new in the office of the prime minister. Coincidentally, one of the first things that Modi had to face, shortly after assuming office in 2014, was 'attack on Christians.'

During the Modi era, the 'attack on Christians' narrative, which included the so-called attempts of 'ghar-wapsi' (i.e., re-converting Christians into Hinduism), fell flat as most attacks turned out to be petty crimes. That could happen because the dynamics of communication and tools of narrative had changed during the Modi era, but back in 1999, Vajpayee didn't have this luxury. The narrative was entirely one-sided, as if Christians were being beaten up all over India. Yet, Vajpayee stood his ground. While assuring safety to the Christians and to the Christian missionaries, he also called for a national debate on conversions.

However, the debate was soon lost by Hindus, at least in the eyes of Congressi Hindus like me—the biggest reason being the murder of a Christian missionary in Odisha. The incident happened almost within a couple of weeks of Vajpayee asking for a debate on conversions. Graham Staines, a Christian missionary from Australia who was active in the tribal areas of Odisha, was burnt alive and killed along with his two minor sons in the Keonjhar district of the state.

No amount of logic was going to win over such a tragic story. And that's how the Hindus have been losing narratives most of the times. The other side comprises an endless list of victims, while Hindu victims are systematically erased from public memory.

One of my 'communal Hindu' batchmates, from the group about which I talked about earlier, justified this murder of the Christian missionary. 'Do you even know how these missionaries convert people? They tell uneducated Hindus that your Hindu gods and goddesses are fake, who can't protect you from hell. Such arguments sell with the poor and uneducated people. They see that missionaries indeed don't suffer for insulting Hindu gods. Slowly, they end up changing their religion. Now, the Hindus can shout back that if Hindu gods are so weak and if the Christian god is so strong, why could the Christian god not save Graham Staines?'—this was one of the arguments offered to me, which left me shocked.

The shock at this attempt to justify a murder aside, I didn't even know that Christian missionaries indeed use such arguments to try and convince poor Hindus that Hinduism was an inferior religion. I thought the missionaries might be just telling people how nice and lovable Jesus Christ was. No news report or popular media ever told me that missionaries used supremacist arguments and fraudulent means to convert, such as mixing allopathic medicines in the 'prasad' of Jesus and claiming that the ailments were cured due to the blessings of the Christian god. Even in a Bollywood movie, a Christian priest was invariably a good man.

More than a decade later, I came to know about such means adopted by Christian missionaries only through social media, when various video clips showing such 'miracle cure' events went viral. I could also find a few news reports in the local newspapers, which I accessed via the internet, that showed how missionaries used objectionable means, which included offering inducements and insulting native traditions.

And well, I personally was the target of a Christian missionary, trying to convert me right in the centre of a shopping mall in Budapest, Hungary. This happened in 2019 when I was on a holiday abroad with my family. The rest of them had gone inside a shop to buy something while I waited outside. One guy, presuming that I was an Indian and Hindu, came to me and started preaching the gospel! He told me that the Hindu concept of reincarnation was wrong. He tried to convince me that I should become a Christian, because there were no such 'irrational' concepts in Christianity.

Good that my wife was not around, else the guy would have witnessed the Hindu concept of 'shakti'. Perhaps, a video clip showing an Indian woman shouting at a European man in Budapest would have gone viral. I decided not to create any scene or argue with him. I just smiled and asked the guy not to waste his and my time and politely asked him to go away. Even while going away, he repeated that Hindu belief in reincarnation was false.

Imagine, I was just a tourist, and this man had no idea about me or my religious beliefs or even my financial status—maybe he thought I was a poor guy in need of a better lifestyle, as I don't really wear branded designer clothes—but in full public view in a European capital city, this man had the temerity to tell me to my face that my religion was inferior. What such Christian preachers would do in the remote Indian villages, that too decades ago, was easy to guess.

Such information asymmetry is humongous, which acts as a big handicap for Hindus in putting forward their arguments. Not that being aware of these things would have convinced me that burning a man alive was justified, but at least that college batchmate wouldn't have appeared an entirely deranged liar to me. His claims about what missionaries do were not wrong, but I assumed them to be made up because justifying a murder was entirely unacceptable to me.

Let me clarify that I have absolutely no knowledge or memory to claim that this particular batchmate was an RSS member or supporter. I currently don't even remember his name and can't trace back and contact him to ask whether he was a shakha-going Sanghi. In all probability, he was not; he was just an angry Hindu, which I was not.

That one friend who actually went to a shakha never came up with such extreme arguments while discussing anything with me. In fact, he didn't try to convert me at all through debates and discussions. We mostly used to discuss mathematics and what to do if we failed to get admission in the IITs.

And well, we indeed had failed to get into the IITs. There was an option of going to other engineering colleges. I remember that a lot of Bihari students would go to engineering colleges in Maharashtra and Karnataka, where, if I remember correctly, you didn't need to take some gruelling entrance exam. Your Class 12 marksheet was enough to apply for admissions. However, I had decided to stay back in Patna and complete my graduation studies in maths from Patna Science College, the same college where I attended Classes 11 and 12, and where, later, I was subjected to the argument about Christian missionaries.

I had chosen maths because I really liked solving mathematical problems, and its application in physics. I was clueless about chemistry, which proved to be my nemesis in the IIT entrance exams. I was so scarred that I decided not to study chemistry, even as an elective subject, for my Bachelor of Science degree. The future career plan was to prepare for the UPSC exams. It was the religious duty of every Bihari student to either become a doctor/engineer or become an IAS officer, nothing better if one becomes both.

I was not too excited about the UPSC plan though, so as an alternate plan I thought of studying further after graduation and get an MCA degree (Master of Computer Application), a course that was supposed to be the next big thing back then, as the use of computers was being adopted widely.

I was among those very few students who decided to stay back in Bihar for a graduate degree. Most Biharis become non-resident Biharis during college days itself. As a result, the same college during the graduation days felt a little alien. I was left with a very few friends, and started exploring other ways to engage myself. This was the time I started listening to a variety of music—from Urdu ghazals by Jagjit Singh to popular songs in English by the likes of Bryan Adams and MLTR, the latter being discovered thanks to MTV launching in India and dial-up internet helping with the lyrics.

My shakha-going friend too had stayed back in Patna for graduate studies, but he was in a different college. He was least impressed by either of these two interests that I had picked up, but he didn't scoff at them either. We used to frequently hang out on our college campuses.

With our IIT dreams shattered, our conversations revolved mostly around future studies and banal things in life, though a few times politics was discussed too. How could one not? In four years, India witnessed three Lok Sabha elections between 1996 and 1999.

How much invested I was in electoral politics can be gauged from the fact that I did not vote even once, though I had attained the minimum age for voting in January 1998 and could have voted in two of these elections. However, that didn't mean that I was not interested in keeping myself aware about politics or political developments.

I distinctly remember the first BJP government that lasted barely two weeks in 1996, especially the televised vote of confidence discussion that ended with an emphatic speech by Atal Bihari Vajpayee. After giving an impassioned lecture about democracy and respect for mandate given by the people, Vajpayee suddenly went on to announce that he was resigning, even before the voting on the motion could take place. It was watched and talked about all over India, and it created sympathy for him. He was seen as a person who was wronged, and against whom some bullies had ganged up.

The Congress-supporting me also felt that this person should get a chance, as he came first in a race but was denied the rewards. But, it was essentially sympathy for the person named Vajpayee, not any warming up to the ideology called Hindutva. A personal liking for Vajpayee could have led me to explore more about the BJP's or RSS' ideology, but in those years I was too busy, and mostly concerned about my chances of getting admission in the IITs, and didn't have time for exploring such topics. I understood politics and ideology only to the extent that was propagated by the mainstream media.

The person who can be credited to have first exposed me to a different set of ideas—in contrast to the ideas propagated by the media—was a senior colleague of my father who was also teaching abroad. He was originally from Lucknow and his name was D.D. Sharma. He had come to Patna to meet us once and gifted me two books—*Beyond Belief* by V.S. Naipaul and *Eminent Historians* by Arun Shourie—both were published in the same year, in 1998.

As an 18-year old, having almost given up on my chances of getting admission in the IITs, I was more interested in romantic ghazals and songs at that time. However, I didn't ignore those books altogether. I can't claim that I understood everything written in the books, or that I found them too engaging, but both of them did leave some impact on me, especially the book by Arun Shourie. Suddenly I felt that I didn't miss much by not paying attention to social science during my high school. If those history textbooks were written by such fraud and dishonest academics, I was better off just mugging up answers from 'guides' and not imbibing any learning.

However, those two books did not force me to doubt the mainstream media or its narrative, for neither of those books were critiques of the media or journalism per se. In fact, Shourie himself was a journalist, and that actually made me warm up to the world of media and journalism. On the other hand, *Beyond Belief* by Naipaul revealed that the criticism of Islam, rather of its influence on the society, was possible in a language that was markedly different and better from the street language used against Muslims.

Beyond these two books, the other books that I could find around me were mostly English literature classics, because my father was a professor of English. Some of those that I picked up to read included works by Charles Dickens, Mark Twain and D.H. Lawrence. I even tried to read up *Ulysses* by James Joyce because I loved the term 'stream of consciousness' that my father once told me about. He explained that there was an entire chapter in *Ulysses* that had no punctuation marks, and it figuratively represented uninterrupted stream of thoughts. It all sounded so good, though I couldn't understand anything.

But, I was slowly getting more and more interested in words than in numbers as my graduation days progressed. I won't rule out that perhaps that 1997 Booker Prize to Arundhati Roy could have been the trigger. She was all over the news media as the first Indian to win such a reputed literary award. She became a household name, like Sushmita Sen had earlier become for being the first Indian to win the Miss Universe title.

Our media anyway loves the 'first Indian to do so' type of news and many a times they go overboard. The hype around 'achievers' affects youngsters, who want to emulate those who are being presented as heroes of that time. Obviously, I couldn't have won a beauty pageant like Sushmita Sen, but I could at least have tried to become a writer, a novelist like Arundhati Roy.

So instead of becoming an engineer or a bureaucrat, my new wish was to become a writer. I discovered that many of those writers, such as Charles Dickens, Mark Twain or George Orwell, whose book were lying around in our house, had started their careers as journalists or columnists in newspapers. That led me to conclude that journalism was the best route to become a fiction writer. Oops!

But on a serious note, that indeed was the reason I started exploring journalism as a career option, as my graduation days progressed. Suddenly, the original plans of studying to be a computer professional or an IAS officer were derailed, as I tried to figure out how exactly one becomes a journalist.

There were two obvious routes. First, start taking a keen interest in journalism and in journalists, so that you learn more about the industry and what kind of work is respected and rewarded there. And second, find out if there were any 'IITs of journalism' where you could study and get campus placement. Being a Bihari, why would I settle for anything less than the IITs? And that pain of not having qualified for the original IITs was still there, which needed to be assuaged by achieving something that could be argued to be similar.

And that was it. I started following the news keenly, finding out who were the editors of leading newspapers, and who were considered the best journalists. That was the time when newspapers still ruled and TV news was relatively nascent in India. It was a time when there were no celebrity TV news anchors, except *Doordarshan* newsreaders. I started reading the editorial pages of newspapers, which I would otherwise skip.

And well, that meant visiting an RSS shakha was now definitely not on the cards, despite me having a shakha-going friend. The perceptions against the RSS or the Hindutva ideology was further reinforced as my interest in media and journalism increased. The BJP was in power then and writing against the BJP or Hindutva implied writing against the 'establishment', an act of speaking truth to power. I was increasingly getting exposed to such views.

It was not like there were no counter views. Some like those of Arun Shourie were obviously there, but he had become a minister in the Vajpayee government and was not writing regularly. Then, there were people like Sita Ram Goel, Koenraad Elst, Ram Swarup and many others writing about ideological issues such as inherent problems with Islam or how secularism that was practiced in India was a sham—and they had written prolifically in the 1990s—but I didn't even know they existed.

The mainstream media would obviously not publish them and even my shakha-going friend never gave me any books or booklets written by these people. Years later, rather almost 25 years later, when I would read the writings of Sita Ram Goel, I would feel that I wasted so many years trying to reinvent the wheel.

Nonetheless, in the absence of contrarian views, I imbibed thoughts and arguments that would make me lean towards the Left, while believing that I was being 'neutral' and idealist. Even my own experiences from the real world won't count, as I would now be in the world of idealism.

So, when some opposition leaders would oppose and even walk out from an event organized by the then HRD Minister Dr Murali Manohar Joshi, just because Saraswati Vandana was recited, it won't even register to me that I had sung the same Saraswati Vandana along with fellow Muslim students in my childhood and no one had walked out.

I remember that Dr Joshi had issued a statement, pointing out that even under earlier governments, Saraswati Vandana recital had taken place. He asked why it was being opposed suddenly, as if it were something new that was being imposed by the BJP government.[26]

When the same point was raised during a discussion on current affairs on a TV show, a participating panellist, who was a journalist, came up with the argument that went something like this: 'In that case, Dr Joshi should think that why no one objected earlier but are objecting now? Because people don't trust BJP's intentions. Because they fear BJP is trying to convert a secular India into a Hindu Rashtra.'

As a student who wanted to be a journalist, I was impressed by this logic. However, in reality, it was not the BJP that was forcing any change—it was literally continuing a practice from earlier times—but those who were fighting the 'communal forces' wanted to get rid of Saraswati Vandana at public events. The change was being forced by the secular parties—one Hindu symbol out of public life at a time. It was actually the Left's project of de-Hinduization at work. However, popular discourse was that 'saffronization' of education was taking place under the Vajpayee government.

This is a standard operating procedure of the Left. They first create an illusion of excrescence that they must wipe out, so that they can lay the foundation of their own edifice over it. At that point of time, it was about pushing Saraswati Vandana out of government events, and today it's about a blanket ban on Hindu festivals or puja on educational campuses and eventually from public life.

Actually, the project to de-Hinduize the society today demands that every Hindu festival is stripped off its religious lore and context, and is reduced to just a pagan festival around nature and ecology. The biggest and the most successful example is of Onam in Kerala, where now the liberals insist that the imagery of Lord Vishnu, in the Vaman avatar, blessing King Mahabali is 'offensive'. The same is being attempted around Holi, Diwali and other festivals too.

In the process, they actually de-Hinduize the identity itself. Recently, in April 2020, when two Hindu sadhus were lynched in Palghar in Maharashtra, a far-Left publication called The Wire declared that the sadhus, who belonged to an akhara that had been leading the participation in the Kumbh Mela for centuries, were not Hindus. They kept repeating the lie for over two weeks. The lie was repeated by other publications too. And one fine day The Wire stealthily changed the script. But by then, their lie had already travelled far and become the truth for many.[27]

Saraswati Vandana at public events is passé, that is, a battle the leftists already consider won; Hindu sadhus wearing saffron is now the 'saffronization' that is being fought, by denying dignity and identity to the dead.

Back then, at the time of the Saraswati Vandana controversy, what was more visible and audible appeared to be more rational and acceptable as debating points. I was ready to join the debate, and repeat the same arguments, hoping to become a respectable and successful media person. I had more or less decided to get into journalism.

In retrospect, I think the RSS erred by not caring about what image the media was painting of it. It doesn't mean that they should have kept fighting with the media, but they should have thought of designing alternative strategies to reach out to people who were being bombarded with only one particular narrative.

Not only did the media paint them in certain colours, they would always find someone here and there, whom they would present as a Sangh Parivar guy, who would come up with some stupid statement, and people like me would think, 'These guys are like this only'. The issues that the Hindutva groups raised—as reported in the media—were also something that appeared to make no sense.

I remember the disruption during the shooting of a movie named *Water* in Varanasi that made headlines and triggered many debates, especially on the fast-growing TV news channels. For someone like me, it was like 'Dude, it's just a movie!' (No, as a Bihari, I was not using cool 'angrezi' terms like 'dude' in those days, but I guess you get the drift.).

The RSS obviously toiled hard on the ground and reached out to people and tried to 'convert' them. That's how their tribe grew, but you can't aim to convert everyone into a member or a Swayamsevak. They didn't seem to have any plan to reach out to someone like me, who didn't step into their shakha because the perception was that I should keep away from them.

3

The 'terrorist' batchmate

Patna to Delhi, maths to journalism

While I chose to stay back in Patna to finish my graduate studies, my younger brother had left Bihar after Class 12 to pursue his graduation from Delhi University. He was my Man Friday who would do all the running around for me. And even while being a thousand miles away in Delhi, when he got to know that I was warming up to the world of journalism, he started exploring which were the best institutes for studying journalism.

He soon informed me that IIMC, that is, Indian Institute of Mass Communication was a top institute for studying journalism. It was an 'Indian Institute of ...' and approved by the Government of India. 'So, it was similar to the IITs,' that was my first reaction. The idea was exciting and the pain of not qualifying for the IITs was still fresh. I decided to take a shot at it.

Not only did Kunal, my younger brother, bring me the brochure of the institute, he even managed to get hold of some old question papers of the IIMC entrance exam, which he had 'jugadoed' from somewhere. IIMC offered post-graduate diploma courses in journalism, and their admission process consisted of a written exam and then interviews of the shortlisted candidates. I think at that time the total intake was not more than 200 students across all journalism courses in their two campuses— Delhi, the main campus, and another one at Dhenkanal in Odisha.

In those days, the entrance exam comprised two papers, if I remember correctly—one that tested mathematical skills, and the other testing general awareness about history and current affairs. The mathematics questions were ridiculously easy for me, as I was studying for Maths Honours for my graduation degree; much later would I realize that they should really expect much higher knowledge of mathematics and statistics from a journalist. I didn't find the questions on general awareness tough either, primarily because I was already hooked onto journalism, and thus was tracking news and newsmakers.

This was a child's play as compared to getting into IITs, I thought. Further, who would really be interested in becoming a journalist, at least from Bihar, so the competition shouldn't be tough at all. However, I was surprised to see hundreds of students taking the entrance exam even in a city like Patna. But I was happy—if I get admission, it would mean that I have actually cleared a decent competitive exam.

I qualified and made it to the shortlist of students who were called for an interview at Delhi in May or June 2001 (I don't exactly remember the month correctly). But what I do remember is that thanks to the academic sessions invariably running late in Bihar, due to strikes or some other issues, my final-year graduation exams—exams itself, not results—were still pending.

I was actually lucky to be studying at Patna University, which was the top university in Bihar. In those times, other universities in the state had academic sessions running almost a year or more late—one of the reasons why students would rather study outside the state even for standard degree courses.

The IIMC admission interview date was scheduled for a day that fell on the next day of a final exam paper for my graduation degree. I couldn't have made it on time if I travelled by train, and thus my father decided to send me to Delhi via flight.

Despite my father having saved some money during his stint abroad, we were still not that rich to afford flight tickets. But there was a way out. Air India, the national carrier, used to offer 'student discount' if the principal of the college issued an official letter explaining why a student must travel on a certain date. Fortunately, the Patna Science College principal gave me the letter, though not before wondering why I should become a journalist after having been rather a decent student of maths.

At the age of 21, that is how I took the first flight of my life. It was a late evening flight, so I could not fully experience the excitement of the first flight, where you notice how things on the ground start diminishing in size as the flight takes off and rises up in the sky.

I vividly remember such details about the second flight that I took around 4 years later, from Delhi to Ahmedabad, to embark on another journey for another post-graduate course. All I remember of my first flight is that when I landed in Delhi, I was happy to see Kunal, my younger brother, waiting for me at the airport with his friend. I knew that I didn't need to worry about anything after that.

The next day at the IIMC campus, I remember being interviewed by Sunit Tandon, a Doordarshan newsreader whom I had seen so many times on TV. In those days, Doordarshan news anchors were celebrities in themselves. I was so excited to see him, but was nervous too. He was nice to me and asked me some standard questions, such as why I wanted to be a journalist and what I thought were the required traits a journalist should have.

I remember saying something that made him laugh. I told him and a couple of other people who were on the interview panel that I believed that a journalist should have a cunning mind too, so that he can think like corrupt or criminal politicians and anticipate their moves. I don't know if that clinched the deal, though it clearly made them chuckle. I was offered admission to Post Graduate Diploma in Radio & Television Journalism, that is, broadcast journalism.

I had indicated broadcast journalism as my first preference over print journalism during admission, even though ironically my interest in journalism was born due to journalists-turned-novelists who had started their careers with newspapers. I think the popularity and influence of the newly launched 24-hour TV news channels impacted my decision.

The Kargil War of 1999 was one of the biggest events that helped the 24-hour TV news channels in India grow in popularity and become the preferred and more authoritative source of news. As the news of the war spread, people were hooked on to their TV sets to know the latest—whether our territory was safe, whether our uniformed men were safe, whether the rest of the country would remain safe. This was also the event that propelled the career of Barkha Dutt, eventually making her a celebrity journalist.

Another incident that made people remain glued to their TV sets was the hijacking of Indian Airlines Flight 814, that is, the Kandahar hijacking, which took place just a few months after the Kargil War. That's when the TV journalists in India, perhaps for the first time, realized how much influence or power they can wield. The visuals of the families of those trapped in the hijacked plane, crying and appealing to the government to do anything to save their loved ones, were quite absorbing for a society that would get emotionally attached even to fictional characters on screen.

The hijackers had killed one passenger, soon after the incident came to light, perhaps to ensure a morbid fear among the family members of surviving passengers, whom we could see on our TV screens in tears, helpless and seeking our support in convincing the government to rescue their parents, kids, friends and other loved ones. These were real people in real grief. The TV coverage had created a huge pressure on the government to negotiate with the hijackers and not take any risky decision.

I believe I too was taken in by the aura and impact of live TV news, and that's why I decided to opt for broadcast journalism over print journalism as the first choice of course at IIMC.

My admission to IIMC was provisional because my final-year graduation results were pending. If Patna University inordinately delayed the final results, I could have been asked to leave the course midway. The post-graduate diploma course at IIMC was barely a year long, in fact less than a year long, so this risk was real.

Amid uncertainties around what lay ahead in the future, but with loads of hope and excitement, I left Bihar in the summer of 2001, this time in a train, and came to Delhi to embark on a new journey. My younger brother was already in Delhi for his graduate studies and was living with some friends. But, when I moved to the national capital, he moved in to stay with me. We rented a small house that was near IIMC, at a place called Ber Sarai in South Delhi.

Our mother too joined us in Delhi, as our father decided to take another shot at teaching abroad. However, the primary reason for our mother moving in with us was related to a past experience of mine. The last time I lived in another city, as a student away from the family, it had turned out to be a disaster. No, I had not started taking drugs or joined a

criminal gang, but I fell seriously ill and had to rush back to my hometown.
Those were a couple of months that I spent in Bokaro Steel City, then
a city in the undivided Bihar and currently in Jharkhand, where I had
secured admission for Classes 11 and 12 at Delhi Public School (DPS)
around March 1995. DPS Bokaro was known to be hugely successful at
sending its science stream students to the IITs. Cracking the entrance
exam of DPS Bokaro was supposed to be a job half done—that of cracking
the IIT entrance exams, which would follow two years later.

I could crack the entrance, but had to quit soon as I fell ill living
a 'bachelor life'. Eating food that was not cooked by mom and general
homesickness made me fall ill. I ran back to Patna and took admission
in Patna Science College, where academic session started a bit late. The
admission fees and my living expenses of those two months at Bokaro
were wasted. I think my mother decided to move to Delhi along with
me lest I fell ill and end up wasting time and money again.

We had always lived in rented houses all our lives, and it was just a
year earlier when my parents finally bought a house for themselves in
Patna. My mother desperately wanted to have her own house, so that
she didn't have to be a kiraayedaar (tenant) all her life. But, she couldn't
even spend a couple of years in the house she proudly called her own,
as I pushed her into a cramped rented space again. This was just one
among so many adjustments and sacrifices that Indian parents take upon
themselves to secure a better future for their children.

Our belongings, which included a TV set, my desktop computer and
3–4 suitcases that had utensils and clothes, were loaded on a train and
we left for Delhi. We were almost fined by the railways for carrying so
much of luggage and not using the goods train or the luggage coach
for the transportation of our belongings. We also had to bear snarky
comments of co-passengers for travelling with so much stuff—all of which
was tolerated for the sake of my better future.

Ber Sarai, where we took this small one-BHK flat on rent, was next
to IIT Delhi. On my way to attend classes at IIMC, some days I would
feel as if 'this is where I was meant to be', as I passed by the IIT campus.
That is how strong the craze to study at the IITs was among Biharis of
my generation. Even though I had taken a conscious decision to become
a journalist, that feeling did not leave me.

But as time progressed, that nagging feeling slowly went away. I was in a new city and learning new things. The students at IIMC were from various parts of the country and that in itself was an enriching experience. There was a guy from Kerala who would speak only in English (a huge thing for someone like me who hailed from Bihar), another from Nagaland who played the guitar beautifully and some from other states, such as Odisha, Rajasthan and Bengal, with whom I would interact and learn.

And then there were girls. This was for the first time since that girl scratched me all over in my junior school that I sat next to a girl in a classroom. Gyan Niketan, the high school at Patna, was an all-boys school, while the section I was allotted at Patna Science College for my intermediate classes (Class 11 and 12) did not have a single girl for some reason. Neither were there any girls in the maths classes I took for my B.Sc. (Honours) course at Science College. It took me a while before I could feel comfortable interacting with the girls at IIMC.

Soon I started enjoying IIMC, not because of girls, but because I was praised on at least two occasions for my class work. One was when we were asked to write a TV news report on bandit-turned-MP Phoolan Devi being killed—she was shot dead in Delhi just a few days earlier in July 2001. I started my report with the latest information available on her killers, while most of my batchmates had started with the incident when she was shot at. 'You don't start with a week-old information on TV news, as things get stale in a matter of hours'—this was the reason given to the class explaining why my script was better.

On another occasion, a sample piece-to-camera, that is, what a TV news reporter says in front of the camera as part of his report, performed by me was also singled out for praise. The teacher told us that I did not appear too nervous or too lost regarding what I should say on camera. This gave me the confidence that I can face the camera and be a good TV reporter or a news anchor.

I also got to learn that I was not pronouncing my own name correctly. As a Bihari, I was pronouncing all 'sh' (श) sounds as 's' (स), including the 'sh' in Roushan. This was slightly embarrassing. I was told that I must correct my diction if I wanted a career in broadcast journalism. And before I could figure out how to pronounce श, or not mix up the र and ड़, as many Biharis do, I got to know that there are even more complex sounds, known as nuqtas, that are essential to master in order to correctly pronounce the Urdu words. For some reason, many Urdu words were used in Hindi TV news. It was *Samachaar* on Doordarshan, but became *Khabar* on Aaj Tak.

But it was fun and a good learning experience. I would practice some tongue twisters, which they used to give as a challenge if you wanted to be a newsreader at the All India Radio, and learn new Urdu words. Suddenly, my focus was more on the pronunciation of the words of the ghazals than on the meaning of the poetry!

And it was not just ghazals; Urdu words were used in popular songs too. I loved to imitate Kumar Sanu and Kishore Kumar, and used to hum so many of their songs. And I realized how I was mispronouncing almost every word in the line *Tere bina zindagi se koi shikwa toh nahi* from the movie *Aandhi* sung by Kishore Kumar. I got the diction correct over time, but lost the melody in the process.

Those were also the times when I had a culture shock in Delhi after having spent all my life in Bihar, especially in Patna. People generally appeared rude in Delhi. Back in Patna, one would normally use 'aap' for strangers, especially for elders, but here in Delhi that was entirely absent. In fact, even at the college in Patna, we started conversations with 'aap' before moving to 'tum' as the friendship evolved. But almost everyone was addressed as 'tu', not even 'tum', in Delhi. The only 'aap' that Delhiites would seem to love would be Arvind Kejriwal's party, some 12 years down the line!

Another culture shock, in a pleasant way this time, was how freely boys and girls would interact on campuses or even in public places, something that I wouldn't witness frequently back in Patna. There used to be a self-deprecating joke among us Biharis—a Bihari student boards a DTC bus in Delhi to go somewhere. At the next stop a girl boards the bus and takes the seat next to him. And this Bihari immediately thinks of the following phrase: Papa maan jaayenge na. (Hope my father agrees.)

To explain, that is, to ruin the joke, it means that the Bihari dude immediately starts thinking about getting married to the girl, because never in the past had he had an experience where a girl voluntarily sat next to him. Well, I wasn't really this desperate, but yes, I was indeed impressed by the way boys and girls would talk to each other like friends.

Remember, I grew up watching *Maine Pyar Kiya*, which said 'Ek ladka aur ek ladki kabhi dost nahi ho sakte.' ('A boy and a girl can never be friends.')

The flyovers in Delhi gave me a culture shock too! Back in Patna, I had seen only two flyovers (till 2001), and both were built over railway tracks. I grew up thinking that flyovers are meant to cross railway tracks, so that buses, bikes and cars don't have to halt every time a train passes, and to avoid any collision. But Delhi had so many flyovers, and hardly any of them passed over railway tracks. That was posh!

And the final culture shock was facing direct or indirect ridicule for being a Bihari, especially because Bihar had become synonymous with Lalu Yadav by then. Lalu's party had won three state elections in a row—1990, 1995 and 2000 Bihar assembly elections—and these tenures were first marred by incidents of violence—the caste militias that I had talked about earlier—and later by allegations of corruption, that is, the fodder scam.

Fortunately, I didn't have any unpleasant experience where I was at the receiving end of some ugly insult for being a Bihari. Further, Ber Sarai, the locality where we lived in Delhi, was inhabited by many Bihari students who stayed there and in neighbouring areas like Katwaria Sarai or Jia Sarai. Most of them were preparing for the UPSC exams. So locals in these areas didn't really treat Biharis as aliens.

JNU was nearby too, where many Bihari students resided. In fact, IIMC was located just next to the JNU campus, virtually forming a part of the larger campus. We could easily walk inside JNU without any inquiries or security guards asking us to show our ID cards after we told them we were from IIMC. And there were many occasions when we did walk inside the JNU campus to have 'better and cheaper' food at one of the JNU hostels.

Even though JNU was really well-known even then—and not for 'controversies', as it would be known for later—I was not in awe of it like I was for the IITs. The food available at the hostels or the snacks available at the dhabas were what attracted my attention and not the posters or the stupid-if-not-toxic slogans written on the walls. Frankly, I didn't even understand half of it.

However, one has to admit that their posters were attractive, with neatly done illustrations and slogans written in eye-catching fonts. As much as the Left may hate the 'MBA types', they are masters at marketing for sure. Those pamphlets were basically attractive advertisements of their ideology. Far more attractive, visually, than the booklets that my shakha-going friend had given me.

That's where the Right wing or rather the non-Left wing loses out on campuses. They are not good when it comes to marketing. At best, they come up with some anti-terrorism or patriotic slogans and posters, and young guys will be like, 'Dude, these are Independence Day celebrations level stuff that we have been seeing since our school days. So boring. Give us something cool!'

The Left knows how to appear cool, even compassionate, while planning to burn down the world.

Nonetheless, it was good being in a new city, observing new people, noticing new trends, learning new things, though I was still ideologically agnostic, or rather ideologically unaware. Definitely not a Sanghi.

Whitewashing Islamism

While I was a student of journalism at IIMC, three major incidents took place, almost at equally placed intervals. First was the 9/11 terror attack in the US in September 2001, then the Parliament attack in New Delhi in December 2001 and finally the 2002 post-Godhra riots in February–March 2002 in Gujarat. Incidentally, all three, especially 9/11 and 2002, were incidents whose impact was magnified multiple times due to live TV.

Although there was no official confirmation, the suspicion was on Osama Bin Laden almost immediately after the 9/11 (or September 11) attacks. There were also reports of some people in Palestine celebrating the attacks, which strengthened the suspicions that Islamic terrorists were behind the act.

The use of the term 'Islamic terrorists' by the media was not that rare or controversial in those days, because it was frequently used by the US media, including liberal outfits like *The Washington Post*. It was only later that some started objecting to the term, saying it aided in 'Islamophobia'—a term that wasn't heard much back then but gained currency pretty fast once it was introduced in the market of political correctness.

Unsurprisingly, our Indian media was more liberal and politically correct than their Western counterparts when it came to such matters. The Indian media usually avoided using 'Islamic' as an adjective for the terrorist acts that were explicitly carried out in the name of Islam. India had been wounded multiple times, not just in Kashmir but in the rest of the country, by Islamic terrorists, but rarely the term 'Islamic terrorists' was used by the Indian media.

There is a viral video clip[28] from a TV show named *The Big Fight* hosted by Rajdeep Sardesai, which aired on NDTV sometime after the September 11 attacks. In that particular episode, Narendra Modi, who was not the chief minister of Gujarat yet, is seen talking about the 'mindset' that gives rise to Islamic terrorism. Modi then congratulates Sardesai and NDTV for finally using the term 'Islamic terrorism', adding that it was possible only because the US media had been using it. Almost upset over being congratulated, Sardesai immediately clarifies that NDTV had not used the term even after the 9/11 incident. Years later, the same lot would use terms such as 'Hindu terror' or 'Saffron terror'.

Due to this political correctness, the jihadist or Islamist ideologies were hardly blamed for acts of terror in India. Pakistan was liberally blamed, but the mindset that created Pakistan was never blamed. Even in the BJP, barring a few leaders like Modi in that TV debate, most leaders talked only about Pakistan when raising the issue of terrorism.

The BJP was in power in 2001, and one of the official reactions of the Indian government to 9/11 was to hope that the US would be able to see how Pakistan was a rogue nation that harboured terrorists. Well, at least they were right on that count as Osama was finally found in Pakistan 10 years later, but the point is that the Islamist mindset was rarely called out. At least someone like me was not exposed to such debates or discussions or statements.

Yes, there were writers like Sita Ram Goel who had written cogently about Islamic imperialism and Muslim separatism back in the 1980s and 90s itself, but I didn't even know they existed. IIMC had a library, like any other educational institute, but I can hardly recall books by such authors being kept there. There were a couple of books by Arun Shourie though, possibly because Shourie was a known and influential journalist and a cabinet minister at that time.

Once, when I picked up a book by Shourie in the IIMC library, a classmate of mine sarcastically congratulated me for picking up a book of an 'intellectual'. He was basically mocking me for my preference. The sarcasm escaped me then and thus I didn't put down the book. Later, I discovered that he was a leftist, though we became rather good friends.

Anyway, coming back to the days at IIMC immediately after the 9/11 attacks, we were given a task to create a TV report on the attacks. We had one full day at our disposal to talk to people, use available TV footage and any other material to create this report. The class of 25 students was divided into five groups.

My group decided to talk to various students on the campus itself and create a news report on how people were reacting to the incident. At that time, some foreign students from African and Middle Eastern countries were also present on the campus, attending a short-term course around 'Development Journalism'. We thought we'd get multitude of opinions for our news report.

However, we got the usual reactions from these students, condemning terrorism and hoping that the incident wouldn't disturb world peace, but the one reaction that stood out came from an Indian. A student of Hindi journalism, he said, 'The US is the biggest terrorist nation in the world,' further adding, 'We cannot say who did it. There should be an investigation. But what the US had been doing in different countries is terrorism too.'

The guy virtually gave a clean chit to Osama Bin Laden! To be fair to him, Osama had actually denied his role in 9/11 in the immediate aftermath, before he accepted the responsibility and warned of more attacks a few months later. However, this student's reasoning, where he declared the US a terrorist nation, was borne out of the belief that the US was unfair to the Muslim world. Essentially, here was a man—his name was Shahbaz—talking primarily as a citizen of the Muslim world, something not even those from the Middle Eastern countries did.

However, at that point of time, I didn't really see his statement the way I can analyse it now. I just took it as an unusual but interesting opinion. Further, why should I feel offended if someone was attacking the US? I was happy that at least he wasn't saying anything against India.

The fact that an Islamist mindset will ultimately lead one to target

India too didn't strike me at all, for such discussions were not part of the popular narrative. Terrorism in India meant proxy war by Pakistan, and whatever strife was happening outside India was all due to the US's greed for oil—these were the two popular discourses—the former from the Right and the latter from the Left.

The Partition of India, which was the result of nothing but an Islamist mindset, was never discussed honestly in popular discourse or school textbooks. The Congress blamed the Partition on the so-called 'Divide and Rule' policy of the British and Jinnah's complicity, while the Sanghis blamed it all on Gandhi and Nehru, in addition to Jinnah.

The two-nation theory is presented as some modern construct that came up only in the twentieth century, and was used as a political weapon by the Muslim League. However, the fact is that the two-nation theory is nothing but a political variant of the concept of 'Ummah', that is, universal Muslim brotherhood, which is central to Islamic theology.

The leftists have tried to spread canards about the two-nation theory, blaming it on the RSS or Veer Savarkar, conveniently ignoring what Sir Syed Ahmed said in 1876: 'I am now convinced that the Hindus and the Muslims, as their religion and way of life was quite distinct from one another, could never become one nation.'[29] He had said these words almost 50 years before the RSS was formed and when V.D. Savarkar was not even born.

But the leftists are masters at subterfuge, so they say that Sir Syed Ahmed was 'hurt' with Hindus not warming up to his attempts of Hindu-Muslim unity, and thus he was 'forced' to come up with such a statement. Somehow, they are desperate to blame the Hindus and Hindutva for the two-nation theory. Perhaps, they need to read Karl Marx again, who in 1854, around 22 years before Sir Syed Ahmed, had said the following about Islam:

> The Koran and the Mussulman legislation emanating from it reduce the geography and ethnography of the various people to the simple and convenient distinction of two nations and of two countries; those of the Faithful and of the Infidels. The Infidel is 'harby', i.e., the enemy. Islamism proscribes the nation of the Infidels, constituting a state of permanent hostility between the Mussulman and the unbeliever.[30]

Did you read 'two nations'? The prophet of communism virtually declares that the two-nation theory is inherent in Islam itself. The leftists should at least listen to what their prophet said.

The point I'm trying to make is that the dangers of this Islamist mentality was never discussed in popular discourse at all. Forget the dangers, one didn't even know what this Islamist mentality was, even though the country had paid a heavy price for it in 1947. So, when a man—Shahbaz at IIMC—spoke up as a citizen of the Muslim world instead of as an Indian in 2001, it didn't send any alarm bells ringing that he could be an Islamist.

I obviously forgot about him or his statement soon after. Since we belonged to two different courses at the IIMC, I didn't bump into him much often either, even though IIMC has a rather small campus.

More than seven years later, at a time when India had seen various bomb blasts in civilian areas and many were arrested on terror charges, I happened to read a news report titled 'Shahbaz gives details of SIMI training camps' while surfing the internet.

The name 'Shahbaz' didn't ring a bell immediately, but I proceeded to read the news report as internal security was in a serious mess then. It was a news report about some arrests made in connection with the serial bomb blasts in Jaipur, which had left more than 60 people dead in May 2008. The first one to be arrested was Shahbaz in August 2008, who was identified as a SIMI (Student's Islamic Movement of India) operative by most media reports.

A part of this particular news report by *The Indian Express* caught my eye—'The police believe (Shahbaz) Hussain was the head of SIMI's legal and journalism cell. He is a mass communication graduate from the Indian Institute of Mass Communication.'[31]

Wait, what? Shahbaz and IIMC! Was it the same guy? I immediately called up some of the Hindi journalism batchmates with whom I was still in touch. They too were shocked to know about the incident. They told me that in all probability it was the same guy. Though, they added that *The Indian Express* had got one tiny detail wrong. The Shahbaz, who had declared the US a terrorist nation within a couple of days of the 9/11 attacks, never got his journalism diploma from the IIMC, so he couldn't be called a 'mass communication graduate' from the Indian

Institute of Mass Communication.

Shahbaz had left the course mid-way as SIMI was banned in 2001 after the 9/11 attacks. In all probability, he had gone underground to evade arrest after the organization was outlawed. No one knew where he went, and now they were shocked to discover his possible role in the Jaipur serial blasts.

The friends from the Hindi journalism course further informed me that a couple of IB (Intelligence Bureau) guys had even visited the IIMC campus in those times and inquired about his whereabouts. Whoa! I had no clue about all these developments until that day when I happened to read that news report while surfing the web.

So, I had interviewed a student who was already a member of an Islamist organization, which was outlawed a few weeks later, and who, seven years down the line, would be accused of facilitating a series of bomb blasts in an Indian city, veritably waging a war against India.

He declared the US a terrorist nation, but an average Hindu around him didn't bother, because who cares about his hatred for the US as long as he did not say anything against India? And seven years later, he is arrested for killing over 60 fellow Indian citizens on the Indian soil in the name of Islam. It was a natural progression for a person with an Islamist mentality.

Even today as I write this, an entire industry of Left-liberals is active out there whitewashing this Islamist mentality, giving cover to every contortion, giving context to every crime, and in the process making sure that the Hindus can't hear and see even the obvious, like I couldn't hear and see an Islamist even when he was standing right in front of me.

The boundaries that define what is normal and acceptable have been consistently pushed towards far-Right when it comes to the Islamist mentality, and it has been done with active aid from the leftists and liberals. Any statement or belief that shows that an Indian citizen considers himself first and foremost a part of a transnational identity based on religion should have been a cause for concern from a secular point of view, but such statements and beliefs have only been normalized more and more over the years.

One example of such normalization is the support for Pakistan by some sections of Indian Muslims during cricket matches. Initially, the liberals and leftists used to vehemently deny that such a thing even happens, even though I myself had witnessed crackers going off in some pockets of Patna when Pakistan beat India in ODI cricket matches during the 1990s—and unfortunately many matches had such results, except in the world cups. That did bother me, but my parents wouldn't blame the entire Muslim community for it, so I too blamed only a few rogue elements.

But the fact was that some folks did indeed celebrate, but liberals would insist that it was a 'Sanghi propaganda' that Pakistan's victory over India in cricket matches is celebrated by some Indian Muslims. Years later, when we'd have social media, some people uploaded videos with sounds of crackers being heard in the background in the Muslim-dominated areas when Pakistan beat India, the liberals would have no option but to admit that some Indian Muslims indeed celebrate Pakistan beating India in cricket matches.

The liberals then proceeded to normalize this behaviour—which was primarily a manifestation of considering yourself a member of the Ummah before considering yourself a citizen of a nation-state—and bring in ridiculous arguments like 'even British citizens of Indian origin support India during India vs England cricket matches, what's the big deal?'

To normalize the behaviour further, they organized social media campaigns, especially on Twitter during the 2015 ICC Cricket World Cup, where a bunch of Indians supported Pakistan and vice versa. It was supposed to defeat 'jingoism' and 'hypernationalism', which was supposedly growing with Modi becoming the prime minister a year before.

It could all sound humanist and 'cool' to support each other's countries, but it indirectly normalized an activity that was born out of a religious mindset—supporting Pakistan because it was an Islamic nation. By exaggerating the supposed dangers of jingoism, effectively the focus was taken away from the issue of Islamism.

It is a standard operating procedure actually. Smokescreens of bigotry, jingoism and communalism are created, and the Islamist mentality is given cover and context. You are rendered incapable of seeing the obvious. If someone wanted to argue how the two-nation theory is alive and kicking in modern India, and how another 'Direct

Action Day' cannot be ruled out, that argument will be drowned out by shouting about other 'real issues'.

I can give you dozens of such examples where an Islamist mindset and a belief in the two-nation theory have been normalized and intellectualized—be it supporting Pakistan during cricket matches or opposing Vande Mataram, insistence on Shariat-compliant businesses or boycott of businesses with Hindu symbols such as a saffron flag or an 'angry Hanuman' poster on a cab, or glorification of leaders who demanded the Partition of India to carve out an Islamic Republic of Pakistan.

When they fail to normalize or intellectualize the Islamist mindset or justify an act of Islamism, they resort to muddling of facts. It starts with denials (Muslims didn't do it), then shifting of goalposts (the real issue is Islamophobia or injustice to Muslims) and then orchestrated propaganda to confuse people, so that ordinary people simply give up arguing or talking about the original issue.

The latest tool in this standard operating procedure of whitewashing the Islamist mindset is use of 'fact check', where, ironically, an attempt is made to blur the line between truth and lie. For example, if a Muslim mob has chanted 'Pakistan zindabad' during an event in India, the fact checkers will find a clip from Pakistan where obviously a Muslim mob will chant 'Pakistan zindabad' and declare that the 'Viral video clip showing Muslims chanting Pakistan zindabad slogans is from Pakistan'. Keep repeating it, and people will get confused which viral clip is being talked about. And finally, they will conclude that any claim of Muslims in India chanting 'Pakistan zindabad' is fake news.

This is why conspiracy theories are so popular in the Muslim world—9/11 was an inside job, ISIS was created by the US, Mumbai terror attacks were carried out by the RSS, the Pulwama terror attack was done by the Government of India, the Godhra train carnage was an accident, no Muslim mob ever attacked doctors or policemen during the coronavirus lockdown—you name a conspiracy theory and it has an audience. An average Muslim is perpetually in victimhood mode due to this. Such theories convince him that everyone else is conspiring to give Muslims and Islam a bad name.

Such conspiracy theories not only get support from the Right-wing groups among the Muslim community, but from seemingly neutral and erudite intellectuals of the society too. Ironically, the Islamists privately celebrate or take pride in each of these incidents, but with active support from the leftists and liberals, they publicly deny it. And the common person is left confused about what the reality is and what is fiction.

Not only the boundaries of what is acceptable and normal have been pushed too far, your ability to identify this boundary has been compromised too. It has been made very difficult for you to spot an Islamist around you.

Back in 2001, I too couldn't spot an Islamist despite him standing right in front of me, and almost no one could, not even the slightly Sanghi-type students from the Hindi journalism course. They told me that they never had any inkling as Shahbaz hardly ever spoke against Hindus or Hinduism. In fact, he was pretty friendly with them, talking about shared experiences from Uttar Pradesh, the state he belonged to.

Seven years later, Shahbaz was accused of sending emails to media houses taking responsibility of the Jaipur serial blasts. The emails reportedly talked about finishing Hinduism and establishing the rule of Muslims in India.

Today, a Shahbaz can openly talk about finishing Hinduism, wearing the veil of Ambedkarite–Periyarite activism, and the Left-liberals would defend his right to free speech. Many Hindus would still be blind and deaf to his utterances because a smokescreen of Hindutva and Brahminism will be created around them. In fact, forget spotting an Islamist when one shows up in front of you, many Hindus would cheer such a guy, hailing him as an oppressed person fighting for the rights of the marginalized. That is the length of brainwashing that has happened over the years.

It is not just my conjecture, but the truth. We saw in early 2020, how many young Muslim students and professionals, including journalists, had openly defended the likes of Jinnah and idolized Ali Musliyar, the architect of the Moplah massacre, where thousands of Hindus were butchered by armed Muslim gangs in 1921. Such folks were dressed up as faces of dissent, and promoted as brave young men and women opposing the CAA and standing up to a 'fascist government'. And guess what, many Hindus were out in the streets holding placards against the CAA and NRC (National Register of Citizens), standing shoulder to shoulder with them. The more things change, the more they stay the same.

I just hope that seven years from now they don't end up discovering that the guy holding an anti-CAA placard next to them has joined a terror outfit. I won't be shocked at all. What else do you expect from a movement whose poster boys and poster girls consider architects of the Pakistan movement and the Moplah massacre their icons? What else does one expect from a protest that ended up in the 2020 Delhi riots? You have to be suicidal, brainwashed or braindead to not see these issues. At least today the narrative is not entirely one-sided as it used to be back in 2001.

There was no social media in 2001. Even Orkut was not launched then, neither was Gmail. The mainstream media reigned supreme in that era, and I was pretty happy and eager to be part of the same after finishing my studies at IIMC.

But just think about it, the guy who was caught for carrying out the serial bomb blasts was also on his way to become a journalist in the mainstream media.

The Godhra carnage

The second big event, while I was studying at IIMC, was the terror attack on the Indian Parliament in December 2001. We were attending our classes when suddenly the news about the attack came in. Since our course was 'Radio and Television Journalism', there was a TV with a cable connection in our classroom. The class had to abruptly end as we watched the live news coverage of the terror attack on the Parliament.

Rather sadly, neither us students nor any teacher saw the attack as a direct attack on the Indian democracy. It was just a TV spectacle. In fact, one of my batchmates—the same friend who had tried to mock me for picking up Arun Shourie's book in the library—would snidely remark 'Yeh toh sab bach gaye' ('All of them survived.'), referring to no casualties among politicians or the ruling class. Perhaps from his point of view—he was a member of the leftist student organization (SFI or Student's Federation of India) during his college days—being against those in power meant even going to the extent of violently attacking the representatives of the government.

But I'm not blaming him only; we perhaps didn't realize the gravity of it all. And we still don't. The attack on the Parliament is barely considered as some great tragedy or warning for the Indian society, except in formal statements made by the political class.

I feel the reason is the same—normalizing an Islamist mindset. Kashmiri terrorists are inspired by nothing but the two-nation theory. They are fighting for Nizam-e-Mustafa, that is, the Shariat rule. And they have been fighting for this for decades. And to hide this fact, smokescreen of 'Kashmir is a political problem' is created. Human rights, army deployment, rigged elections—everything is talked about and analysed threadbare, except the Islamist mindset that drives and keeps terrorism alive.

As a result, the attack on the Parliament by Kashmiri terrorists was seen just a 'great day'[32] for TV news coverage as any political drama, and not as a consequence of Islamism. I would be surprised if any journalist mentioned the Parliament attack in the same breath as communal incidents.

And when they talk about a communal incident, not one of them miss the 2002 Gujarat riots, when violence had erupted in parts of Gujarat after an Islamist mob of over 1,000 men set the S6 sleeper coach of the Sabarmati Express train on fire, killing 59 Hindu pilgrims, including 10 children and 27 women, burning them alive on 27 February 2002.

These deaths are not talked about at all, as if they never happened, and one fine day Hindus in Gujarat decided to unleash the violence because they had always disliked the Muslims. Just like Kashmiri Pandits are not to be talked about when one discusses death and destruction in Kashmir, the Hindus burnt alive at Godhra are not talked about when one mentions the 2002 riots. But I will mention.

I was interning with TV Today, with their Hindi news channel Aaj Tak to be precise, around that time. This short internship—around three weeks—was part of the course curriculum at IIMC, and we had to rejoin the institute after finishing it.

I, and two other batchmates who were interning at Aaj Tak, were given jobs such as guest coordination, research work or assisting senior journalists with clerical work that they may not have time or inclination to do. I remember printing dozens of invitation letters to be sent out to various people on behalf of Aaj Tak, where I had used the 'mail merge' feature of MS Word to create multiple copies of the same letter that was addressed to different people, without having to manually create a new page in the document for every addressee. The senior journalist was quite impressed.

The horrific attack on the train at Godhra took place in the morning that day, at around 8 a.m. At that time, I was on my way to catch a DTC bus from Ber Sarai to Jhandewalan, where Aaj Tak had their office. By the time I reached, it was already making headlines. The initial news reports didn't term it as a terror attack or even an incident of violence. Information was still trickling in. I too assumed that it could have been an accident, may be the pantry car of the train caught fire.

Within an hour, as reporters from Gujarat started sending more information, everyone in the newsroom knew that it was not an accident. As the reporters talked to the authorities and other people who were travelling on the same train, it became clear that the fire was set by a mob.

Curious to know the details of what had happened, I filled a paper cup with tea from the vending machine in the office, and stood near the desk where a bunch of copy editors typed away information that would be either made into news reports ('package' as they were called) or read out by the news anchor, while visuals played on screen ('voice-over'). Copy editors received information from what was known as 'input desk', which in turn got raw information and reports from reporters in the field or from news agencies.

I saw one input guy standing next to one such copy editor while the news of the Godhra incident played on the TV sets in the newsroom. Assuming that they will have the latest information, I sneaked up to them and stood there to overhear their conversation as I pretended to watch the news being played on the nearest TV set.

'Pata chala kaun kiya?' ('Do we now know who did it?'), asked the copy editor to the input guy, who immediately replied 'Musalmaan sab aur kaun?' ('The Muslims did it, who else?') in a hushed but disgusted tone. After a brief pause, the copy editor said, 'Ab yeh toh nahi likh sakte na.' ('Now, we can't really write this.')

I furtively tried to have a look at the input guy. He didn't say anything after this. Anger was discernible on his face and so was the disgust. His eyes met mine and I immediately averted them, lest he thought I was trying to spy. He then walked away, leaving some fax or photocopies at the desk of the copy editor, presumably the raw reports sent by the reporters from the ground. I too walked back to my desk, silently.

This conversation of barely ten seconds, which would include some uncomfortable pauses, too, revealed so much in retrospect.

The mainstream can write headlines like 'Frenzied Hindu mob brings down sixteenth-century mosque' and 'Dabang Rajputon ne Dalit dulhe ko ghodi se utaara' (when some men from the Rajput community force a Dalit groom to alight from the horse during a wedding procession), mentioning the religion or caste of the perpetrator of a reported crime in some cases, but it feels greatly uncomfortable about mentioning the religion when the perpetrator of the crime is a Muslim—this when religion was clearly the main element in the crime committed at Godhra. 'Muslim mob sets a train carrying Hindu pilgrims on fire' is not seen as a legitimate or 'responsible' headline, even though it is factual.

It is a template that Indian journalists have religiously internalized over decades. Any attempt to break away from this template is seen as losing your 'moral compass'. Highlighting and shouting about caste is seen as fighting for justice, while hiding and keeping mum about religion is seen as indulging in responsible behaviour, except of course when the religion of the perpetrator is Hindu and the victim a Muslim. In which case, the same journalists shout with double the intensity and even exaggerate the incident with made-up claims about 'beef' and 'Jai Shri Ram' slogans.

This unwritten rule or the moral compass of the Indian mainstream media ensures that we grow up with a strong ingrained belief that a Hindu cannot be a victim of any injustice or hate crime, unless he belongs to the so-called lower castes (and in which case the perpetrator has to be a Hindu too). The Hindu–Muslim relationship in this country has been presented as that of the oppressor–oppressed, where Hindus by default are the oppressors.

This induces an element of guilt in an average Hindu, who tries to go the extra mile to appease and accommodate Muslims, including and invariably the ones with Islamist mindset. That's what we saw when thousands of Hindus came out in the streets to oppose the CAA, standing shoulder to shoulder with those who idolized Jinnah and the leader of the Moplah massacre.

I can literally give hundreds of examples from just the past few years where the Indian mainstream media has indulged in such glaring double standards, and this in the era of social media where people have other means to know the ugly truth. You can imagine how skewed the reporting and beliefs would have been almost two decades earlier. This is the 'truth' that was fed to unsuspecting consumers by the media, and when people started speaking up and showing the other side, the media talking heads invented the term 'post truth.'

For now, I'll go back to 27 February 2002 and that moment in the newsroom. The conversation between the copy editor and the input guy, which lasted barely 10 seconds, showed that most journalists knew within an hour that the Godhra incident was not an accident but an organized act of violence. They knew that it was veritably a terror attack by an Islamist mob against helpless, unarmed Hindus. Yet, around two and half years after the carnage, when the Congress returned to power in the Centre, cobbling up a post-poll alliance, and when it announced the formation of a commission to declare the carnage an 'accident', hardly any journalist protested saying it was a mockery of justice.

What that short conversation also showed is how a journalist, even if he wanted to speak the ugly truth, would have to surrender to the moral compass. Since he won't be able to control the narrative, he would be left to control his anger and disgust, failing which he will be branded a Sanghi and unprofessional and whose career path would be cut short.

I distinctly remember the face of that input guy, though I don't remember his name. Maybe he is still there at Aaj Tak or in some other news channel, working as a senior person managing the affairs behind the screen, if he escaped being branded a Sanghi. If I happen to see him even today, I'd be able to recognize him. The anguish and disgust in his tone, and the anger subdued by helplessness on his face are visuals I can't forget.

Umm...well, this is a book where I can't be politically correct or try to hide what I know or feel. So, let me correct the first and the only slip-up I have committed. I actually do remember who the input guy is and know where he is employed. How could I have forgotten that expression on his face? Today, he is indeed at a senior position at one of the leading Hindi news channels.

I actually looked up his social media posts before writing this paragraph to check whether he is vocal about his beliefs. His Twitter timeline makes him appear 'neutral', so I won't name him and spoil his 'image'. The liberal mafia of the mainstream media is ruthless and I have no reason to unleash them on this guy who was just an angry helpless Hindu on 27 February 2002.

I too, perhaps for the first time, felt angry as a Hindu on that day. I was 22 years old then and I could have felt angry as a Hindu on many occasions earlier, especially when Kashmiri Pandits were being killed or when kar sevaks were killed at Ayodhya in 1990, but I was just a boy then, and neither of these incidents were talked about much in the media in the coming years, as if those incidents were erased from public memory on purpose. Compare it with how the media never forgets to talk about the Babri Masjid demolition every year on 6 December.

The 2002 Gujarat riots

Within a week or two, the anger that I had felt as a Hindu on the day of the Godhra carnage was replaced with guilt—something Hindus already had in plenty thanks to the moral compass—as the media started covering the riots that erupted in many parts of Gujarat in the aftermath of the Godhra incident.

It was independent India's first televised riots, and thus the impact was unparalleled. Not that India had not seen Hindu–Muslim riots earlier, and nothing beats the obscenity of state involvement so far as the anti-Sikh pogrom of 1984 is concerned, but the 2002 riots in Gujarat appeared to be the most monstrous thing independent India had ever witnessed— because people indeed 'witnessed' such an incident for the first time, on their TV sets. It seemed as if entire Gujarat was up in flames.

Over time, we came to know about many cases related to the riots. We became aware of names like Zakia Jafri, the wife of Ehsan Jafri, the former Congress MP who was killed in the riots. We also heard stories of Zahira Sheikh, who was seen with Teesta Setalvad much often and later Setalvad was accused of pressurising her to change statements. The horrific story of Kausar Bano was also told, who was raped while she was pregnant and killed with her foetus being pulled out with a sword—something that the doctor who performed the post mortem disputed.[33] And we came to know about Qutubuddin Ansari, the teary-eyed man with injuries on his fingers as he pleaded for mercy with folded hands—his photograph epitomizing the riots.

There are many more stories, and many more names that we couldn't forget as the media widely reported the 2002 riots, and those cases were followed up and reported for many years thereafter. I'm sure most of you remember these names. With Muslims bearing the brunt of the violence, it's natural and logical that most names and stories would be about Muslim victims. But how come we don't know a single name or story about a Hindu victim, when the riots started with 59 Hindus being burnt alive?

Ask yourself, do you know the name of even one Hindu who was burnt alive at Godhra, or any survivor who lived to tell the story about the carnage? Further, those killed at Godhra were not the only Hindu victims. You must have repeatedly heard about the Shah Alam relief camp that housed Muslim victims of the riots, but do you know that there was another relief camp at Kankariya,[34] not far away from the Shah Alam camp, which sheltered hundreds of Hindu victims who were targeted during the post-Godhra riots?

Hindu victims are numbers, Muslim victims are narratives.

As someone who was studying mathematics but suddenly fell out of love with numbers to fall in love with words and shifted to reading literature and poetry, I was bound to be influenced more by stories than statistics. Not just TV news reports, there were hordes of documentaries and short films made on the Gujarat riots in the following weeks and months, many of which I happened to watch, as we were recommended to watch good documentaries too, as part of our broadcast journalism course.

The anger that I could feel as a Hindu on 27 February 2002, consequently evaporated and was replaced with a guilt that Hindus went too far and took revenge from ordinary Muslims who were not responsible for what happened at Godhra.

One can raise a valid question: What stopped the Right-wing Hindus from creating similar stories about victims of the Godhra carnage? Social media or YouTube did not exist back then but they emerged a few years later; so, why no stories even then?

There are no easy answers. The traditional media is too biased and they will not tell your story. And if somehow you muster the courage to tell your story, you'd be maligned and your work will be discredited. However, that alone can't be the reason why someone shouldn't even attempt to tell those stories. One has to admit that such skills and perhaps even dedication is missing on 'our side'. But things are changing slowly. Even this book is an attempt to tell 'our own story'.

Without digressing further, let me go back to the time when I was an intern at Aaj Tak and the Godhra carnage, and later the riots, had taken place.

During those days, I was assisting the guest coordination team of the channel. It meant talking to politicians, celebrities and experts, and requesting them to take part in interviews or debates on the channel. The senior people did the talking, while my job as an intern was to fetch them to the studios and attend to them while they were the channel's guests.

On the evening of the Godhra train burning incident, I was sent to the VHP (Vishva Hindu Parishad) office to bring some Hindu leaders to the studios. When I reached the office, I remember seeing Giriraj Kishore, the senior VHP leader with a big flowing white beard and red tilak on his forehead, in conversation with a few people who had gathered at the office.

He was saying something like 'Hindu jal ke marne se nahi darta,' that is, 'The Hindus are not afraid of dying by the fire.' He then referred to something about cremation, probably explaining why he thought that those who died at Godhra would attain 'sadgati' even though it was not possible to perform the last rites for them, as their bodies had been reduced to ashes.

He was talking fast, and talking about many things. I could sense that he was distressed and furious. He averred that this ghastly carnage won't be successful in intimidating Hindus into submission, and that if Muslims thought that by carrying out such attacks they can scare away the Hindus from asserting their rights on Ram Janmabhoomi, they were greatly mistaken. It's pertinent to note here that those who were burnt alive were returning from Ayodhya, where they had gone on a pilgrimage.

I don't recall bringing Giriraj Kishore to the Aaj Tak studios that evening. He was just too agonized and distracted to take part in a TV discussion or give an interview. He said that his priority was to reach Gujarat and talk to the survivors of the carnage and families of the victims.

But I do recall Praveen Togadia being in the studio. Whether it was the same evening or some other day, I don't exactly recall because it was not me who was sent to fetch him. Once he was inside the TV Today building, I was asked by the guest coordination team to accompany him to the make-up room and stay with him until he is called inside the studio. In TV news, a basic make-up is also applied on the guest panellists, so that their faces look fine under the bright studio lights.

In the make-up room, a couple of news anchors were occupying the chairs in front of the big mirrors, getting ready for their shows. So, Togadia was asked to sit on a sofa and wait for his turn. Usually off camera, the political guests would indulge in niceties with the journalists or news anchors, but Togadia started talking about Godhra and other things in the make-up room itself. The anchors sitting there appeared totally uninterested, plus they were not supposed to talk too much while make-up was being applied, so I had to lend my ears to keep the guest humoured.

I don't think I understood much of what Togadia said, as he was not just ranting about the Godhra incident. He was broadly talking about Islamic imperialism, Hindutva ideology and other such issues, about which I didn't have much knowledge back then. However, as someone who was tasked to take care of the guests, I pretended to be interested and eager to understand what he said.

I didn't pretend for too long though, and soon admitted to Togadia that I lacked the knowledge or information to appreciate the many things he said. He was carrying a small diary. He immediately wrote his email ID on a page, tore it off and gave it to me, asking me to write to him, after which he will send articles that would help me understand his point of view.

I felt pretty honoured, to be honest, because it was the first time that a man, who was a public figure, cared to share his contact details voluntarily with someone who was a mere intern and who had been given such a small and 'unintellectual' job of fetching and humouring guests to the TV studio. That Togadia was Sanghi types, who I thought were regressive and intolerant, didn't matter at that very moment, because someone had cared to notice my small existence in the big world of TV news.

It was a special gesture by him, though that doesn't mean that other guests I had fetched had entirely ignored me, except Congress leader Kamal Nath, who didn't even care to let me sit in the same car that I had taken to fetch him to the studio. Leaders like BJP's Madan Lal Khurana or Congress leaders Arun Nehru and Anil Shastri, whom I had earlier brought to the studios, were pretty courteous too. Khurana and Shastri made sure that I sat in the same car next to them and indulged in small conversations with me, as the car drove to the studio. But once in the studio, they had the senior journalists and editors to hang out with. I would become irrelevant as soon as I entered the TV Today building.

But Togadia cared about my existence and talked to me even while we were inside the TV Today building. Not just that, he also asked me to keep in touch, which is where he stood out for an intern like me. Interestingly, one of the news anchors who was in the make-up room, had a smirk on his face when he saw Togadia handing out his email address on a piece of paper to me. A couple of days later, the anchor bumped into me in the office and advised me to keep a safe distance from the 'Togadia types' if I wanted to become a good journalist.

I had already sent an email to Togadia by then. A few days later he replied too. He had sent me an article on some historical events, the details of which I currently can't recall, maybe because I had taken the advice of the news anchor to keep a safe distance from him. I wanted a career in media, so I gave more importance to the words of a news anchor than Togadia's.

Further, that gesture by the news anchor was also heartening, because a senior professional cared to give a friendly advice to an intern. As a result, I didn't bother to read the entire article sent by Togadia, nor did I send any emails to him in the future. That slight chance that I could have been exposed to counter a set of arguments rather early in my life was gone.

We were back on the IIMC campus after the internship. Making a documentary was one of the last remaining tasks that had to be completed before our diplomas in journalism were handed out to us. That's when I discovered a few documentary makers, and they were even more Left-leaning than an average journalist. I remember reading a news report where a documentary maker had claimed that he had cut off his janeu after being disgusted with what was done to the Muslims in the 2002 riots.

I didn't wear the janeu back then, but such strong statements affected the psyche. For someone who wore a janeu, his sense of identity was turned into a sense of guilt. To unburden himself from that guilt, to dissociate himself from those who killed innocent people, he will have to remove his religious markers, as those have been meticulously turned into symbols of hate. You don't need to publicize a treatise against Brahminism to push a person into cutting his janeu; you just need a good personal story. That is the power of storytelling.

4

Lessons in journalism

Perils of 'responsible' journalism

Apart from learning how to pronounce my name correctly, and how to pronounce Urdu words correctly, I learnt the basics of broadcast journalism at IIMC. I also got to know the basics of cameras, video editing, scripting, various formats of reporting, live studio production and of course, storytelling, that is, the narrative.

The term 'narrative' doesn't just mean the art and craft of storytelling, but also the agenda that you want to set along with the story. I don't recall any in-your-face kind of ideological narrative being peddled by any teacher or guest faculty in the broadcast journalism course. My friends from the print journalism courses though would share some stories about heated debates around such issues in their classes.

Perhaps the print journalists were more into bitter ideological battles than the TV journalists at that time. Television journalism had just started taking off in India and not many were ready to become a flagbearer of ideological battles from the beginning itself. Today, obviously you can name a dime a dozen of TV journalists who indulge in such battles. You can imagine what they would teach if they were to be invited as guest faculty in any journalism school, but I was more or less spared any direct ideological preaching in the classrooms.

The general ideological bias in media narratives is not due to some grand universal conspiracy by the Left to control the world—at least that is what I personally believe, even though some people do believe that such a conspiracy exists—but because of the widely held belief that the mass media is hugely powerful and thus this power has to be used 'responsibly.'

Stan Lee wrote in *Spider-Man*, 'With great power comes great responsibility.' Incidentally, alter egos of some fictional superheroes too worked in newspapers, such as Peter Parker and Clark Kent, that is, Spider-Man and Superman, respectively. Journalists, too, seem to have alter egos, who must save the world from the villains and promote good over evil.

And I am not being flippant about it. Journalists, for sure in those times, did solemnly feel that they were very powerful and thus they had a very important job. Dileep Padgaonkar, a long-time editor at *The Times of India*, is reported to have said, 'I have the second-most important job in the country,' presumably after the prime minister's.

This sense of self-importance is the result of the widely held belief that the traditional mainstream media is hugely powerful, which consequently leads to ideology playing a part in the overall scheme of things. Let me explain.

Among various communication models applicable to the mass media, I remember being taught the oldest and the original theory of 'hypodermic needle model' very early at IIMC. Also known as the 'magic bullet' theory, this model equates messaging through the mass media with medicinal injections. The messages carried by the media are supposed to be like the medicinal fluid in a syringe, which can be injected into a receiver's body and the desired affects can be achieved to almost clinical perfection. Alternatively, the media is supposed to be a magic gun that can inject bullets right into a person's head—without killing him—but the person's beliefs and thinking changes according to what was contained in that bullet.

There is also something called the 'agenda-setting theory', which effectively argues that the media is not anything like a 'mirror to the society'—an adage often used by journalists or media professionals—but the press and the media actually go on to shape the character of a society by altering its thinking and sensitivities. So, far from being just a commentator—which is how journalists present themselves by offering 'Don't shoot the messenger' and such maxims—a journalist is actually an active player and on occasions, even an umpire.

These are not conspiracy theories but communication theories taught at journalism schools. To be fair, there are other theories too, which argue that the recipients or the masses are not so passive. Such theories are taught too, and I'm sure that over the past few years, new models would also have come up, given how new technologies have diluted this power of the old mass media. I hope those are also being taught in journalism schools today.

But the original and earnest belief among journalists was, and perhaps remains, that the traditional mass media is too powerful and can bring about mass changes and revolutions by altering people's thinking.

Since the media is a hugely powerful tool, if not THE powerful tool to control the masses, that one must be responsible in using this tool was an unquestioned wisdom. I too believed that a journalist's job was to educate the masses about what is good and bad, to make them take note of the right issues by deciding which news deserves what kind of space and to fight for justice on behalf of the masses—that would be 'responsible journalism.' A student of journalism would feel that a journalist was no less important than a teacher or a doctor or a soldier for the society.

Possibly many of you are thinking—'But what is wrong in that belief? Journalists must feel that sense of responsibility.' However, the moment you bring in a moral aspect, things are bound to get influenced by the ideologies you subscribe to, because what is 'responsible behaviour' will be guided by your ideology, especially your political ideology.

Similarly, answers to questions such as 'What is good for the society?' that you should promote and 'Who or what is evil?' that you should fight against would also depend upon, and sometimes be dictated by, your personal and socio-political ideologies.

Let us take a very simple case. Say, in a small town, the local administration gives sanction to a builder to construct a shopping mall. The land is acquired or small shops are bought in some area to be demolished, so that a new mall can be built there. Now, if your political ideology is old school communism, a big builder demolishing small shops itself would be an act of evil, which is pushing the society towards capitalism. And you would earnestly believe that this evil should be fought against and defeated.

Such a journalist, whether reporting from the ground or rewriting the ground reporter's copy from his desk, will act 'responsibly' and present the development as evil, which should be resisted. Depending on how much committed and devoted such a journalist is to his ideology, he would even go on to cherry-pick data and incidents to build a narrative that is against the construction of the mall. And he would be acting 'responsibly' in his head, and not in a 'biased' or unethical way.

So, when that copy editor in Aaj Tak said he could not mention 'Muslim' in the report about the Godhra train carnage, he was simply acting 'responsibly' by hiding a piece of information from the public, because putting out that information at that point of time would be 'irresponsible'. While in your mind, the role of an ideal journalist would be that of someone who is objectively reporting every piece of information he comes across, here a piece of information was not reported—because the media must act 'responsibly'.

The world of journalism is replete with various such examples. No matter how much journalists deny, they do subscribe to political ideologies and many cherish them. So many Delhi-based journalists have been card-carrying members of various leftist student organizations during their college days. It's ridiculous to believe that suddenly their ideological beliefs disappear when they get employed with a media organization. In fact, these beliefs become more pronounced as they start acting even more 'responsibly' after becoming journalists.

From a simple communism vs capitalism ideological divide decades ago, we are now in an age when various shades of ideologies have sprung up and original ideologies have morphed into something else altogether. The Left was supposed to speak for the 'unwashed masses' for a long time and raise issues that resonate with that crowd and class, but today almost all the pet activism of the Left resonates with those who are 'elite' and well-off. The leftist used to be a pen-wielding jholawala wearing faded chappals at one point of time, but today's leftist is often a mobile-wielding individual wearing torn jeans along with facial piercings. The constituencies of the Left and the Right have virtually been swapped.

Hence in today's world, a journalist's ideas of what will be 'responsible' have become even more complex and sometimes borders on the absurd. For example, in January 2018, a lady reporter with The Wire, a far-Left news and opinion website founded by a former editor of *The Hindu*, was manhandled and heckled in Ahmedabad by a mob of 15–20 men who were supposedly 'Dalit activists'. Distressed and disturbed by what had happened, the reporter wanted to write about her ordeal, but she was told to 'let it go' by the leftist activist and editors.[35]

Forget writing about it in any mainstream publication, she was advised not to even file a police complaint against the goons. By advising a woman to forget that she was manhandled and attacked, the leftist editors were acting 'responsibly' in their minds, because the evil of Brahminism had to be defeated. Apparently, Brahminism can't be defeated if Dalit men are identified as aggressors, even in isolated incidents.

Similarly, in June 2019, in the Hauz Qazi area of Delhi, a Muslim mob had attacked Hindu shops and homes as well as vandalized an old Durga Mandir, after a fight over parking space turned ugly and communal. The mainstream media not only decided to downplay the incident, especially the desecration of the temple part, they entirely ignored the wails of a poor Hindu couple whose son had gone missing for over a day. The parents had filed a police complaint for their missing son and insisted that their son was kidnapped by Muslims. The mother was crying inconsolably while the father threatened to commit suicide if his son was not traced.[36]

Despite a police complaint and parents sobbing right in front of them, no mainstream media journalist reported about their claims. The incident came to light via social media, and subsequently some 'pro Hindu' publications, including OpIndia, picked it up after talking to the parents and having a look at the FIR. Later, when the son was traced and found to be safe, the mainstream media journalists behaved as if their decision to ignore the incident was justified and 'responsible.' They claimed that they were waiting for verification and confirmation from the police and did not want to worsen an already volatile environment. So responsible!

Somehow all this responsibility goes for a toss if a Muslim couple were to claim something similar. Recall how allegations of many Muslim men who claimed that they were beaten up and forced to chant 'Jai Shri Ram' were reported without the mainstream media waiting for verification or confirmation from the police. The bulk of such cases, incidentally reported after Modi won the 2019 Lok Sabha elections, was found to be baseless or downright fake after the police carried out interrogations and investigations; yet reporting on such lines continued unabated.[37]

Earlier in June 2017, the media never cared for any verification or confirmation before claiming that a Muslim teenager named Junaid Khan was killed on the Delhi-Mathura train because he was suspected to be carrying beef. Later, the Punjab and Haryana High Court observed that the death had happened because of a fight between two groups of daily travellers over occupying train seats and not due to 'lynching' over any suspicion of carrying beef.[38]

There are countless such examples—a Muslim model claiming to have been denied a flat in Mumbai due to her religion while in reality many Muslims were already living in that building,[39] a Muslim boy in Delhi claiming some men beat him up and asked him to chant 'Jai Mata Di', but later his friends, who were Muslims too, revealed that nothing of that sort ever took place,[40] a man in Mumbai claiming that an auto-rickshaw driver beat him up because he was carrying a leather bag, which the driver suspected to be made of cow skin, but subsequent reports revealed that the story was entirely made up by the man who reportedly admitted that he hated Hindus[41]—and all of these were reported by the media without waiting for any verification or confirmation by the police. But somehow the same journalists decide to wait and become 'responsible' if a Hindu man or woman claims to be a victim of communal hatred.

And this is not just limited to Hindu vs Muslim or upper castes vs lower castes. Journalists indulge in editorializing news reports almost without exception. Thus, while most of us grew up thinking what we consumed in the newspapers or saw on the news channels was pure unvarnished truth, the fact is that more often than not, those were selectively picked and carefully presented narratives, shaped by ideologies that respective reporters or editors believed in.

The bulk of the journalists would not have done this as part of some grand conspiracy to ensure the triumph of some political ideology—this is my personal belief because I would like to give most of them the benefit of the doubt—but because in their minds that would have been the right thing to do, the right thing for the masses, all done in good faith. Journalism is perhaps the best manifestation of the aphorism, 'The road to hell is paved with good intentions.'

Coming back to my IIMC days, as I said, fortunately I didn't have any teachers or guest faculty trying to seed their own version of truth and responsible journalism among the students, but I do remember at least one instance, which in retrospect I believe was an example of how ideological slants are seeded as virtues of responsible journalism.

Our course director had introduced us to a young documentary maker, who had apparently visited the campus just to meet the director but was nevertheless asked to give a guest lecture. Since he was also a student of IIMC from earlier batches, we were interested to know what he was doing in life, so that we could get an idea of the career paths we could take up. He talked about his journey and then gave us some suggestions to write better scripts.

One of his suggestions was to get rid of 'footprints of the government' in our scripts. He gave an example to explain what he meant. He said that a phrase like 'Police had to resort to lathicharge' was an example of footprints of the government, because by using that phrase, we were giving a clean chit to the police by suggesting they had no other option but to wield lathis. Why should we blindly trust the government or the police and use a language that is favourable to them, he challenged us to think.

We found it pretty thought-provoking as well as logical. And honestly even now I'd say it was not a bad suggestion. My only concern now would be: Why should a logical mind only doubt the government? If we should get rid of the footprints of the government, shouldn't we also get rid of footprints and handprints and all the marks left behind by the so-called 'civil society' and 'eminent citizens' too?

Why should the utterings of a few people be reported in the newspapers as sacrosanct conclusions of a 'fact-finding committee' just because they call themselves a fact-finding committee? How are we so sure that the self-appointed committee's interests were never to find facts but to invent one? Or at best, to selectively find 'facts' to support a predetermined conclusion?

When you sow doubts only about the government but paint another set of people, often unelected and unaccountable, as selfless activists whose pronouncements can't be doubted or questioned, you are not creating a vibrant democracy but a parallel governance system. This is what causes many people to argue that what certain journalists do are not innocent ideological misbeliefs but a grand conspiracy to destabilize the existing democratic systems and replace them with their own power structure and governance systems.

I didn't have such counter-arguments or thoughts then. I just imbibed what appeared to be a logical and novel line of thinking. Fortunately, there were no committed communists or 'Urban Naxals' teaching broadcast journalism at IIMC back then, else who knows what I would have been writing and where I would have been working today. Perhaps, I would have been doing 'responsible journalism' too, instead of writing this 'irresponsible book.'

Nonetheless, IIMC days were good. I learnt new things, acquired new skills, explored a new city, got exposed to new cultures and gained the confidence that one could get a job—and a respectable job of a journalist—even without studying at the IITs or taking the UPSC exams.

The course duration at IIMC was hardly of 10 months, which meant two successive batches never shared any time together on campus. So, we didn't get to know the 'seniors' in person, who could share their experiences of finding a job or help us get a job. Employment prospects were entirely left on the campus placement process, or they depended upon how enterprising a student was in finding a job of his own.

Only a handful among us from the batch of 25 could get jobs through campus placement. Some were promised jobs during their internship period itself, while a few others got them during the final placement process, but most of us were without a job.

This was around April–May 2002 and we were told not to lose hope, as some new TV channels were to be launched. At that point of time, NDTV used to air as Star News, and murmurs had begun that soon they will part ways. NDTV would launch their own news channel, leading to new jobs. Sahara India Pariwar—a business house spread out in multiple sectors, from finance, retail, real estate to even airlines—was also supposed to come up with their own news channel. The Times group—the richest media house—was expected to come out with a TV channel too, though they came up with one much later.

A couple of my friends, who were more enterprising and outgoing, had taken unpaid or very lowly paid jobs at some production houses that made programs for various TV channels. Their logic was that at least they will get exposure to the industry and start developing contacts and network, which would eventually help them in getting a better job. But I was never good at networking, so I didn't opt for it and rather sat at home, looking for job vacancies in the newspapers.

My parents were a little worried, though they never really opposed any of my career decisions, or for that matter any life decisions. Honestly, even I was worried. In order to avoid wasting an academic year, I even applied for admission in Delhi University, for an M.Sc. degree in mathematics. I also appeared for a competitive exam to become some Grade A or Grade B officer at the RBI. However, I really wanted to pursue a career in media and my heart was not into any of these steps that I had taken.

After three months of unemployment and confusion, I spotted a huge ad of Sahara India, soliciting job applications for their TV news channels. They declared that they were not launching just one but multiple news channels—one channel catering to the national audience and others catering to a few regional ones. I applied and was called for a job interview.

I was pretty happy, and nervous too. I mugged almost everything that I had studied and memorized for the entrance test at IIMC—names of the editors of major newspapers at that time, and topics that were making news.

I was interviewed by a few senior journalists on the D-day. It was not a comprehensive interview as I had applied for an entry-level job. I didn't really know who they were, but they were seniors as I'd later see them in senior positions in the newsroom. They asked me generic questions, such as why I'd want this job, what I learnt at IIMC, what role I'd prefer in a newsroom—a reporter's or a desk editor's, etc. And then, there was one question about who my favourite journalist was.

I don't know if they were expecting me to name some historical figure, but I thought they wanted me to pick one from among the active journalists of that time. That was a problem, because I didn't really have any favourite journalists. As I have recounted earlier, I chose journalism because I wanted to be a writer, a novelist to be precise, and only when I started digging more facts about novelists and their writing careers, I warmed up to the world of journalism and journalistic writings. But I was still to become a fan of any journalist. I didn't have any role models in journalism whom I wanted to emulate.

So, I just blurted out some names that I could recall as leading editors and columnists of those times. I remember having come up with names like Dileep Padgaonkar, Vinod Mehta, Prabhash Joshi, and...wait for it, Siddharth Varadarajan. The last one is the founder of the far-Left website The Wire, about which I have mentioned two dishonourable incidents in this book so far.

When I came up with these names, one of the interviewers asked me, in Hindi, 'The names that you have taken are of people who have a certain way of looking at things. They have a certain ideology. Do you have a similar ideology?'

I had absolutely no idea what the question meant. I still remember the exact words in Hindi—'Inki ek khaas vichardhara hai'—and back then I didn't even know what the word 'vichardhara' (ideology) meant. I was 22 years old and had just completed a post-graduate diploma in journalism. I was clearly too naïve, or rather incompetent, to not even know what 'ideology' meant.

I gave a random answer, stating why I like their work, that the issues they raise are important for the society, etc. The interviewers could sense that I was basically clueless or maybe too 'innocent' to understand the question. They let me go. But I got the job. Maybe because they could figure out that at least I didn't subscribe to the 'wrong ideology'? Further, if a person's ideology was irrelevant to the job in the media, I shouldn't have been asked that question in the first place. I'm sure I would not have been hired if I had shown any Sanghi leanings.

Back then, I didn't bother. I didn't even care to find out more about the word vichardhara. I was just happy to get a job, even though the designation that I (and everyone at the entry level) was given was named 'intern', which was pretty unfair as it suggested a lack of regular employment. Further, the monthly compensation was a mere ₹5000, which was stingy even in 2002, and there was some deduction at source even for this amount! I remember getting ₹4691 per month in my first job.

But none of these were really important. All that mattered then was that I had a job, that I had a career and that I was a journalist.

Rewards of secular journalism

At Sahara, the work used to progress at its own pace, or at the pace decided by 'Sahara Shri', that is, Subrata Roy, the founder and Chairman of the Sahara India Pariwar. When I joined, there was still no clarity on when the channels would be launched. We didn't even know what they would be called. If I remember correctly, the channels went on air and were available for public viewing almost six months after my joining. They were branded 'Sahara Samay'.

In those six months, juniors like me were given various dummy reports to write. We used the time to understand how a newsroom works and familiarized ourselves with the work flow and machines. It also helped me to get to know the other 'interns' better. It was like an extension of the journalism course at IIMC, with the added advantage of modern machines and real-time work.

Out of these six months, three months were almost non-productive, while another three were when the channel was virtually operational, but the programming feed was not yet made available to the public—a period known as 'dry run', which shouldn't have run for so long.

I was put in the team of the regional news channel, catering to the Uttar Pradesh and Uttarakhand regions, unimaginatively named 'Sahara Samay Uttar Pradesh-Uttarakhand'. To start with, I worked in the roles of copy editor, package production guy and voice-over artist, even though my designation continued to be 'intern' for the next two years, during which I would go on to work as a bulletin producer and a news anchor too.

As a copy editor and production guy, you are supposed to take the raw copies filed by the field reporters and rewrite them into a TV news report format, based on available video footage and sound bites. One could use tapes from the video library too, if the cameraman had not recorded enough shots. Library footage or file footage could also be used to complement any extra information or add context during the process of copy writing to enhance the report. Reporter's copies were supposed to be dry and banal, sometimes even incomplete, and copy editors were expected to make them ready for broadcast by filling up the information gaps.

At Sahara, the field reporters used to send handwritten reports that were faxed to the 'input desk'. The input team screened these to select what information should be passed on to the desk of the copy editors. As a copy editor, the bulk of my job was to rewrite the colloquial Hindi used by the reporter and replace them with literary-sounding script, sprinkled with Urdu words. And then proudly pronounce those Urdu words while doing the voice-over.

You could also produce 'desk reports' when no relevant field reports by reporters were available. You could make use of publicly available information and the footage sent by news agencies, and add your own analysis around it to create a desk report. There was one such report that I had filed, which attracted high praise from a senior person in the newsroom.

It was a report on the US invasion of Iraq in March–April 2003 to overthrow the Saddam Hussain regime, which was suspected to be hoarding weapons of mass destruction (WMD) and helping Osama Bin Laden's Al Qaida. The report was made based on file footages from the video library and the latest footage that came from the Iraq War via agencies. I wrote the script after reading various articles, including conspiracy theories, as I searched for information on the internet as part of my research. I was given special access to a computer with internet, something that was available only to bosses at that point of time, to do the research work for this special report.

The report basically argued that Iraq having weapons of mass destruction was a sham and that the US was actually eyeing the oil fields of the gulf countries. It explained how US-based oil companies 'illegally' controlled the oil production in the gulf region. The report also talked about how Saddam was actually working on creating a trading conglomerate that would have weakened the US dollar.

Essentially, it was an out-and-out US-bashing report, holding them responsible for the mess the gulf was in. And well, should I say that had Shahbaz from IIMC not run away in the middle of the journalism course, and if he had got a job in some TV news channel, he would have possibly written a similar report, with an added focus on how Osama Bin Laden didn't even exist.

I had basically rehashed some leftist literature bashing the capitalist US, which would suit an Islamist narrative too. But, I was proud of my work because my senior patted my back. What also made it special was the fact that I could get to sign off the report with my own name, else copy editors had to sign off with the name of the original field reporter, even if they might have rewritten the entire copy and given it a new direction.

This is how someone in media and journalism, who doesn't even know what vichardhara is, slowly starts following and subscribing to the leftist ideology. It comes with rewards and privileges. I was rewarded with a public endorsement that I was among the brighter guys in the junior lot, while I gained the privilege to sign off a report with my name. It was such a satisfying and proud moment to hear your own name, in your own voice and on public TV; so, why wouldn't I repeat the same in the future?

I didn't get much opportunity to repeat it though, primarily because I worked in a news channel that catered to Uttar Pradesh, where such reports didn't need to be frequent. I had to focus on developments and politics of the state, where the BJP, and by extension Hindutva politics, was progressively losing strength and becoming irrelevant. From a pole position in the 1990s, the BJP was pushed to a sorry third position in the 2002 assembly elections.

The BJP had supported the BSP (Bahujan Samaj Party) and helped Mayawati become the chief minister of Uttar Pradesh after the 2002 assembly elections, a move that can be argued to be an unintelligent one as it gave a signal to the electorate that the state had only two options—SP (Samajwadi Party) or BSP—and others would have to play a second fiddle to either of them.

Around mid-2003, that is, in my first year as a working journalist, Uttar Pradesh saw multiple political upheavals, with many BSP MLAs becoming rebels. Soon, with help of these rebels, Mulayam Singh Yadav of the SP became the chief minister and Mayawati the prime challenger, with the BJP and Congress looking like Bangladesh and Zimbabwe in a four-nation cricket championship involving India and Australia.

It appeared that Uttar Pradesh was moving towards becoming a state that could soon see Tamil Nadu-type political landscape, with the SP and BSP taking turns to win the elections, similar to the DMK (Dravida Munnetra Kazhagam) and AIADMK (All India Anna Dravida Munnetra Kazhagam) down south—something that actually happened in the subsequent 2007 and 2012 assembly elections, before the BJP scored a miraculous victory in the 2017 state polls.

Essentially, the BJP was on the wane and state politics was about SP vs BSP, about Mulayam vs Mayawati, about boisterous OBC vs resurgent Dalits. The politics that I was exposed to as a working journalist was less about ideology and more about one-upmanship, muscle power and personality clashes. The national-level politics, however, was surely about 'defeating communal forces', with the BJP in power in Delhi, the Gujarat riots having taken place the year before and general elections scheduled to be held the following year.

However, it wasn't so bad either that Hindutva politics would be entirely dead in Uttar Pradesh in 2003–04. That simply can't happen with Ayodhya, Kashi and Mathura being in the state—three holy cities associated with Hindu gods, and where mosques were built after destroying the temples.

It was sometime in late 2003 when the VHP called for a meeting or perhaps a symbolic puja at Ayodhya. However, the VHP claimed that the proposed meeting was a non-religious gathering and thus not against the orders of the Supreme Court, which had banned any religious activity in Ayodhya around the disputed site.

The immediate and natural reaction of the media, acting 'responsibly', was to toe a narrative that the move was aimed at whipping up communal sentiments ahead of the Lok Sabha elections that were due next year, and that it was irresponsible on the part of the VHP to indulge in such an act when the wounds of 2002 riots were yet to heal.

But the VHP was adamant. Mulayam Singh Yadav's government deployed police forces in Faizabad and Ayodhya, which I believed was a right step because the VHP was trying to 'disturb peace'. The role of the media in my mind was to stand with the people. I automatically assumed that the people were not with the VHP, because no normal person would want peace to be disturbed.

In such a scenario, responsible journalism meant airing reports about how the lives of common people were being negatively impacted by the VHP drama. It also meant airing reports that argued that people didn't care about mandir politics. It would have been the best to air reports about Hindu–Muslim unity to show how the VHP didn't have any popular support and how they were dividing people.

A story with such a potential arrived at our desk very soon. The local reporter had sent a report about some Muslim garland sellers who used to supply garlands to a few temples in Ayodhya. The report claimed that these garland sellers had been doing this job over many generations and they didn't want their work to suffer. In fact, the handwritten report claimed that the garland sellers didn't want to stop serving the Hindu temples, as they apparently derived some divine pleasure from it.

As Ravi Shastri would say, 'It was just what the doctor ordered.' This was a perfect story depicting Hindu–Muslim unity and harmony and which showed how pathetic the VHP was. If I were working for a magazine or a newspaper, I'd have just rewritten the story in a flowery language and submitted it for approval to the seniors, who would have not wasted a minute in giving the green signal for its publication.

But since I was working for a TV channel, I had to do a little donkey work. I had to go through the entire video footage sent by the reporter and identify the relevant sound bites that would support the script. So, armed with an earphone, I sat through half an hour of the video recording to find those lovely words that would drown out the loud speeches made by the VHP leaders. And I couldn't find any.

The garland sellers had essentially told the reporter, 'Yes, we have been selling these garlands that are used in temples, but we are not educated. We can't do any other work. We can't leave this work just because the VHP people are here; how will we earn our living?'

One of the garland sellers actually went on to say, and rightly so, that he would leave this menial job if he finds a better paying one. None of them said anything like they derive happiness or satisfaction by doing something that was in service of gods.

These were perfectly normal sentiments. One could sympathize with the plight of these poor garland sellers, but it was nowhere as romantic and harmonious as the script sent by the reporter made it out to be. So I asked my editor what to do.

The editor asked to me to not go into such 'technical details' and create a story that was as near in tone and tenor as possible to what the reporter had originally sent. He said it was a 'good story' and we must carry it on our channel. Basically, we would be acting very 'responsibly' if we sent out a message of communal harmony.

So, I, a young TV journalist, employed my newly acquired skills and used only the 'We can't leave this work just because the VHP people are here' part of the sound bite to create the story. The rest of the script conveyed what the local reporter had imagined or wished the situation to be, that is, the Muslim garland sellers taking pride or pleasure in providing their services to the Hindu temples.

Do note that what was aired was fabrication and manipulation, but it was a fair thing to do because in our minds we were acting responsibly. I had essentially helped create a fake Hindu–Muslim harmony story, similar to the various stories I had grown up hearing.

This is how a particular narrative is kept alive. You don't even realize that you become an active player in keeping this narrative alive.

The story was aired multiple times on the TV channel. It was a script I had written and it had my voice-over too. Again, I received rewards that come naturally when you toe a particular line. That's how the system itself is designed to perpetuate a particular narrative.

And do remember, this is one of the most benign examples of fabrication and manipulation that you can get. Stories have literally been manipulated to the extent of turning the original one on its head to keep a narrative going, with victims turned into oppressors—for example, news reports about skirmishes between cattle farmers and cattle thieves—and facts muddled to the extent that you can't know the truth at all.

Slowly, you not only start believing your own lies but you become a soldier fighting to perpetuate them because your moral compass says that those are not lies or manipulation, but responsible journalism. Your career and reputation become dependent on ensuring that the moral compass keeps pointing to a secular equilibrium—where a Hindu is always under the guilt of having committed some injustices while a Muslim is perpetually in the victim mode. This state of equilibrium is what is known as communal harmony and peace. Anything that strays from this state of equilibrium is undesirable and is understood to have caused injustice, intolerance and violence.

Therefore, whether an incident is an example of injustice, intolerance or violence is not dependent on what the incident is in reality, but whether it maintains or upsets the 'secular equilibrium'. Consequently, an incident involving a Muslim mob indulging in violent protests over CAA is presented not as an act of violence but 'dissent'—because it keeps the victim mode among Muslims alive—while a Hindu talking about Islamic persecution of his fellow Hindus is painted as 'hate speech' that can lead to violence.

There is a popular cartoon that shows people standing in a long queue in front of a desk selling 'reassuring lie' while the desk selling 'ugly truth' or something similar has no buyers. I have seen many journalists sharing it at some point of time to buttress their point. I go 'Dude, that's precisely what you have been doing in the name of responsible journalism for decades!' in my mind when I see that.

Nonetheless, I was happy buying as well as selling these reassuring lies as I completed a year in my first job. As someone who was not aware of ideological nuances, I thought such minor manipulation—the one I did in the story about garland sellers—was not a crime. It was indeed responsible behaviour and had nothing to do with any ideology.

Why should communal harmony or Hindu–Muslim unity be about the Left? It was a responsible thing to do irrespective of what ideology you believed in—one could as well have argued like this and justified the manipulation.

Even the BJP leaders talked about Hindu–Muslim unity. Noted Urdu poet Bashir Badr had joined the BJP along with many other Muslim poets, and Arif Mohammad Khan, who had quit the Rajiv Gandhi government over the Shah Bano issue, too had joined the party in those years. Even as I write this, the current BJP leadership talks about 'Sabka vishwaas', that is, winning the faith and confidence of everyone, including Muslims—a call that was given by Prime Minister Narendra Modi himself.

Further, there were many Muslim colleagues in the newsroom too, some of whom were 'interns' like me. We would hang out together, gossip about bosses, bitch about each other and talk about our career paths, and thus the Hindu–Muslim harmony would hardly appear to be anything that was captive to a particular political ideology.

The Left is very good at initiating someone into their ideological fold using seemingly universal virtues as baits—caring for the poor, fighting for justice, social harmony—while the Right starts attacking these very ideas as being utopian and impractical—both as a reaction to the Left appropriating these ideas, and because the Right, or the non-Left, gives more importance to cold hard facts and impassive analysis over raw emotions and trendy idealism. However, that's not how you can win over starry-eyed poetry-smitten youngsters.

Whenever I meet youngsters, some of whom are still in their teens, I am actually shocked if I find any of them subscribing to the non-Left ideology. How can someone so young be able to see through the utopian chimera that the Left is adept at building? I have met guys, barely 17 or 18 years old, who would reject the leftist view with a stunning ideological clarity. I had none as a 23-year-old media professional. Even now, I don't have the confidence to declare that I understand everything, but at least now I do know what ideology is!

Anyway, as time progressed, and when debates around politics would take place inside the newsroom or in canteen or at a chai ki tapri, I'd slowly understand the broad nature of ideologies. Since I had not flunked my high-school social sciences exams, I certainly had heard about communism and Karl Marx, but didn't know that Left-wingers considered their ideology to be a perfect science, which can help them find solutions to almost every problem. I even remember a CPI leader saying 'Marxism is science' during a TV debate. It was actually a religion to them, not science, as I'd discover much later.

I had developed good friendship with one senior person named Pawan, to whom I'd usually go to seek help or understand issues that I found a bit complex, primarily while dealing with current affairs. Fortunately, he was not a leftist, though he was not Right wing or followed the Hindutva ideology either. I'd put him more in the classical liberal or libertarian category.

In the office, he would mostly keep his dealings very professional and didn't meddle in the personal lives of people. He didn't even get into needless political debates, but once he somehow got into a debate with a man from JNU. This man's appearance was exactly like a quintessential leftist guy, with unkempt beard and who appeared to be allergic to taking a bath daily. They ended up discussing how various ideologies were violent. Pawan cited the staggering number of people, including dissidents within his own party, whom Joseph Stalin had got killed, in response to which this JNU guy declared that 'Stalin was not a communist' and that anyone claiming so had not read enough.

In retrospect, I think the communists were first to invent 'this is not real communism' chicanery before Islamists learnt the trick. Back then obviously I didn't think this way and was left scratching my head. Pawan too gave up, because he realized he was better off limiting himself to strictly professional discussions. I stopped bothering about ideologies and decided to just do my job and be happy with the salary that I got at the end of the month.

'Hindu groups' and headlines

How I was not at all invested in any political ideology can be gauged from the fact that the only memory I have of the BJP losing the 2004 Lok Sabha elections is that I had worked extremely hard, spending almost 16 hours non-stop in the newsroom during the live coverage of the results, and the drama thereafter as it was a hung parliament. I was neither in delirium nor in depression—how most people ideologically committed to either the Left or Right were. I was just hungry, and looked forward to the company providing free food because I had worked so hard and for so long.

The 2004 loss was catastrophic for BJP supporters and Hindutva ideologues. The nation and Hindus not only lost a full decade, they were actually pushed back by several decades—this is how many of them saw the event, while I saw it as just another TV coverage.

And it made for good coverage. It was a hung parliament, even though today it is touted as some grand success of Sonia Gandhi's strategy that led to Congress victory. There were political parleys in the days following the results to finalize the candidate for the post of prime minister. It was accepted wisdom that the Congress party wouldn't put anyone from the Nehru–Gandhi family in the chair, unless the party had a majority of its own. The standard modus operandi was to support someone from outside and then bring down that government to win a majority of its own in the ensuing elections.

However, it had been eight long years since Congress was out of power and the party couldn't have afforded to extend it more. They had to be in power and the supporters were adamant that Sonia Gandhi should become the prime minister. There were 'protests' by Congress supporters outside 10 Janpath, the residence of Sonia Gandhi, when news broke out that Sonia herself may not lead the government. A Congress leader named Ganga Charan Rajput had climbed atop a car in Delhi, brandishing a pistol, threatening to kill himself if Sonia Gandhi didn't accept the post of prime minister.

The live scenes made for good TV coverage, and those were the only things that interested me then. Rajput was a new recruit to the Congress at that time (earlier he was with the BJP), and perhaps this drama was to prove his loyalty to his new party, rather the family. Rajput later joined the BSP and is currently back in the BJP. How can anyone see the broader issue of Hindutva or Hindu civilization amidst such drama? Politics appeared just a funny thing to be covered on TV for TRPs (Target/ Television Rating Point).

As a 'Congressi Hindu', I didn't bother much about Dr Manmohan Singh replacing Atal Bihari Vajpayee, even though I had a personal liking for Vajpayee. His style of speaking, despite those awkward pauses between sentences, his friendly demeanour, his face, which carried either a reassuring smile or vivid expressions matching his powerful oratory—all these made him stand out from the usual caricature of a Hindutva leader, who would be boorish, speak crude language, always have expressions of anger and frown on his face and who would be ever ready to get into a fight.

Vajpayee was thus carefully termed as the 'right man in the wrong party' by his detractors and by the people in the media. The term made sure that a signal is sent that Vajpayee was just an exception, an aberration. That phrase was used not to compliment Vajpayee as the 'right man' but to perpetuate the BJP's image as the 'wrong party', and by extension the RSS as a group with the 'wrong ideology'.

It is generally believed that Vajpayee's moderate approach or image didn't really help him or the BJP, because 2004 was lost after all. But that is quite an unfair assessment of the man. While it's true that Advani's Ram Rath Yatra of 1990, which was anything but a moderate step, made the BJP a powerful contender at the national-level politics, it was Vajpayee's image that helped it gain allies and be in power eight years later. It was also due to Vajpayee that an average, rather clueless, Hindu like me started looking at the BJP as a natural alternative to the Congress party.

During a party meeting in Mumbai after the 2004 electoral loss, Vajpayee had said 'Aata baari nakko' ('No next time') in Marathi when party supporters were chanting slogans asserting that he will be back as the prime minister in the next elections. This left people wondering whether he was retiring from active politics. A Congressi Hindu like me definitely thought that the BJP as an option was over if there was no Vajpayee.

At that point of time, for someone like me, Advani's image was that of a hardliner, who would be blamed for the riots after the Babri Masjid was demolished. Modi obviously was not supposed to be an option at all, with Atal Bihari Vajpayee's 'rajdharma' remark post the 2002 riots, widely reported as a snub to Modi.

For those who may not know, sometime in April 2002 at a press conference in Gujarat, when media persons asked Vajpayee, the then prime minister of India, what message he'd like to give Modi, the then chief minister of Gujarat, Vajpayee had said that the only message he had for a ruler was that he should be following rajdharma—where a ruler is morally duty-bound not to differentiate between his subjects based on caste, religion and gender. He later added that he had full faith that Modi was following rajdharma, but the first part of the statement was enough for a theory to be developed that Vajpayee did not like Modi. Such theories made sure that Congressi Hindus like me didn't see Modi as an option for national leadership.

Perhaps among the top leadership of the BJP at that time, the only person apart from Vajpayee who was not overtly painted as communal and obscurantist was Pramod Mahajan. He was seen as a committed worker of the party, who belonged to the younger lot, and who was tech savvy and a good orator like Vajpayee. However, he did not have the kind of mass appeal and charisma that Vajpayee had. He died after his own brother shot him fatally in a family dispute two years later, in 2006. Nothing seemed to be going well for the BJP after the 2004 loss.

Meanwhile, the Congress, after being back in power, had started 'de-saffronization' and 'detoxification' projects, which initially appeared to be removing everyone who was appointed at government or quasi-government posts by the Vajpayee government. One of those was the popular Hindi news reporter Deepak Chaurasia, who had earlier quit Aaj Tak to join DD News as the consulting editor. Within three months of the Congress getting back in power, Chaurasia had to leave Doordarshan and go back to Aaj Tak. Another person who was pushed out was Anupam Kher—he had been appointed as the head of the Censor Board by the Vajpayee government.

To me, these things appeared more political than ideological. The fact that this whole exercise also meant reverting the changes introduced by the BJP government in school textbooks didn't appear anti-Hindu, because the Congress would do these things so swiftly that you won't even realize it had been done. Also, any changes in the educational system, when introduced or even attempted during a BJP government, were always presented in the media as if they were teaching some pseudo-science of 'wrong history', so the Congress appeared to make 'genuine corrections'.

One could as well blame the BJP for not making enough noise about such issues as compared to the noise they made about, say, Sonia Gandhi's Italian origin. Maybe, they thought that these issues won't resonate with the masses or were issues where they would not get any attention from the media. The BJP did not appear to be attacking the Congress on ideological grounds as much as they attacked on political grounds.

One incident that could have painted the Congress party as anti-Hindu was the arrest of Kanchi Peeth Shankaracharya Jayendra Saraswati. The manner in which he was arrested made shocking TV visuals—an old man being pushed around and dragged out on Diwali night. Even though I was hardly a practising Hindu—a Congressi Hindu as I said earlier—it felt pretty odd that an old man was being arrested like that, and that too someone who is supposed to be one of the senior-most priests of the Hindus.

That was perhaps for the first time a 'Sanghi' counter-thought ever came to my mind—will any government dare to arrest the Shahi Imam or some Christian padre in a similar fashion, especially on Eid or Christmas days, respectively, regardless of what the charges were against them?

I didn't know much about that particular case or politics in Tamil Nadu back then—being a journalist in a regional news channel didn't help either—but I felt angry seeing those visuals. I also thought that there could be some protests in the following days.

And there were. Saints from various akharas in North India condemned the arrest and announced a protest, while people from the VHP, the Bajrang Dal, and the BJP too, joined the protests. The words 'Hindu groups protest' dominated the headlines.

Now, such a headline might look factual, but this is also how narratives are built. When Hindus protest over something that could be even remotely seen as a legitimate grievance—in this case the way a 70-year-old priest was dragged and kicked—it's always the 'Hindu groups' or the 'Hindutva outfits' that come out to protests, never the 'Hindus' themselves, as if the average Hindu is not concerned and doesn't feel that anything wrong was done, and by corollary, the original grievance might not be that legitimate.

This effect is achieved by prejudicing the term 'Hindu groups' itself, by repeatedly using the term on other banal occasions during news reporting. So, the 'Hindu groups' will invariably be in news for something silly—some outlandish statement made by someone, someone being accused of causing trouble or the group organizing some seemingly senseless events.

When any of these Hindu groups happen to do something good, for example, the RSS helping people during a natural calamity or accident, then those are flat reports—if at all such an activity is reported—that would either be headlined as something like, 'RSS extends a helping hand' or 'Local residents come together to help accident victims' with the body of the report mentioning the RSS. The term 'Hindu groups' would be missing even if other Hindu outfits might have joined the RSS in such activities, which they normally do.

As a result, an ordinary Hindu starts thinking that if 'Hindu groups' are involved in a case, something has to be wrong. Even if the cause appears to be genuine, the presence of the term 'Hindu groups' would make them feel that maybe there is something amiss somewhere. He starts downplaying the causes being championed by them. Even a genuine Hindu cause and concern is reduced to something shady and political in the eyes of an average Hindu because of the prejudicing of this term.

Now this is how it plays up—first of all, the media doesn't report any hate crime against Hindus because of 'responsible reporting' practices, and if at all it's forced to report it, as Hindus start building the pressure, the reports would invariably read something like 'Hindu groups protest over XYZ incident', where XYZ could be a case of desecration of a local temple, or obscene comments against Hindu gods and goddesses, or cases of 'love jihad' or sexual harassment on communal lines, or worse, a targeted assassination by Islamist gangs.

All such incidents are real, and rather frequent in many parts of our country, but because the term 'Hindu groups' has been maligned so much, an average Hindu starts downplaying those 'XYZ incidents' itself, merely because they are being raised by such groups. He starts suspecting that there is 'something more' to the story because these Hindu groups rarely make news for the right reason. This is soft 'genocide denial' in action against Hindus, where you make the narrative so lopsided that either victims become invisible or victim-blaming becomes normal.

How such narrative insidiously affects the psyche and ends up having undesired—or maybe desired, if the objective is to strengthen Hinduphobia—outcomes on an average citizen is something I had personally witnessed in the winter of 2014.

On Twitter, some users had highlighted how dozens of Hindu families, living in a makeshift camp in an area known as Majnu Ka Tila in Delhi, were struggling with their livelihood, and winters were making their troubles only worse. These families had fled to India after facing persecution in Pakistan.

Some guys on Twitter got together to help the families and sought support from people. I transferred some money to one of the guys who led the cause, and asked whether donating blankets to these families could be helpful, to which the guy obviously answered in affirmative. I asked this because I knew a friend in NCR who had been distributing blankets among the homeless during each winter for a few years. I thought I'd ask this friend of mine to join these guys and go to Majnu Ka Tila to hand over the blankets.

So, I called up this blanket-distributing friend and asked him whether he could help this group provide relief materials to the Pakistani Hindus. He inquired about the people involved. I told him that they were basically vocal Hindu activists who were active on Twitter. One of them was Tajinder Pal Singh Bagga, incidentally a Sikh and technically not a Hindu activist, who is currently the spokesperson of the Delhi BJP. Bagga didn't have any official post in the BJP back then, but had gained popularity as a fan of Modi when he distributed chai at a Congress gathering after Congress leader Mani Shankar Aiyar had tried to 'insult' Modi by terming him 'chaiwala'.

After hearing terms like 'Hindu activists' and 'Modi fan', suddenly my charity-loving friend was a little unsure whether he should be partnering with this lot. He told me that he would like to avoid being seen as an active partner of this group. He further told me that he didn't do the blanket distribution alone and there were other people helping him, and he was not sure if they would be comfortable in associating themselves with 'Hindu activists' who wanted to help only Hindus.

I was a little disappointed, but didn't argue or insist. Also, the Twitter guys told me that they had received enough support and would be able to help the Pakistani Hindus in a meaningful way even without any blankets.

I don't really blame my friend for suddenly developing cold feet. This is how narratives play their part. Because of a narrative that has prejudiced an average Indian citizen into thinking that 'Hindu groups' are invariably involved in useless things, some poor Pakistani Hindus could not get blankets in the winter of 2014.

I don't know if the journalists who indulge in 'responsible reporting' realize what they have done. Not only do they deny the existence of Hindu victims, they actually aid the creation of more such victims. I put the blame entirely on them, and not on my friend. He was just a guy trusting the 'responsible media' and getting affected by their narrative.

This 'responsible reporting' by the mainstream Indian media effectively ensures that an average Indian is convinced that Hindus can never be victims of religious hatred or religious persecution. Any step or statement that officially acknowledges Hindus as victims starts sounding 'communal' to their ears. This was one of the reasons why many urban millennials opposed the CAA later in 2019–20.

Coming back to the arrest of Shankaracharya in 2004, the Hindu groups protested and a Congressi Hindu like me took note. However, the Congress at the Centre planned their moves smartly. Either they kept mum or tried to put the blame on the state government of Tamil Nadu, which was being ruled by J. Jayalalithaa then. I am sure that the Congress–Left ecosystem, even then, would have had people who bared their Hinduphobic fangs and attacked every Hindu priest as a potential criminal, but there was no social media where such guys' rants could be heard and witnessed by an average Hindu.

Rather, the average Hindu saw a Congress which was trying to distance itself. In fact, Congress leader and former chief minister of Madhya Pradesh, Digvijay Singh, someone whom the Sanghis love to hate, condemned the manner in which Shankaracharya was arrested. This was followed by usual statements by the Congress leaders that the BJP and Sangh Parivar were 'politicizing' the issue.

Things became normal in a few weeks. I was back to being an average Hindu, more concerned about mundane things, such as my career and colleagues, than grand ideas like ideology or civilization.

Leaving the world of journalism

Though I largely liked the mass media and the world of TV journalism, over time I started getting disenchanted with the kind of journalism one was expected to do at Sahara. An unwritten rule was adopted in Sahara Samay Uttar Pradesh-Uttarakhand—that the channel won't be harsh on the then state government led by Mulayam Singh Yadav.

I have no idea if there were orders from the top, or the senior journalists just decided this on behalf of the management, following the adage 'More loyal than the king himself'. Since Subrata Roy was supposed to be close to Mulayam Singh Yadav, the channel became friendly to the then SP government. I won't rule out that this was being done without any orders from the top.

This unwritten rule had become so brazen that the input desk used to put a red mark on potentially 'negative' news reports, indicating that the decision must be taken by senior editors—whether to run that particular piece of news or to drop it.

Once a local reporter was badly humiliated by Mulayam Singh Yadav for asking some questions, and the entire incident was captured by the cameraman. The footage arrived at the headquarters in Noida and I personally watched it, but obviously that was never aired. If social media were available in those days, the clip could have been leaked, and it could have become viral, and... I could have lost my job.

This was tactless political partisanship to say the least. There was no moral justification of dropping the footage, except that you were trying to appease your bosses. But, now that I think of it, actually it was not any different from what 'responsible journalism' entails, where you tactfully come up with moral compasses and greater causes to hide certain pieces of information or ally yourself with certain groups.

If a reporter of Sahara happened to be the only witness to a crime committed by some SP member in Uttar Pradesh, that news report perhaps would never be aired. But, how is this different from what the far-Left website The Wire or other leftist editors did when they asked that lady journalist in Ahmedabad not to report or even lodge a complaint about manhandling and assault by some so-called Dalit activists? Or how is this different from the mainstream media not choosing to report complaints of the Hindu parents in Hauz Qazi area of Delhi, who said that their son was missing and feared he was kidnapped by Muslim rioters?

The difference lies in how good your spoken English is and how deftly you can weave a web of illusion using highfalutin words about social justice, class conflicts, communal harmony and other such grand ideas to delude yourself into believing that what you are doing has some higher purpose and objectives than the antics of lowly stupid people who are loyal to a political party.

The blatant bias in favour of a political party, however, disheartened and disillusioned me, because at that time I too used to think that journalism should be and could be 'neutral'. This is not what I had signed up for. Even the salary wasn't so good. And worst, my designation still read 'intern'. So, I started looking for a change of job, thinking that maybe other channels were not so bad. I tried to apply at almost every existing channel then, dropping my CV at the reception counters.

I asked some of the senior guys, working at Sahara itself, whether they could help me get a job elsewhere. I primarily complained about the salary and designation, not about the work culture. A couple of them tried to help. The weirdest, or maybe not so weird, suggestion came from a man who asked me to meet a particular journalist who also hailed from

Bihar and who belonged to the same caste as mine. He was supposed to favour people from his own caste during recruitments.

This 'Hire Bhumihar' guy is currently active in public life and has an active Twitter account, too, with considerable following. These days he is fighting Hindutva, fascism, intolerance, Modi, Amit Shah, Yogi Adityanath and the trolls. How convenient it is to become a virtuous guy!

I never met this guy for a job, because by then—sometime in late 2004, after I completed around two years in my first job—I had decided that I would take a break from the world of journalism. I had decided to go for higher studies and equip myself with a better degree and hopefully more useful skillsets in order to acquire a better job, though I wanted to remain in the media industry.

I zeroed upon MICA (Mudra Institute of Communications, Ahmedabad) for higher studies, as it could possibly give me a better career path in the media industry. One needed to take the common admission test (CAT) conducted by the IIMs and a separate entrance test conducted by MICA to apply. Shortlisted candidates, based on their CAT percentiles and performance in the MICA exam, were invited for group discussions and personal interviews.

That's how I started preparing for CAT, studying outside the working hours, and sometimes inside those too, during the night shifts, when one didn't have much work to do. I was fortunate to have a helpful boss who allocated frequent night shifts to me, so that I could get more time to prepare.

Despite the low salary, the time spent at Sahara was not that bad. Not just a good boss, I had decent colleagues around me too, which included three other guys from my batch at IIMC. At work, I was far more confident and comfortable with girls around, having overcome the initial 'culture shock' and awkwardness that I had felt after moving to Delhi.

So comfortable and confident I was that I flirted with a few too, and fell for at least one. But I would keep that part out of this book. Not that Sanghis are not supposed to fall in love or talk about romance—something NDTV's Ravish Kumar seems to believe in—but something should be saved for my autobiography too, if I ever write one.

Okay, the real reason for not divulging any further details is because I am scared my wife too will read it.

But, let me write about some wife-proof things I noticed and experienced in my 2.5-year-long stint in journalism, between 2002 and 2005. I discovered that the presence or representation of Biharis in journalism was actually not poor at all, something I had not expected or was aware of when I had decided to choose journalism for my higher studies while staying in Bihar. I thought as a Bihari you can either be a doctor/engineer or an IAS officer later. So, when and how did these Biharis discover that they could be journalists too?

I'm being guilty of stereotyping here, but I found out that many Biharis in journalism were also UPSC aspirants. Either they were still trying or they had given up and settled for a career in journalism. I am not too sure how they landed up in journalism in the first place while preparing for the UPSC exams. A wild guess could be that maybe some of them became friends with journalists who lived in the same locality, for example, many Bihari UPSC aspirants used to reside in the Ber Sarai area, where I and many other students of IIMC lived. You don't really need a degree in journalism to become a journalist.

At least a couple of such Bihari guys, working in Sahara and having been UPSC aspirants earlier, were from JNU. Later, I discovered that they were still living on the JNU campus in their hostels, possibly enrolled at some Ph.D. course, while working as a full-time journalist.

My first reaction then was that of envy, because they were saving so much money—living in a subsidized hostel, eating subsidized food and earning not only the salary from their journalism jobs but also the stipend or scholarships for their 'research work.' I didn't think of them as people who were freeloading on state resources.

I don't know if social media at that time could have made me shift towards the Right. Maybe it would have, because insults like 'commie freeloaders' would have made sense to me, having witnessed the above. Or maybe not, because I'd have broadly thought of all of them as being part of the same fraternity, that is, journalism, and I might have actually tried to defend them, for social media encourages tribalism.

By the way, Orkut had come into existence around this time, that is, in second half of 2004, though it was not yet popular or widely adopted in India. Facebook, too, technically existed but only for select university students in the US. Even Gmail was not open to everyone, and you needed an invite to sign up for the service.

Many things that would today become topics of outrage on Twitter were found to be normal by me in the newsroom at that time, primarily because I had no exposure to other points of views at all. For example, the first time I heard about Zakir Naik was from a Muslim colleague at Sahara who spoke very highly of him. I was generally chatting about issues with various religions and why I leaned more towards atheism—yes, that made me an average Congressi Hindu as well—and this guy told me that I should listen to Zakir Naik as 'he debates logically' and can answer most of the issues I had raised about religions as a wannabe atheist.

I couldn't listen to Naik as there was no YouTube then, but now I realize how popular this guy was among a certain section of Indian Muslims, before controversies stopped his free run in India. Even without any YouTube or WhatsApp, his debates and sermons, which preached and propagated stricter and 'original' version of Islam, were already reaching many Muslim households in India. Remember this is before he had founded Peace TV, which further amplified his reach.

Then there was another Muslim colleague, who in the course of discussions on random topics, told me how the 'O Paalanhaare' devotional song from the movie *Lagaan* was something that a Muslim could also enjoy, because the lyrics didn't explicitly mention the name of any Hindu god, and that while the picturization of the song depict Hindu themes, the lyrics in itself were about god who was 'nirgun', that is, formless, and thus in line with the Islamic concept of god.

Back then I found this to be an interesting take and an opportunity to understand other points of view, but I could as well have taken it as proof of how Muslims look at even a Bollywood song from an Islamic lens while Hindus are supposed to entirely forget about their religious sensibilities and accept 'Sab but uthwaaye jaayenge' and 'Bas naam rahega Allah ka' (All idols would be removed and only the name of Allah will prevail) as mere metaphors. We will come to this specific *nazm* by Faiz later in the book.

One may term my view as 'competitive communalism', but it will be competitive communalism only when I start behaving in the manner that deeply religious Muslims behave, for example, reject all syncretism as 'shirk' (Islamic word for sin that involves having polytheistic beliefs or accommodation for idolatry), aspire for parallel systems of governance and justice that is in line with puritan religious beliefs and insist on living in modern times as per the standards of ancient times.

Merely pointing out certain things, which otherwise could be ignored for the sake of personal relationships or social harmony, is not competitive communalism. It should more appropriately be termed as 'calling out casual communalism'.

Just like liberals call out casual sexism, casual racism and casual casteism in daily behaviour and lexicon of people, one should be free to call out casual communalism, or casual Islamism to be precise, by highlighting certain beliefs or manners of the Muslim community. And Islamism has to be called out because it is solely responsible for the Partition of the country and for the millions of deaths, not only in India but worldwide.

Here, I must recommend books like *Muslim Separatism—Causes and Consequences* by Sita Ram Goel (and for that matter, I recommend most of his books), which mince no words and elucidates in detail how the Partition was the result of nothing but Islamism, and how the whole business of blaming the 'Divide and rule' policy of the British is actually a copout.

Blaming the pre-Independence Indian National Congress for not doing enough to win the trust of Muslims is quintessential Nehruvian secularism. It might sound ironical that blaming an outfit where Nehru was one of the tallest leaders is being termed as Nehruvian behaviour, but that is how it is. There is no irony involved because liberals blame Mahatma Gandhi and not Nehru when they blame the pre-Independence Indian National Congress for alienating Muslims.

Mahatma Gandhi's support to ideas such as cow protection has been blamed by some liberals as reasons why the Muslim League and the idea of Pakistan gained strength.[42] All these are elaborately created smokescreen to not let you see the real reason—Islamism. I got to read books by Sita Ram Goel only after or around 2016. That's pretty embarrassing to admit. Back in 2002–05, I was an entirely different person.

To be fair to my colleagues in the news channel, I don't think anyone was an out and out Islamist, though a few of them clearly had the 'symptoms', for example, one guy would insist that the Godhra train carnage was not done by Muslims. I wouldn't say anything back then despite knowing it was a white lie. Perhaps, that's the kind of 'tolerance' liberals want Hindus to have.

I used to take these beliefs or statements just as good or bad statements, and didn't really see them from a political or ideological lens, primarily because I was unaware and secondarily, because there were other issues, too, that troubled me more, so far as problematic beliefs were concerned.

For example, there was a guy in a senior position (well, everyone was a senior to an 'intern' like me!) who would say that it was impossible that any woman can be raped. He contended that some element of consent from a woman has to be there for sexual penetration to take place. When I said that it was utter nonsense, he came up with an even more nonsensical retort, asking how would I know if I never had sex before. That was the most absurd thing I had ever heard in my life, despite me being in an all-boys school and a virtually all-boys college earlier. I don't even need to explain how that statement was shocking on so many levels. It was rather criminal, and it came from a journalist. And as per him, I can't counter-argue because I was a virgin!

Such people and beliefs further made me uncomfortable, and strengthened my resolve that I should study further and be among better people. I just linked it all to education and thought these guys were just BA pass people and had no class. Obviously, that was a wrong diagnosis, but that was one of the reasons I wanted to quit journalism.

As always, my younger brother Kunal came to the rescue. The CAT study material was brought and given to me by him, days after I discussed my plan of going for higher studies. I did not find the subject expanse of CAT so tough. Having prepared for the IITs earlier and not having forgotten all the mathematics that I had learned during my graduation, I found the 'quant' section of the CAT to be relatively easy, though speed was needed. The 'verbal' section was not easy but not too tough either, because being in journalism I was accustomed to reading materials on myriad topics. The data analytics and logical reasoning parts certainly needed lots of practice and alert thinking.

I am not trying to make it sound as if I had it easy. But, I was not under a huge pressure to get into the 99.9+ percentile group, because I was not targeting admissions to the IIMs at all. I wanted to get into MICA. Further, even if I failed to get a good percentile, at least I had a job to fall back on. So, my preparation as well as taking the CAT was rather stress-free, which I think helped me.

Almost immediately after I took CAT, I was informed that I had passed the screen test to become a news anchor. Earlier, I had made it to the shortlist for the screen test because of my frequent and better voice-overs for Sahara.

Being a news anchor made me temporarily forget about other issues that were bugging me at Sahara. I thought that not only could I become a celebrity who would be recognized in public places, I would also get a raise in my salary in the form of allowances. News anchors were supposed to spend on better clothes, appearance and on their general well-being, and at Sahara they paid extra money to spend on such endeavours. I did buy a pair of new shirts, tie and a blazer with that money. Trousers were not visible on screen, so I didn't bother to buy those.

I almost forgot that I had taken the CAT exam, as I was busy dreaming of becoming a celebrity news anchor. I thought I would work hard on my anchoring, which could get me noticed in the fraternity, and which in turn could help get me a job in 'better' channels like Aaj Tak or NDTV.

NDTV used to have a promotional video extoling the virtues of their journalism, which was titled 'Sach dikhaate hain hum' (We show the truth). It was written really well in Hindi, with liberal use of Urdu words, whose *nuqtas* were pronounced perfectly by a male baritone voice. I simply loved it. I had memorized each word of that 1-minute long promo by heart and often used to recite that.

When CAT results were announced sometime in January 2005, I didn't even bother to check my score. I was actually alerted about it by a guy, with whom I had developed a friendship at the MICA examination centre. He called me up to congratulate me, informing me that my name was among the shortlisted candidates selected for group discussion and personal interview. I was obviously happy, but no more as desperate as earlier to leave Sahara or TV journalism.

My younger brother was always more serious about my career than I ever was. He took pains to go to a cyber café to reconfirm that it indeed was true. He not only found it to be true, but he also came back with the 'shocking' news that I had actually qualified for the group discussions and interview rounds even for admissions into IIM Kozhikode, IIM Calcutta and IIM Ahmedabad, that is, half of the IIMs at that time.

Now, that made me far more excited! I had failed to get admission into the IITs, but here was an opportunity to study at a place that had a similar reputation. Further, every year there used to be news reports about fat salaries being offered to IIM graduates during placements. There was no way I couldn't have been excited about it, even though I was fairly happy being a news anchor by then.

Although I can write a lot about this phase and excitement, I will desist. Since this book is more about my ideological journey than a personal one, I'd straightaway jump to the fact that I could get final admission offers from IIM Ahmedabad and IIM Kozhikode, and from MICA too.

Entirely due to the brand image of IIMs and due to the fat salaries IIM students were supposed to command, I forgot my love for media and MICA, and decided to take admission at IIM Ahmedabad for the regular two-year-long MBA course. To be technically correct, it was not MBA, but PGP, that is, Post-Graduate Programme in management, for IIMs were autonomous institutes and not universities that could offer post-graduate degrees, until the IIM Act became a law in 2017. The first MBA degrees were awarded by IIM Ahmedabad in 2019. The year I am talking about is 2005.

So, at the age of 25, I took my second flight in the summer of 2005. This time it was an afternoon flight, when I could see how the houses and trees and roads appear to diminish in size as the plane rose up in the air. I still remember that excitement of glancing down from the plane window to find that the world below looked like a miniature model made by an architect. And as the plane rose even higher, the scene below looked like those 'physical maps' from Google. And finally, you found yourself surrounded by clouds.

Incidentally, it was a plane operated by Sahara, though I didn't get any discounts in fare this time. I was amused to find the flight attendant doing the 'Sahara pranam'—a greeting gesture mandatory for employees at Sahara, where you had to put your right hand on your heart and say those two words. I used to do that too as a news anchor at the beginning of news bulletins. I realized that I won't be doing it anymore, that I was not just leaving a city, but a phase of my life altogether.

The friends that I had made, the skillsets that I had picked up, the career that I had just started—I will be leaving all of them behind to virtually start afresh. I didn't have much idea about life at a B-school campus, as virtually no one I knew in my social circle had studied at any IIMs. I was happy to be in the sky, but a bit nostalgic about the land I had just left as the plane cruised.

And yeah, the plane was taking me from Sonia Gandhi's New Delhi to Narendra Modi's Ahmedabad.

5

In Modi's Gujarat

The first days in Gujarat

I landed at the Ahmedabad airport carrying a medley of emotions, ranging from the excitement of beginning a new life to the anxiety of surviving in a top educational institute—the latter being partly triggered by the fact that the last time I was away from my family to lead the life of a student, it didn't work out. But there was hope too, because I had gained confidence about my abilities during my professional stint in a media house, and there was a lot of curiosity about the city and the people, about whom so much had been written and discussed in the preceding three years.

There were not many cities I had visited earlier, so I was curious as a tourist too. In Bihar, as I had said earlier, people would hardly spend on tourism. The only cities apart from Patna, Delhi and Bokaro—cities where I had lived some parts of my life—that I had seen were Varanasi, Ranchi and Jamshedpur. I had literally just 'seen' these cities, as I visited them just for a day or two because they were centres of IIT or other engineering entrance exams.

We used to opt for cities other than Patna as a preferred centre for exams purportedly because of the fear that an exam conducted at Patna or some other place in North Bihar might get cancelled over allegations of unfair practices or leaked papers. I don't know how much of this fear was justified. It might as well have been an excuse to see new cities because otherwise you didn't get a reason to see new places.

Ahmedabad was now the farthest city from my hometown that I was in. The first thing I noticed, rather felt, was that it was really hot. Even though Delhi or Patna were not really hill stations and summers were hot in these two cities too, Ahmedabad felt much worse. It was scalding, and I was there in the month of June.

The other thing I noticed was that it was clearly a far more developed city than Patna. It might not be as grand as Delhi, especially when compared with Lutyens Delhi, but it was a modern city with roads that were as good as the ones you'd find in Delhi, in fact they were in better shape than some of the roads in the interiors of Delhi.

The third thing that almost immediately struck me, as I looked around sitting in an auto-rickshaw on my way from the Ahmedabad airport to the IIM campus, was better presence of women in public places. It was higher than what I had seen in Delhi, and obviously much higher than what I had seen in Patna. Many of those women would wear the saari in a particular style—the 'ulta pallu' style—which was similar to those seen in *Kyunki Saas Bhi Kabhi Bahu Thi* and other TV soap operas with Gujarati characters, which were quite a rage back then.

And it wasn't so that women used to disappear after sunset due to safety concerns. One would find women in public spaces till late at night, and it was not just during the Navaratri or Garba, as stereotypes suggested. There was a culture of eating out and hanging out in the late evenings, and women would be there, not really under the watchful eyes of men from their families. On the contrary, men appeared to be acting on their orders. Ahmedabad certainly was a more women-friendly place.

As someone who had spent the bulk of his life in Bihar, that is, in the eastern part of the country, I also happened to notice that sunsets would happen 'late' in Ahmedabad. I don't know why I never felt this distinction when I had moved to Delhi, which too was decently westward when compared to Patna. Maybe because I was determined to learn and observe new things in Ahmedabad, and was possibly overdoing it!

I was indeed overdoing it, for I would have a good look at everyone whenever I used to go out of the IIM campus and would often wonder how these Gujarati people—who appeared easy-going and not in a ready-to-fight mode as people in Delhi would be—indulge in wide-scale violence and killings that were reported just three years before.

The IIM campus in Ahmedabad is nicely nested in the city. Unlike some other IIMs or big educational institutes, it is not situated in some remote corner, far away from civilization. It was very easy to step out of the campus and go to the city to eat out, or hang out, or buy something for yourself or just have a cup of chai across the road. Basically, quite often you'd be among the Gujaratis—nice folks who looked ever ready to enjoy life to the fullest.

So, who were those Gujaratis who were killing wantonly in 2002, I would wonder. The middle class of Gujarat, especially the ordinary Hindus of Gujarat, were painted as being fully complicit in the riots by the intelligentsia and the chatterati, and that had clearly affected me. That normal guy in the street or at the shop could just be easy-going from the outward while being deeply violent inside, I would think. And if I found some rare over-aggressive Gujarati man with a frown on his face, I would be convinced that this guy must have killed some Muslims three years ago.

The vanguards of communal harmony and secularism had overused the 'Gujarat' motif. Gujarat was declared a laboratory of the Sangh Parivar, as if it was not a city with its own soul and free will but a dystopian society, where each person was being controlled and manipulated by some evil force. They declared that 'Gujarat won't be allowed to be repeated elsewhere in India', making 'Gujarat' synonymous with riots and a symbol of evil. No wonder Modi would make 'Gujarati asmita', that is, 'Gujarati pride' a rallying point around which he won the elections thereafter. Gujarat indeed was maligned way too much over the 2002 riots.

I never tried to initiate any conversation with any local about the riots. The first time a local guy talked about the riots was when a jamaadaar, or a janitor, came to sweep the hostel rooms. It was during my early days at the IIM campus. I think he was part of some temporary work force employed at the campus, as some portion of the IIM's new campus was still being built.

He was a young Gujarati man who loved to talk—which I think most Gujaratis do. He started a conversation in flawed Hindi. He asked me questions like from which part of the country I belonged to and how I was finding his 'desh' (Gujarat) and the 'Amdavad' city. I told him that I really liked the place though the heat was unbearable. He agreed that heat and dust were big problems, as he dusted off my study desk in the hostel room.

And then, as an afterthought, he added that there was one more problem apart from the heat and dust—the Pakistanis, who want to ruin the city. He suggested that I should not venture towards a certain locality in the city. Though I couldn't exactly get the name of the place the way he pronounced it, I understood that he was talking about a Muslim-dominated area. He termed the area as 'Mini Pakistan' where 'dangerous people' lived.

And then he talked about the 2002 riots. He claimed that the Muslims had made a huge pool of acid in that area during the riots and used to throw Hindus into that.

I listened to him silently but rejected most of his assertions in my head. How could Muslims have killed anyone in the riots, because it was an anti-Muslim pogrom the way I knew it from media reports and thousands of op-eds after that. There was no point of arguing with this rather semi-literate guy who could be lying, I told myself.

But I would hear such sentiments more often in the coming days. An auto-rickshaw driver would claim how they were scared to go inside the Muslim areas earlier because many guys (*miyabhai*, as he would call them) would not pay the full fare, and some would simply refuse to pay anything. And the drivers had no option because if they objected, they risked being physically beaten up and their auto-rickshaw being damaged. The goons in those areas have become 'disciplined' after 2002, the driver went on to add.

It is easy to scoff at these thoughts and statements as deeply bigoted and justification for riots, and I too wondered why many of them didn't appear too 'ashamed' of what had happened in 2002. Since most of the guys who came up with justifications for the 2002 riots were from a particular socio-economic class, I blamed it all on education and 'class'.

On the IIM campus, at least during the first year, we hardly had any time or interest in discussing politics or current affairs. The grind during the initial months, especially for a non-engineering and non-IITian like me, was almost unbearable. The surprise quizzes (class tests) and the case-study pedagogy were new to me, so there was no time to discuss politics or ideology.

However, once things started settling down and the initial grind was over, such topics were discussed. There was a Gujarati student in my dorm (hostel) who was a good friend too. When this topic was broached, he didn't say anything that could be remotely seen as justification of the riots, but he did point out that Gujarat was unfairly targeted, and he blamed the media and journalists for it.

He also talked about how Gujarat was not really alien to communal violence, and so were other parts of the country, so why keep harping on 2002 all the time? That's when I dug out more and realized that he wasn't really wrong. I got to know about gangsters like Abdul Lateef, who was accused of starting many such riots, and who would later be played on screen by Shah Rukh Khan in the 2017 Bollywood movie *Raees*.

Lateef was one of the dreaded Muslim gangsters who had friends in the Congress party that ruled Gujarat in the 1980s and earlier. Initially a rival of Dawood Ibrahim, Lateef became his ally and had become the face of terror in Gujarat. The rise and popularity of the BJP in the state is tied to him as well. The following report in *The Times of India* refers to the 1990s, when the BJP started winning in Gujarat:

> That was the time when the terror of mafia don Abdul Latif was at its peak in Gujarat and his was the most hated name in Hindu households. Having finished off all Hindu gangs in Ahmedabad, he had also emerged as a frontman in Gujarat for Dawood Ibrahim and the Pakistan ISI... No election speech of a BJP leader was complete without the mention of Latif and his connections with Dawood Ibrahim and the Congress. The BJP got two-third majority in that election and Keshubhai became the chief minister for the first time.[43]

It is said that the Congress used to take help of such Muslim gangsters to get even with their opponents. Many communal riots happened because the party used Muslim gangs to crack down on political opposition. Ahmedabad especially used to witness such riots pretty regularly—I had no idea about these issues earlier, and got to know them only after I landed in Gujarat and was exposed to counter-arguments.

This also helped me put a context to possibly why those 'Muslim areas', which the janitor or the auto-rickshaw driver talked about, would have gained notoriety. Lateef was able to win the local body elections from such areas. It is not hard to guess how supporters of such gangsters would be behaving with the vulnerable sections.

Within two years of the BJP forming its own government in Gujarat in 1995, Lateef was first arrested by the anti-terrorism squad, and later killed in an encounter when he tried to flee from police custody. The BJP has been in power in Gujarat ever since, except for a gap of two years when a rebel faction had formed the government with outside support from the Congress.

Not once back in Delhi circles had anyone cared to put these as factors of BJP's popularity in the state. It was painted in a different light, which portrayed that an ordinary Gujarati was happy to see people being killed around in 2002 and rewarded the BJP for that. No wonder my Gujarati dormmate was not amused.

The interactions with the Gujarati people did convince me that they were a state and people who were wrongly maligned, but that didn't really mean that I had started warming up to the Sanghi ideology while being in Gujarat or on the IIM campus. However, I was now increasingly questioning the 'wisdom' I had acquired as a journalist earlier.

Another time I got to discuss the 2002 riots on the IIM campus was during a class that was part of a subject aimed at exploring yourself. Yes, such a subject existed to impart some soft skills or 'liberal values' and of late, there has been a demand to have more and more such subjects as part of the curriculum in engineering and business schools.

I had used a video clip from a documentary about the 2002 riots in a presentation during one of the classes. A Muslim kid, who was orphaned during the riots, was seen and heard saying that he will kill Hindus when he grows up. After so many years, I don't really remember what the presentation or the class was about, but I think using that particular clip was seen as an attempt by me to link the possibility of radicalization among Muslims to the 2002 riots.

One of the teaching assistants of the professor who taught that course later caught me after the class. She told me that she was working with many riot victims and would want me to meet such people and work for them. She mentioned stuff like the need to heal the wounds and how such kids (like the one in my presentation) need our help and attention. I told her I'd try my best, but I could hardly take time out in the future.

But this shows how the Left-leaning people are really active on educational campuses. The Right wing or the Sanghis appear to have no plans at all to win over people who might not be politically or ideologically aware. On the contrary, young students end up associating killjoys against Valentine's Day as representative of the Hindutva ideology.

Fortunately, at IIM Ahmedabad, there were no overtly political groups. There was a 'students union', which was called the 'Student Activities Committee' (SAC). We had elections, too, to elect various post holders, but there were no ABVP, NSUI or SFI candidates contesting in these elections. Individuals contested and won. I too had contested and won the post of media secretary. My batchmates voted for me because I was a journalist earlier. There was no political or ideological angle at work here.

However, I did start developing a sense of ideological understanding as time progressed. Not political, but ideological, and life at IIM Ahmedabad played a role.

The IIM Ahmedabad days

A place like IIM Ahmedabad is as much about learning just by virtue of being on the campus, as it is about what you study in the classrooms. The life experience that you gain by interacting with your batchmates, or with your professors outside the classrooms and by dealing with various issues as part of the hostel life teach you as much, if not more, than what case studies inside the classrooms can teach you. Much of the cost accountancy that I could learn was thanks to a guy from the senior batch in my dorm, else I'd have flunked the exams.

Having engineers from top institutes as your batchmates helped too, as many of them were really sharp with varied interests, and not robotic and unidirectional as engineers are stereotyped to be. The bulk of the batch was made of engineers, mostly freshers, but there were those with work experience similar to mine too. The batch had diversity as well. There were a few chartered accountants, a couple of lawyers and doctors, a man from the armed forces and obviously me, the lone journalist. The batch also had ample diversity in terms of the different regions of India from where we came from. The gender ratio could have been better though.

At the campus, one gained from each other's perspectives, even while chatting on random things that were unrelated to studies. As a journalist, I never felt the need to question the established narratives—such as the ideas I had around the 2002 riots—but these guys were under no such moral obligation.

On occasion, their arguments or queries were due to a lack of awareness and information about a particular topic, but that assured that things would be debated and dissected from the first principles. That approach forced me to revisit my own assumptions on many topics, not just the riots.

The scope of such debates was mostly about history, philosophy or religion—to whatever extent we could understand these topics. And in retrospect, much of the 'gyaan' that we threw at each other was after the research undertaken via Google search, but it was an enriching experience. This culture of discussing or debating anything and everything, and not treating anything as taboo or sacred, intuitively shifted me towards a classical liberal, or rather a roughly libertarian ideology.

The availability of internet right in the dorm room was another factor that enabled me to acquire more awareness. Beyond killing time on Orkut or searching for the lyrics of English songs, it helped in digging out information that was otherwise not highlighted by the mainstream media. This was also for the first time that I had access to the internet, where, unlike cyber cafés, I didn't have to worry about speed or time.

Although I had a personal computer and dial-up internet even in Patna, the speed used to be quite bad and I had to judiciously be online for a very limited time to save telephone bills. Today's generation may not know, but earlier when you went online through a dial-up connection, your landline phone would be 'busy' and you would not be able to make or receive calls.

In Delhi, since we didn't have a landline phone, we had no internet at home. Once a week I used to go to a cyber café, where I would be either stuck with bad speed or a clunky computer. So, it was a relief to have your own brand new personal computer as well as broadband internet connection in your dorm room.

The service was not really free though, because the study and stay at IIM Ahmedabad had to be paid for. Fortunately, the costs were not too high back then, though they were not ridiculously low either, as they were in various other universities, such as the JNU. If I remember correctly, it was around ₹4 lakhs for the entire two-year program back in 2005. Since I had saved almost my entire salary that I earned while working at Sahara, thanks to staying with my family, I could pay the first instalment of the fees with my own savings. I took an education loan from the SBI (State Bank of India) to finance the rest of it.

With unlimited internet, I started exploring all kinds of things on the web, the mentionable and the unmentionable. I created a Gmail account for myself and joined Orkut, both of which, I think, were still 'by invitation only' around that time (mid-2005). I could get invites because many IITians—who were now my batchmates—were already using them. I would then show off my new digital addresses to my journalist friends by sending them invites for these services.

Back then, internet was mostly about finding interesting stuff online that you could send as email forwards to multiple accounts—similar to the WhatsApp forwards these days—or exploring the world of Orkut, which was the first initiation for the Indian audience into the world of social media.

There were bloggers, too, and some of them had developed their own readership. I think the bloggers should thank the controversial businessman Arindam Chaudhuri for suing some of them. He had sued Rashmi Bansal, who incidentally was an alumnus of IIM Ahmedabad and was running her own magazine and blog, for publishing an article against his B-school IIPM (Indian Institute of Planning and Management). He sued a couple of other bloggers, too, for defamation in 2005, which made the mainstream media talk about the 'blogosphere'. People like me also took notice, and I too tried my hands at blogging.

Unlike what the Left wants an average person to believe, the very first bloggers or digital content creators in India were not Right wing or Sanghis. They were either Left-leaning or classical liberals. A few of the early bloggers were actually radical Left, who regurgitated and published the same old things about how Hinduism was oppressive, why Dalits were not Hindus, etc.

Primarily, the 'Left' was not really a bad word in the online world in those days. The only popular blogger active during this period (roughly the UPA-I [United Progressive Alliance] years of 2004–09), who perhaps would have actively resisted the 'Left' label on himself, even the 'Left-liberal' variant, can be argued to be Arnab Ray, popularly known as 'Greatbong'. He was acclaimed for his witty sharp takes on current affairs, especially on pop culture and Bollywood. However, he was not your typical Sanghi or Hindutva guy, and not a Right-winger either, except in some economic matters.

It seems that the Sanghis—the popular vocal ones—came online only after 2009, when the BJP lost the second successive Lok Sabha elections. It could very well be a coincidence or the 2009 Lok Sabha elections results could have been a trigger as well, I don't know. But, someone like MediaCrooks, which was led by 'Ravinar', apparently an anagram of his name Ravi Narayan, debuted only in 2010. His articles arguing how the media or the journalists were inherently biased against Hindus and Hindutva used to get insanely viral.

A group blog called 'Centre Right India' was launched in 2010, which argued not only for Right-wing economic policies but also batted for cultural issues. Then you also had many popular pro-Hindutva handles on Twitter, some of which were temporarily blocked by the Congress government in 2012. And you could also find Sanghis in the Rediff discussion boards and comments during that period.

We will come to that period later. For now, let us go back to 2005 and the subsequent few years—the Orkut years—when despite web 2.0 shaping up, the narrative was still controlled by the old media.

While Orkut appeared to be inhabited mostly by people who left cheesy messages on girls' scrapbooks, hoping to become 'fraands', there were also many active 'communities' where thriving debates took place. These communities were hugely popular among the youth, and it was a badge of honour to become 'moderators' of the community or even an active participant.

This changed one thing—ordinary people were subconsciously deciding the tone and contours of a debate, without the direct involvement or gatekeeping by the mainstream media. Even though many things they were writing about could have been hugely influenced by what the media fed them, the mere fact that ordinary people were writing—and it was being read by a large number of people—was a huge development. It was going to have pronounced effects in the coming years.

By 2006, Orkut had become quite popular, though internet connectivity was still not widespread across the country. Commercial broadband services to individual households were still evolving. Most of those who were online were either those who could afford dial-up connections at home or students like me who had access to internet on campuses, and obviously people who went online from offices and accessed websites that were allowed by their IT administrators.

The 24x7 access to internet from the comfort of my room also brought in major behavioural changes within me. I lost the habit of reading newspapers, and my news consumption shifted to reading articles on news websites. Not just news, I had started reading even short stories and books online.

In the later part of 2006, author and scientist Richard Dawkins had come up with the book *The God Delusion*, which became an instant hit. I got a digital copy of the book and loved reading it. Even though I had never hated my Hindu identity, I used to fancy myself as an atheist, so far as belief in supernatural entities was concerned. Hinduism was primarily a cultural identity for me.

Dawkins' book didn't change that fortunately, because fundamentally it was a criticism of the concept of god as defined by the Abrahamic faiths, that is, Judaism, Christianity and Islam. Although Dawkins did have some comments on why 'Looking East' and finding solace in religions such as Buddhism or Hinduism was not a solution either, he spared these religions the lashing. As a result, I continued to put myself in the zone of 'religiously atheist, culturally Hindu.'

There were many more avenues on the campus that made me learn new things and unlearn old ones.

For example, there was this dreaded subject in the first trimester itself, called WAC—Written Analysis and Communication—where you learned how to write business reports. My experience of writing news reports didn't prove to be of much help there. One needed the skillsets of writing academic research papers as well as writing business plans.

And the assignments had strict submission deadlines. Even if you wrote a fantastic report, you would be failed if you were late by even a minute while submitting the report, both online and offline.

WAC was a dreaded course, as students didn't know what could get them the best grades. Unlike quantitative subjects, there were no right or wrong answers here. It depended on the how well you analysed a case, and how lucidly you presented the analysis as well as other pieces of information. Having been a media person, I thought at least my communication skills would help me get good grades. I was mistaken.

After my very first WAC submission, I was called in by the professor for a personal meeting to discuss my submission. I was a little scared, but I later realized that it was part of the feedback process, as there were no right or wrong answers. Many students were called in for such discussions.

The professor started with the positive part of my report, and there was only one—my narration was good. He asked me what I did earlier and I told him I was a journalist, to which he said that it reflected in my writing. He explained that my narration of business history and business challenges was good, but my report lacked substance, so far as hard numbers and data were concerned. He further added that my analysis was mostly qualitative. Perhaps, he meant 'journalistic.'

He told me that I needed to cite data to back up my arguments and propose solutions, even if they appear obvious. Further, I shouldn't assume that data will be readily available in the reading material that was provided to me. In such cases, one was expected to employ logical assumptions and research beyond the given reading material to add external but relevant data to back up the analysis and propositions.

That's it. I knew what was the 'problem'—I had fallen in love with words towards the end of my graduation days, and I had almost forgotten about numbers during my journalism days—now it was time to unlearn that.

I think this was one of the most crucial changes that IIM Ahmedabad triggered in me. I was trained to look for hard data, and mere awesome storytelling was not enough. This is where I think I ended up unlearning a few things that I had imbibed during my journalism days.

This conflict between MBA learning and journalism learning came up during my summer internship too. As part of the MBA course requirement, I interned with the news channel Times Now. My internship project was about figuring out ways in which the management could measure the productivity of journalists.

As a former journalist, I scoffed at the idea of 'intellectual' work being quantified and judged, as if salesmen were being evaluated on whether they met their sales target. But then, management education had taught me the importance of data, and that perhaps the job of a salesman was far more challenging than that of a journalist. Further, running a media house was a legitimate business at the end of the day and the management should have an idea about the business processes and productivity.

Times Now was launched just a few months before my internship began in May–June 2006. Arnab Goswami was leading it editorially, though he was yet to take on the avatar that we later saw on Times Now and then on his own channel, Republic TV.

I familiarized myself with the newsroom process, though I already knew much of it, having been a TV journalist earlier. However, this time, instead of focusing on the headline column of a news bulletin rundown (a table basically), I was looking at numbers, for example, the duration of the news report. Not just that, the bulletin rundown now appeared like a database to me.

It was a bit challenging as editorial systems are not really designed with such aspects in mind, but I tried my best. I finally came up with some ratios and percentages that could hint at productivity or measure the work done by the journalists.

The then CEO of Times Now, Sunil Lulla, had attended my presentation, which I had presented at the end of the internship period. He had said that he liked the idea. Arnab Goswami was supposed to attend it too, but he didn't. Maybe he didn't like the idea of journalists' productivity being measured in numbers, or maybe he was too busy. There were rumours that the Times Group was already thinking of replacing Arnab Goswami because the channel was not topping the TRP charts. This was obviously before Arnab changed gears and became virtually irreplaceable.

Anyway, the time spent at IIM Ahmedabad was quite valuable. This is where I picked up ideological nuances and started identifying myself as a libertarian. Shifting towards the libertarian ideology made sure that I entirely disliked communist and socialist ideas.

The initial reason for this dislike was the much-hyped high salaries that one could earn after graduating from IIM Ahmedabad. As someone who was earning merely ₹4691 per month as a journalist, I couldn't believe my ears when I was told that McKinsey, a leading global management consultancy firm, was offering ₹90,000 per month to summer interns. Man, capitalism was so cool!

I fancied getting a job at an investment bank or a top consultancy firm, which were supposed to pay crazy money. During the summer placement process in late 2005, I was shortlisted for an interview at Deutsche Bank. It gave me the hope that my newly acquired dream of earning millions of dollars by becoming an investment banker would finally come true.

I don't think I came across as a bright spark in the Deutsche Bank interview. I was rejected. And I was dejected. Just one rejection put me under so much stress that I fared even worse at interviews for the Indian banks on the second day. I was not picked up for any summer placement job even after more than half of the batch had been placed. That made me even more dejected.

I received some counselling by a batchmate and dorm mate of mine, whom we used to call 'Sambha' (all of us had dorm names and that's how we addressed each other. I was 'Softy'.). He had done his MS from a US university and had already earned decently in the US. He had joined IIM Ahmedabad primarily to come back to India and take care of his ageing parents. He was adamant that he would not take part in the summer placement process but was asked by the institute to attend at least a few interviews. He finally did his internship at a start-up, but effectively used those two months of internship to get married. He was the most 'chilled' guy on campus.

Sambha had a word with me like an elder brother and it really helped me. It was not really some serious pep talk given to a depressed guy, but just a light conversation aimed at lifting my mood. His approach of not caring about the entire process—because life was far bigger than these things—was reassuring. He further reminded me that I had not really come to IIM Ahmedabad to become an investment banker, so I shouldn't feel sad for something that I didn't even aim for, to begin with. He also told me to not forget my original pursuits and plans just because everyone else wanted to become a banker or a consultant. The conversation made me feel better and that's when I decided to intern with Times Now.

But this didn't mean that I no longer saw any merit in capitalism and the perks associated with it. Though I was not chasing a high-paying career in an investment bank any longer, I was influenced by the ideas of a professor who encouraged students at IIM Ahmedabad to become entrepreneurs. He was Professor Sunil Handa. He would convince students that an entrepreneur creating wealth was much more important than a professional getting an astronomically high salary.

I found the idea of running a business pretty exciting, though I didn't have any business plan that I could pursue to become an entrepreneur at that point of time. I founded *Faking News* in September 2008, more than a year after graduating from IIM Ahmedabad, while my first interaction with Professor Handa must have been around July 2006. He was not teaching us any course, but had offered to give a few voluntary lectures when we were in the second year. I happened to attend one such lecture and I was quite impressed.

In these two years, before I founded *Faking News*, which marked my return to the world of news media and political commentary, I donned many hats. I founded and sold off a website—my first venture was an online game called 'Cricket Stock Exchange' or CricStock—undertook management consultancy projects, did some freelance work, including public relations, tried to raise funds for a TV channel and even tried to set up an ethanol factory in Bihar!

Exciting as they are, I'll have to skip the details, as they are not directly related to my ideological journey, so far as cultural issues are concerned. But these experiences helped me in one way—most of them made my belief stronger that the free market economy was the best. I had definitely become a committed 'Right-winger', so far as economic matters were concerned.

The non-meeting with Narendra Modi

So, broadly from 2005 to 2008—the IIM Ahmedabad years and then pursuing various projects before I founded *Faking News*—I was busy exploring new ideas and new opportunities. I had started understanding ideological nuances and fancied myself as libertarian, but I still had no reason to warm up to the Sanghi side.

In the same period, India faced multiple terror attacks in various cities, which targeted civilians, where hundreds of people lost their lives. Some of the major attacks were—Delhi blasts (twice in 2005 and 2008), Varanasi blasts (2006), Mumbai (the 2006 bombing in trains), Samjhauta Express bombing (2007), Jaipur blasts (2008), Ahmedabad blasts (2008) and the Mumbai terror attacks (2008). All of these were carried out by Islamic terrorists, but as always, there was hardly anything in the mainstream media that pointed fingers at the Islamist ideology.

In fact, this series of terror attacks by Islamic terrorists during the UPA-I had begun with an attempted attack at the makeshift Ram Temple (the Janmabhoomi site) in Ayodhya in July 2005. Fortunately, the attack was not successful and the makeshift temple or the idols of Ram Lalla couldn't be damaged. All the terrorists were killed before they could reach the temple site.

If at all the discussion around terror attacks moved beyond condemnation and little Pakistan bashing, it was invariably linked to the Babri mosque demolition, as if that exculpates the mindset that inspires to carry out such 'revenge' attacks. And how many revenges, really!

The BJP did try to portray the Ayodhya terror attack as an attack on the Hindu faith, but they didn't use the words as explicitly. Further, what made the BJP's position a little awkward was the fact that just a month before the attack, L.K. Advani had gone on a visit to Pakistan, where he had termed Mohammad Ali Jinnah, the founder of Pakistan, a 'great man.'[44]

Advani had to offer his resignation after the outrage that ensued, and finally quit the post of BJP president a few months later, but the Congress did not let this opportunity go waste and tried to paint the BJP as a party that was not serious about the fight against Pakistan, and by extension, the fight against terror.

All the terror attacks by Islamic terrorists were conveniently, though rightly too, blamed on Pakistan or Kashmir-based groups, but the debates in the media never hovered around the ideology of radical Islam that primarily motivated the terrorists. I can't recall such criticism being offered even in the digital domain. Or maybe I missed it, because from

2005 to 2008 I was too busy with my own life.

What I do recall however is some commentary in the media that brought the element of 'class divide' in the aftermath of the Mumbai terror attacks of 2008. A few talking heads argued that there was extraordinary outrage and focus on the Mumbai terror attacks only because posh hotels and hangouts were targeted. The rich and influential were scared for the first time. They apparently didn't bother earlier when common people were dying in blasts that targeted various Indian cities.

That's how cleverly you propagate a communist agenda while appearing to be logical and compassionate about common citizens. The Mumbai terror attacks were not about class, what made it stand out from the earlier blasts in various cities was the sheer vulgarity of the attack and the audacity of the terrorists.

For the first time one saw images of terrorists moving around with assault rifles in areas that were normal urban spaces—roads, railway stations, restaurants, hotels. The city was veritably under siege. Apart from posh hotels, the terrorists had killed ordinary and poor citizens, too, at a railway station. Yet, a narrative was built around class divide.

One can argue that the BJP too failed to make it about radical Islamism. Granted that they couldn't have decided the narrative or topics in primetime shows in the mainstream media, where any such attempt would have been shot down as 'irresponsible' and 'communalism', but they could have tried. As a normal person, who was decently active online in those years, I can't remember any such attempt by the BJP.

Further, the party leadership appeared confused. Vajpayee had all but virtually retired from active politics, while Advani had made the Jinnah blunder, which kept coming back to embarrass him and the party whenever Pakistan was blamed for terrorism.

While the BJP appeared confused—at least to someone like me when I try to recall that era—the Congress seemed to have pre-empted any such move by the BJP. They had started work on the 'Hindu terrorism' theory, so that if at some point in the future radical Islam is blamed, the secular-liberal ecosystem can hit back saying 'But terrorism is not exclusive to Islam, here is the proof of Hindu terrorism'.

It started with the investigative agencies arresting Swami Aseemanand and then Sadhvi Pragya for the Samjhauta Express bombing and the

Malegaon blasts, respectively, even though earlier the agencies had blamed Islamic terrorists for the act. Suddenly, the secular-liberal ecosystem, which had earlier blamed the same investigative agencies for framing innocent Muslim youths in various terror cases, started treating the words of these agencies as gospel truth.

The secular-liberal ecosystem was so devoted to further and protect the 'Hindu terrorism' theory that even the Mumbai terror attacks were blamed on Hindutva groups, and some Congress leaders played active role in that. Not less than a union minister tried to further this theory within a month of the terror attacks. A.R. Antulay who was the minority affairs minister in the UPA-I government, tried to insinuate that Hemant Karkare was killed by Hindutva groups.[45]

The Congress party had 'distanced itself' from his remarks immediately. It was the same old strategy of the Congress, where they said different things to different groups, so that the Congressi Hindus don't see it as an anti-Hindu party. The Congressi Hindu in me was not impressed though. That was one of the earliest incidents that made me amenable to the idea that the Congress was following a brand of secularism that was not just absurd, but dangerous.

Two years later in 2010, when Digvijay Singh attended the launch of a book that termed the Mumbai terror attacks 'an RSS conspiracy,'[46] the Congress party had stretched it a bit too far. Perhaps, the likes of Digvijay Singh put too much faith in the traditional ability of the Congress to speak in different voices to different groups, not realizing that the world was changing.

While things were changing, the narrative was very much in Congress' favour until 2010, or rather in favour of the corrupted secularism practised in India. No wonder the BJP could not win the 2009 Lok Sabha elections, even though it had made national security a major issue in their campaign.

Hundreds of people had died at the hands of Islamic terrorists and a weak prime minister like Manmohan Singh was not able to save them— this was BJP's pitch against the incumbent. The party said that India needed an 'iron man' like Advani. However, that pitch didn't work. The BJP got even less seats in 2009 than in 2004.

All this while, Narendra Modi was getting ready for a long innings.

Between 2002 and 2007, that is, in his first full term as the chief minister of Gujarat, Modi was relentlessly projected as a 'controversial' leader who won the 2002 elections riding on the wave of 'hate'. He was accused of having turned Gujarat into a police state, where fake encounters and political killings were routine. Whether it was the encounter of Ishrat Jahan and Sohrabuddin Sheikh or the murder of BJP leader Haren Pandya, it was all blamed on Modi, holding him directly responsible for these events.

When I had landed in Ahmedabad in 2005, I too had a similar image of Modi in my mind. Forget his image, I had a very prejudiced image of Gujarat itself, as I have recounted earlier.

As I spent more time in Ahmedabad, it was not too difficult to shed those prejudices against Gujarat or Gujarati people—first on the IIM campus and later in a residential society full of Gujaratis. One of our professors, Professor P.K. Sinha, had a flat in that society, which he had given us—me and my business partner Karthik Laxman from IIM—to stay for free.

Karthik and I had worked on a few projects for SEWA (Self-Employed Women's Association) while we were in Ahmedabad post our IIM studies and after scouting for consulting projects. It was literally an all-women organization. We had also travelled to a rural area in Gujarat to talk to a few members of SEWA about their activities and challenges, which we were to document and analyse. The rural women appeared to be quite confident in their dealings. They would be farmers, artisans, running small shops or homemakers, but bubbling with energy and confidence.

I would later fall in love with a Gujarati girl to whom I am married now, but these observations are truly independent of that fact, and have been made by a guy who had seen only Bihar and Delhi, until then.

While it was rather easy to shed prejudices about Gujarat or Gujarati people, I didn't care much about Modi, mostly because, as I had mentioned earlier, the 2005–08 period of my life was focused on learning new things at IIM Ahmedabad and taking my first steps in the world of entrepreneurship, and dealing with a range of issues related to these. I was so engrossed in my own life that I don't have a single memory of the 2007 Gujarat assembly elections, which took place at a time when I was living in Ahmedabad.

The 2007 elections were a litmus test for Modi. Not only was he up against incumbency, he was up against a hostile national media too, which had tried to delegitimize his 2002 victory, accusing him of winning it in a polarized environment post the riots. This was also the election where Sonia Gandhi termed him 'Maut ka saudagar' (Merchant of death), raking up the issues of riots and supposed fake encounter killings.

Modi won the 2007 Gujarat assembly elections with an absolute majority. The people of Gujarat trusted him and his work, and gradually the sentiment 'Modi means business' started resonating beyond Gujarat. The demand to make Modi the prime ministerial candidate had started quite early, the first of which were just a few months after the BJP lost the 2009 Lok Sabha elections.

I, too, had my own little 'Modi means business' moment, and that was before he won the 2007 assembly elections.

This was in early 2007 when we were still students at IIM Ahmedabad. By that time the entrepreneurship bug had bit us, and we had informally formed a 'company' to offer consulting services. We had been sending emails to various companies or groups, thinking we could help them with our 'great' intelligence as soon-to-be graduates from the best management institute of India.

We also decided to send emails to government agencies, expressing our interest to work with them. We looked up the official websites of many state governments—most of which were quite cumbersome to navigate—and sent emails to the principal secretaries of various chief ministers. In retrospect, I find it funny. We had so much confidence, rather overconfidence, that we felt that we were ready to help chief ministers, even though we were yet to complete our MBA course.

The only office of chief minister that responded to our emails was that of Narendra Modi. K. Kailashnathan, who was then the principal secretary to Modi, had written back to us, asking us to come to the state secretariat in Gandhinagar for a meeting. We were pleasantly surprised and mighty excited.

Ahmedabad and Gandhinagar are neighbouring cities, with seamless connection to each other via public transport. There were no cab aggregation apps back then and travelling by bus would have been a little too 'middle class', so we hired an auto-rickshaw from outside the

IIM campus and reached the Gandhinagar secretariat around noon.

Fortunately, it was February and not May or June, else we'd have been drenched in sweat by the time we reached. All we needed to do after getting down from the auto-rickshaw was to wipe our faces and comb our hair. We then had to walk for around 100 m as the auto-rickshaw was not allowed inside the secretariat for security reasons.

The security was definitely far more alert and stricter than what I witnessed when I had visited the secretariat in Bihar a few weeks earlier (while pursuing the business plan of setting up an ethanol factory). And it became even stricter as we reached the block where the Chief Minister's Office was situated.

After waiting in the common area of the ground floor for some time, we were called upstairs to the floor where the Chief Minister's Office was located. We had to pass another layer of security, and were finally brought to the office of Kailashnathan. He treated us well, offering chai and refreshments, and began the conversation, which initially centred around us, where he asked us questions such as, 'Which part of the country we belonged to', 'How was IIM', etc.

'The chief minister likes to work with young talents like you,' he said, which made us feel pretty good about ourselves, 'He (Modi) is of the view that bureaucracy should benefit from people who have professional skills, and what you guys have planned (working with the government instead of going for private jobs) will really be appreciated by him.'

Then he asked us whether we had the time and can wait for a while. When we replied in the affirmative, he said that he would like us to meet the chief minister and have a few words with him. I think Modi was held up in the state assembly or was away to attend a meeting. We were obviously thrilled. Meeting a chief minister was going to be a good 'CV point'—a term we used frequently to refer to any kind of achievements in our lives that we'd like to put on our curriculum vitae.

We waited, and we waited for long. To keep us engaged, Kailashnathan continued to talk to us. He spoke about how Modi liked to solve issues and how he especially liked using technology, whether simple or advanced. He told us a story about how Modi, after becoming the chief minister, killed retail corruption by simply installing CCTVs at a few places near the secretariat. Those places were apparently the meeting points of touts and some corrupt government officials.

This was virtually the first time when I had heard anything positive about Modi, who was always painted as a scheming politician in the media. 'He is making sure the system works for the people and there is all round development,' Kailashnathan continued. We were intrigued and looked forward to meeting the man himself, and were quite excited at the prospect of getting our first consulting assignment.

The meeting with Modi couldn't take place that day. He was stuck somewhere—either in an assembly session or some other meetings—and his principal secretary also had better things to do than keep a conversation going with two management students. Sensing that we too were feeling a bit awkward, just sitting there in his office as he got busy with his work, Kailashnathan said that we could go back to the IIM campus and he would try to arrange a meeting with the chief minister some other day when his schedule permits.

We were not crazy Modi fans who would not mind waiting for hours and hours just to have a glimpse of our 'favourite' leader, so we opted to go back to the campus and return some other day to have a meeting. In retrospect, we should have waited. Who knows, today we would have been working at the Prime Minister's Office!

We were foolish not to pursue this lead aggressively. We sent just one reminder via email for the next meeting, which never happened. One of the reasons was our first venture—the 'Cricket Stock Exchange' or CricStock website—which kept us really busy and which gave us our first mini success too.

I don't know if an early meeting with Modi would have made me a 'Sanghi' much earlier. Maybe yes, maybe not. Maybe not, because we would have been working on projects that had nothing to do with ideology. And maybe yes, because Modi definitely was a huge factor, if not THE factor, for making people warm up to Hindutva or Hindu nationalism. He impressed them with his oratory, with his focus on development, with his image of a hard-working leader—all of which are 'secular' qualities—and subsequently he indirectly invited his newly gained fans to warm up to his ideology, which he would not be apologetic about.

So, I was exposed to this 'Modi means business' image in early 2007 itself, but it was only much later that I would buy this image, along with most of India, almost 4–5 years later. Incidentally, these 4–5 years would see social media expanding like crazy, and many other small and big events would take place during this period, which would further help this transition.

6

Internet, Anna, 'paid media'

Signs of things to come

During the bulk of the first term of the UPA government (2004–09), which was led by Manmohan Singh and 'super-led' by Sonia Gandhi, the narrative was shaped entirely by the mainstream media. Even though social media had taken birth by then and Orkut had become hugely popular in India, these platforms were not 'countering' the mainstream media narrative.

As I mentioned earlier, the first blogs or the first websites were hardly being run by Hindutva proponents. On many occasions, these blogs or websites were actually supplementing the mainstream narrative. Many of the leading or active bloggers were classical liberals, while some others were radical Left who hated Hindutva. Thus, despite various cities in India being mauled by Islamic terrorists, the dominant narrative, even in the virtual world, could not be about the mindset of Islamism, which had given birth to a wounded and partitioned India in 1947.

However, two separate incidents took place in 2008—the murder of a young girl named Aarushi Talwar in Noida and the Mumbai terror attacks. Though both were different cases, they had affected the relationship between social media/blogosphere and the mainstream media/journalists. One can argue that they laid the foundations of weakening the hold that the mainstream media enjoyed thitherto.

The Aarushi case happened in May 2008, when a 13-year-old girl was found murdered at her Noida residence. Apart from Aarushi, Hemraj, the 45-year-old domestic help of the house, was also murdered in the same building. Hemraj was initially thought to be the suspect, as he used to

159

live in the same building and had been missing after Aarushi was found murdered. His body was discovered almost a day later in the course of primary police investigation. The discovery of his dead body was broken 'live' on TV news.

It was not as if India had not seen shocking murders earlier, but since the incident happened in Noida, where head offices of many TV news channels were situated, this double murder was converted into a non-stop TV coverage, with ludicrous sensationalization by the TV news channels.

The TV reporters were moving around the crime scene unchecked, with most of them shouting like overexcited cricket commentators. The media was interviewing anyone and everyone in the neighbourhood to talk about the personal lives of the parents and the girl. In fact, many more ridiculous things were done in the name of news coverage. One reporter had put red colour on his palm and demonstrated how the blood on the hands of the murderer could leave stains on walls and other places. Genius.

Then one fine day, TV journalists discovered the Orkut profile of Aarushi. Detailed analysis of the kinds of communities she had joined, what 'scraps' she used to receive or send, her 'testimonials', her friends and her photos—all of them were beamed on national TV. The entire incident was turned into a televised tamasha.

This was possibly the first time the mainstream media was criticized by many for their role and conduct. Earlier, the criticism of the media would be limited to living rooms, or at best a few people would send 'Letters to the editor' to register their protest, but now people had the internet and social media platforms, where their criticism would be read and shared by others.

The journalists might have not realized this, but the threadbare analysis of the Orkut profile of Aarushi was putting off the youngsters who were active on the social media. It may sound counterintuitive, as the coverage of something like Orkut should only appeal to the young, but there was a reason why it didn't appeal to many such youngsters. While everything on Orkut was virtually public, there was still an unwritten understanding of 'What happens on Orkut, stays on Orkut.'

To give you an example, as students at IIM, we had taken screenshots of Orkut messages ('scraps' as they were called) of one of our dormmates who had left cheesy pick-up lines on the profiles of girls. One of the girls wrote back something that was funny but 'insulting' to our Romeo. We immediately took screenshots of this and shared it on the 'dorm notice board', which was a private digital forum. Everyone joined in mocking our Romeo, but later, when sobriety returned, everyone broadly agreed that it shouldn't have been done. Orkut was a place to indulge in things like trying pick-up lines, so let those stay there only—this was the accepted wisdom.

The TV media was essentially doing what we had done. We shared screenshots with our dormmates, while the news channels shared it with the entire country. They ended up telling millions of Indian parents what happens on Orkut—how guys can leave messages on a girl's profile with ease, and how their pictures can be seen by anyone with an internet connection. Some amount of parental censorship was being triggered, which the young did not like. It discomforted them.

While the Aarushi case was about principled criticism and mild discomfort with the mainstream media, a couple of incidents around the media coverage of the Mumbai terror attacks in November that year left many in the virtual world extremely critical of the media. And at least one incident turned the relationship between the mainstream media and the virtual world hostile and confrontational.

By 2008, Mumbai, the financial capital of India, was already targeted multiple times by terrorists, be it the bomb blasts of 1993, at least five incidents of bombings at various places in 2002–03 or the deadly serial blasts in 2006 that targeted the local trains. All of them were carried out by the terrorists in the name of giving justice to Indian Muslims, and were linked by liberals to either the 1992 Babri Masjid demolition or to the 2002 Gujarat riots.

Although the 1993 bomb blasts and the 2006 train bombings remain the deadliest in terms of the number of people who lost their lives, the 2008 terror attack was the most terrifying, as it was a barbaric warfare unleashed in civilian areas in modern times.

Terrorists with assault rifles moving in civilian areas and firing indiscriminately at people was not something one had seen earlier or even heard about. The terrorists had entered two hotels—Oberoi Trident and Taj Mahal Palace—to kill people and take hostages. The Mumbai Police tried to fight them, but finally the NSG (National Security Guard) commandos, the Black Cats, had to be called in to salvage the situation. It led to three days of non-stop TV coverage about counter-terrorism operations.

Four years later, while upholding the death sentence awarded to Ajmal Kasab, the lone terrorist who survived and was captured alive during the terror attacks, the Supreme Court had made the following scathing comments over the media coverage of the attacks:

> The reckless coverage of the terrorist attacks by the channels thus gave rise to a situation where, on the one hand, the terrorists were completely hidden from the security forces and they had no means to know their exact positions or even the kind of firearms and explosives they possessed and, on the other, the positions of the security forces, their weapons and all their operational movements were being watched by the collaborators across the border on TV screens and being communicated to the terrorists.[47]

The SC bench of Justices Aftab Alam and C.K. Prasad had further said that, 'it is not possible to find out whether the security forces actually suffered any casualty or injuries on account of the way their operations were being displayed on the TV screen. But it is beyond doubt that the way their operations were freely shown made the task of the security forces not only exceedingly difficult but also dangerous and risky.'[48]

The court had made other unfavourable comments too. It said that the TV channels put commercial interests ahead of national interest by competing against each other for the highest TRP and by showing gory details of the mayhem. The bench cited specific incidents where they felt that crucial information about the location or movement of forces were given out by the media during their live coverage. The bench wondered why the TV channels couldn't have waited for some time before making such pieces of information public.

While such comments came from the Supreme Court in 2012, many people on social media and in their blogs (me included) had spoken up against this irresponsible, thoughtless and sensationalized coverage in 2008 itself, right during or immediately after the attacks.

Now, here I might appear to be contradicting myself, saying that I expected responsible journalism from the TV media after having criticized 'responsible journalism' many times in this book. But there is no contradiction. First of all, do note that I had used quotes on earlier occasions! But the basic premise remains unchanged—what you think is responsible, what you think is the greater cause, what you think is good for the society or what you think is evil, all of these are dependent on your ideological beliefs.

A belief in nationalist ideology will translate to an idea of responsible journalism where the media actively helps the security forces in their combat operations. For some, this help might even extend to the extent of airing fake news, which might confuse the terrorists and help the security forces. Do remember that airing fake news is bad journalism, but it would be responsible journalism in someone's head because their nationalist ideology says that terrorists have to be neutralized at any cost. So I'm still not deviating from my theory that 'responsible journalism is nothing but putting your personal ideology into action.'

In 2008, my ideological moorings were still at a nascent stage, even though I had started aligning myself with the classical liberal or libertarian positions. Theoretically, a deeply nationalistic ideology would be in conflict with libertarian positions on many socio-political issues, but no such conflict was seen in terms of the media coverage of the terror attacks.

I think this 'nationalist' part of my ideology, which expected responsible journalism from the TV channels during the Mumbai terror attacks, was basically an outcome of being patriotic. I earnestly believe that an overwhelming number of Indians are naturally patriotic, thanks to all the Republic Days and Independence Days one celebrates since childhood, and the love one develops for the tricolour thanks to even factors like cricket matches. These emotions further develop into respect for the armed forces, and you start caring for them and their safety.

Anyway, my blog post, which happened to be an article written in a serious tone on the *Faking News* website, was hardly the most famous criticism of the mainstream media back then. This was primarily because *Faking News* was yet to become popular. It had just been three months since I had started blogging anonymously on the website.

Regardless of how popular they were, many bloggers had criticized the media coverage of the Mumbai terror attacks. It was a prevalent sentiment in the virtual world that the mainstream media had behaved irresponsibly, both by giving away locations of the security forces and by not showing enough compassion while interviewing the common people affected by the chaos.

One such blog post that became really famous was titled 'Shoddy Journalism' by a man named Chyetanya Kunte. It was a rather short blog post, under 1000 words, but what made it different from the others was its specific criticism of Barkha Dutt. Around half of the blog post was about her reporting.

Kunte had given two specific incidents accusing Dutt of being insensitive and irresponsible. In one incident he claimed that Dutt had caught hold of a man who had just ran out of the hotel and interviewed him live. In the interview, she apparently made the man disclose where his wife was hiding in the hotel, which arguably made her vulnerable to being located by the terrorists.

In another incident, a security officer is supposed to have told Dutt that the Oberoi Trident was free of hostages, but Dutt had apparently called up a top manager at the Oberoi who contradicted the security officer. Kunte suggested that probably the security officer was being clever by falsely claiming that there were no more hostages, so that the terrorists—who by now were certainly being briefed by their bosses in Pakistan, who were tracking updates on live TV—try to move out of the hotel and in the process get killed by the security forces, but Dutt and that Oberoi manager possibly spoiled the plan.

I cannot guarantee that both these incidents did happen, as I don't have access to the archives of NDTV's broadcast to cross-check this, but these criticisms were in line with what the Supreme Court went on to say four years later. Kunte had written this blog on the second day of the terror attacks and there is a fat chance that he might have invented the incidents while the city was under siege. Maybe, he confused some other TV journalist as Dutt and wrongly accused her?

When published, Kunte's blog post was one among the many criticisms available online, but what made it become the talk of the town a few weeks later was the fact that it was no longer available online. On

26 January 2009, he deleted the 'Shoddy Journalism' post tendering an unconditional apology[49] to Dutt. The wording of the apology seemed to convey that Kunte had received a legal notice of defamation from Dutt and NDTV.

In his apology, he specifically withdrew his allegations that claimed 'a lack of ethics, responsibility and professionalism by Ms Dutt and NDTV Limited', and 'that Ms Dutt and NDTV's reporting at the scene of the Mumbai attacks during November 2008 resulted in jeopardizing the safety and lives of civilians and/or security personnel caught up in and/or involved in defending against the attacks in Mumbai in November 2008' and 'that Ms Dutt was responsible for the death of Indian servicemen during the Kargil Conflict.'

Except for this post, which was now gone, other posts on Kunte's blog had nothing to do with the media or politics. His blog suggested that he was based in the Netherlands and worked in the IT sector. He came across as just another blogger writing about life abroad and software issues, who possibly ended up writing on the media because of strong emotions that arose after seeing the mayhem in Mumbai.

The deletion of the post and the apology to Dutt were met with widespread indignation and condemnation by the bloggers. 'The big media has arm-twisted and insulted one of us when they could have simply ignored or proved the claims false' and 'If it can happen to him, it can happen to any of us' were some of the reactions by the bloggers on this incident.

It made Dutt a mini villain. Some bloggers, as an act of defiance, retrieved the deleted post of Kunte from Google cache and uploaded it on file-sharing websites. Some even republished it on their blogs or posted it on Facebook—which was becoming popular and rivalling Orkut in the beginning of 2009.

Perhaps, this is when, for the first time, the mainstream media was seen as a hostile force and as an entity that should be confronted. And perhaps this is when Barkha Dutt for the first time came to know what a Streisand effect was.

Fortunately for Dutt and for the mainstream media, Facebook and Twitter were yet to become popular in January 2009. These two platforms, along with YouTube and WhatsApp, are the most effective in making anything 'viral'. Orkut was good, but the viral phenomenon, as we know it today, was yet to happen. Mobile data was painfully slow and not many apps were in vogue. 3G services were yet to be launched.

As a result, Dutt and the media appeared to be villains to a very small section of the society. While the mainstream media faced condemnation and even hostility, it didn't affect their clout.

There was another incident that took place in between these two incidents in 2008, which in a way proves why the criticism of the mainstream media didn't really affect their clout. It was the 'cash for votes' scam of July 2008, where the BJP claimed that the Congress and its allies, especially Amar Singh of the SP, had offered bribes to some of their MPs to vote in favour of the Manmohan Singh government in a trust vote. The trust vote was necessitated after the communist parties withdrew support from the government over the issue of Indo–US nuclear deal.

The entire country had seen the dramatic images when some BJP MPs flashed wades of notes in the Lok Sabha, claiming that those crores of rupees were given to them as bribe for voting in favour of the government. The BJP demanded the resignation of Manmohan Singh for subverting democracy by trying to win the vote of confidence using corrupt and illegal means.

The BJP further claimed that the entire act of offering bribes to their MPs was captured on camera, as they had planned it as a 'sting operation'. The full tapes were with the news channel CNN-IBN (currently known as CNN-News18), they said, which was then editorially led by Rajdeep Sardesai.

While CNN-IBN aired some part of the sting operation, they didn't air all of it. It refused to endorse the BJP's version, even though the party had claimed that they had taken the news channel and their journalists into confidence. The BJP leaders accused CNN-IBN and Sardesai of backstabbing them and succumbing to pressure from the Congress.[50]

However, that charge never took off in those days. People, including me, were more inclined to believe the media than any politician.

Also, in both the Aarushi murder case and the Mumbai terror attacks, the criticism of the media and the feelings of hostility against the media in the latter case were not due to strictly political or ideological reasons. The criticism of the media was restricted to what it widely covered and how it covered the events. The criticism of what it did not cover adequately, and why it did not cover certain incidents, was yet to come.

For example, in August 2008, a Hindu leader Swami Lakshmanananda Saraswati was killed along with his four disciples in front of young children in Odisha, but that did not generate the kind of outrage as the killing of Graham Staines a few years earlier could. The media started covering it only after 'Hindu groups' started protesting. The protests and violence were covered as 'Kandhamal violence' and it was the Hindus who were painted as aggressors even though the issue was murder of a Hindu leader.

Much later in April 2020, when two Hindu sadhus were lynched in Palghar in Maharashtra, the media had to cover and debate the issue owing to pressure and outrage from the people, who demanded that the media can't report and obsess over only 'certain kind of' lynchings. However, back in 2008, the criticism of the media from an ideological perspective was missing.

The mainstream media was yet to face criticism on why it employs certain double standards. It was yet to be questioned on its ideas of 'responsible journalism'. It was yet to be seen hand in glove with politicians and fixers.

And all that would happen within a couple of years.

Sanghis start getting online

The 2009 general elections were held in the aftermath of various terror attacks, including the Mumbai terror attacks. Hundreds of people had died in various cities during the UPA-I regime. The BJP had made internal security a major poll plank, with Advani projected as a tough leader who would take tough decisions. They promised to bring back tough anti-terrorism laws, such as POTA, that was repealed after the Congress came back to power in 2004.

The Congress on the other hand talked about their welfare policies, especially NREGA (National Rural Employment Guarantee Act), and how the Manmohan Singh government helped the poor. They said they were committed to an all-round development that included the urban areas too, which is why they had refused to bow down to the Communist parties earlier over the nuclear deal. And obviously they talked about communal harmony and protection to minorities.

Both the BJP and the Congress had pre-poll alliances, known as NDA (National Democratic Alliance) and UPA, respectively. The Communist parties and some random parties were also in the fray with their alliance, which was called the Third Front, and which claimed to be equidistant from the BJP and the Congress. But, it was well understood that in case of a hung parliament, they will support either a Congress-led government or a minority government, led by one of their own to keep the 'communal forces' out of power.

There was a Fourth Front too, comprising the RJD (Rashtriya Janata Dal), the SP and some other parties, which was basically a group that couldn't cut a direct deal with the Congress for a pre-poll alliance.

In the eyes of a BJP or an RSS sympathizer, perhaps the BJP alliance had a better chance at the elections. A BJP supporter could argue—what will you do with development if you were to die in terror attacks? And that life and dignity, even in death, should be the top concern of people.

With the elections getting into campaign mode, the BJP had a fresh chance to talk about internal security and safety, as the IPL, the Twenty20 tournament that the BCCI had introduced just the previous year, had to be hosted outside India because the Government of India expressed its inability to provide security for the tournament in the wake of the impending Lok Sabha elections.

Are we so weak that we can't even host a cricket tournament safely? Will we not allow terrorists to win if the fear of terror attacks stops us from playing even cricket matches? The BJP raised such questions and Narendra Modi, as the chief minister of Gujarat, offered to host the entire IPL in Gujarat. Lalit Modi, the then IPL commissioner, however, decided not to accept this offer. The tournament was held in South Africa—the only edition to have been hosted outside India before the coronavirus pandemic forced the tournament to be shifted to UAE in 2020.

But, as I had recounted in the previous chapter, the narrative portrayed by the media around the terror attacks didn't really lead to a deep anger against the ruling 'party', which could have been legibly accused of being a sleeping partner in promoting radical Islam. Instead, it was fashioned to elicit anger against the ruling 'class'—a nebulous construct of the rich and influential, which included 'all' politicians, including from the BJP.

Consequently, the internal security and 'tough on terrorism' pitch by the BJP couldn't really convince ordinary Indians, who perhaps had also become numb to the frequent terror attacks. The 'Spirit of Mumbai' was celebrated each time an ordinary person ended up proving how his fear of losing livelihood was bigger than the fear of losing his life.

The BJP couldn't raise the issue of 'big-ticket scams' either. Although the 2G scam had already taken place, details about it was known only during the UPA-II tenure. I can recall two scams that had made headlines during the UPA-I tenure—the fake stamp paper scam where a man named Abdul Karim Telgi was arrested and the Satyam computers scam where its Chairman Ramalinga Raju was arrested for accounting fraud in one of the biggest IT companies of India. The top leadership of the Congress or any top personality of UPA-I was not directly linked to either of these scams, at least not in popular knowledge. The 'Cash for votes' scam was there, but it was already sabotaged by the media as per the BJP, so the party didn't have any big stick of corruption to beat the Congress with.

As someone identifying with libertarian ideology, personally I didn't care much about who may win. I feared that a period of political instability, like the one seen during 1996–99, could come back to haunt India. The third and fourth fronts had a rather muscular presence in the then Lok Sabha, and their dreams of being the kingmakers or the brokers didn't appear misplaced.

Further, on a personal level, I had gotten busy with a project we had taken up with TV Today, where we—Karthik and I, working on one of our last projects together, as I had already started Faking News by then—were to develop a website for Aaj Tak for the IPL. The website would have allowed common users to bid for players before every IPL match, just as the IPL teams bade for cricketers before the tournament.

Actually, the initial conversation and understanding we had with TV Today was to develop a 'Political Stock Exchange' for the 2009 Lok Sabha elections. A Political Stock Exchange, running on virtual money obviously, was my original idea, which was converted to Cricket Stock Exchange on suggestions by my IIM dormmates. I thought of trying out that original idea ahead of the 2009 Lok Sabha elections.

I had pitched the idea to the TV Today representatives that the movement of share prices (based on the political valuations decided by the public) of Sonia, Manmohan, Advani, etc., as the election dates draw near will be good drama for TV. The TV Today representatives liked the idea and we signed an agreement where Aaj Tak would create a show out of it.

Aaj Tak even promoted the website for a day or two before their legal team developed cold feet. They thought that a website like Political Stock Exchange could be seen as violation of the ban on opinion polls during the polling phase, because the rise and fall of shares of a political leader or a party was virtually like a continuous opinion poll being carried out. We were called in for an emergency meeting and informed that the TV channel won't be able to promote or make a show out of it.

We were shocked, but TV Today clarified that the agreement in itself was not being cancelled and the promised money will be paid in full. But now, instead of politics, we were told to make a website on cricket, specifically around the IPL.

We couldn't have converted it into a Cricket Stock Exchange, as that would have been unfair to the party to whom we had already sold off CricStock, so we converted it into a bidding game around cricket, which would also be more in line with the novel 'player auctions' element of the IPL.

For the short duration when the Political Stock Exchange website was active and promoted by Aaj Tak, the most popular stocks were those of the BJP and its leaders. Assuming that the limited data we could collect via the website was representative of the internet-savvy politically aware Indians, one could conclude that the 'Sanghis' had certainly started getting online, and were possibly 'dominating' the virtual world, too, by 2009. But, most likely, their presence and influence extended only to numbers, not to narrative, which was still by and large controlled by the talking heads of the mainstream media.

In the TV Today meeting, which was called to discuss the apprehensions raised by their legal team, once the anxieties over the continuation of the agreement were laid to rest, we indulged in some chit-chat. We asked the Aaj Tak team what they thought about the fact that the BJP was attracting the maximum support on the website. This was almost immediately laughed off by Qamar Waheed Naqvi, the then editorial head of Aaj Tak, who said that this must be due to 'manipulation'.

'The RSS has a special cell to manipulate such things to influence the mind of the media,' he said. That was perhaps the first time I had heard a journalist complaining about something like an 'IT cell' though the exact phrase was not used. To explain what he meant, Mr Naqvi talked about the time when he was the editor of some newspaper or magazine, and used to get many letters complaining about bias in coverage or expressing anger on some articles.

He claimed with confidence that all such letters were written by members of some special cell of the RSS, who were tasked with influencing the media. Convinced that those letters were not from the general public, he said that he used to throw them in the dustbin. He suspected that some similar cell must be manipulating the Political Stock Exchange data to show that the BJP had an edge in the 2009 Lok Sabha elections.

Mr Naqvi can surely say that he was not off the mark because the 2009 Lok Sabha elections saw the BJP losing both seats and vote share, when compared with their 2004 performance. It meant that the popularity of the BJP online, as reflected in that short-lived website we had created for Aaj Tak, was nowhere reflective of the ground realities.

But, did it essentially mean that the mismatch between the real and virtual world performances of the BJP was due to a group of people who were manipulating data? One could as well have concluded that the popularity of the BJP among the internet-using urban Indians was disproportionate. Why should the first reaction be about doubting the sanctity of data rather than seeing it in its proper context?

And regarding the 'Letters to the Editor', why should one conclude that anyone complaining about some political or ideological bias necessarily has to be an RSS member? Maybe those guys were also Sanghis who never went to any shakha. As an aside, while I was in high school, I had written a letter to the editor and sent it by post to the local Times of India office. It was even published, and I was so thrilled that I ended up sending many more letters, though I didn't get to see my name in print again.

In essence, rejecting those letters (by Mr Naqvi) meant rejecting feedback. Remember the communication theories, such as the 'magic bullet theory' of mass communication that I mentioned earlier? There was no place for feedback in such communication models.

Traditionally, there has been no meaningful avenue for reader's feedback in the mainstream media. 'Letters to the Editor' is the only avenue one can think of, and even that was being thrown in the dustbin. We were rarely encouraged to write letters to a local newspaper as feedback. In schools, our teachers would ask us to write such letters—as part of language classes—where we were supposed to talk about some lamp post in the area that was not working.

The mainstream media, rather the journalists, don't appear to have any appetite for feedback from the public. They still haven't changed and are loathsome of social media, where common readers can give them feedback—good, bad and often ugly.

I didn't make much of the comments made by Mr Naqvi back then. Honestly, he appeared to be a nice man and I don't hold those comments against him even today. Neither have I heard any scandalous things about him—something you get in plenty in the media industry.

The only 'controversial' thing that I heard about him was his resignation from India TV in April 2014—he had left Aaj Tak by then—allegedly to 'protest' against Narendra Modi's interview by India TV's Rajat Sharma, because he thought 'no tough questions' were asked by Sharma.

I will come to 2014 later, but in retrospect, his comments in 2009 reflected a rigid and closed mindset, where you reject divergent points of views by delegitimizing them as some organized attempt by a political organization.

Ironically, this trait of being rigid and not being open to dissenting views is known as being liberal in India. Such comments also betray that journalists have mostly been in a battle of ideologies, not ideas.

Nevertheless, the BJP's pitch for a strong government that would uproot terrorism didn't work, despite the multiple terror attacks and incidents such as the Batla House encounter, which took place just a few months prior to the scheduled elections of 2009.

As always, Pakistan was blamed for all terror attacks, but the issue of radical Islam, and how it was receiving support in domestic quarters aided by domestic politics, was hardly raised. Maybe the party tried to raise it, but the popular narrative was not conducive for it. The moment you try to talk about such issues, you'd be accused of trying to create a 'Hindu–Muslim issue' and using 'communal' means to win elections.

A controversy around 'communal' politics did arise, when a video clip of Varun Gandhi's speech during his campaign went viral. Varun was the BJP's candidate for the Pilibhit Lok Sabha seat. In that clip, he could be heard saying that the names of other parties' candidates sounded like the names of terrorists, such as Osama, to him.

He was apparently referring to the Muslim gangsters being given tickets by non-BJP parties, but was accused of stereotyping every Muslim as a terrorist. He further topped it by threatening to cut off the hands of any Muslim who dared to harm Hindus. This short clip was played over and over again on TV channels, and the BJP was accused of anti-Muslim hate speech. The BJP leaders had a tough time defending Varun in TV debates, though the party refused to drop him from their list of candidates or take any punitive action against him.

As a budding libertarian and someone who had read and liked Richard Dawkins, I was no fan of shielding Islam from criticism, but I was not impressed with this seemingly crude 'anti-Muslim rant' either. At least in the clip that went viral, Varun Gandhi was not really talking about Islamic extremism as such, and it indeed appeared that he was equating every Muslim with a terrorist, just because they had similar names.

Not that it affected my voting choice, because as always, I didn't vote. I was yet to vote in any parliamentary or assembly elections; so passive I was about electoral politics, supporting or opposing any political party or ideology with full gusto was unthinkable for me back then. I was a typical 'youth' who didn't make much of the voting process, thinking nothing is really going to change or the sky will not fall irrespective of who wins.

When the election results were declared in May 2009, the BJP had slipped even further, compared to its last performance in the 2004 Lok Sabha elections. It must have elated the seculars and depressed the real Sanghis, but I was not really bothered. I was actually happy with the results because the communists had lost badly, which meant that they won't be able to hold the government at ransom with their regressive economic ideas. The libertarian in me was happy. The Congressi Hindu in me was happy.

Unlike the 2004 Lok Sabha results that saw a rather accidental victory of the Congress and a shock defeat of the BJP, the 2009 verdict indisputably was a victory of the Congress, even though it had not got a majority of its own. If somehow the Congress were able to revive itself in UP and Bihar, it could have even dreamt of forming a government of its own and going back to the old days of glory.

However, it seemed as if the Congress had become comfortable being in power at the Centre through alliances. The party, which was supposed to be the default operating system of a computer called India—in the words of Rahul Gandhi—was happy being one of the frequently used programs of the computer.

Maybe one of the reasons the Congress was happy with this was because its main rival, the BJP, appeared to get only weaker. After the Lok Sabha loss, the BJP failed to win in Maharashtra and Jharkhand assembly elections, which were held later in 2009. The BJP however formed a post-poll alliance in Jharkhand and supported the JMM (Jharkhand Mukti Morcha) to keep the Congress out, but the JMM was notorious for being politically promiscuous. The Congress would have thought that there was nothing to worry because such allies could dump the BJP any time.

Coincidentally, this was also the period when many Indians started getting online. If you look at the numbers, 2009 is one of the years that saw a sharper growth in the number of users who started using the internet in India.[51] Facebook had rapidly started to replace Orkut as the preferred place to hang out online. Facebook also had better features in terms of sharing and making things viral. Twitter too had started getting popular, especially after Congress leader Shashi Tharoor made that 'cattle class' tweet, which became a controversy and grabbed the headlines in the mainstream media.

For the uninitiated, in September 2009, the Congress had launched an 'austerity drive' to cut the costs of running the government. Not just ministers, Congress leaders too were expected to be austere and adopt means to save money. Tharoor, who was then the minister of state for external affairs, had already got embroiled in a controversy, as media reports suggested that he was staying in a 5-star hotel instead of a government accommodation. Though Tharoor clarified that he was paying from his own pocket, he was asked by his party to move out of the luxury hotel.

In the wake of this, he was asked by journalist Kanchan Gupta on Twitter whether he would be flying cattle class—a slang for economy class in airlines—the next time he visited Kerala, his home state. Tharoor replied, 'Absolutely, in cattle class out of solidarity with all our holy cows!'

This created a controversy and people questioned whether the union minister had insulted the middle class of India by terming them as 'cattle class'. It was a silly controversy, and most people on Twitter knew that Tharoor didn't mean it that way, but the popular narrative was still being set by the mainstream media. Tharoor had to apologize for his remarks. The Congress party did not support him on this matter either. I think they were more offended by the term 'holy cows', which appeared to refer to the Congress high command Sonia Gandhi. Earlier, she had taken a flight in the economy class, and which was perhaps the trigger for the question put by Kanchan Gupta.

Tharoor was known as a prolific writer and speaker, and someone who could have become the Secretary-General of the United Nations, thus bringing laurels to India. This was his first year in Congress, and I think the party thought that the earlier he was disciplined, the better.

I don't know how that controversy impacted Shashi Tharoor—he definitely is a loyal and disciplined servant of the party and the Gandhis now—but it certainly had a positive impact on Twitter. Newspaper headlines and TV debates around his 'controversial tweet' gave free advertisement to Twitter. Many signed up on Twitter out of curiosity to check out the tweet that almost took the job away from a minister! I myself decided to use it more effectively to promote *Faking News*. Incidentally, Tharoor started following *Faking News* (i.e., me) on Twitter soon after.

It won't be an exaggeration to say that Twitter subsequently led the change in popular narrative in India. Unlike today, when Twitter is employing more and more censorship tools and increasingly appearing to be an ideological ally of the cultural Left, back then Twitter was the quintessential free and independent platform that democratized the narrative. Twitter was liberal then, it is woke now.

Debates happened on Twitter, even though in painfully limited characters, and counter-views were not suppressed as they were in the mainstream media. Ideas that often originated on Twitter were featured in blogs and Facebook posts, and they travelled far.

The criticism of the media that was earlier limited to a few blogs—such as the critical post written about the media's coverage of the 2008 Mumbai terror attacks—was now getting a bigger audience on Twitter. Television journalism, especially, came under attack for sensationalism and discussing non-issues to increase TRP.

One of the reasons for the popularity of *Faking News* on Twitter was the name itself, as it was parody of the term 'Breaking News' that the TV news channels had started overusing. Articles that satirized the news media generally got more attention and were decently popular.

The growth in internet users and the phenomenon of new narratives being born in places like Twitter, proved to be one of the most favourable developments for the Hindutva supporters. They were waiting for something like this. With no gatekeepers or censorship involved, as in the mainstream media, they could now offer their points of view to the masses.

The people's letters to the editor, which were earlier being thrown in dustbins by Left-leaning editors, were now being published online, 140 characters at a time.

How the narrative shifted

Things were going fine for the Congress for around a year after the 2009 Lok Sabha elections victory before they were caught in an avalanche of corruption charges.

It started with the Comptroller and Auditor General (CAG) report published in April 2010, which talked about the 2G scam. Earlier, there had been stories about little-known firms getting licenses and later being acquired by big telecom companies, leading to speculations whether this was done as part of some fixed match. Now, the CAG report put a number to the presumptive loss to the government exchequer—₹1.76 lakhs crores—which went on to make big headlines in the following weeks.

Initially the Congress stood by A. Raja, the telecom minister under whom the 2G spectrum licenses were sold, but towards the end of 2010, they started feeling the heat. Raja's party, DMK, stood by him throughout the fiasco, claiming he was being targeted because he was a Dalit. But these arguments didn't cut ice with the majority of the people, as the narrative around corruption kept growing stronger.

Around June 2010, as people still wondered about the sheer expanse of the 2G scam due to the humongous numbers being quoted, news started coming in about the mismanagement and irregularities in organizing the Commonwealth Games (CWG), which were slated to be held later that year in October. Congress leader Suresh Kalmadi became the second face of corruption under UPA-II. He was the Chairman of the CWG organizing committee as well as the long-serving president of the Indian Olympic Association, which oversaw the preparations and management of such events.

From allegations about inflated bills in procuring materials, sporting equipment and even toilet papers for the event, to allegations of taking bribes in awarding contracts, the CWG scam had it all. It was further marred by mismanagement as the venues didn't appear to be on the path of being readied on time. There were concerns whether India was heading towards an international embarrassment.

For the common public, the details of the CWG scam were easier to understand and talk about than the 'complicated' 2G scam. They could even see where the money was being wasted or how it was being looted, unlike the 2G scam that literally was about an invisible spectrum.

Barely a month ahead of the scheduled start of the games, a foot-over bridge that was constructed as part of the CWG infrastructure collapsed, triggering massive outrage. Engineers from the Army had to be called in, who rebuilt the bridge in just four days, which led to further outrage about the quality of work done by the government agencies.

Some athletes from other countries announced that they feared for their safety and didn't want to come to India for the Games, while some others complained about the bad facilities. Lalit Bhanot, the second-in-command after Kalmadi for organizing the games, created further outrage and anger by declaring that the Indian standards of hygiene and cleanliness were different from those in the Western countries, and thus the complaints by the athletes were just a matter of perception.

The huge numbers mentioned in the 2G scam and the negative stories of the CWG scam led the Congress party and the UPA government to lose the narrative, just a year after coming back to power. Further, a man from their own party added to their embarrassment. It was Mani Shankar Aiyar, who went on an unhinged tirade against the Commonwealth Games.[52]

Aiyar declared that he will be happy if the Games failed, as it will 'teach India a lesson' not to waste time and money on such events. He wished so because India was a poor country, which should be focusing on 'real issues' than trying to 'show off' to the world that she could host international sporting events—a typical Brown Sahib mentality that wonders why should a country launch satellites when there are people below the poverty line. I think the Sanghis should someday felicitate Mani Shankar Aiyar and Digvijay Singh for their crucial roles in shifting the narrative away from the Congress and secularism.

While both the 2G and CWG scams dented the Congress-led UPA government's image—which they tried to salvage later by getting rid of A. Raja and Suresh Kalmadi from the government and party, respectively—it didn't exactly shift the ideological narrative towards the 'Right'.

The political narrative evidently shifted away from the Congress due to the scams, but the shift in the ideological narrative was incidentally triggered due to anger against the mainstream media. And coincidentally, the first incident that dented the mainstream media's image happened almost in parallel with the news of these scams coming out.

In June 2010, the Press Council of India (PCI) came up with a rather average report on the problem of 'paid news' in the media. PCI had appointed a committee after receiving complaints from some journalists themselves about this phenomenon, where newspapers were providing or denying news coverage to any party or politician based on the kind of money they could pay to the media houses. It wasn't just positive coverage that was given in lieu of money, even negative news was published against rivals if the party or a leader paid enough.

Apparently, the 2009 Lok Sabha elections had seen this practice of paid news being adopted by many on a widespread level, which led to such complaints. Even relatively small publications are believed to have earned crores of rupees by publishing news reports and articles that favoured particular candidates or painted opposition candidates or parties in negative light. The readers consumed the information thinking those were objective analysis and observations by 'neutral journalists', but in reality they were paid for advertisements.

I had heard about such claims before the controversy of 'paid news' became public. After coming back to Delhi from Ahmedabad in 2008, I had been living with a couple of journalist friends. During the 2009 Lok Sabha elections, when I was busy working on that project for TV Today, my flatmate had told me that many reporters and editors had earned a good amount of money by publishing paid news.

I didn't take him too seriously then, thinking it was the usual exaggeration that journalists indulge in by extrapolating a few individual experiences to the entire universe. But now it seems that it was a real issue that was plaguing the industry, which is why the PCI subsequently constituted a committee to look into it. The committee was supposed to check the veracity of these allegations and propose solutions to combat paid news.

When it was finally published and put up for public consumption, the PCI report was criticized for being a 'watered down' version of what it was apparently supposed to be. It was alleged that the report had been deliberately delayed and diluted under pressure.[53]

The report indeed read like a glorified essay on the topic rather than a serious paper that attempted to look into the specifics and provide effective solutions. While it acknowledged that the paid news phenomenon was real and the elections saw its worst form, it didn't name anyone who indulged in paid news, nor did it cite incidents that could have indirectly identified the culprits, and the solutions it proposed were really simplistic.

Since the report did not name anyone or any incidents, it largely remained an academic criticism. However, it introduced the term 'paid news', which was going to be used often in the future by the 'trolls', who would further use variants like 'paid media' and other unparliamentary versions.

Ideas or information don't get viral by themselves; they need accompanying stories and story-tellers who can connect with the masses. The PCI report had no stories as it didn't name anyone, while the story-tellers were mostly the journalists who were talking to each other about an issue that they thought was an internal matter of the industry.

But in November 2010, another incident took place, and this time it had many stories, and it attracted many story-tellers—the Radia tapes controversy.

It all started with online murmurings and some tweets alleging that there were some leaked tapes that contained telephonic call recordings of some journalists, which showed them working for corporate houses and lobbying for political parties.

These phone calls had been recorded by investigating agencies while probing the 2G scam. Copies of the tapes containing these recorded calls were apparently leaked and sent to some lawyers and media houses in sealed envelopes by a whistle-blower. On Twitter, it was alleged that the news was being supressed because many big names from the field of journalism were involved.

Journalists were mostly tight-lipped about the whole controversy, especially those on Twitter, except someone like J. Gopikrishnan, who had originally broken the stories about the 2G scam in *The Pioneer* newspaper. He had reported about Niira Radia and her phones being tapped in April 2010 itself, though names of any journalist were not published then.[54] Now the tapes were being talked about, and people were wondering who the journalists were.

I (as *Faking News*) wasn't too vocal about it, but many Right-wing accounts were. I was still a libertarian, not a Sanghi, and tapping of phone calls being an 'invasion of privacy' was one of the things that bothered me rather than rumours about journalists being power brokers. Additionally, having seen how some journalists indeed used to be allies of politicians during my short stint in media houses earlier, I thought this was not a big deal.

Further, I wasn't really hostile to the celebrity journalists around that time. In fact, on many occasions I had been invited to be a part of their TV shows by the likes of Barkha Dutt, Rajdeep Sardesai, Ravish Kumar, Nidhi Razdan and others, and maybe that was an additional factor why I didn't take them on.

But there were accounts like MediaCrooks that had become quite popular by then. It took on the mainstream media and celebrity journalists head on,[55] and mercilessly if I may add. 'Ravinar' was so popular that on several occasions the title of his blog posts ended up becoming trending topics on Twitter in India, so widely were they shared.

Unlike my criticism of the media, which was mostly benign, sarcastic and came from a libertarian point of view, criticism by MediaCrooks was sharp, scathing and with a declared and definitive Hindutva point of view. The articles on his blog would seldom be something that would ever be published by a mainstream media house, but they were well-written. MediaCrooks was surely among the early voices online that made many people realize that the mainstream media had a problem of ideological bias.

Once influential accounts like his and other users started talking about the Radia tapes, and once the information spilled over to Facebook from Twitter, it became increasingly clear that it was just a matter of time before the details came out in public. And they came out in style.

Two magazines—*Outlook* and *Open*—uploaded the audio files and transcripts of the call records on their websites, making them easily accessible to the public. They made the leaked tapes their cover story in the print copies too. They even put outdoor ads of their cover story, one of which had the faces of the journalists who featured in these tapes. Suddenly, journalists had become news stories. It was a turning point in the news industry.

Names such as Barkha Dutt, Vir Sanghvi, Prabhu Chawla, M.K. Venu and many others featured in the tapes. All of them were heard talking in very friendly and helpful manner with Niira Radia, a public relations professional plus corporate lobbyist, whose PR company had Tata Group and Reliance Industries as clients. In many of these conversations, Radia was seen as someone who was keenly interested in the cabinet formation. She appeared to be lobbying to make A. Raja the telecom minister again in the UPA-II government.

Raja was accused of the 2G spectrum scam during the UPA-I government, so why was Radia pushing for him to become the telecom minister again? Was she acting on behalf of some of her corporate clients who wanted the telecom ministry to go to Raja again as some sort of reward or in expectations of future gains? Many such questions were raised about the nature of these calls.

And questions were also raised about why these journalists appeared so comfortable interacting with a corporate lobbyist. Were they taking editorial notes from a lobbyist and passing them on to the public as independent pieces of information? Were they also part of the lobbying process? Were they helping in fixing ministries? The topics and tone of some of the leaked calls appeared to answer these questions in the affirmative.

Barkha Dutt became the face and centre of a controversy yet again. 'Tell me what should I tell them?' was the title of a transcript that *Open* magazine had published, which contained her conversations with Radia, and which were about the talks that broke down between the DMK and the Congress.[56] That particular line, which one could hear in Dutt's voice, was taken to mean that she was acting as a courier for passing information between two political parties that indulged in a power tussle over ministerial berths. Dutt later broke her silence and rejected the allegations and interpretation of that line, but by then, this perception had gained much ground.

Journalists were fixers, they brokered political deals, they worked for political lobbyists—such sentiments started growing as the media was forced to discuss the Radia tapes after the magazines made them public.

For the common person, the revelation that there was a nexus between journalists and politicians was somewhat similar to the revelations of links between the underworld and the Bollywood (when such news reports first appeared). An average TV news viewer felt the same way that an average movie lover had felt back then—that their heroes were heroes on screen only. Off screen, they had feet of clay. Everyone is sold, everyone is part of a cartel—'Sab bike huye hain, sab mile huye hain'—such sentiments grew stronger and someone was to take advantage of it soon.

This anger against the mainstream media pushed many people to explore ideas and narratives that were contrary to what talking heads in journalism, especially those who were 'caught' in the Radia tapes, would profess. And this is where many ordinary social media users, even if they didn't know what Hindutva was, started warming up to accounts like MediaCrooks.

I too followed him on Twitter. Although later he attacked me, that is, *Faking News* for 'selling out' to Network18. But, I have to admit that he played a crucial role in the change of narrative, especially on Twitter. Under mounting pressure over the 2G spectrum scam, Raja had to resign as the telecom minister in November 2010. The Radia tapes too had become the talking point around the same time. As a result, journalists were being directly linked to political corruption, which had become a huge issue by the end of 2010.

By this time, Modi was yet to become a national alternative, at least for people like me. While online buzz had started about his good governance record, which focused on development, he was still to become a political heavyweight on the national stage. There were just too many challenges in front of him to rise up to the national stage. The biggest challenge was that of 'acceptability'.

The 2010 Bihar assembly elections took place towards the end of 2010, by which time the Congress had started losing the narrative around corruption, Modi was 'forbidden' from campaigning for the ruling BJP-JD(U) [Janata Dal (United)] alliance. This was done apparently on the insistence of JD(U) supremo Nitish Kumar, and the BJP had to oblige. Modi was indeed kept out from the campaigning in Bihar.

Earlier in June 2010, Nitish Kumar, as the chief minister of Bihar, had returned a donation of ₹5 crore that Modi, as the chief minister of Gujarat, had given to Bihar in 2008 for flood relief. Kumar claimed that Modi had 'insulted' the people of Bihar by putting up advertisements in newspapers about that donation, which was given two years ago. Due to such incidents, it was assumed that Modi will find it challenging to make it to the national level, and it also contained the risk of the BJP losing its allies.

Perhaps, the Radia tape controversy came just at the right time for Modi. Since he was hardly a favourite leader of the mainstream media and celebrity journalists, anger against the media indirectly helped him too. And it definitely helped the overall ideological shift towards the Right wing, as people started distrusting the mainstream media and the journalists, who broadly leaned Left in sociocultural matters.

Earlier, it was fashionable to attack and mock only politicians, bureaucrats and celebrities, but now media houses and journalists were added to that list. The criticism of the media, which was earlier limited to them being TRP chasers or sensationalist, was now extended to include criticism of their bias, agenda and deeds. This is where the Sanghis had an upper hand. The Radia tapes thus proved to be a blessing in disguise in more ways than one.

Vinod Mehta, the editor of *Outlook*—one of the two magazines that published the Radia tapes—had revealed that NDTV had banned him from appearing on the group channels as punishment for publishing the stories about the Radia tapes. This only added to the resentment against the big media houses and celebrity journalists, and people wanted to attack and mock NDTV.

One of the ways of mocking NDTV was to turn the phrase 'Blow to Modi' into a joke because NDTV had become predictable with its use. So, while you might not be a big fan of Modi, you would use this template as a joke to target NDTV in the aftermath of the Radia tapes controversy, and in the process, all the blows that NDTV had managed against Modi till then, softened a bit.

Non-allied alliance of the Left and Right

Incidentally, the leftists too had their problems with the mainstream 'corporate' media, because they thought the media was not leftist enough, especially in economic matters. The leftists solemnly believed that the media ought to have a leftist bias in order to be 'responsible'. The Radia tapes were an abhorrence for them too, but for different reasons. While the Sanghis focused on the 'journalists helping the Congress' part of the Radia tapes, the leftists focused on the 'journalists helping the corporate houses' part.

The Left's criticism of the 'corporate media' had been running almost since the 1990s, both in the West and in India, but these criticisms were too academic and too laborious for the common people to understand and process. Basically, the Left didn't have 'wokes' at that time, who could tone down the criticism in memes and forwards and make it appear cool.

The non-Left had the memes and parodies though. They came from the libertarians and the Sanghis. Journalists joining Twitter further helped this process, because they exposed themselves to public scrutiny of their beliefs, arguments and behaviour. They came across as flawed and superficial on many occasions, or ignorant and stupid on others.

Many ended up being parodied due to their predictability.

This unusual alliance of the Left and Right was present not just during the Radia tapes controversy, but for most part of the UPA-II tenure. It wasn't an 'alliance' technically, as there was no written or assumed partnership, but the targets of criticism and attack were common.

On the Right side, Libertarians and Sanghis had their own reasons to mock the media or the government. There was no alliance between these two either, but they ended up helping each other. For me personally, the anti-government satire worked well and so did my tweets or articles mocking the media. I got valuable and monetizable traffic to the website and the number of followers on social media also increased, so I had no reason not to indulge in it. An ideological reason was there too—the libertarian in me wanted free market and capitalist policies to be pursued by the government, while the ideas championed by Sonia Gandhi's NAC (National Advisory Council), which was the real power centre, were all socialist.

On the Left side, there were committed leftists, who thought the Congress was not being socialist enough. Further, UPA-II had declared an all-out war against the Naxals, which was popularly referred to as Operation Green Hunt. This was launched within months of the Congress coming back to power in 2009. Many so-called activists were detained or arrested. Arundhati Roy had come up with a long laborious fiction, painting the Naxals as the innocent Na'vi species (from the Hollywood movie *Avatar*) and the Indian state as the selfish brute occupying force, which aimed to uproot and destroy them and their habitat.

In April 2010, 74 CRPF men were killed by the Maoists in the Dantewada district of Chhattisgarh. The incident was reportedly celebrated by the leftists at JNU.[57] They took it as the defeat of an oppressive state in the ongoing war, where the UPA government was the belligerent force; by the way, such incidents and events at JNU did not feature in prime-time TV debates until after Modi won.

Then towards the end of 2010, there was unrest in Kashmir over alleged fake encounters. Arundhati Roy, again, poked her nose, and that is when I had written an open letter against her, which went viral, earning me Right-wing fans and making me a figure of hate among the committed leftists—something I have mentioned in the introduction of this book.

Incidentally the 2010 protests in Kashmir, which were purportedly about fake encounters by the Indian security forces, had turned into a protest against the burning of the Holy Quran. The sacred book of Muslims was rumoured to have been burnt thousands of miles away in New York, while violent protests were held in Kashmir and in some other parts of India.

A US pastor had announced that he would be burning a few copies of the Quran on September 11, 2010, as 'punishment' for the September 11 attacks of 2001, but the burning didn't take place on that date. However, many people were killed in protests all over the world. In Kashmir too, over a dozen people were killed. The protestors had set a Christian missionary-run school on fire to avenge the threat of burning the Quran.[58]

Not a word about this insane behaviour was uttered by the likes of Arundhati Roy, who painted the raging Islamists as innocent people who were wronged. She virtually called for the independence of Kashmir in her writings and speeches thereafter. As a result, there were demands to arrest her under sedition charges, but the then Home Minister P. Chidambaram said that there was no need to act against her. He had justified his decision with a cryptic 'Not taking action is also an action.'

Perhaps those words epitomized what the Congress was doing, rather not doing, and thinking towards the end of 2010, which could be argued to be the inflexion point in the shift of narrative away from the Congress— you had problems in Kashmir, you had an ongoing domestic war against the Naxals and Maoists, you had charges of massive corruption in the 2G and CWG scams, inflation was at an all-time high since 1999 and you had the halo of the media and journalism, which was part of your broad ecosystem, taken away—and you thought that 'not taking action was also an action.'

But, in January 2011, the Congress got a stick to beat the BJP on the issue of corruption. The Karnataka governor had sanctioned the prosecution of the then Chief Minister and senior BJP leader B.S. Yediyurappa. The case helped the talking heads in the media to claim that there was no difference between the Congress and the BJP, so far as the issue of corruption was concerned.

This was almost similar to what had happened after the multiple terror attacks. The anger was not directed at the ruling Congress, but against the ruling political class. Similarly, with the Yediyurappa angle to the rescue, the anger and resentment around corruption was also directed at the entire political class, and not just the Congress.

This entire narrative against corruption and political class was further amplified by the 'India against Corruption' movement led by Anna Hazare, which hit TV screens in April 2011, just a day after India had won the cricket world cup. It seemed as if the euphoria around the world cup victory, which had come after a gap of almost three decades, was transferred to the Anna movement.

Though the Anna movement was primarily directed against scams that took place under the UPA regime, many people associated with it targeted the entire political class. Anna Hazare had once ended up saying that Gujarat, then governed by Narendra Modi, didn't have any major problem of corruption, but soon his team members had to intervene and 'correct' him. Anna clarified soon afterwards that his statement shouldn't be seen as an endorsement of Modi or the 'Gujarat model' of governance.

Team Anna, as they were called, further pointed out the charges against Yediyurappa, and argued that every political party was corrupt. The 'Sab mile huye hain' sentiment, which was triggered during the Radia tapes controversy, was now the all-pervasive sentiment around the anti-corruption movement.

The BJP subsequently gave in to this narrative and Yediyurappa had to resign as the chief minister of Karnataka in July 2011. Perhaps the BJP thought that this will show them as being a party with a difference, but it only went on to reinforce the narrative that for every Kalmadi in the Congress, there was a Yediyurappa in the BJP.

Yediyurappa consequently went on to quit the BJP for being treated unfairly and formed his own party, which proved to be one of the reasons why the BJP lost Karnataka in the 2013 assembly elections.

While the BJP tried to 'appease' the Anna movement, even though it painted the entire political class as corrupt, the Congress tried to claim that the Anna movement was some clandestine project by the RSS.

Obviously, that didn't cut ice with most people, because that indeed was not the truth. The anti-corruption movement or the Anna movement was a mysterious fight between the Congress and the ecosystem that it had nurtured all these decades. Arvind Kejriwal, the architect of the entire movement, was anything but a Sanghi.

There were a couple of names from the movement who later went on to join the BJP, such as Kiran Bedi and General V.K. Singh, but the majority of the influential and founding members of the Anna movement were nowhere pro-BJP or pro-RSS. People like Prashant Bhushan, Yogendra Yadav, Swami Agnivesh, Medha Patkar and others were as anti-Hindutva as anyone can ever be.

I think the Congress erred massively by claiming that the anti-corruption movement was an RSS-sponsored drama. They indirectly ended up telling many urban Indians that the RSS was perhaps not so bad. They undid their own propaganda of decades, where the RSS was linked with issues that were farcical, hateful and regressive. The Anna movement on the other hand was seen as an apolitical, secular and 'honest' movement.

The movement had almost unequivocal and unconditional support from the mainstream media, because many members of Team Anna came from the same ecosystem from which the journalists came. Consequently, there was no dearth of good PR for the team and the movement. By associating the RSS with the Anna movement, the Congress ended up giving good PR to the RSS too.

Imagine, for decades the same mainstream media was careful enough to make sure that the RSS was never seen as a 'respectable' organization, but the Congress messed it up by associating the RSS with something that the media was all set to paint as respectable and righteous. The Sanghis must pause here and say a heartfelt thanks to Digvijay Singh, who was at the forefront of blaming the RSS for the Anna movement.

I personally was never impressed by the entire idea of a Lokpal bill being a panacea for corruption, which was the main pitch of the Anna movement. How can a new law remove corruption, which was systemic, I wondered? By then, I was convinced that corruption was an offshoot of the socialist legacy and the outcome of an idealist illusion, where politicians are supposed to serve selflessly and where profit-making is seen as a sin.

I was rather impressed with libertarian solutions, such as 'legalizing' bribery and institutionalizing lobbying, where bribes or kickbacks transform into performance bonuses. People will make money, which everyone wants to, but not by taking 'cuts' and commissions and hampering the quality of public work, but by earning incentives and bonuses for ensuring better quality of work, which benefits everyone. The libertarian in me believed that the solutions lay in free markets, not in more and more regulation. I found the Anna Hazare movement just good for TV and drama.

But I certainly marvelled at the public and media support that the movement attracted. A big chunk of youth, who had become passive and uninterested in politics or social issues, suddenly found something to talk about. Having a photograph of the septuagenarian Anna Hazare as a display picture on social media was almost a proof that the user was a young urban Indian, possibly just a teenager.

Arvind Kejriwal, too, was slowly but steadily becoming popular. The youth had started idolizing him as well, apart from Anna. That he was an IIT alumnus also helped his image a lot. Supporting Team Anna meant supporting a loving and caring grandfather like Anna Hazare, and also a logical and educated elder brother like Arvind Kejriwal. The youth didn't want the maai-baap Congress, as they had now found the dada-bhaiya anti-corruption crusaders.

Associating such a movement with the RSS would indeed have led many people in urban India, especially the youngsters, to think that the RSS was after all not a bad organization. How can anyone supporting a movement against corruption be bad?

While most of Team Anna's core members were not pro-Hindutva, the RSS had made public statements saying that it supported the Anna movement for the greater public good. This made the Congress double down on its claim that the Anna movement was indeed the handiwork of the RSS.

This set alarm bells ringing in the core team of Anna, which realized that they had to make sure that the RSS or pro-Hindutva guys don't benefit due to this reckless move by the Congress and some smart statements by the RSS. This was the reason why they actively kept a saffron-clad Baba Ramdev away from the mainstream anti-corruption movement, and replaced the picture of Bharat Mata with that of Mahatma Gandhi on the stage where Anna Hazare fasted for the second time in August 2011, this time during Ramzan, the Islamic month of fasting.[59]

However, by then, the Anna movement and its perceived RSS connection had already mainstreamed the Sangh in some sections of young India, which otherwise was rather uncaring and indifferent to politics. The Sangh generally doesn't appear to have any strategy to reach out to and influence this bunch, but now they had a window, thanks to Congress!

'RSS ka haath hai' (The RSS is behind this) became a joke to target the corrupt Congress like 'Blow to Modi' had become to target the corrupt media. The RSS indirectly gained acceptability, first in the lexicon, and then in the narrative.

In a way, the Anna movement was a mini Janata Party experiment for the RSS. The RSS supported the movement, even though they were not treated as a welcome ally after the movement gained prominence and acquired influence.

The 'secular-liberal ecosystem' becomes uncomfortable the moment it sees an alien element trying to become a part of it. They make sure that this alien element is weeded out. It happened during the Janata Party government, then during the V.P. Singh government and on a very limited scale with the Anna movement. The RSS or Hindutva is never welcome in the ecosystem, which otherwise is comfortable accommodating all kinds of elements.

7

Hindutva vs the 'Ecosystem'

The anti-Hindutva ecosystem

It is a little intriguing why the same ecosystem that was nurtured and nourished well by the Congress party ended up giving it a fatal blow in the popular narrative through the 2011 anti-corruption movement, which had the face of Anna Hazare and brains of the likes of Arvind Kejriwal, Yogendra Yadav and Prashant Bhushan.

But before that, one has to understand what exactly is this secular-liberal ecosystem—a term that I must have used over a 100 times in this book. One may wonder how can the same people, who had attacked or criticized the Congress not just in 2011 but even on many earlier occasions, be accused of being part of something that sounds like a Congress-supporting outfit.

The best way to comprehend this is to understand the word itself. Most probably, the first time you came across the word 'ecosystem' was in your high-school biology classes. All animals, including human beings, plants, land, the water bodies and the air in a particular geographical unit are defined as parts of an ecosystem. There is a common source of energy in this ecosystem—the sun—and this energy keeps all of them alive. The energy passes from one to another in the form of food chain. If one of the constituent units is removed, the entire ecosystem risks collapsing.

The key element is interdependence, not alliance or union.

It is not rare or unimaginable to see the constituents of an ecosystem attacking each other. If you take the case of ecological ecosystem, the food chain itself is proof of how they 'attack' each other, even to the extent of killing and eating each other! Essentially, the ecosystem is not a syndicate, where members must stick to some strict rules and where they must not oppose each other.

Take the case of communists, for example, and their place in this secular-liberal ecosystem. While the communist parties have always been the rivals of the Congress party, so far as electoral politics is concerned, the Congress co-opted the communist ideologues to a large extent, right from the time of Nehru itself. As I had mentioned earlier in the chapter on 'Congressi Hindus', the communists then gained a crucial foothold in the corridors of power during the Indira Gandhi days.

Many Left-leaning ideologues or intellectuals can point to various incidents when they stood up to the Congress, as proof of their 'independence'. But that doesn't negate the 'interdependence'.

The CPI (Communist Party of India), in fact, didn't even oppose the imposition of Emergency by Indira Gandhi, though many leftists can say that their 'intellectuals' had spoken up. They can similarly cite them for speaking up against Rajiv Gandhi on issues like Bofors and when he tried to censor the press through his defamation bills. They can even claim that their opposition led to Indira and Rajiv losing the subsequent Lok Sabha elections.

However, the truth is that most of them bask in reflected glory. Both Indira and Rajiv were defeated not because of an intellectual uprising but because the rival political parties formed a potent unified opposition, where they let go of various personal and ideological differences to unite under one banner. If the Sanghis had not extended support on either of these occasions, the results could have been different. But, Sanghis are never given that credit by the ecosystem.

There is no doubt that the intellectuals or the intelligentsia of India have criticized and opposed the Congress multiple times, and that's how they appear 'neutral' or 'independent' to a common Indian, but hardly any of them have attacked any member of the Nehru–Gandhi family with the same viciousness that they have attacked someone like Modi. The ecosystem has always been soft on the family.

The ecosystem doesn't harbour any special dislike or ill-will for the Nehru–Gandhi family, because it has only flourished whenever someone from the family has been in power. It's well-known and obvious that some of them are literally devotees (yes, 'bhakts') of someone like Nehru. The historian-cum-cricket-expert-cum-conscious-keeper-cum-columnist-cum-activist Ramachandra Guha is a renowned specimen of such a 'bhakt'. When it comes to other members of the family, the fawning devotion might not be as brazen as in the case of Nehru, but the ecosystem players make sure that their criticism is not caustic.

As I write this, the most recurring theme of criticism of Modi by the so-called intellectuals is how there is an 'undeclared emergency' in the country. All that they have to offer in support of this claim are hyperbolical histrionics. Modi is a despot who somehow allows them to shout every day on every platform that he is a despot. Comparison of Modi with Hitler is tossed around regularly by the same bunch. Again, Modi is such a Hitler that he allows this comparison to go unchecked, almost on a daily basis.

If Modi has spectacularly failed at something, he evidently has failed to be the despot and Hitler that he is supposed to be in the eyes of the liberals.

Talking of despots and Hitler, one of the first things that led Hitler to acquire dictatorial power was the Reichstag Fire Decree. In February 1933, the president of Germany issued an emergency order, which was based on Article 48 of the German Constitution, on the advice of Chancellor Adolf Hitler, which massively curbed many civil liberties and led to the imprisonment of many of his political opponents.

Cut to India in June 1975, when the president of India issued an emergency order, which was based on Article 352 of the Indian Constitution, on the advice of Prime Minister Indira Gandhi, which massively curbed many civil liberties and led to the imprisonment of many of her political opponents.

Despite this chilling parallel, how many times has Indira been called Hitler by the intelligentsia? On the other hand, Modi is compared with Hitler based on ridiculously loose parallels on every possible occasion.

It's the same with Rajiv Gandhi too. The ecosystem players never cease to claim that Modi had tried to justify the 2002 post-Godhra riots by saying that 'Every action has an equal and opposite reaction'. Now consider this—2002 was veritably the first televised communal riots of India, but where is the video clip of this alleged statement of Modi where he is supposed to have justified the killings of Muslims as a revenge for Hindus being burnt alive? In the era of TV, shouldn't it have been played again and again on TV, and in the era of internet, shouldn't it have gone viral?

Such a clip is not viral because Modi never said such words to justify the riots. On the other hand, Rajiv Gandhi literally justified the 1984 anti-Sikh riots by saying, 'When a big tree falls, the earth shakes.' The video clip of him saying so was hardly ever played on TV. It became public more than 30 years after he said it. A lawyer named H.S. Phoolka somehow managed to get a recording of it from the archives, and only then people could see and hear Rajiv saying these words.

The point I'm trying to make is that the ecosystem is meticulously soft on the Nehru–Gandhi family. Poor Rahul Gandhi comes under attack once in a while these days, but it's mostly because he has not been winning elections. If in the future he becomes the prime minister, the same set of guys would race against each other to write how great he is and how misunderstood he was during the 'dark days' of India, when the country was ruled by a fascist Modi.

By attacking the Congress on various occasions, and by offering token criticisms of the members of the Nehru–Gandhi family, the ecosystem is able to present itself as independent, non-partisan and 'anti-establishment', but effectively it helps both the Congress as well as the Nehru–Gandhi family because others, especially the Sanghis, are criticized more scathingly and much more frequently, leaving a common person to believe that the Congress is the best option among all.

As I had mentioned earlier, over decades the Congress party has become a party that practically has no distinct and definite ideology. Its current ideology is just to survive and self-preserve, and to keep someone from the Nehru–Gandhi family in power. This has only made the Congress a preferable option for the ecosystem, as they can get the party to work on their pet projects without any ideological opposition.

By not viciously attacking the Nehru–Gandhi family, the ecosystem makes sure that it is at least supporting half of the Congress party's non-ideology, that is, of keeping someone from the Nehru–Gandhi family in power. It additionally buys peace and patronage from the family by behaving that way. And most importantly, in the eyes of the common man, the ecosystem appears 'neutral' and not an ally of the Congress, because it is seen as attacking the party and its policies on various occasions.

Even when the Congress party had some ideology to talk about, it didn't have any major ideological differences with this ecosystem. We will soon know why. But practically, it was not just the Congress that ruled India, it was also the ecosystem that ruled India. This ecosystem *is* the establishment.

The establishment is an entrenched bunch of people and institutions that systematically control the thoughts and beliefs of the masses. It is often achieved via control on the media and academics. The establishment also aims to control the citizens' speeches and actions, so that the status quo is maintained, and counter-thoughts and movements are supressed. This control is achieved through judiciary, and through advocacy and activism.

For example, the establishment can launch a campaign to remove you from modern tech platforms if your thoughts are not aligned with them. Or, if you are a regular employed civilian, they can launch a campaign to put pressure on your employer to remove you from your job. It is to ensure that you're left with no choice but to surrender, and that is the real power of the establishment.

The establishment does not comprise the bunch of people who sit in government offices for a 5-year term after winning the elections. Such political power is transient, but the power that a real establishment enjoys is potent and lasting.

It doesn't mean that political power means nothing. After all, to make sure that 'your people' become the real establishment, you need political power too. The Congress played that role for the most part, by winning election after election.

However, the birth of this establishment, or the origin of this ecosystem, predates even the birth of the Congress. We will come to that soon.

The ecosystem not attacking the Nehru–Gandhi family acerbically was seen during the anti-corruption movement too. None of the influential leaders of Team Anna, especially someone like Arvind Kejriwal, took the name of Sonia Gandhi as one of the corrupt leaders who should be kicked out.

Had Anna Hazare's fast ended differently, say without the whole acrimony where the Congress tried to attack the movement and brand it as RSS-sponsored, it would have only helped the Congress. Perhaps, the ideal end to the entire drama would have been Rahul Gandhi promising to constitute the office of the Lokpal, and endlessly played TV visuals where he is seen offering a glass of orange juice to Anna Hazare, ending his fast-unto-death pledge.

The cases of corruption, such as 2G, CWG, coal scam, would have been effortlessly blamed on Manmohan Singh in the popular narrative, which would have been built once Rahul Gandhi became UPA-III prime minister in 2014.

A few weeks before the 2014 Lok Sabha elections, the then Prime Minister Manmohan Singh had expressed confidence that history will be kinder to him. It was virtually a farewell statement that hinted that he too knew that regardless of what happened in the 2014 elections, he won't become the prime minister again.

And had the Congress won—and there could have been a fat chance of it winning had the anti-corruption movement ended the way I described in the earlier paragraph—history would definitely *not* have been kinder to Manmohan Singh. The darbari historians would have painted him as the villain to make Rahul Gandhi the hero. A rehearsal of the same was already done in September 2013, when Rahul Gandhi tore an ordinance by his own government that protected convicted lawmakers.

I have my reasons to believe that the anti-corruption movement, when it was launched, was not really aiming to pull down the Congress-led government. Swami Agnivesh, one of the original members of Team Anna, was once heard talking over the phone—purportedly to Congress leader Kapil Sibal, though he later said that it was another Kapil—where he compared his colleagues with wild elephants (mad elephant or pagal haathi to be precise).[60]

Agnivesh was heard saying that Team Anna had lost their way and were behaving like wild elephants who were not ready to stop their onslaught. So, was Team Anna supposed to behave in a restrained manner and end their movement after a certain period of time?

Maybe they were, because a short-lived movement by the ecosystem would have helped the Congress. It would have created an environment that was against a corrupt 'political class', where the Congress and the BJP were to be equally seen as corrupt, thus denying the BJP any political advantage on the issue of corruption—similar to what had happened ahead of the 2009 Lok Sabha elections, where an environment was created against the political class over the issue of domestic security and not against the ruling class or party. That would have been a job perfectly done by the ecosystem, but somehow it decided to stretch it beyond the comfort of the Congress party.

It seems that the global developments around that time, especially the 'Arab Spring' of 2010-12, which resulted in regime changes in many countries of the Middle East and North Africa, gave a false hope to the ecosystem that they, too, could bring in such a revolution in India. If successful, it would have allowed them to rule directly, without needing the crutches and crumbs from the Congress party. Perhaps, that dream made them run amok like wild elephants, in the words of Agnivesh.

In fact, TV journalist Rajdeep Sardesai, in a viral video clip presumably recorded sometime in 2012, is heard saying in Marathi that he had advised Arvind Kejriwal to do a 'Tahrir Square' in India around the anti-corruption movement.[61] Tahrir Square is situated in Cairo, the capital of Egypt, and it had seen mass protests in February 2011, which went on to be one of the crucial events of Arab Spring. It resulted in the overthrow of President Hosni Mubarak, who had ruled for almost 30 years non-stop, before the protests broke out.

It can't be ruled out that the ecosystem actually thought that they could pull off something similar to an Arab Spring in India too. If so, they were essentially trying to capture power directly, instead of getting a share of it via the Congress. This possible plan and desire of the ecosystem could be crudely likened to a criminal or local dada deciding to fight the elections himself, instead of lending his muscle power to some other candidate and being his sidekick.

That plan, if it existed, didn't really fructify as Anna Hazare movement fizzled out over time. It couldn't gather mass support like the movements in the Arab world did. Team Anna especially failed to attract any meaningful support outside Delhi. Some planned protests in Mumbai attracted very thin crowds and subsequent protests in Delhi had started losing sheen. Other parts of the country too gave very tepid response to calls for local protests. However, the passion and energy kept running high among the dedicated team and it often reflected on social media platforms.

The ecosystem soon realized, if at all it was hoping to rule directly by overthrowing the Congress in some popular uprising, that their plans were impractical. However, they didn't lose all hope. Their desire of bypassing the Congress and capturing power directly resulted in the formation of the Aam Aadmi Party (AAP), which did exceedingly well in the December 2013 Delhi assembly elections. It gave them hope that they could make an impact in the 2014 Lok Sabha elections too, only to find out that Modi was too good for them.

Basically, both the Congress as well as its friendly ecosystem made grave mistakes. The Congress attacked the Anna movement and linked it with the RSS, thus indirectly giving positive PR to the RSS. Further, by virtue of attacking an 'anti-corruption' movement, it unwittingly accepted that it was 'pro-corruption'. On the other hand, the ecosystem overestimated its abilities in electoral politics and thought that it no longer needed the Congress party, a group that had patronized its various constituents for decades.

Let me come back to where this chapter had started, that is, understanding this ecosystem.

As the term itself indicates, it is not supposed to be an organized clique that secretly meets and strategizes how to maintain the status quo, where it enjoys enormous power and privilege to influence public opinion.

The constituents of this ecosystem include journalists, academics, jurists, bureaucrats, activists and artists, and of course the politicians. They end up helping each other. For example, a journalist gives credence and legitimacy to an activist or artist through positive media coverage of their work, and in return the artist or activist wouldn't say anything about the kind of journalism being practised by that journalist. An academic will make sure that impressionable young minds are willing to recognize only a particular type of journalists and artists as 'real' journalists and artists, while a politician or bureaucrat would reward such academics by giving them posts in policy-making bodies. Such bodies would come up with helpful policies that jurists would uphold.

This is just an indicative set of interrelationships. There can be many other permutations and combinations, where the constituent units can help each other. The constituents feed each other as their interests feed into each other. In the end, everyone needs each other to keep their own interests safeguarded. This interdependence is what makes it an ecosystem.

The question then is why and how did all these professions and institutions, to which each of these constituent units belong, get captured by a particular type of people who share similar ideologies, or at least share a common hatred for Hindutva?

One of the explanations about why a particular ideology ends up capturing most of these professions or institutions is what is known as the O'Sullivan's First Law, named after British columnist and commentator John O'Sullivan who coined it in 1989. The law states that 'All organizations that are not actually Right wing will over time become Left wing.'

The reason for this gradual capture of spaces and institutions by the Left is because the Left wing is observed to be more and more tribalistic—which is ironic in a way—and is more likely to hire and promote people with whom they agree on ideological issues. Not just that, they actively push out people with whom they disagree. So over time, an institution is left with only Left-leaning people.

If one goes by the current 'cancel culture' that is so popular among 'wokes', one can see this law in action on steroids. In the name of 'safe spaces', the Left is increasingly monopolizing institutions where every voice of dissent is silenced after being labelled 'fascist' and 'hate speech'.

So, one explanation of how this ecosystem was stuffed with people following the same ideology is—that it was destined to be so; that's what O'Sullivan's First Law essentially says. Another, but associated, explanation is what I have mentioned in the chapter about 'Congressi Hindus'. The leftists got access to the corridors of power during the Indira Gandhi years due to her politics and possibly due to Soviet influence. And once they get in, they allow only people like themselves to get in next.

The third, and the most important, explanation lies in the legacy, in the roots of how this ecosystem was born. It is specific to India, and which also explains why this ecosystem compulsorily hates Hindutva.

It should be noted that this network of various professions and institutions was not set up by the Congress party but by the British rulers. While one can argue that roles and occupations such as those of academics, artists or jurists have existed for centuries, the way we know them today and the market dynamics that make livelihoods around these occupations viable, are all modern constructs. These models were broadly developed in the European countries in an era that is known as the 'Age of Enlightenment' or the 'Long eighteenth century'. Professions such as those of journalists and bureaucrats, and even of politicians contesting elections, can all be argued to be born in this period.

It is not as if without the European models India wouldn't have seen these professions or institutions developing and flourishing. On the contrary, our civilization had such systems in place already, which were destroyed by invaders. I don't want to get into that debate around history here, but the truth is that virtually every system that we follow today was set up by the British.

The market dynamics, the interdependence of various professions and the hierarchies were set up by the British rulers, who were influenced by developments back in Europe in the eighteenth and nineteenth centuries. Essentially, the blueprint of the ecosystem was developed by the colonial rulers of India.

It is not rocket science to guess what objectives and interests the British had in mind when they set up these systems in India—to perpetuate their rule and to exercise control over the natives. Thus, they put up systems in place that not only helped them colonize the land, but also the minds of the subjects.

Thomas Babington Macaulay, the British historian and politician who is credited for having shaped the modern education system in India under the British Raj, believed that 'there was no culture beyond Europe'. Remember that education system is the base on which the other systems are developed.

In 1835, Macaulay had conceitedly claimed that 'a single shelf of a good European library was worth the whole native literature of India and Arabia'—something that should give you a fair idea of what he thought about India and its native culture.

And what he wanted to achieve by setting up the modern education system in India is reflected in the following sentences, which are a part of his Minute on Education, dated 2 February 1835:

> We must at present do our best to form a class who may be interpreters between us and the millions whom we govern—a class of persons Indian in blood and colour, but English in tastes, in opinions, in morals and in intellect. To that class we may leave it to refine the vernacular dialects of the country, to enrich those dialects with terms of science borrowed from the Western nomenclature and to render them by degrees fit vehicles for conveying knowledge to the great mass of the population.[62]

This is the class that went on to become the members of the ecosystem—Indians, who were Indian only in blood and colour, but colonizers in their outlook.

You create such a class of natives—as proposed by Macaulay—by convincing the natives that their original ways were inferior and they needed to be 'civilized.' You have to make sure that the natives start hating their roots, and if not hate, at least they start being ashamed of their roots. And for the bulk of the Indians, those roots lay in the Hindu culture. That's how the ecosystem was destined and designed to be anti-Hindu.

The Congress party simply inherited this ecosystem once the British left. In fact, the Congress itself was formed as part of this ecosystem by the British. Let us not forget that it was founded by a British civil servant named Allan Octavian Hume in 1885 to avoid repetition of the 1857 revolt, which is often known as the first war of Indian independence. As the administrator of Etawah, Uttar Pradesh (then known as the North-Western Provinces), Hume had personally witnessed the 'problems' due to the revolt.

It is true that people, places and organizations evolve over time. The Congress too evolved and changed its character. It was not exactly an anti-Hindu organization, with the likes of Bal Gangadhar Tilak, Lala Lajpat Rai, Madan Mohan Malaviya being some of its tallest leaders in the coming decades. It was born out of a system created by the British, but it was soon at odds with it.

However, the broad nature of the ecosystem that the British had imagined, designed, legitimized and empowered, remained more or less the same during the British raj and even after the Independence of India. Congress, rather Nehru, didn't bother to change that.

During the British Raj, the ecosystem had identified the native culture as a 'problem' and it set on a path to 'civilize' the natives—via modern education, social reforms, legal interventions and even force and proselytization.

There is honestly nothing in history that suggests that there was an attempt to overhaul this basic DNA or character of this ecosystem after Independence. Nehru was pretty comfortable inheriting it the way it was. In fact, Nehru can be argued to be the embodiment of the class of Indians that Macaulay wanted to create.

Nehru had no special pride for his Hindu identity, and he also put the burden of secularism and communal harmony squarely on the shoulders of Hindus, that is, he continued to believe that Hindus needed to be civilized. In his letter dated 17 November 1953 to Kailash Nath Katju, the then home minister of India, Nehru wrote, 'I am convinced that it is the duty of the majority to behave in such manner as to create a feeling of security in the minority.'

If you think that this possibly reflects the faith Nehru had in Hindus, that he perhaps thought that Hindus were magnanimous enough to behave in a 'big brotherly' way, you are wrong. In the same letter he further wrote, 'In practice, the Hindu is certainly not tolerant and is more narrow-minded than almost any person in any other country except the Jew.'[63]

Basically, Nehru wouldn't have felt the need to change the basic objective of the systems set up by the British, which were aimed at civilizing the natives, especially the Hindus, because he too was of the same view. So it's not at all inaccurate to say that the Congress, especially Nehru, happily inherited the ecosystem and decided to maintain it.

Recall that Macaulay had spoken condescendingly not just about India, but Arabia too. However, he was not exactly referring to the Arab world, because that region was not part of British India. He was essentially referring to the Muslims of India, who he thought were more interested in getting their education in Arabic than in English. If he were to randomly insult every non-English or non-European culture, he could have mentioned Africa or Americas too, which he didn't do in that very speech. He had referred to Arabia in the context of the Muslim population in India.

However, the ecosystem put in place by the British didn't really need to shame the Muslims of India into hating their 'Arabic roots', because of people like Syed Ahmad Khan, the founder of AMU and the ideological father of Pakistan. Khan, or Sir Syed as he was known after being knighted by the British government, especially collaborated with the British, both in the fields of education and governance, and helped the British safeguard their interests, without them having to paint the 'Arabic roots' or Islam as a problem.

The mantle of Syed Ahmad Khan was taken forward by the likes of Allama Iqbal and Muhammad Ali Jinnah, who made sure that the British ecosystem never had to take on the Islamic beliefs or introduce any 'reforms' among the Muslims of India. On the contrary, the British made blasphemy a punishable offense because Muslim leaders demanded so after the *Rangila Rasul* incident.

Rangila Rasul, literally meaning the 'colourful prophet', was a short book that outwardly appeared to praise Prophet Muhammad, but was actually written to criticize his deeds, especially his marriages and relationship with women. It was published, presumably under a fake name, as a work of revenge against a pamphlet that insulted Hindu goddesses.

Although the identity of the writer was not known, the publisher of the book was known. Some Muslims assumed that it was the publisher, Mahashe Rajpal, who wrote the book. Rajpal was killed by a Muslim fanatic named Ilm-ud-din in 1929, who was later sentenced to death under the British Indian laws. But, he was declared a martyr by the likes of Allama Iqbal and Jinnah.

Section 295a of the Indian Penal Code (which is still a part of legislation in India) was introduced by the British rulers after the controversy around *Rangila Rasul*. That was the kind of bargain the Muslim leaders could extract from the British, and obviously later they could extract the Partition of India itself.

The Muslim leaders made sure that the ecosystem created by British never trained its guns against Islam—something that the Hindu leaders clearly failed to do when dealing with the British rulers. Hindus and

Hindu culture continued to be the primary targets of the 'civilizing mission' of the British and its ecosystem.

Let it be clear that the British-created ecosystem was not exclusively designed just to eradicate Hinduism, but it became one of its main objectives while trying to create a class of Indians who would not resent the British rule. Indians who were not proud of their roots, Indians who would lack self-esteem, Indians who would willingly be ready to be civilized—such a class of Indians would be easier to govern by a foreign force—and it will be easier to create such a class of Indians if their faith and identity were diluted and drained. Furthermore, it was driven by a messiah complex, as flaunted by Macaulay, where you must look to reform and 'save' a bunch of people.

The British were pretty successful in creating such a class of Indians, primarily among the Hindus, who didn't really resent the British rule. The existing issues within the Hindu society were exploited—and I won't entirely blame the British for that because they were just being opportunist and smart—to promote and strengthen varied theories and ideologies that were soft on the British rule. So much so, that when the British were ready to leave India in 1947, there were a bunch of people, such as Periyar E.V. Ramasamy of Tamil Nadu, who declared it 'a day of mourning.'[64]

Such voices have only gone shriller and more 'mainstream' after Independence. A so-called Dalit thinker named Chandra Bhan Prasad had written a laborious article extoling the virtues of Macaulay in 2006, where he declared that 'Lord Macaulay was a rationalist extraordinaire' and chastised fellow Indians, including Left-leaning historians, as 'brown men' who had failed to acquire the intellectual capacity to appreciate this great British reformer.[65]

This is one of the main reasons why the 'white guilt' among the British is not as pronounced when it comes to their colonial rule in India, as compared to their exploits in Africa. A survey, findings of which were published in July 2014 by YouGov, a data and analytics group headquartered in London, had revealed that 59 per cent of the British public felt that the legacy of the British Empire in India was something they were 'proud of'. Only 19 per cent said they were ashamed of what the British did in India.[66]

And why should the British be really ashamed when there are thousands of Indians, paraded as 'scholars' and 'intellectuals', who subscribe to ideologies that propagate that the British rule in India was better for the 'depressed classes' or the 'non-Aryan' people. The British will rather see themselves as saviours for having rescued these groups from 'oppressive Hindoos'.

Groups naming themselves after Periyar and Ambedkar still insist that the British rule was better. They rue that on 15 August 1947, there was a transfer of power from the British to the Brahmins, which was a 'setback' to their development. Such voices and ideologies were born and promoted during the British era, and they still call the shots in the secular-liberal ecosystem, which was also born in the British era.

After Modi's return to power in 2019, such voices—claiming to represent Dalits and 'marginalized' communities—have become hyperactive abroad, perhaps realizing that the hold on domestic narrative is weakening. They are yet again looking at foreign powers as saviours and messiahs, somehow hoping that some extreme foreign pressure will 'reign in' Modi and Hindutva politics.

A Dalit or a South Indian or a tribal who doesn't subscribe to these extremist and exclusivist ideologies is denied a voice and delegitimized. A Dalit leader like Babu Jagjivan Ram is hardly celebrated by the so-called Dalit activists, because he didn't advocate the mass conversions away from Hinduism.

It is not as if Babu Jagjivan Ram didn't fight for the political rights or dignity of the Dalits. He was the railways minister during 1956–62, and he is credited to have created a new post in the railways, where a person was tasked with the responsibility of providing drinking water to passengers at platforms. Candidates from the scheduled castes were recruited for this post.[67] This rather simple step has not been appreciated enough for the role it could have played in removing untouchability.

In peak summers when you have a parched throat, you must accept the water touched by a Dalit. You either risk your life or change your belief in untouchability. That was no less radical a step. But one is radical or revolutionary for this ecosystem only if there is an element of anti-Hinduism in his ideas or words.

Neither the mindset nor the objectives of the ecosystem have changed since it was created by the British. The ecosystem is there to help control the thoughts and actions of the masses and come up with moral justification for this control. Further, the ecosystem continues to be driven by the messiah complex or a superiority complex, and is on a continuous civilizing mission.

After Independence and Partition, even if the ecosystem were to continue with these objectives and a superiority complex where they must civilize the unwashed masses, perhaps the target of this civilizing mission could have been changed. Perhaps, they could have chosen to reform and refine those whose mindset demanded Pakistan and ended up partitioning India. But Nehruvian secularism didn't allow that, because Nehru had put the burden and guilt of Partition entirely on the shoulders of Hindus.

And then came the assassination of Mahatma Gandhi. And that was it. The ecosystem that the Congress party, rather Nehru, had inherited from the British, 'officially' identified a bunch of people who needed to be civilized—those who killed Gandhi. 'Hindutva' was declared the culprit of Mahatma Gandhi's assassination, and the anti-Hindu nature of the British-created ecosystem was cosmetically changed to 'anti-Hindutva' ecosystem. Nothing changed in practice though.

The Murder of Mahatma Gandhi became, and remains, the greatest tool in the hands of this ecosystem to morally justify their existence and exploits. The ecosystem players don't exactly love Mahatma Gandhi, who after all was a practicing and conservative Hindu. The Hindutva ideologues could have their own issues with Mahatma Gandhi and his philosophy or politics, but even they would concede that Gandhi, unlike Nehru, had a Hindu outlook after all—which singularly makes Gandhi a misfit in the Macaulay-created-Nehru-inherited ecosystem.

The murder of Mahatma Gandhi was one of the biggest setbacks to Hindu politics, or Hindutva politics if one can say so, as it gave a moral excuse to the British-era anti-Hindu ecosystem to continue in independent India with the same mindset and objective. It also put the Hindus permanently on the back foot, from where they just couldn't assert their rights.

Sita Ram Goel, who otherwise has criticized Mahatma Gandhi for various reasons, especially for turning his illusion of Hindu–Muslim unity into a cult, has aptly described this phenomenon in the following words:

> It was a tragedy indeed that this great Hindu (Mahatma Gandhi) ended becoming the bridge over which all sorts of Hindu-baiters— Marxists, Mullahs, self-alienated Hindus, and the rest—crossed into the Congress camp, and captured it completely soon after this death. The Muslims in the Congress had only to drop a hint, and any Congressman could stand accused as a 'Hindu communalist' in the eyes of Nehru and his henchmen. The only thing that can be said in favour of the Mahatma is that he himself never indulged in or encouraged Hindu-baiting. He never used the expression 'Hindu communalist' for those who championed Hindu causes, and opposed his pro-Muslim pursuits.[68]

I would say that had Nathuram Godse not killed Mahatma Gandhi, over the years Gandhi would have been obliterated by the same ecosystem that today pretends to respect and follow him; just like Anna Hazare was sidelined and made irrelevant by Team Anna once the AAP performed exceedingly well in the Delhi assembly elections of 2013, something that also gave hope to the ecosystem that it could enjoy power directly without needing the patronage of the Congress.

Hindutva in the time of 'vikas'

While a considerable section of the online-savvy youth in urban India was impressed with the idealism of Anna movement, I was not really enamoured with it. During 2011–12, I was a neither-Congress-nor-BJP person, though the Congress obviously remained a usual target of my satire and humour, because it worked better among my audience.

I was happy when the communists lost West Bengal in the 2011 state assembly elections, ending their 34-year long rule. Later that year, Maoist leader Kishenji was also killed in a counter-insurgency operation, giving Left-wing terrorism a deadly blow. As a pro-market libertarian, these things appeared to be significant developments than believing that a new law could end corruption.

Around the same time, the image of Modi as a pro-market leader was also rising. Various reports in the media talked about the Gujarat model of development, and how the state had adopted pro-industry policies, securing growth on various parameters, especially economic.

There were credible voices, such as economists Arvind Panagariya, Surjit Bhalla, Bibek Debroy and others, who argued that the Gujarat model of development was indeed something that the rest of India should learn from. Such developments made someone like me warm up to the idea that Modi wouldn't be a bad choice to lead the country. The fact that around four years ago, I had almost met Modi and heard about his pro-development focus also propelled this thought further.

The image of Modi as a 'development man' was growing steadily during 2011-12, while the Congress invested its energies in fighting some 'rogue elements' of the ecosystem, that is, Team Anna. Soon both of them—the Congress party as well as the friendly ecosystem—realized that Modi could seize this opportunity to pitchfork himself on the national stage, and they tried to fight back, in their own ways.

The ecosystem wasted no time, and news articles and opinions 'exposing' the Gujarat model were almost immediately offered. The arguments mostly ranged from 'Gujarat was always well-developed' to pointing out that this was not 'real development' because the state didn't have a good record on social indices, such as human development and social justice.

The Congress started claiming that a PR agency named APCO was the reason why there were certain pro-Modi or pro-Gujarat articles in the media—as if by default the media shouldn't be publishing anything positive about Modi or Gujarat.

The desperation to bring down the 'Gujarat model of development' by the Congress as well as the ecosystem only ended up giving it more prominence. Not just that, the discussions on Modi invariably meant a discussion on development and good governance. Perhaps, the Congress party and the ecosystem didn't realize that they were undoing their own hard work of almost a decade, where they had made sure that the discussions on Modi revolved around a discussion on communalism and riots.

Modi too appeared very careful to keep the focus of his statements around good governance and good economics. He talked about the need to have policies that were more market-friendly than the ones pursued by the Congress and the UPA government. Around that time, the UPA government was also accused of suffering from 'policy paralysis', which was seen as an outcome of innumerable scams, bad investments and tax laws, and lack of coordination among various ministries, with the environment ministry especially being attacked for delaying work on many projects.

Things were just going from bad to worse for the UPA government. In August 2012, the Government of India asked the ISPs (Internet Service Providers) to block various URLs, many of which were Twitter handles that regularly attacked and exposed the central government or the Left-leaning media. Among them were the Twitter handles of journalist Kanchan Gupta, @barbarindian, which was famous for its quote 'Media is a crime scene, always take screenshots', and a parody handle of the then Prime Minister Manmohan Singh, @PM0India—with a zero instead of the letter 'O' in the username.

The action by the government was seen as blatant censorship and an attack on free speech. It caused massive outrage online. Many Twitter users uploaded black banners as their DP (display picture) to register their protest against this move. Rather unexpectedly, Modi also changed his DP to the same, and tweeted in support of the outraging netizens. After free markets, Modi was now associated with free speech too. The libertarian in me was impressed.

I can hardly recall anything that Modi said in that period, which could appeal to the 'culturally Hindu' part in me. But, I started believing that he should be given a chance to govern due to his views on development and due to him appearing as someone who understood social media.

While Modi might not have explicitly said anything on cultural issues, many on social media, especially on Twitter, had started to throw political correctness out of the window while talking about such issues, especially around Hindu–Muslim relationships. They had started seeking parity in the narrative that if Hinduism could be criticized, why shy away from criticizing Islam? If you can name Hindus as aggressors and Muslims as victims in news reports, why not do the same when the roles are reversed?

Essentially, questions that were similar to the observations about the media and popular narrative that I have documented in the preceding chapters of this book were finally being asked now. A website called

'Niti Central' was launched in 2012, which declared itself 'Bold and Right'. It vowed to be different from the mainstream media, which it, rightly, accused of setting an agenda in favour of the (secular-liberal) establishment.

I won't say that I was immediately attracted towards these handles and initiatives, but they gradually exposed me to a counter-set of views, many of which sounded logical and convincing to me. Instead of countering them on facts, many of the celebrity journalists decided to discredit and label these voices by using terms such as 'Internet Hindus' and 'trolls'—which was not a very smart strategy, as it made the Sanghis appear to be victims of vilification. I personally ended up following many such handles that were 'under attack' from the celebrity journalists, and most of them were not really trolls. The real trolls arrived much later.

Even though I had followed many 'Internet Hindus' on Twitter, it didn't really turn me into one. The 'credit' for triggering the Hindu in me actually goes to the mainstream media and its approach towards two incidents in 2012, both of which were related.

The first one was the Assam riots that took place in July 2012 between ethnic Bodos and Bengali-speaking Muslims, who are seen as illegal settlers from Bangladesh. The mainstream media was not reporting about it in detail while multiple claims were being made on social media about the violence. Many pictures and short videos were uploaded on Twitter and other social media platforms, where it was alleged that the Muslims were the main aggressors in the riots. Many claimed that the rioters had modern assault rifles, hinting at the involvement of terrorist groups.

In fact, these riots were used as an excuse to block those Twitter handles and other URLs by the government. So apart from being seen as an attack on free speech, this step was also seen as an attempt to supress information when Muslims were allegedly the aggressors. Not just the government, the mainstream media too was accused of supressing information by not covering the riots properly. 'Why did the same TV media, which was hyperactive during the Gujarat riots, not covering the Assam riots now?'—such questions were being raised, tagging the journalists on Twitter.

Such questions were answered in a rather 'controversial' way by Rajdeep Sardesai, who came up with the phrase 'Tyranny of distance'.

In an article,[69] and later on Twitter, he tried to argue that it was not the religion of the perpetrators, but the accessibility of the region, that was the main factor why the Assam riots were not being covered prominently by the media. He pointed out how news channels didn't have enough modern broadcast equipment in their offices even in the capital city of Assam. Thus, he argued that the lack of means of travel and equipment were the reasons why a coverage similar to that of the Gujarat 2002 riots was not possible in Assam.

Sardesai had made the same error that the 'Right wing' often makes—relying on cold hard facts to make an argument while the topic was attracting emotional outbursts. Being a journalist, he should have known that the mahaul (mood) is always more important than data or facts—that is how journalism has been influencing public opinions for decades. He erred, and till date he is trolled with the 'Tyranny of distance' barb.

Further, while Sardesai was technically right about why the Assam riots were not being covered the way the Gujarat riots were, he opened the floodgates for similar cold hard facts about the 2002 Gujarat riots. By the corollary of his own argument, he virtually admitted that the Gujarat riots were covered widely by the media not because it was especially inhuman or shocking, but because it was easier for the media to cover it, and that the riots looked so 'unique' because it took place at a time when modern technologies were available. It was India's first televised riots. So, if access and technology were the only factors, why make it about Modi? Why single him out, when 2002 riots were certainly not the only communal riots to have taken place in India or even Gujarat?

I hope you noticed how Modi didn't need to talk about the 2002 riots at all, but arguments in his support were already getting out there in public. The narrative was shifting. Modi didn't need to trigger any communal sentiments at all; his detractors, knowingly or unknowingly, had started doing that.

The second incident that triggered communal sentiments took place a couple of months later in August 2012—the Azad Maidan riots of Mumbai. Various Muslim groups in Mumbai had called for a protest against the Assam riots because there were counter-claims that Muslims had been killed in bigger numbers. The protests were also supposed to be against the issue of the killing of Rohingya Muslims in Myanmar, which they said was not getting the attention it deserved from the media and the world.

These protests turned violent, leading to the death of at least two people. The protesting Muslim mobs set police vans and media vans on fire. Not just that, a few female constables of the Mumbai Police were even molested by the protesters. The rioting Muslim mob also desecrated the Amar Jawan Jyoti—a memorial dedicated to the war heroes of India.[70]

The Mumbai Police was accused of not acting quickly to rein in the protesters. The critics said that the police should have acted as soon as they saw signs of the protestors turning aggressive and hostile. Questions were raised as to why did the police not pick signals when incendiary speeches were being delivered. There were claims that the police commissioner had even shouted at one of the DCPs who had caught a rioter by collar. The rioter was allowed to leave.

Over the next few days, however, many arrests were made, including of the man who had desecrated the Amar Jawan Jyoti. He had fled to Bihar and was arrested from his hometown.

This incident surely triggered the Hindu in me. Why the hell should Muslims in India go berserk over alleged atrocities on Muslims in Myanmar? How was the Indian government responsible for what was happening in Myanmar? Why desecrate a symbol of war heroes of your own country? It was a manifestation of the two-nation theory at work, where Muslims felt a sense of belonging to one common nation beyond national boundaries—the Ummah.

The last comment obviously is in retrospect. At that point of time, I didn't link it to the two-nation theory. But apart from the violence, what triggered the Sanghi in me during those days was an article by Teesta Setalvad and her husband Javed Anand in *The Indian Express*, barely a week after the rioting at Azad Maidan.

The husband-wife duo, who had gained fame by accusing Modi of orchestrating the Gujarat riots of 2002, wrote an article praising the Mumbai Police commissioner for not 'repeating history', pointing to the police inaction against the Muslim rioters. The duo recounted how the Mumbai Police had shot dead many Muslim rioters during protests against Salman Rushdie's book *The Satanic Verses* in 1989 and then later when Muslim mobs came out to riot in the immediate aftermath of the demolition of Babri Masjid in 1992. The duo then went on to commend the police for not having acted in a similar manner in 2012.[71]

The hypocrisy was staggering. Setalvad and her husband were virtually arguing that the police did the right thing by letting the Muslims vent out their anger against perceived injustices. Well, that's exactly what they accused Modi of saying and doing—that he asked the police in Gujarat to let the Hindus vent out their anger over the Godhra train carnage.

It was not just someone like me who found it odd and shockingly hypocritical. Madhu Trehan, a senior journalist, too, was surprised at the tone and objective of the article written by Setalvad and her husband. Trehan wrote an article[72] in response to the original article by Setalvad and Anand, in which she also referred to the viral clip that showed the Mumbai Police commissioner shouting at a DCP and threatening to have him suspended for having caught a rioter. The concluding paragraph of her article read:

> Gujarat 2002 upset and shook me up. Many Tweeters have sincerely tried to convince me that Narendra Modi was not responsible. I, sincerely, have not been convinced so far, since I have seen stories with evidence and footage that show the opposite. But an article like this one by Setalvad-Anand is enough to turn me into what is called an Internet Hindu.

So there you go again. Modi didn't need to utter a single word about 2002 or how Indian secularism was deeply flawed and designed to give a raw deal to the Hindus, but such topics still ended up being discussed and debated. This was because his haters, like always, were hyperactive in shielding Muslim aggression, and ended up exposing the double standards of Indian secularism. Not only that, they elicited reactions that made an average secular Hindu feel like an 'Internet Hindu'. The Hindu identity in me too was triggered due to these incidents.

Later in November 2012, the lone surviving terrorist of the 2008 Mumbai terror attacks, Ajmal Kasab, was hanged to death as the then President Pranab Mukherjee rejected his mercy petition. This set a bunch of liberal activists in action, who started a campaign against death penalty—something that didn't go down well with ordinary people, who could feel no sympathy or mercy for someone like Kasab.

To rake up an issue on the morality of death penalty around the execution of someone like Kasab made no sense to ordinary people. This was one of those instances that painted activists as being people with superiority complex—who must raise some issues about high-sounding principles and ideas of justice when almost everyone wants to just go with the flow. And well, didn't I say earlier that this ecosystem—of which sundry activists are part of—continued to be driven by a superiority complex even after the British left.

As a libertarian with preference for cold hard facts or logic over emotions, such stands by activists didn't really shock me, as I could see that they had a 'larger point' and on occasions I even agreed with them, but I was also a pop satirist, where my curiosity was to understand what the masses were interested in and what they preferred. I saw the masses, especially the unwashed masses, as the market, and the ideas as products. If your ideas are unwelcomed or rejected by the masses, the pro-market guy in me was more inclined to believe that it was a failure of the product, not of the market.

Then there were the usual voices online that claimed that the liberal heart was bleeding because Kasab was a Muslim. I didn't believe so, and I still don't believe so. I don't think the religion of Kasab was the factor why some people started talking about death penalty at that time. It was just a standard liberal itch to indulge in virtue signalling and show yourself to be superior to the common people, many of whom were literally celebrating the death of Kasab.

Not all were celebrating though. Hafiz Sayeed, the mastermind of the Mumbai terror attacks, offered funeral prayers for Kasab. While that was hardly shocking, there were reports about funeral prayers offered for Kasab even in Kashmir and Kerala[73] back in India. All of these went on to add to the narrative about how secularism in India had turned a blind eye towards radicalism among Muslims. Again, Modi didn't need to say anything.

The year 2012 ended with Modi winning his third successive assembly elections in Gujarat. The Congress and many 'experts' had earlier tried to suggest that while Modi was aiming for a national role, he might lose Gujarat itself. An anti-incumbency of two terms plus rebellion by BJP leaders like Keshubhai Patel, who had formed his own party and vowed to defeat Modi in the upcoming elections, were offered as reasons.

The Congress had tried to make even the national popularity of Modi an electoral issue in the assembly elections. They termed the positive press coverage of Modi and the 'Gujarat model' as 'prasiddhi ghotala' (reputation scam) of Modi. It obviously sounded pretty desperate—that a party embroiled in endless scams could only come up with something as senseless as prasiddhi ghotala to attack the Modi government for its preceding two terms.

On the other hand, Modi projected his pitch as 'good economics can be good politics too'. He talked about how his government had been and will continue to focus on development. While he had already demonstrated how he was willing to use the digital medium to communicate, he also demonstrated that his interests in modern technologies went beyond the internet. He used 3D holographic images of himself to address rallies at multiple locations simultaneously—a campaign technology that was later used during the 2014 and 2019 Lok Sabha elections too.

In the 2012 Gujarat assembly elections, the BJP won 115 out of 182 seats, almost winning two-thirds of the total seats. When asked about Congress' poor performance and whether it was a setback for the party, Congress leader and then union minister Kapil Sibal, who by then had become famous for claiming 'zero loss' in the 2G spectrum scam, pointed out that the BJP had won two seats less than what they had won in the previous assembly elections of 2007.

It was no longer clear what was serious and what was satire. The Congress was losing the narrative really fast, and Modi was rising really fast.

Once Gujarat was won three times in a row by Modi, it was almost clear that he was now going to be the prime ministerial candidate of the BJP for the 2014 Lok Sabha elections. His victory speech post the assembly election results started in Hindi even though it was given at Ahmedabad—signalling that it was meant for audiences beyond Gujarat—and it continued for over 45 minutes, where Modi repeatedly thanked the Gujarat voters for 'showing the direction in which India was already progressing.'

The audience shouted 'PM-PM' (prime minister) many times, which was answered with a content smile by Modi. A few among the audience also shouted that it was time Modi went to Delhi, that is, became the prime minister, to which Modi playfully responded by saying that in the coming days he will visit Delhi for a day to attend a meeting. The mood and signals were clear—Modi was all set to play the next innings on a bigger stage.

Modi or the BJP didn't make a national spectacle of Modi's third consecutive victory in Gujarat, because around the same time massive anger over the 2012 Delhi gang rape and murder case had started simmering. Just a day after the Gujarat election results, student protests broke out in various parts of Delhi, including outside the Parliament and Rashtrapati Bhavan and at public places like India Gate. It was covered and supported by the mainstream media in the same way that the Anna movement was covered.

Although the unfortunate incident could have been used to attack the Congress party, Modi didn't put out any political statement about it immediately, despite the incident making national and international headlines. That was in sharp contrast to what Arvind Kejriwal did. AAP was just a month old then and party members took part in the protests. AAP also went on to make women's safety an election issue in the Delhi assembly elections the following year, and it paid rich dividends.

Modi could have easily 'played politics' around the issue and claimed how Gujarat was a safer place for women, but he refused to make that a political issue in the immediate aftermath. In fact, the media did ask him to comment about the gang rape incident, but he said that politics should not be done over such issues. Perhaps, he knew that the anger was against the political class in general, and if he tried to get any political mileage out of, it would immediately backfire. Kejriwal could raise the issue because he was not seen as a typical politician around that time. But Modi remained focused on the issues of development.

And this is where he was able to check-mate his detractors as 2014 neared. While he kept his arguments almost entirely focused around the issues of economics, governance, corruption and poverty, his detractors had to go back harping on fascism, communalism, 2002 riots and RSS. While in their minds, they might be highlighting the 'real issues' and winning the arguments, they appeared prejudiced and pig-headed to an average person, as they raised unrelated topics to derail a discussion.

Most of these debates happened online. I had seen many of my batchmates from IIM Ahmedabad debating these topics passionately on their Facebook profiles or groups. I mostly kept quiet and just observed. I could see that the pro-Modi crowd had better arguments and they were clearly winning the debates around development and economics. I believe the discussions elsewhere might not be too different, either. Above all, the best thing was that at least the discussions and debates were happening.

The year 2013—when these debates started shaping the online political narratives—saw an even sharper upswing in the number of internet users in India compared to 2009, which was the earlier turning point in internet adoption in India.[74] This round was largely led by easier availability and affordability of smartphones, and 3G services being widely adopted across the nation.

In early 2013, yet another scam by the UPA government had come to light—this time it was the helicopter scam or the AgustaWestland VVIP chopper deal—reinforcing the image of the Congress as being synonymous with corruption. On the other side, in February 2013, Modi gave a speech at SRCC (Shri Ram College of Commerce) in Delhi, where he reinforced his image as the development man or vikas purush, apart from the fact that he was connecting with the youth.

At SRCC, Modi talked about how India should become a nation of 'mouse charmers'—referring to the computer mouse—replacing the old image of snake charmers, which underscored his image as a tech-savvy leader. He also popularized the term 'Minimum government, maximum governance', signalling that he could go for disinvestments and lean bureaucracy if elected.

While he was touching the right chords on the issue of development and governance, the Congress continued to look like a party that was busy with scams and mismanagement.

Among the pre-2014 liberals

The year 2013 brought a turning point in my life too. Actually, it had come a year earlier itself, in 2012, when I got married. The money I had made via consulting projects and selling off CricStock was good enough to sustain my mundane lifestyle for most part of my post-IIM life as a struggling entrepreneur, but once I started courting my would-be wife and spending on our romantic escapades, I realized that Google was not paying enough for clicks on ads.

Not that my then-girlfriend-now-wife demanded a sophisticated lifestyle, but I just took it upon myself that I should earn more if I were to marry. My wife had actually told me to continue doing what I was doing—writing pop satire and cracking one-liners on Twitter and Facebook—while she would take up a job, but my middle-class sensibilities made me decide that a man should be the primary earner of the family.

Consequently, around a month before our wedding—which happened after a lot of twists and turns, and included a scene at a railway station too; somewhat embarrassingly similar to *Dilwale Dulhaniya Le Jaayenge* but fortunately without any running or injuries involved—I had got into a partnership with an ad-tech company, where they assured me of a minimum monthly income in lieu of having exclusive advertising rights on *Faking News*.

While that worked fine for a few months and *Faking News* got some advertising campaigns too, things didn't work out that well by the end of 2012. The partnership with the ad-tech company was mutually terminated and I had to start looking for a fresh beginning in 2013.

I could have tried bootstrapping, or accepted an angel investment offer diluting 49 per cent of equity, or sold off 100 per cent equity to a couple of big media houses—The Times of India Group and Network18 Group—with whom I had a few rounds of discussions.

After much deliberation, I decided to sell it off. It was a rather early exit, like in the case of my first venture CricStock, and in retrospect I could have tried bootstrapping or taken some modest investment in exchange of much smaller equity dilution, but I was in a hurry to get some money in my bank account due to my imagined financial burdens post marriage.

Moreover, I was a bit unsure about my own plans in the long term. When I started CricStock, I didn't know a thing about how websites worked, and I had literally written just a couple of satirical articles before I started *Faking News*. Basically, I myself didn't know what I would be doing in another five years and I couldn't convince myself that humour or satire was all I wanted to do in the long term. Therefore, I settled for something that was giving me the best return in the short term, that is, selling off *Faking News* completely.

While the Times of India Group was offering marginally better money, I decided to go with Network18 Group's offer as I liked the leadership team of Firstpost—Durga Raghunath, who was in charge of the overall product and business, and R. Jagannathan, who was leading the editorial operations. *Faking News* was to become part of Firstpost, a digital news and opinion website that Netwoork18 had launched in 2011.

Based on a couple of interactions, before I decided to go ahead with the offer of Network18, I found Raghunath as a no-nonsense person who liked taking quick decisions and making things work—something I thought would suit me, having been an entrepreneur before, whereas I already liked Jagannathan, or Jaggi as he was and is popularly called, due to his simple but impactful writing on Firstpost. In person, I found him to be quite agreeable and even funny; almost invariably, he had a quirky take on any ongoing discussion. Together, they appeared to form a good leadership team.

The results were visible too. Firstpost was changing the grammar of digital publishing in India. It used a language that was conversational, and content that was often opinionated and many times provocative. The aim was to trigger debates, and its comments sections used to be on fire most of the times. It was one of the earliest mainstream outlets that didn't consider its solemn duty to toe the usual leftist narrative. It gave space to all kinds of voices, and that was enough for many to brand it a 'Right wing' outlet.

Jaggi definitely was Right wing so far as economic matters were concerned, and his takes on socio-political matters were also regularly in conflict with what the leftists would say, though he had differing views from the Sanghis too. Add to that the fact that he had written a few pro-Modi articles already. Those were enough to declare not just him, but the entire Firstpost a Right-wing outlet.

However, the fact was that the number of Left-leaning opinion or commentary pieces on Firstpost used to be higher, perhaps in any given period. But, the Right-leaning or the pro-Modi ones used to get more traction and used to go viral more quickly, giving an impression that Firstpost was Right-leaning.

This ideological 'comfort' too was a minor factor in choosing Network18 over Times of India, as I was not sure of finding a parallel to Jaggi in the Times Group, though it was not really a deal breaker.

Sometime in April 2013, we (my wife and I) left Gurgaon, where we had spent just over a year of our married life, and shifted to Mumbai. As part of the contract with Network18, I was supposed to stay with the company for a minimum of two and a half years to get the full consideration for the sale of the *Faking News*. The contract was designed so because *Faking News* virtually comprised just one person (i.e., me) at the point of sale, and it would have made no sense for Network18 or anyone to buy it without me continuing to run it. I too looked forward to creating a proper team and business around it, where the website was not entirely dependent upon me. A new beginning awaited me in Mumbai.

When we started searching for a house, rather a two-BHK flat, to live, we realized how crazy the real estate prices, even rentals, were in South Mumbai, where the Network18 office was. Having balconies was a luxury, while back in Delhi or in Patna, you couldn't imagine a house without balconies. We had to settle for a 1-BHK flat, obviously without any balcony, but fortunately it was barely 700 m from the Network18 office. I didn't want to stay too far from the office and waste time travelling by road. The rush in the local trains was terrifying, so travelling by them was ruled out even though they are called the lifeline of Mumbai.

As a Gujarati, my wife definitely found Mumbai better than Delhi. The city had better representation and influence of Gujaratis in some pockets, though we went on to live in areas that were either Marathi-dominated or had mixed population. I was also happy to be in Mumbai as the Delhi gang rape incident had forced many people, especially men, to realize that the city was indeed unsafe for women. It wasn't just about Delhi, but the realization that we need to correct many things in our society. For example, it dawned upon many that 'rape jokes' were not just another joke and they should be discouraged. Just three years earlier, the entire country was laughing at one such joke in the Aamir Khan starrer *3 Idiots*.

In Mumbai, life automatically appeared to be in fast gear, even though I was doing the same things that I did in Delhi. Each city indeed has some unique character that it passes on to its residents. This could sound entirely counterfactual as it's the residents who define the culture and vibe of a region, which is just a mass of land otherwise. But over generations, these landmasses acquire a life and character of their own and start affecting new entrants.

Obviously, if the new entrants overwhelm a region due to their sheer numbers or if they are inherently insular individuals, the effects could just be the opposite, that is, the character of the city will start changing rather than the other way round. It's a complicated topic, and controversial too. I would just say that life was a bit laidback in Delhi, but once in Mumbai, I felt I was always busy and didn't even feel bad about it. I wanted to do more, start new things and explore new opportunities.

By virtue of *Faking News* becoming a part of Firstpost, I was in a way back to the mainstream newsroom. Though I was not exactly a journalist in my latest avatar, I could see again, literally, how newsrooms function. I witnessed the same sense of urgency about breaking news as I had seen earlier in a TV newsroom, for digital news is also like a 24x7 broadcast.

Since Firstpost was led by Jaggi, the usual manipulation and leftist bias in the name of 'responsible journalism' was not evident, but it was not absent either, because that bias simply can't go away. Let me give two very minor examples.

Although Firstpost was part of the Network18 Group, which had its own band of ground reporters for various media properties owned by it, the website itself didn't have any big team of ground reporters. It had to depend on news agencies and other media outlets for news reports. It used to 'curate' content, that is, take information from multiple sources or publications and present them at one place in a single article, with due credits, somewhat similar to what Huffington Post (now HuffPost) had earlier done in the US.

Due to this curation policy, Firstpost was pretty liberal in using content from various sources. However, it was not liberal with one source. A copy writer had once curated the content, or perhaps just linked back the content to 'Niti Central'—the website led by Kanchan Gupta that had declared open its ideological leaning towards the 'Right'—and I remember one of the editors pointing it out as a mistake. 'Guys, we don't link to Niti Central' was announced as an unwritten rule or policy in the newsroom.

I was slightly shocked. Except for its declared ideological slant, Niti Central had done nothing to earn a place in some sort of a blacklist. Any random media house could have made the same set of mistakes or slips that Niti Central could be accused of at that point of time. Yet, it was treated as an untouchable and unreliable source.

Then I recalled my pre-MBA journalism days, and I knew that it was pretty normal and maybe a 'responsible' thing to do for the journalists—deciding what is good or bad based on ideological beliefs, not on logic or facts. But imagine, this was the balance of narrative in a newsroom that was supposedly being edited by a 'Right-winger' and 'Sanghi' Jaggi in the run-up to the 2014 Lok Sabha elections. So, you can imagine the situation in other newsrooms.

However, to be fair to Firstpost and the editorial team, including the person who put Niti Central on the blacklist, I was never asked to censor anything on ideological lines in my satires. On the contrary, I was often asked and encouraged to write opinion pieces on Firstpost too. By then, they definitely knew that if I wrote serious articles, and I did write a few, I will be writing Right-leaning articles, as I had started liking Modi's pitch for the top job. Not just that, I had made various comments on Twitter, say around the Azad Maidan riots or against the likes of Arundhati Roy, which did reflect that I was clearly anything but a leftist.

Still, I couldn't find any anti-Hindutva website or blog on the blacklist—no official blacklist existed, just to clarify once again—the way Niti Central was supposed to be avoided, and that was absolutely not right.

I remember another incident when an anti-Hindutva blog called Kafila was temporarily unavailable. Their website was not loading. Suddenly, one of the senior guys in the Firstpost newsroom declared that the BJP members were behind it. He insisted that pro-Hindutva hackers or people in the BJP IT cell had brought down a website that was critical of the party and its ideology. He confidently asked the copy editors to build a story around it.

But before such a story could be written, a couple of bloggers associated with that blog clarified that there were some server-related problems and the website will be back soon. Imagine what would have happened if they had not clarified, or if this Firstpost guy had actually colluded with them to create this news and controversy about the attack on free speech. Such collusions to 'create news' indeed happens and it is not just a fictional scenario that I'm asking you to imagine.

Again, let me reiterate that these were individual instances and there wasn't an institutional ideological bias in Firstpost, at least till the time I was with them.

But do note that these individual incidents demonstrate how the O'Sullivan's First Law works, that is, how institutions that are not avowedly Right wing turn Left wing over time. The Left-leaning guys are more vocal, more aggressive and get away with their whims, while a Sanghi like me would just keep quiet, observing the events from a distance.

Forget me, for technically I was not in the core editorial team and should have perhaps kept quiet anyway minding my own business, but the 'Sanghi' Jaggi, who was the editor of Firstpost, could have stepped in. He was the polar opposite of these folks. I don't recall a single incident when he shouted and demanded that something he had in mind must be done, or insisted on a particular narrative to be taken up by the team, despite the fact that he had the top editorial job and he could have easily bulldozed his way. Put a leftist in that position of strength and he'd paint every corner red in an organization.

The only thing I was requested to censor at Firstpost was making fun of Rajdeep Sardesai and Sagarika Ghose, because both of them were part of Network18 too at that time. But, it would have been very unfair on my part if I continued mocking other journalists while sparing Sardesai and Ghose, so I started to avoid direct attacks on journalists altogether on *Faking News*.

Jaggi was especially worried that if I mercilessly attacked the duo, perhaps they might get an impression that I, a member of 'Team Jaggi', was attacking them because Jaggi and they were not on the same ideological page. I decided to heed to that request.

However, I couldn't really stick to that promise for long. Contradicting and 'exposing' journalists had become a part of the popular narrative and I couldn't have ignored it entirely as a pop satirist. So I told Jaggi and Durga that while I might avoid a biting or hostile attack on these folks, I can't really keep them entirely out of bounds. As a result, Sardesai and Ghose started featuring in a few articles after a gap of few months. I still avoided a direct attack or articles exclusively devoted to mocking them, as I didn't want to put Jaggi in a tight spot and spoil his personal or professional equations within Network18.

These experiences also pushed me away from liberals. Even though Jaggi took special care to ensure that he doesn't end up offending a Sardesai or Ghose, I didn't sense any reciprocation from the other side. Many of the self-declared liberal journalists used to attack and mock Jaggi regularly, but I never saw a Sardesai or Ghose intervene and support Jaggi. In every sense, liberalism and secularism were quintessential one-way streets, and I was getting uncomfortable with it.

I feel that many others would have had similar experiences, obviously in very different set-ups and circumstances, in the most part of 2013 and early 2014, where they would have felt that there is no element of mutual respect or reciprocation from the liberals. When the ideological debates would start getting heated, it would invariably be the pro-Modi guy who had to step back and assuage the feelings of his liberal friend, who just couldn't stop ranting about how fascism must be stopped.

While the liberal friend might end up thinking he won the debate, he had essentially pushed a not-so-Sanghi guy an inch closer to the Sanghi camp. Do remember that Modi had started to impress many, especially the urban online-savvy educated class, many of whom had no special ideological affinity for the RSS or Hindutva.

These were the incremental votes that Modi was able to draw towards the BJP, but he was drawing them primarily to himself, not to the Hindutva ideology as such. However, such people were liberally being painted as Sanghis and fascists. It was the intolerance of the liberals that was all set to convert those incremental votes into ideological and numerical strength of Hindutva.

When losing a debate, the liberals threw labels such as Sanghis, fascists and bigots to assume moral superiority. They also assumed some sort of victory arising out of that labelling. When you put any label on a person, that person can either actively try to shed that label, or get curious and start exploring the 'truth' about those labels—I think the majority of the pro-Modi folks fell in the latter category. I certainly was one of them.

The liberals were rendering the word 'liberal' meaningless, just like politicians had earlier made the word 'secular' meaningless. Once there is no innate pressure to be a liberal, because the connotation of the term has changed, one becomes more open to explore what the 'bigots' are saying.

This was one of the reasons why I had started listening to the 'trolls' and 'Hindutvawadis', as I followed their accounts on Twitter. At least during those years, most of those who had been labelled so had rational arguments and hardly any of them proposed or postulated any supremacist theories—something that Hindutva is popularly accused of by the liberals.

A common theme among most of the arguments forwarded by the pro-Hindutva voices was to oppose the hypocrisy and double standards of the liberal and secular crowd. Most of the times, these people, the Sanghis, were seeking parity, not supremacy—treat Hinduism the way you treat Islam. Treat Gujarat riots the way you have treated any other riot. Treat grievances of the Hindus the way you treat the grievances of 'minorities'. Treat our voices the way you treat any other voice. Give us a platform to speak too, the way you give everyone else. And so on and so forth.

Now, the Left has all the required framework and theories to justify their double standards and deny this demand of equal treatment, but those don't really cut ice with an average person, or even with a classical liberal or libertarian person on many occasions. Being brazen about these double standards and practising them on steroids is being 'woke' as we know the term today, but wokes were not that vocal and ubiquitous in that era. Perhaps, they would have only added to the population of neo-Sanghis, thanks to their fanatical behaviour.

The self-styled secular-liberals were not doing any great service to their cause despite the absence of wokes. For someone like me, it became increasingly apparent that the liberals indeed were hypocrites. They showed symptoms of having almost every single vice that they accused the Sanghis or the Right-wingers of possessing.

The usual criticism of the liberals was that the Right-wingers were abusive. First of all, in those times, not many abusive accounts were active on Twitter, as compared to today, when abusive language really flies high and fast, and which targets anyone and everyone. The self-declared liberals, especially the celebrity journalists, would invariably ignore valid and well-reasoned criticism and instead pick a tweet from some random account that used abusive language or came up with a stupid response. These stray comments would be used to declare any criticism as abusive and invalid. It was a typical strawman strategy to silence or sidestep genuine criticism.

Secondly, talking from the first principles, abuses or insults at the end of the day are just verbal expressions aimed at hurting one's feelings or sentiments, and 'hurting sentiments' is a very grey area, which is often used as an excuse to clamp down on free speech. As a libertarian, I was not at all fine with the business of hurting sentiments being seen as some crime or offense. Well-written scholarly articles can also hurt sentiments. You should actually be proud if someone came up with only abuses and insults in response to something intellectual that you came up with—it only proves that your verbal and cerebral abilities were of no match to those of the other guy.

Finally, 'abuse' in itself is a vast and subjective term. What can indeed be termed problematic in any verbal expression is libel, obscenity (again a subjective term), direct threat of physical harm or targeted mental harassment. Barring these, I won't really lose sleep over random abusive words intended to unsettle or hurt me. How is calling someone a ch***ya any different from calling someone a fascist? Why is the latter not an abuse? The latter is actually an example of libel.

If not abusive, the liberals would claim the Right-wingers are intolerant and narrow-minded, that their interest was not in the debate or discussions but in talking down to people and coming up with diktats. Perhaps, they never realized how ironical it sounded. I would just go back to what I had written about the 'ecosystem' and the attitude that drives it—a messiah complex is at its core, which makes them talk down to people and come down with diktats.

It was actually the liberals who were intolerant of the dissenting voices, and they continue to be so. For decades, they didn't want to publish articles or books by authors they saw as pro-Hindutva or anti-Left, and even now they want to drown out such voices. In April 2014, a 'progressive' and 'liberal' publishing house decided to cancel the book contract of a Sahitya Akademi-winning author, Joe D'Cruz.[75] The fault of D'Cruz was that he had dared to praise Modi's Gujarat model of development. How exactly is one supposed to consider these set of people as open-minded and tolerant?

The liberal attempt to counter the bad ideas (that they claim to be fighting) is to rarely come up with better ideas. Rather, they attempt to de-platform individuals and de-monetize entities that come up with a counter set of ideas, which they declare as bad ideas. They behave this way perhaps because they have no counter at all.

This quintessential intolerant behaviour is now widely promoted across the world on the pretext of fighting 'hate speech' and creating 'safe spaces'. Big tech companies and corporates are being arm-twisted into adopting this extremist behaviour as a 'responsibility' towards the society.

The justification for shutting down dissent by branding the dissenting voices as fascist, bigoted and hateful is offered by pointing to the Karl Popper's paradox of tolerance. The paradox says that for a tolerant society to continue being tolerant, it must be intolerant of intolerance. The rationale is—if the intolerants are tolerated, that is, if they are allowed to promote and propagate intolerance, there would be no tolerance left, as the intolerant would obliterate it once they prevail.

This is a paradox, not a law, but the liberals treat it as a law. However, in essence they use it as an excuse to justify their intolerance—just paint the other side intolerant by drawing random parallels with the Nazis, and then 'punch a fascist'.

Without going into the debate of who is a real fascist and who really is intolerant, let us look at Popper's paradox of tolerance from the first principles framework. The same can be extended to every proselytizing religion, such as Christianity or Islam. Taking inspiration from the policy of being intolerant of intolerance, a multi-cultural or multi-faith society must not allow preaching by those religions that are monolithic/ monotheistic and those who consider apostasy as a sin or crime. If such religions are allowed to preach and prevail, the multi-faith characteristic of a society will vanish (because of monotheistic nature of the prevailing religion), as there will be no further proselytization allowed (because apostasy will be punished).

So taking cue from Popper's paradox, liberals should actually work towards altering Article 25 of our Constitution, which allows all citizens to 'propagate' their religion. Thus, only those religions should be allowed to propagate, which extend the rights of propagation or proselytization when they are in majority. To put it bluntly, since Islam doesn't allow proselytization once it becomes the dominant religion, and it even punishes apostasy, Islam shouldn't be allowed to be propagated in a society that aims to remain multi-faith and multi-cultural—that will be Popper's Paradox of Proselytization.

We all know how a liberal will react to such an idea. Essentially, they will betray their hypocrisy. And they betrayed it quite liberally, as India, especially digital India, debated Modi and ideologies.

Hypocrisy and contradictions appeared to be the defining traits of a liberal. The criticism about Hindutva politics being just an obsession about religious identity was the most hypocritical one, because liberals and every ally of liberals indulge in nothing but identity politics all the time.

If a Hindutva guy can't see beyond religion, the liberal can't see beyond caste. You can't really find a caste angle in everything, including food and cricket, and then rue that certain people just talk about 'Hindu–Muslim' all the time. Well you too talk about 'Brahmin–Dalit' all the time. How come caste is a bigger reality than religion? Both are social identities and both impact the daily lives of people. If you feel religion doesn't impact people's daily lives, then you're just living a cocooned privileged life, where you're safe from these impacts.

When an upper-caste Hindu says that he doesn't believe in caste, he is immediately attacked and lectured that he can afford to say so because of his privilege, which allows him to be blind to certain realities. Granted. I do see a merit in that argument. But how about employing the same wisdom and realizing that you too are blind to certain harsh realities about religion, and thus you get on your moral high horse and start preaching everyone not to talk about Hindu–Muslim?

These blind spots have been meticulously created by our education system and the media. As I had said earlier, the practise of not reporting

Muslim aggression in the name of 'responsible journalism', the maligning of the term 'Hindu groups', the whitewashing of atrocities during the Islamic period, the justification of Islamic radicalism in modern period and many such factors go on to develop these blind spots. Further, living in your safe 'upper-middle-class Hindu colonies'—your privilege—you go on to preach those who are living in 'mixed societies' and who have to suffer the consequences of such preachings.

It is you who choose to be blind when a Chandan Gupta is killed for shouting Vande Mataram in a 'Muslim lane'.[76] It is you who choose to be mute when Islamic radicals kill a Kamlesh Tiwari in broad daylight as a punishment for blasphemy.[77] It is you who would ask a Hindu to shift his house instead of asking a mosque to lower down the volume of the morning azaan.[78] It is you who can't see the plight of the Hindus once monotheistic religions are in majority in a region. It is you who gives a 'political context' to the exodus of Kashmiri Pandits or the murder of Hindu activists at the hands of Islamists. It's your privilege that allows you to ignore issues arising out of religion; others can't, as they have paid with their lives, since centuries.

And such an incident did take place in 2013. In the month of August, riots broke out in Muzaffarnagar in western Uttar Pradesh. They were triggered after two Hindu brothers, allegedly enraged over the sexual harassment of their sister, were killed in clashes with Muslim men.[79] The usual reaction of the liberals was obfuscation of facts, blaming the BJP, blaming the victims and doing everything under the sun rather than remotely acknowledging the fact that members of the Muslim community can indeed indulge in such acts.

The liberals can delude that every Hindu–Muslim issue is artificially engineered by the RSS or the BJP, but the truth is that they have existed for centuries. The Moplah massacre took place when the RSS was not even founded. And there have been so many religious issues around the world; are all of them engineered by the RSS?

To his credit, my friend who was a member of a leftist student's union (SFI) and whom I have referred to a couple of times earlier in this book, acknowledged that Muslims in western Uttar Pradesh were indeed rowdy and their gundaism was no different from that of some dominant castes, such as the Jats. Obviously in public, only Jats can be accused of being rowdy and violent, and saying the same about Muslims will amount to bigotry; which is why I am not naming him.

Ironically it was from him, a leftist, that I first heard claims about a 'Modi wave'. He claimed that there was support for Modi in western Uttar Pradesh, as Jats wanted Modi to 'teach Muslims a lesson'. He said that he won't be surprised if the BJP wins from those areas instead of the usual Jat and so-called farmer leaders.

I was unsure about his claims then, which were made a few weeks after the Muzaffarnagar riots, and by when Modi was officially declared the prime ministerial candidate of the BJP. This declaration happened in September 2013, until which time Modi had not made any statement over Hindu–Muslim issues. But as I wrote earlier, Modi didn't really need to say anything. His detractors kept the Hindu–Muslim issue alive by raking up 2002 and by selling fear.

Modi sold hope—there will be no corruption, there will be better governance, inflation will go down and obviously, 'achchhe din aane waale hain'—while his detractors sold fear—if Modi wins, India will lose international reputation, Muslims will be disenfranchised and citizens' freedom will be taken away. His detractors didn't include just the political opponents, but the entire ecosystem. As the elections drew nearer, the commentary only grew shriller and more desperate.

In December 2013, *The Telegraph*—the newspaper published from Kolkata that is now famous for showing the spine to Modi and melting it away in the service of Mamata Banerjee—published an anonymous article that essentially argued that if Modi wins, India will be overrun by Taliban.[80] While another article published on a digital platform in March 2014 shamed the Indian voters by saying that 'India crosses the moral line of no return if Modi becomes prime minister.'[81]

I remembered the message and headline, respectively, of these two articles for many years to come. At that point itself, I found them to be totally irrational. Such extremist polemics only made me more convinced that Modi was the right man for the job, and that these set of people were suffering from some messiah complex—that they must save the stupid Indians who can be fooled by Modi. This only led me to question where this superiority complex comes from, and well, you already know the answer, reading my conclusions and inferences since the beginning of this book.

8

Making of Modi's India

The 2014 Lok Sabha elections

In retrospect, while it might appear that Modi's 2014 victory was a given—the Congress having lost the narrative badly after its own ecosystem went rogue, clubbed with Modi's rising image as a development man—it wasn't apparent at all in the run-up to the elections. At least, I didn't think that he could achieve such a spectacular victory.

I certainly backed the man for the top job. I had even taken my first steps towards the ideological shift by agreeing to the many points raised by the pro-Hindutva voices. I had started becoming conscious of my sense of belonging, though I was not yet assertive of my identity.

I was not sure that Modi would win easily because I thought that I belonged to a rather small bunch, which doesn't have the numeric strength to shift the results of the elections. In my own eyes, I was just a 'privileged' upper-caste urban male, living in a big city and drawing my experiences from the virtual world, while the real India lived in small towns and villages.

There were other reasons too that suggested that it was not going to be easy for Modi. Firstly, and primarily, he appeared to be battling alone. Advani, the prime ministerial candidate of the BJP in the 2009 Lok Sabha elections, had resigned in June 2013 as a knee-jerk reaction to Modi being appointed the chief of BJP's poll campaign committee for the 2014 Lok Sabha elections. He later withdrew his resignation, but not before proving to everyone that all was not well within the BJP over the issue of Modi's leadership.

Within a week of Advani's resignation, Nitish Kumar, the then chief minister of Bihar and JD(U) supremo, announced that he was breaking up the 17-year-long alliance with the BJP in Bihar. Bihar was one of the states where the BJP-led NDA used to perform well, and now even that state became 'difficult'. As *Faking News*, I had tweeted that the NDA was reduced to being 'Narendra Damodardas Alliance'. That was immediately re-tweeted by many Modi haters too, who saw it as a commentary on Modi's supposed inability to win allies, without whom you couldn't possibly form a government at the Centre.

Starting with the 1989 Lok Sabha elections, every government at the Centre was a coalition government, where no single party could win a majority of its own. Thus, everyone had assumed that India was now in a 'coalition era' for an indefinite period of time and it was unimaginable that anyone would be able to capture power at the Centre without building coalitions. And here, Modi was losing even existing coalition partners.

Secondly, the BJP was supposed to be a spent force in Uttar Pradesh and more recently in Karnataka—they had lost the 2013 assembly elections and Yediyurappa, their tallest leader down south, had left the party—with no hope of bouncing back. Traditionally, it was weak in states such as West Bengal, Odisha and Haryana, and regions such as the North East and South India. The BJP's presence appeared limited to around 300 Lok Sabha seats. It was unimaginable that it will end up winning 282 seats.

And finally, I thought—what if all the support for Modi was just an online phenomenon, which was limited only to the urban crowd? What if the ground realities were different? After all, the BJP was winning in that 'Political Stock Exchange' that we had created for Aaj Tak during the 2009 elections, but the final results were just the opposite.

Being hugely popular among the Twitter and Facebook crowd is not the same as being popular in a tier-II or III city or village of India, where the bulk of the voting population resides. I felt that the issues surrounding ideology didn't matter to them, because their daily battles revolved around livelihood. The Congress could be argued to be losing support in these constituencies, thanks to inflation and a 'jobless growth', but would all of them put their faith in Modi as an alternative? I was not sure.

There certainly were some 'helpful' factors, similar to what my leftist friend had told me about western Uttar Pradesh, that is, the frustration of the locals with Muslim aggression in those areas. This was fanned further by a Congress candidate named Imran Masood, who threatened to cut Modi into pieces ('boti boti kaat denge') if he dared to harm the Muslims. Do notice that yet again, Modi didn't need to say anything against Muslims in the run-up to the Lok Sabha elections, but his haters volunteered to 'polarize' the elections, at least in certain areas.

However, I thought that such factors were too localized and could at best affect a handful of seats, where the religious identity of a Hindu starts affecting his daily life. There didn't appear to be a pan-India 'Hindu' feeling—except online—that could trigger a wave and propel the BJP to attain the pole position. The BJP had called their campaign 'Mission 272+', that is, the target of winning a majority of their own. I found it overambitious.

Primarily, my apprehensions were born out of the belief that the changes that I had witnessed and felt since 2010 might not be shared by a large chunk of the population that didn't care about Twitter or the virtual world. Maybe, I too was underestimating the impact of the new media and its trickle-down effect on the population that might not be directly touched by this new chaotic narrative-building process, much of which happened online. The Congress party and the ecosystem definitely underestimated the impact of the internet and social media.

I now realize that while issues such as hypocrisy of the liberals—that dominated online discourse during those times—might not be of any relevance to someone living in a small town or village, the weakening of the faith in the mainstream media and celebrity journalists—thanks to the Radia tapes controversy and the gradual effect of the shifting online narrative—definitely would have impacted their thinking and the way they looked at political developments and current affairs.

During and after the Radia tapes controversy, an average person could somewhat see, though not discern, that the media too was part of the establishment while pretending to be anti-establishment. In simple terms, people could see that many journalists were too close and friendly with politicians from the ruling parties. The effects went beyond the virtual world.

The same mainstream media had painted Modi as a 'controversial leader' and a 'divisive figure', who appeared to invest all his time plotting conspiracies against the Muslims. A weakening of faith in the mainstream media meant a weakening of this media-created image of Modi too. Further, as we will see in this chapter later, media indeed could not dent the image of Modi as they had lost clout.

In order to be effective and influential again, certain sections of the mainstream media needed to get back that halo of being anti-establishment. Ironically, Modi's victory proved to be of great help to them, as they could attack a section of the media and brand them 'Godi media' or pro-BJP, and by corollary paint themselves as anti-establishment heroes. Unfortunately, for most people, the 'establishment' still means the ruling party. I won't blame the people. It is easier to see who are occupying some government spaces than realizing who are occupying your mind space.

Nevertheless, many liberals apply this 'Godi media' theory retrospectively and try to argue that in the run-up to the 2014 Lok Sabha elections, the mainstream media, especially the Hindi TV news channels, was soft on Modi, that is, they were Godi media even before Modi had won. That's far from the truth. What can be conceded is the fact that some sections of the media, especially the Hindi media, did not hate Modi the way the English liberal media did and continues to.

The vernacular media, especially some Hindi news channels, had essentially treated Modi the way they would have treated any other politician who had won three consecutive state elections with convincing margins. And that was the only 'crime' of those channels. It's amazing how the same English media never felt it necessary and relevant to talk about scams or 'jungle raj' of Lalu Prasad Yadav when talking about him in the post-2010 era, but when it came to Modi, they expected everyone to be stuck in a time warp and keep harping about 2002.

Also, it is not true that the mainstream media, including the Hindi news channels, was entirely 'soft' on Modi. In the run-up to the elections, Modi was attacked at least three times, and all those controversies were aimed at painting him as a misogynist with no personal morals. The first was the '50 crore girlfriend' comment on Shashi Tharoor, then his marital status, as Modi had to acknowledge his child marriage due to a change in rules by the Election Commission of India, and finally a controversy called 'Snoopgate', where it was insinuated that as the chief minister of Gujarat, Modi was illegally spying on a woman.

All the three were aimed at destroying the personal integrity and character of Modi, and made prime-time headlines on TV. These were not small controversies. In a largely conservative society like India, such allegations about a leader being 'characterless' and immoral can make or break careers. Even in a progressive and modern society like the US, an 'affair' by a president was a huge controversy, which eventually led to his impeachment.

The mainstream media, including the Hindi news channels, had debated and amplified all these controversies, so it really is a bit far-fetched to claim that the media was soft on Modi. On the contrary, you can hardly recall the mainstream media 'helping' in any such attacks when it came to Rahul Gandhi's personal life and character.

These controversies couldn't hurt Modi, not because the media was soft on him, but because the media had lost much of its credibility and clout. Thus, their ability to influence people's thinking and shape their opinions had weakened considerably. Furthermore, these controversies appeared to be engineered and malicious, and people didn't find Modi guilty of any transgression.

The '50 crore girlfriend' comment was a matter of semantics than character, and people by and large knew what it referred to. While the phrase might sound inappropriate, the target was not any woman but Shashi Tharoor and the endless list of scams involving Congress leaders. The comment was about the worth of equity that had allegedly been pocketed by Tharoor by using Sunanda Pushkar, whom he later married, as a proxy owner in lieu of helping a company get an IPL team franchise.

The statement was made by Modi in October 2012 and by 2013, the IPL was marred by various scandals, including spot fixing, so people know that all was not well with the way money moved in IPL. And in January 2014, the shocking news of the sudden death of Pushkar came in. Just a couple of days before her death, tweets were posted from Tharoor's account that showed that all was not well between her and Tharoor. The tweets suggested that Tharoor was having an extramarital affair with Pakistani journalist Mehr Tarar. While Tharoor claimed that his account was hacked, Pushkar spoke to a few people in the media and confirmed that it was she who had been posting from Tharoor's Twitter account to show how Tarar was stalking her husband. She was angry and anguished.

'I took upon myself the crimes of this man during IPL. I will not allow this to be done to me,' Pushkar was reported to have said about Tharoor during her conversations with the media. She also talked about the very incident to which Modi had referred, and said that 'they didn't take my permission to put my name... for the equity.' She further added that she was 'advised' by the Congress party not to raise these issues as elections were approaching.[82] She virtually confirmed the veracity of what Modi had alluded to earlier.

Within hours of this scandal breaking out and Pushkar talking to the media, an official joint statement was issued by both Tharoor and Pushkar, downplaying all the tweets and her statements to the media. The statement said that they were 'happily married and intend to remain that way'. The statement further informed that Pushkar was ill and taking rest. The next day she passed away.

While some in the media, especially the English-language media, somehow concluded that that the death was not suspicious, the sequence of events proved to be too much of a coincidence for the common man. The case and the mystery surrounding her death still linger on. Consequently, the charge against Modi—of semantics—didn't really stick, because other issues around the incident proved to be of a much serious nature.

The marital status of Modi could also not paint him as an immoral guy though the Congress tried its best to do so. Leaders like Digvijay Singh and others made a host of personal comments against Modi—and they continue to do so—trying to depict Modi as someone who abandoned his wife. But his wife Jashodaben never portrayed herself as a victim. She had gotten over the fact that their marriage, which was result of their families deciding on their behalf when they were teenagers, didn't work out as Modi chose a different path for himself in his adulthood.

Furthermore, it was not as if Modi had tried to lie about his marital status earlier. The old rules of the Election Commission of India didn't make it mandatory to fill the 'marital status' field, and thus Modi used to leave it blank, signalling that he would rather not want to talk about this aspect of his personal life. But when the rules were changed and it became mandatory to fill up that field, he acknowledged the marriage, thus respecting the sanctity of whatever had happened decades ago, even if it was against his wishes. There was nothing 'immoral' about it.

And finally, the Snoopgate. The entire controversy was replete with insinuations and conspiracy theories. In the supposed 'leaked tapes' one could not hear 'Narendra Modi' even once, while conflicting claims emerged about who was spied on and on whose commands. The Congress tried to take full political advantage of this 'scandal', with its women leaders demanding the resignation of Modi and Shah, but surprisingly the Manmohan Singh government didn't announce any inquiry into the incident.

Once the news gathered momentum, it was Modi's Gujarat government that announced an inquiry. In the end, the father of the woman who was allegedly being snooped upon clarified that he himself had requested the state government to watch over and guard his daughter due to security concerns. But that did not stop the media from talking about it and debating it. How exactly was that being 'soft on Modi'?

In his book, which documented and analysed various incidents in the run-up to the 2014 Lok Sabha elections, TV journalist Rajdeep Sardesai, who has often used the 'media not asking tough questions to Modi' line in his public utterings, himself concedes that Snoopgate was debated in the media and had become a huge issue before the elections. However, he also goes on to concede that it couldn't hurt Modi's image. This is what he writes:

> That the Snoopgate 'revelations' were met with some scepticism perhaps reflected the credibility crisis afflicting the ruling UPA government. In normal times, the audio tapes would have merited a detailed investigation, with tough questions being asked. But in the build-up to the elections, it was perceived as yet another 'hit job' on Modi and his man Friday. Had the Snoopgate story broken a year or two earlier, it might have resonated more strongly. The UPA had got its timing wrong—yet again.[83]

Now, the above paragraph by Sardesai is pretty interesting. Snoopgate was not brought out in public by the Congress party or the UPA government.

It was 'broken' by a website founded by Aniruddha Bahal, who was the co-founder of the Tehelka magazine of Tarun Tejpal fame. Tehelka is credited for having damaged the image of the Vajpayee government by conducting a sting operation that suggested bribery in defence deals.

The then BJP President Bangaru Laxman had to resign as he was seen accepting donation in cash for the party, allegedly without issuing any receipt and purportedly to help in defence deals. The image of the then Defence Minister George Fernandes was also tarnished and he was relentlessly attacked based on the 'revelations' by Tehelka.

It is important to note here that Tehelka's brand name was sullied after Tarun Tejpal was accused of sexual assault by his own employee in November 2013. The management and editorial leadership of the magazine was also accused of not giving the victim a fair hearing. The entire controversy led to other skeletons in Tejpal's cupboard tumbling out, such as the properties he had amassed as well as allegations of Tehelka killing negative news stories of companies that sponsored its ThinkFest event. Although Bahal had left Tehelka much earlier, in public perception, the Tehelka brand of journalism had already taken a hit.

In such a scenario, shouldn't the failure of Snoopgate in creating any impact be tied to the credibility crisis around Tehelka (and by extension, around the mainstream media), given that one of the co-founders of that magazine broke the story? If 'revelations' were not believed by the general public, did it not reflect the weakening of faith in the same media, which earlier prided itself with damaging the image of the Vajpayee government? Why did Sardesai then argue that it reflected the 'credibility crisis' of the UPA government?

Was that a Freudian slip that admitted that outfits like Tehelka were part of the same ecosystem—the Tehelka magazine being the media arm and the Congress party being the political arm—and that it was not really the credibility crisis of the UPA government alone, but a credibility crisis that afflicted the entire ecosystem? Or did he mean to suggest that investigative journalism in India is basically handouts given by political parties to do 'hit jobs' against their opponents? That the timing of publication of such investigative reports depends not on the journalists' ability to dig information, but on a political party's strategic planning to 'time' the exposé? In which case, it also becomes evident that journalism is part of the same ecosystem.

Whatever be the reason, the media was not giving any free pass to Modi the way some would like to believe. Moreover, some Hindi news channels had aired a 'sting operation'—the Tehelka brand of journalism again—where they claimed to have 'exposed' how opinion polls were rigged. By that time, almost every opinion poll was showing the BJP under Modi having an edge over the Congress in the ensuing Lok Sabha elections. Effectively, an attempt was made to tell people that the popularity of Modi, as reflected in those opinion polls, was all make-believe and paid for.

So essentially a section of the media, including Hindi media, tried to delegitimize even the natural popularity and support enjoyed by Modi—this is far from the media being 'soft on Modi.'

It was clear that Modi as a brand had become quite strong, something even I didn't realize. And various factors—not all of them triggered or employed by Modi or his team, such as the rise in consciousness around the Hindu identity, thanks to global and technological developments—contributed to making this brand. Critics couldn't understand this phenomenon, and in frustration they blamed the media for having created this brand, while in reality Modi had reached a stage where his brand was growing despite the media, and not due to the media.

With issues raised in the mainstream media unable to dent Modi's image, and with social media having truly democratized the narrative, many people decided to trust Modi on various issues—development, governance, personal character, 'achchhe din' promise and much more—and give him a chance.

However, one may wonder that why did Hindutva—the bogey raised by the media and intelligentsia over decades—not prove to be an impediment? Was brand Modi, or the Modi wave, so strong that it just carried people away with itself, even if they were not necessarily pro-Hindutva? Or had people made peace with Hindutva?

I have explained why it didn't prove to be a bother for me, because I had started seeing merits in the arguments of the pro-Hindutva ideologues, but what about the others? Not everyone was on Twitter and reading those tweets and blogs.

Hindutva and the Modi wave

Since 2009 itself—after the BJP failed to win the Lok Sabha elections that year—many BJP supporters and leaders had started talking about the possibility of Modi leading the party in the 2014 elections. In fact, leaders like Arun Shourie and Arun Jaitley had wished to see Modi as the prime minister even before the 2009 results were known, with the caveat that Advani should become the prime minister in 2009, followed by Modi in 2014.[84]

Every time such a suggestion was thrown in or the idea discussed, Modi's 'image problem' was assumed to be the biggest handicap in his journey to Delhi. And that image was that of a hardline Hindutva leader who failed to stop the 2002 riots, and was accused by his haters of enabling the riots. The argument that was put forth was that India was not Gujarat, and that he will not be accepted by people elsewhere.

Those concerns and cautions proved to be wrong in 2014. Did the general population make peace with Hindutva or did they simply ignore it and focused only on the new 'vikas purush' image of Modi? I believe that while many must have voted in favour of Modi for issues other than Hindutva, they did not really have the luxury to entirely ignore the Hindutva aspect, for that was how they had known Modi in the popular narrative.

For someone like me who fancied himself to be a libertarian, Modi's image as a development man and his pro-business policies proved to be a factor why I started liking him initially. For someone else, his aggressive stand against the Congress could be the reason why they started liking him. There indeed existed a crowd that just hated the Congress for various reasons and were not necessarily pro-Hindutva or pro-market. Some could have liked him just for his oratory and personality, while some others could have liked him due to the modest background he came from—something that Mani Shankar Aiyar helped the entire country know and sympathize with, thanks to his 'chaiwala' comment.

Obviously, a good majority liked him for reasons none other than Hindutva, but I'm talking about the voters who swung towards the BJP in 2014, and it was a huge swing. A bulk of them, I would argue, started liking Modi due to reasons other than Hindutva, and eventually ended up being comfortable with his ideology too.

Due to the weakening of faith in the media, many would have gotten rid of an image of Modi where he was painted as someone who was directly complicit in the riots, murders and fake encounters, but they would not have gotten rid of the image of Modi as a 'Hindutva leader.' That was not an option.

I have reasons to believe that there was no luxury for any set of voters to settle for something like 'Modi minus Hindutva', even though a tiny set might have tried that.

Remember that Atal Bihari Vajpayee, the only other Hindutva leader to get popular support across India and who became the prime minister consequently, was labelled as a 'right man in the wrong party'. The phrase had a subtle message for Vajpayee fans—'It is okay if you like Vajpayee, but don't end up liking Hindutva—because Vajpayee is right, but Hindutva is wrong.'

But the media didn't leave any space for a similar subterfuge in the case of Modi. He was the 'wrong man' in the 'wrong party' from the very beginning. If you liked and supported Modi, you were pushing India to the 'moral point of no return'—that was the message propagated by the liberal media, and that's how it was passed down to the masses by his political opponents too. Sonia Gandhi had attacked Modi and the BJP using the term 'Zeher ki kheti'—people sowing the seeds of poison—in February 2014, after earlier having termed them as 'Maut ke saudagar', or merchants of death, in 2007.

Some even declared that they will leave India if Modi became the prime minister. They shouted that the very idea of India would die if Modi won. These were strong pronouncements, seeped in a sense of moral superiority. While such explicit pronouncements might not be widespread, the implicit superiority complex manifested in many forms and on many levels. Essentially Modi supporters were forced to take a moral stand on Modi's 'earlier politics' and on Hindutva—either literally during debates in the run-up to the 2014 Lok Sabha elections, or it played on their minds due to the legacy of the narrative built around Modi.

While an Atal Bihari Vajpayee supporter could convince himself or argue with others that he liked Vajpayee but did not support Hindutva, a Modi supporter couldn't have argued that convincingly. It is true that

Modi did not make any anti-Muslim or even pro-Hindutva speech as part of his pitch for the top job, but he always left enough signals for people to pick that he was a Hindutva guy all through.

In an interview with Rajat Sharma of India TV in April 2014,[85] Modi was asked about his refusal to wear a Muslim skullcap that a Maulana had offered him during the sadbhavna fast of 2011. That incident had made news back in 2011 itself, and since then it had been used and overused by his critics to show that while Modi may want to reinvent his image as a development man, he remained a communal person in his heart. He was asked that if every other politician can wear a Muslim skullcap during an Iftaar party or some other event, why would a Modi refuse to wear it?

'I have never seen any picture of Mahatma Gandhi wearing such a cap,' Modi retorted when asked about his refusal to wear the Muslim skullcap. In that one short sentence, he not only ended up showing how the meaning of secularism had become corrupted over decades, he also gave the signal that he was not apologetic about his deeds, which were branded communal by the secular-liberal lobby. He further said that he had not seen 'even Nehru' wearing such a Muslim skullcap—a subtle take on the father of one-eyed secularism in India, which I believe has not been appreciated much.

In the same interview, Modi further said that he would respect other's traditions and beliefs, but he would also follow his own traditions and beliefs—again a signal that he was not diluting his core beliefs. He was essentially inviting his new fans, who would have become his fans only due to his track record of governance and development, to check out his ideological beliefs too.

Basically, Modi was a Sanghi (he literally was, as he started as an RSS pracharak) who not only knew how to reach out to those who had never been to a shakha, but he possibly also had a plan to convert them too. I was being converted for sure, and so were a million others.

Earlier in July 2013, in another interview, this time by Reuters,[86] he was asked, 'People want to know who is the real Modi—Hindu nationalist leader or pro-business chief minister?' Modi answered this by saying that he was a nationalist and also a Hindu, so one can say that he is a 'Hindu nationalist'. He further added that he saw no contradiction between the two images—that of a Hindu nationalist and that of a person who is pro-business.

Now, in strict intellectual and ideological terms, that answer, rather that definition of 'Hindu nationalist' was pretty inadequate and tangential. But it attempted to achieve something else. Modi was attempting to change the connotation around the term 'Hindu nationalism' rather than diluting his image as a 'Hindu nationalist.'

He was normalizing a term that had been meticulously maligned over the decades through a carefully crafted narrative. He was attempting to tell his fans that they should be amenable to the idea of 'Hindu nationalism'—that he didn't find any contradiction between the two terms (Hindu nationalist and pro-business) and was at peace donning both hats, and so should they, too, be. He was helping people break free of the taboo that was created around his ideology.

And finally, there was a distinct symbolism behind his decision to choose Varanasi as the second seat from where he would fight the 2014 Lok Sabha elections. One of the holiest cities of Hinduism, Varanasi or Kashi or Banaras is considered the home of Lord Shiva. A dip in the Ganga cleanses you spiritually, while the ghats are a gateway to attain moksha.

Out of the 80 seats in Uttar Pradesh, he chose Varanasi, which was in no way a 'safe seat.' The BJP had lost it in 2004 while in 2009, even when a senior leader like Dr Murli Manohar Joshi was contesting, the victory margin was less than 3 per cent of the total votes polled. The BJP's vote share was 30.5 per cent, that is, a joint opposition candidate could have won the seat.

Varanasi is important not just from the point of view of religious beliefs, but it symbolizes the awakening and assertion of Hindu political identity too. It is the birthplace of Rani Lakshmi Bai, who fought against the British in the first war of Indian independence, and it houses the BHU (Banaras Hindu University), which was founded by Madan Mohan Malaviya, who also founded the Akhil Bharatiya Hindu Mahasabha. He was one of the earliest leaders in the Indian National Congress who could see the threat that the Muslim League and Muslim separatism posed. Incidentally, a few months after Modi won, Malaviya was awarded the Bharat Ratna (the highest civilian award of India) posthumously.

Subtly, one step at a time, Modi was making it clear that while his pitch is for all-round development and 'Sabka vikas', he was not moving away from Hindu nationalism. He was normalizing one word, one symbol and one belief at a time. He was making it easier for people to become Sanghis without going to any shakha.

Modi's media strategies also helped. Though he did give interviews to various media houses, they mostly came towards the final stages of campaigning. For the most part of 2013 and in run-up to the first phase of voting in April 2014, he was on TV thanks to self-hosted events like 'Chai pe charcha' or his speeches at some or the other events—such as the speech at SRCC in Delhi—and political rallies, which were invariably carried live by almost every channel, for Modi meant TRP.

This meant that Modi was communicating to the people directly, without the journalists being the gatekeepers or filters in the communication process. 'This guy is so different from the way media had projected him' would have been a common feeling among the ordinary citizens who started liking him for non-Hindutva reasons.

Thanks to his communication and media strategy, an average Indian was not only ready to believe that Modi was wrongly vilified by the media and the Congress party, but he was further, directly or indirectly, concluding that Modi's ideology was also wrongly vilified.

Let us be clear here that Hindutva could mean various things to various people, but with limited reference to elections and realpolitik, I'm largely referring to only two things—resistance to Islamic aggression and assertion of one's civilizational identity. The narrative by the ecosystem has always painted this resistance to Islamic aggression as 'communalism' while the assertion of one's identity has been painted as 'bigotry'.

I believe that despite the ecosystem dominating the narrative for decades, a large chunk of the population could discerningly or reflexively question this conditioning, as Modi became the central point of discussions and arguments.

For example, only after 2014 would I realize that the issue of Muslim aggression was not a localized factor that existed in western Uttar Pradesh alone. Such incidents happen almost regularly in many parts of India, including in non-Hindi states. But, these incidents don't make it to the national English-language media. Either the stories are not covered on purpose due to 'responsible journalism' or the journalists convince themselves that these are petty incidents of 'crime being given a communal colour' and thus fit only for local crime coverage.

In an academic or TV studio debate, one can convincingly prove that Hindu–Muslim tensions in an area after a simple incident, say of two bikes hitting each other followed by verbal or physical clashes between Hindu and Muslim mobs, is an example of a petty incident being given communal colours, but the way it plays out locally in real life is entirely different. People see it as an aggression arising out of collective identity.

The Liberals don't waste a second to see a caste angle in seemingly simple crime cases, or a communal angle when the victim is a Muslim. Theories of 'intersectionality' are brought in to argue why the caste or religion of a victim is indeed relevant, even if the crime may not outwardly look motivated by casteist or religious factors. Imagine two bikes, one driven by a person from the Thakur caste and another by a person from the Chamar caste, bumping into each other in some area of Uttar Pradesh, followed by clashes. Can you think of any liberal worth his salt claiming that such a 'clash shouldn't be given casteist colours'? They will colour all corners themselves by claiming that the Thakurs acted violently due to their inherent caste supremacist beliefs.

Basically, they also tie aggressive behaviour to collective identity, and won't mince words on how certain castes behave aggressively and oppress others—but somehow it is always 'giving communal colour' to similar incidents when the belligerent party belongs to the Muslim community.

There are many pockets in different areas of this country where Muslim aggression is witnessed regularly, just like a Jat or a Thakur aggression could be witnessed in other areas. For Hindus living in such regions and feeling the impact of such incidents on their daily lives, the step towards Hindutva won't really need a big push. Perhaps, they were always 'Hindutvawadis' in that sense. They just needed someone around whom they could rally around on that particular point. Earlier they were bucketed in micro-identities, often around caste, and thus they didn't really rally around this point until an 'outsider' Modi came, with whom the only identity they shared was that of religion.

Further, I believe that this whole caste politics, especially the OBC caste politics, unwittingly might have only helped Hindutva. This could sound entirely counterfactual, given that conventional wisdom says that caste politics is antithesis to Hindutva, which aims at building a common identity beyond caste, but there are certain reasons why I believe it could have indirectly helped.

OBC politics, or the Mandal politics, indeed proved to be a counterweight to the 'Kamandal politics'—the term was coined to refer to the Ram Janmabhoomi movement—and Uttar Pradesh is the biggest example of that, where caste politics weakened the pan-Hindu identity and hurt the BJP and Hindutva politics. In Uttar Pradesh, once the Babri Masjid was demolished and a makeshift Ram temple made, the BJP support base progressively thinned. At the same time, both the SP and the BSP—with their own caste-based cadre—grew powerful and their support base swelled. It appeared as if the group that had worked together in the Ram Janmabhoomi movement thought that the 'work was done' on 6 December 1992, and thus they subsequently went back to their micro-identities of caste.

This could have convinced the ecosystem that identity politics around caste can checkmate Hindutva. Perhaps, they thought that the Mandal politics will do to the Hindi heartland what Dravidian politics did in Tamil Nadu, and the Gangetic plains will go barren for any Hindutva politics.

The Dravidian identity politics, or the caste politics in Tamil Nadu, especially the one championed by the likes of Periyar, was rooted in anti-Hinduism. Let us remember that it was born during the British era, when the ecosystem could afford to support overtly anti-Hindu ideas without needing the façade of anti-Hindutva. However, the OBC identity politics of the late 1980s or 90s was not rooted in anti-Hinduism. This is a very basic and obvious difference, and for sure the great minds of the ecosystem knew it. Perhaps they hoped that over time, with help of 'alternative history', they would be able turn the OBC identity into non-Hindu identity, and subsequently into anti-Hindu identity.

The usual first step in this process starts with the anti-Brahmin rhetoric. Every Hindu practice, custom and ritual is declared as 'Brahminism', and the non-Brahmin castes are encouraged to stop following them. That's how they are weaned away from their roots, and then given an alternative history and identity to associate themselves with. Such histories and identities are invented in liberal laboratories, such as the JNU, and popular caste leaders are supposed to take those to the masses.

If you look at the earlier political statements by the likes of Mulayam Singh Yadav and Lalu Prasad Yadav, you will invariably find the rhetoric of anti-Brahminism. Even now many of their supporters keep abusing Brahmins. I remember Lalu Yadav in his early days, asking people not to believe 'pandas' and 'ojhas' (terms used for temple priests). He had made his supporters throw away 'jantar' (amulets) or other religious symbols they might be wearing. Maybe the next step, expected from the likes of Lalu by the ecosystem, would have been to ask his followers to stop going to temples and worshipping 'Brahminical gods'. But that never happened.

The liberal project to de-Hinduize OBCs was always going to be pretty challenging. The backward castes were a central part of the Hindu identity, and castes like Yadavs have identified themselves with Lord Krishna. Not just the OBCs, almost every caste had some god, including 'kuldevtas', or some Hindu icon that they would associate themselves with.

On a societal level, many Hindu rituals and festivals in a place like Bihar require a rather honourable presence of various castes to consider them complete as per traditions. While no one can deny caste discrimination and inequalities, castes in North India, including the Brahmins, had a more symbiotic relationship than its southern counterpart in Tamil Nadu during the British era. Deracinating them from that symbiotic relationship was not going to be easy.

Mulayam Singh Yadav, too, had issued statements in his earlier years that were music to the liberal ears. He had once famously questioned that, how could one be sure that Lord Ram was born at the same spot in Ayodhya that is being claimed as his Janmabhoomi? He had also asked whether there was any 'parchi' (receipt) in the name of Ram that could prove the claim.

Such statements were pure insolence towards Hindu sentiments, and obviously he did worse by firing at the kar sevaks in 1990. But, even he had to mellow down as he realized that he had already won the Muslim support, thanks to his early utterings and deeds, and now his party needed to consolidate support among other Hindu backward castes.

While the ecosystem was building plans and blueprint on how to uproot the OBCs from their Hindu roots, and while those plans perhaps looked invincible in places like the JNU, the OBC politics on the ground essentially strengthened caste identities—identities that were Hindu after all.

Not just that, the support base and even the leadership of the parties founded by Lalu and Mulayam were not exactly 'liberal' in any sense. On issues of women's rights, free speech and free markets, they were far more 'conservative' than what the BJP or RSS could be. You will find it easier to recall a statement by a sexagenarian RSS chief in support of women's rights or gay rights than by young leaders like Akhilesh Yadav or Tejashwi Yadav—the sons of Mulayam and Lalu, respectively.

And how can I forget Tej Pratap Yadav, the other son of Lalu Prasad Yadav, who loves to dress up as Hindu gods? In fact, many of his pictures, where he is dressed up as Lord Krishna and Lord Shiva, have gone viral. He is reported to be quite religious. And I really like that aspect of him. Not kidding.

Anyway, the point is that while the rise of OBC politics clearly checkmated the rise of BJP and the rise of Hindutva, it didn't really evolve the way the ecosystem would have wanted or planned it to be. However, the ecosystem had to continue supporting parties that played OBC politics to keep the BJP at bay. But by supporting such parties in the hope that they will weaken Hindutva, the ecosystem was effectively strengthening identity politics and conservative values. So, basically, the Left-wing ecosystem was promoting the Right-wing value system.

Would it not have been easier for an OBC Modi to get this crowd to the 'real' Right wing? Hindutva as an ideology would not have been an impediment for this crowd, as they were already 'conservative' and proud of their identity, which was part of the Hindu identity.

Even Dalit politics in North didn't turn out the way the ecosystem would have liked. Alternative histories and non-Hindu identities for Dalits were already invented and 'intellectualized' during the British era itself. All it needed was a popular caste leader to spread it in North India.

The liberal ecosystem would have wanted parties like the BSP to toe the sharp neo-Ambedkarite rhetoric. The BSP did start with 'Tilak, Taraju aur Talwar, inko maaro joote chaar'—a slogan against Brahmins,

Baniyas and Kshatriyas—but the party also had to come up with 'Haathi nahi Ganesh hai, Bramha Vishnu Mahesh hai', a slogan associating the party's electoral symbol with the Hindu identity, in fact, Hindu gods.

A few BSP leaders did try a few tricks, such as distributing pamphlets that taught alterative histories to various scheduled castes, trying to convince that they were not Hindus. Many new Dalit groups—promoted heavily by the ecosystem since the ascent of Modi—are still doing it, but these attempts have failed to attract a wide support so far.

Many scheduled castes too identified themselves with Hindu icons, such as Pasi King Raja Suheldev who fought against Muslim invaders, and they too had symbiotic relationship with the rest of the Hindu castes. The Dom rajas of Kashi, for example, play a crucial role in the attainment of moksha. It was not easy to replicate the Periyarist ideology in the 'cow belt'.

Add to that the fact that many of these Dalits have to bear the brunt of Muslim aggression too. When I started tracking such news stories of communal tensions, including those arising out of 'petty reasons', I realized that Dalits were often at the receiving end. For example, pigs reared by a Dalit family would venture into the homes of Muslims, who consider the animal to be unclean, and that would lead to fights. On many other cases, Dalit families were the target of Muslim aggression as they were the most vulnerable.

The 'Jai Bhim Jai Meem' slogan or the Dalit–Muslim unity concept, which could appear unbeatable at places like the JNU, was falling apart in the real world. And why wouldn't it? It had failed during the Partition years itself, when Jogendra Nath Mandal, a Dalit leader and the first law minister of Pakistan, had to come back to India with a heavy heart. Within few years, he had realized that Dalits were not going to be treated fairly in an Islamic state.[87]

Mandal used to believe in the Dalit–Muslim common cause, but he ended up realizing that it was an illusion. Many Pakistani Hindus belong to the Dalit castes, and we all know how they are treated in that country. Many are forced to accept Islam. So in the end, you'll need to forego your identity to realize this dream of Dalit–Muslim unity. That's the antithesis of identity politics.

Essentially, caste politics strengthened identity politics, and largely the identities were sub-Hindu. Hindutva was not going to be a big impediment, as various castes could instinctively see merit in some of the issues that were assumed to be representative of Hindutva. They needed someone who could unite them beyond the sub-Hindu identities, and create a united spectrum of Hindu castes. While liberals were adding letters to the gender identity rainbow, conservatives were adding castes to the Hindu identity rainbow.

Obviously, what also helped Modi was the BJP's poll strategy, which was professionally executed, and attention was paid to as many factors and details as possible. Smart political moves were made. If a Nitish Kumar left the NDA, the party showed political acumen in welcoming back a Ram Vilas Paswan, who incidentally had resigned from the Vajpayee cabinet after the 2002 riots, demanding the removal of Modi as the chief minister of Gujarat. Modi's personal anguish or unhappiness from that era, if he had any, didn't stop him from opting for this alliance.

Chandrababu Naidu too was brought back as an ally and Yediyurappa was brought back in the party, so that the BJP's position improves down south. The party picked up a few NDA allies in the smaller North Eastern states; even though they accounted for just a handful of Lok Sabha seats, it showed the intent that every seat matters. Many 'turncoats' from the Congress party or other parties were also accepted in the BJP to swell up support. Add to these, the much talked about booth management of the party and the role of 'panna pramukhs', who were local volunteers tasked with convincing a set of 50–60 odd voters each.

While such meticulous planning could indeed prove to be a game-changer, as merely a swing of 3–5 per cent of popular votes has seen many political parties score impressive victories, the BJP needed nothing short of a miracle in many places, such as Uttar Pradesh.

And it was no less than a miracle when results were declared on 16 May 2014. The swing in favour of BJP in Uttar Pradesh was almost 25 per cent, a staggering figure. Even an industrial scale of booth management couldn't explain this. It was a wave. Or as Modi haters realized, it was a tsunami.

Once the liberals gathered themselves after this devastation, they concluded that Modi had won by selling hope built on lies. They claimed that people were taken in by his sophistry. It was not a vote for Hindutva, but a vote for development, a vote against corruption and a vote for governance that was better than what the Congress had provided. But, they secretly, and soon openly, hoped that Modi would fail to provide any of these.

The liberals hoped that when Modi fails, people would 'realize their mistakes' and see through Modi's 'Hindutva agenda', and eventually vote him out in 2019. They were basically not ready to accept that much of India had indeed made peace with Hindutva. They were not ready to accept the reality.

The post-2014 liberals

After Modi won the 2014 elections and became the 14th prime minister of India, I didn't really have any plans to become a vocal supporter of him or the Hindutva ideology. I was obviously happy that the man I thought was the best for the job had won, which meant that I was right in sensing what the popular sentiments were. As someone writing pop satire, it was crucial for me to know what was 'pop' at any given time.

Not only was it a validation of my choice, the victory of Modi in a way also meant that those countless debates were finally won by people like us, who scoffed at the show-off of superiority complex and virtue signalling by those who opposed Modi. For many like us, it was like a debating competition that was over, and now was the time to look towards a new beginning. But those who lost didn't just look at it as some debating competition.

The Modi haters, from various shades of Left, were all set to be sore losers, who would soon go on to turn these ideological differences into existentialist inquisition. I had no inkling of that, for I thought ideologies were not the only thing that made a person. But, it appeared that it was the only thing that mattered to the Left.

Ideologically, I was still broadly a libertarian. Yes, I had started seeing a lot of merit in what the Hindutva ideologues had been saying and I empathized with their concerns and grievances, but I believed that one can debate these things and try to look for solutions, or at worst, settle for 'Let us agree to disagree' and go back to normal life.

Little did I know that the concept of 'normal life' itself would be thrown out of the window by the opponents of Modi. The only conclusion they derived from the 2014 verdict was that 'these are not normal times', and that they needed to double down on their efforts to save humanity. The messiah complex was only going to get far worse, and I had no idea of what was coming.

I wouldn't say that it wouldn't have mattered to me if Modi hadn't won such a majority and the 2014 elections had thrown a hung parliament instead. I would have been sad, but that sadness would have been similar to a cricket fan who feels momentarily dejected if his team fails to win a big final match. It would surely have hurt, but it would not have meant the end of life.

Fortunately, Modi won in style. I was overjoyed with the results. But it was still akin to a cricket fan celebrating the victory of his favourite team winning a big final. You celebrate the victory, you see the match highlights again and again on YouTube, but in a day or two, you are back to your offices, schools or colleges and normal life resumes.

I believe most of the newly converted Modi fans or BJP voters would have had similar plans. Elections, a grand event, a festival of democracy, were over, and now it was time to go back to our normal lives and start thinking about the regular, mundane things.

But Modi haters had a very different plan—to create such a vitiated narrative that an ordinary person starts to think that 'normal life' has changed due to Modi coming to power, to create so much negativity that a voter who voted for Modi after buying into the 'Achchhe din aane waale hain' (good days are coming) narrative, starts feeling that 'These are not achchhe din, wish to have those good old days back'; and double down on proving how Hindutva was pure evil, so that those who flirted with it in 2014 make amends in 2019 by dumping it.

I must add or clarify that I'm not suggesting that this strategy of creating negativity and fear—'Darr ka mahaul hai'—was an outcome of some grand meeting that Modi haters had after the 2014 verdict, where presentations were made and group discussions took place, and where they decided to come up with a plan of action after hours and hours of brainstorming.

I would rather want to believe that this plan of action was a natural outcome of the way they are wired. This is how they look at matters of society, politics and ideology. It indeed is a matter of existence and survival for them. They would genuinely believe that these are not 'normal times'.

The various shades of leftist ideologies don't see politics or elections as just some debating game or cricket match, which is how most of the non-Left sees it. For the Left, ideological differences are not like differences in food preferences, where you can ignore such 'minor things' and continue with your 'normal life'.

The Left is much like puritan Islam in that sense, where beliefs are the core of your identity. And the identity is all that makes you. This identity is not something that gets kicked into action only on certain occasions, such as some festivals or life events—that's how the non-Left or Hindus treat matters of identity; a Congressi Hindu is a Hindu only while celebrating some festivals. But for the Left and for the puritan Muslims, every step taken by you, even for seemingly mundane things, must be guided by a set of dogmas and sanctioned by high priests— religious scholars in Islam and these days 'woke' activists for the Left.

And to be fair, any person who is deeply committed to an ideology becomes so 'possessed' that he starts seeing everything from the prism of ideology. The critical difference is that many on the non-Left are not *committed* to non-Left ideologies, most of which anyway don't even insist too much on ideological fidelity or purity tests. Of late, at least on Twitter, there are certain groups collectively termed 'Trads', which is short form of the word 'Traditionalists', who tend to insist on purity tests of ideology and religion, but they aren't that influential in the non-Left camp. In fact, many on the non-Left resist their ways.

I'm using the loose term 'non-Left' on purpose, as most people who are branded Sanghis or Right-wingers, or Bhakts these days, are non-Left. Not only is there no commitment to any particular ideology, there is also no clarity on what ideology they subscribe to or what basic principles—or should I say set of dogmas—they adhere to. The 'Trads' mock this lack of ideological clarity and commitment in some by terming them 'Raitas', etymology of which I would leave out of the scope of this book. But this state of being non-committed to an ideology is fine I think; that's how 'normal' people live their lives.

But that also means that these 'normal' people are always the target of ideologically coloured communication, and are more susceptible to manipulation. The Modi haters needed to tell these normal people that they were not living in normal times after 16 May 2014.

It might look like a Herculean task to talk to millions of people, but even a tiny bunch of committed loony leftists can make a whole lot of difference, as they enjoy a disproportionate control over the tools of narrative building. If they want to prove that these are not normal times, they indeed can. And they tried to prove it relentlessly.

I too was looking forward to leading a normal life in normal times. But before the leftists could create any difference in my personal life, the capitalists did.

A couple of months after the 2014 election results, Mukesh Ambani-owned Reliance Industries announced that they were going to fully acquire the Network18 group of media companies.

Not that it bothered me. Being a pro-market guy, I was only happy that a big conglomerate like Reliance will now directly back the group. Even otherwise, Reliance had indirect control over Network18, owing to a huge amount of convertible loans it had extended to the group via a mesh of legal entities. Thus, Reliance was just exercising its rights by going for a full takeover.

It would have hardly affected me, as *Faking News* was a very small part of the Network18 group. In fact, I looked forward to being an 'Ambani agent'. But after the takeover, one after the other, the top management of Network18 were being replaced with new people. On occasion, some top executive posts even remained vacant. For months, there was no clarity on who was the CEO of the digital arm, after the earlier CEO, Durga Raghunath left.

Some amount of chaos or confusion was definitely expected, as mergers or acquisitions are not always smooth. With a new owner buying a business, there were bound to be new bosses too. I wasn't getting restless immediately, but it meant that there was a long period of freeze on new initiatives or investments until the restructuring process was complete. Although *Faking News* was quite small in the overall scheme of things and its investment requirements were literally loose change for Reliance or even Network18, the decision-makers were either absent or not taking any decisions.

There were no editorial changes imposed by Reliance, and it was only the people in the higher executive and management roles whose jobs and future were being impacted. But, a lot of noise was made in the journalistic circles about 'editorial interference' of Reliance. All of it was obviously linked to the regime change at the Centre. Ambani was apparently kicking out anti-Modi journalists from Network18.

Rajdeep Sardesai, who was not just a senior editorial person but also had an executive role, was also one of the folks who was impacted. He had to leave Network18, and this was turned into a 'media under attack' narrative. Modi was using his corporate friends to control the media; many such conspiracy theories were floated.

It was a laughable charge. Reliance was already controlling Network18 financially, which was a common knowledge among the media circles. Whoever controls finances potentially controls everything. So Network18, technically, was not really free from Reliance interference even earlier.

Furthermore, right since the Anna Hazare's anti-corruption movement days, Ambani was branded as that big evil guy who is supposed to have said that 'Both the Congress and the BJP were in our pockets.' So, if this guy was already controlling everything, including the governments, regardless of who was in power, how exactly was his move to 'officially' own a media company catastrophic?

Did journalists mean to say that it was okay for Ambani to indirectly control everything, and that it was okay for him to buy press and journalists' loyalties through private deals, but it was wrong to become the owner publicly and officially? Why was there so much resistance to transparency?

Anyway, my objective here is not to defend Ambani, but to show how everything was set to be looked from the prism of Modi and 'freedom' after the 2014 verdict. Whatever was normal and accepted earlier was set to be painted as unusual and unacceptable. A new set of revolutionaries, nay messiahs, were all set to arrive at the horizon.

It took time for me to notice this change among the folks with whom I earlier used to talk and discuss various things normally, including our disagreements on Modi or Hindutva. Perhaps if I had gotten busy with work and daily life, I would not have realized it. I would have bought into their narrative that things had indeed turned bad after Modi's victory, and that's why these 'well-meaning' folks were so worked up all the time. But thanks to Reliance owning Network18, I had a lot of free time as decision-making had become stagnant and everything was in a flux. I was asked to wait till the new bosses settle in and new strategies are drawn. And this went on for months.

Since I wasn't too busy with work, I had all the time to psychoanalyse the liberals. This is surely one way in which Ambani helped Modi!

For months, professional life was in neutral gear, and *Faking News* couldn't take any new initiatives or come up with new offerings, such as a video product that I so wanted to launch at that time. I had even identified a couple of creative partners to come up with video offerings, but nothing materialized as I was told that new initiatives that require outflow of cash were on freeze. *Faking News* continued operating as it did earlier.

In those months, especially the first six months after coming to power, the Modi government focused only on non-controversial things. In his first address as the prime minister on Independence Day, he announced the Pradhan Mantri Jan-Dhan Yojana to give every poor family a bank account. Apart from achieving financial inclusion, it was also supposed to do away with the corruption while handing out cash-based schemes or other welfare schemes.

In the same speech, Modi also talked about the need to make our society better for women, asking parents to teach their sons to respect women rather than putting various curbs on their daughters. He also announced the Swachh Bharat Abhiyan, aimed at making Indian cities cleaner to make them more hygienic and tourist-friendly.

And while Modi was doing and saying these things, some of the guys with whom I could interact in a friendly manner earlier suddenly launched a tirade against *Faking News*, asking why was *Faking News* not being 'anti-establishment' and why was it not coming up with a satire against Modi?

This criticism felt pretty odd especially because it came unannounced from a couple of people with whom I was on talking terms. I was actually hurt. I expected at least a basic courtesy, where they could have first tried to reach out to me and raise the issue in private before going public with their criticism, which was unfair to begin with.

First of all, Modi needed to say or do something strange to attract biting satire, and secondly, *Faking News* had already written a couple of satirical articles on Modi. When Modi invited Nawaz Sharif, the then prime minister of Pakistan to his oath-taking ceremony, *Faking News* had made a satirical comment, saying that Modi would next be inviting all illegal Bangladeshi immigrants too to his events. The comment was basically about him doing a 'U-turn' on the issue of India's relationship with Pakistan.

There were other articles on Modi too, and also comments made by me in personal capacity, which were critical of a few moves by the Modi government, such as the government's counsel defending the controversial section 66A of the Information Technology Act. Using the same act and that specific section, the UPA government had blocked many Twitter handles, against which Modi himself had protested by putting up a black display picture. There were other genuine issues on which criticism was offered, as they didn't go well with my libertarian beliefs.

Yet, the brand I had made, the business I was heading, was attacked for being 'soft on Modi'. Yes, I indeed supported Modi before the 2014 elections, and after the elections I was willing to give him time, but that did not mean that I or my website was entirely silent.

Though I was hurt and even offended, I tried to reach out privately to a couple of people whose comments I valued. I sent them the links of satirical articles that were critical of the Modi government. But, it seemed that no amount of proof or reasoning was going to work. They still pontificated that more was expected. Those attacks were the first thing that made me realize that these people were now in the 'either you are with us or against us' mode.

I thought that I might have to ultimately join them or at least appease them, because most of them were in the media industry in some form or the other. If I wanted to survive in the industry, if I wanted to partner with different brands—and I mean brands of other content creators, not just advertising brands—if I wanted to be 'respectable' in the industry, I would have had to 'be like them' to some extent. If I dared to be too different or belligerent, it'd have impacted my career.

But I don't know why I didn't think about my career in that respect.

Maybe the reason was the same as before, which had caused me to sell off *Faking News*—I was not sure what I would be doing in the next five years, and whether I would even want to be in the media industry for long. Further, in order to be concerned about my career, first I needed the normal professional life to resume. My career was already not moving. The Reliance factor had put my professional life in neutral gear. With no big targets to chase, I ended up chasing debates on Twitter and elsewhere.

Or maybe it was just plain ego, where I went 'To hell with you guys and your beliefs if you are not going to treat me fairly' after my initial attempts at having a conversation failed.

I didn't, however, give up within a few weeks of the liberals turning this way, and tried to have conversations with them until around the end of 2015. These debates would be about free speech, religious fundamentalism and caste, where the usual criticism of their double standards came up.

Their initial response was mostly about the denial of such double standards, but when specific incidents would be pointed out, they tried to delegitimize the criticism itself as 'whataboutery'. With time, they either started ignoring the arguments or got more aggressive about it. Maybe, the defeat of the BJP in the Delhi assembly elections in the beginning of 2015 and then the defeat in Bihar towards the end of 2015 was also a factor, which gave them the hope that they were 'winning' and didn't need to accommodate dissenting views.

Or maybe that's how they always were, and I was late in realizing this.

I progressively stopped bothering about their comments and 'feedback', and continued doing what I wanted to. Actually, on many occasions, I started saying things just to rile them up. It almost felt like revenge; your words hurt me, so now my words will hurt you too. I think I entirely stopped worrying about it sometime in mid-2016 and thereafter.

Modi is a very lucky man in this respect. His opponents and his haters are always working overtime to make sure that most of the Modi supporters remain Modi supporters. It is not him who creates a polarized environment, his 'critics' do. Either you can be a Modi supporter or a Modi hater, there is no other option allowed. I gladly chose to continue being a Modi supporter.

But choosing to be a Sanghi was yet to happen.

Adopting the Sanghi label

Even though the Modi government was all focused on 'secular' issues such as Jan-Dhan accounts and Swachh Bharat, an international incident became a trigger to discuss 'communal' issues—it was the rise of the ISIS or the Islamic State of Iraq and Syria.

The Iraq war of 2003 and the consequent fall of the Saddam Hussein regime had sent the region into a long political turmoil, with various tribes and groups trying to capture power in the post-Saddam era. Some of these were backed by US coalition forces, while others termed the US and allied army presence as 'occupying forces.' Initially, reports about ISIS appeared to be just another report on how the region was in deep political and military turmoil, but soon the news of their brutal ways, which included beheadings of 'infidels' and imposing strict laws based on puritan Islamic beliefs, started getting attention, with many realizing that it was altogether a new beast.

What made the incident relevant to India was the news about 46 nurses from Kerala who were reported to be in the captivity of ISIS fighters. Some reports said that they were not exactly in captivity, but were just stuck in a territory that had fallen under the control of ISIS. In either case, there was pressure on the government to bring them back home.

There was a risk that this could be the Kandahar hijack moment for the Modi government, with the Islamic terrorists possibly demanding something for their 'brethren' in Kashmir. Fortunately, nothing of that sort happened, and the government could get the nurses back home safely in July 2014.[88]

Just before that, in June 2014, ISIS had declared that the territories it had captured in Iraq and Syria were now part of a modern Islamic Caliphate, which will soon be expanded into other areas, and one day to the entire world. It further declared its chief Abu Bakr al-Baghdadi as the Caliph of the Islamic world.

That's where the 'communal' element came in. Suddenly, a lot of people became curious about the concept of Caliphate, which led to discussions, rather 'discovery', about Islamic concepts of how the people should be governed.

As per Islamic beliefs and jurisprudence, the world is divided into 'dar al-islam', that is, regions where Islamic laws prevail and 'dar al-harb', the non-Islamic regions where no such laws prevail, with 'dar al-sulh' being the transitionary phase where Islamic laws may not prevail in totality but Muslims have treaties and special rights.

ISIS presented a face of Islam that was by default at war with the non-believers. They didn't need any reason, such as a non-believer saying or doing something hostile, to go to war. The mere existence of non-believers, or kuffars/kaafirs as they are termed, was reason enough to go to war, for they were living in 'dar al-harb', which literally means 'territory of war'.

And that's precisely what they did to the Yezidis—a non-Muslim community living in the areas they had captured—who were killed, converted or traded as slaves, including as sex slaves. A couple of years later, when ISIS was defeated and most of their territories recaptured by allied forces, the world came to know about these horror stories from Yezidi survivors.

What was happening in 2014–15, in the age of modern technology, in the name of Islam was not at all different from what was claimed, and chronicled, by many as atrocities heaped on Hindus by the Muslim invaders in medieval India. However, the liberals rejected those as 'Sanghi history', and it was always claimed that the Muslim invaders or rulers like Aurangzeb were primarily fighting 'political battles' and not religious ones.

Coincidently, and rather cruelly, a thitherto little-known Aurangzeb apologist from a US university would soon be promoted in the Indian liberal circles as some authority on the Mughal ruler, and she would attempt to whitewash the worst of the atrocities committed by the jihadist Mughal emperor.

In the Western world, they were hosting Yezidis who were the living proof of jihadist horror, and in India, we were hosting an apologist of the same jihadist horror.

Due to the widespread use of internet and 3G over smartphones, which were getting affordable, ISIS was now present in the living rooms of many. Many would have come to know about the concept of Caliphate as well as the absurdity of the Khilafat movement that was supported by Mahatma Gandhi.

I personally came to know about the concept of 'Ghazwa-e-Hind', which I earlier thought was some random Urdu phrase used by Zaid Hamid, the self-styled defence expert from Pakistan who comes up with ludicrous conspiracy theories.

Ghazwa-e-Hind is an Islamic prophecy, mentioned in Hadiths—the Islamic records of the words, deeds and behaviour of Prophet Muhammad, though they are not as authoritative as the Quran—which says that Prophet had talked about India being invaded and conquered. Conquering India is supposed to be a crucial step for Islam to prevail over the world, and those who work to achieve it are praised to be the best martyrs, who will reap benefits in the afterlife.

While some believe that it has happened already, with Islamic invaders establishing Sultanates and empires in India, others believe that this prophecy is yet to be fulfilled, because the majority of India is not Muslim yet. Many in the Pakistani Army and in Kashmiri terror groups believe in this prophecy, and they aspire to be martyrs for Ghazwa-e-Hind.

So a Muslim who believes in this Hadith, either has to see the marauding Islamic invaders from the Middle Ages as great servants of Allah who fulfilled this prophecy, and thus be proud of everyone from Muhammad bin Qasim to Aurangzeb, or he has to see India as a land that is yet to be conquered. If the latter, he could aspire to conquer it and become a martyr, who will be specially rewarded after death. How can the idea of communal harmony germinate if one subscribes to either of these two thoughts?

The emergence of ISIS enabled such questions to arise, and expectedly the liberals rejected those as bigoted and offensive. However, more than specific topics like Ghazwa-e-Hind, it was the overall issue of Islamic radicalization that came to the fore, which for some strange reason put the liberals on the back foot.

The issue had become relevant because ISIS was attracting 'fighters' from all over the world, and many from India too—from places such as Uttar Pradesh, Telangana, Kerala, Karnataka and Maharashtra—were reported to have joined the group.[89] Many of them had left for Iraq and Syria to join the 'jihad' while others vowed to create an ISIS arm back in India. Islamic radicalization, as manifested by the ISIS, couldn't have been dismissed as just a local development in a troubled far-off region, for which one could blame the US and its foreign policies as usual.

The liberal responses were simple—ISIS has nothing to do with Islam; ISIS was 'misinterpreting' Islamic scriptures; the number of Indian Muslims supporting ISIS was very low; and what about Hindu terror?

Essentially, they were shying away from admitting that there could be 'some' problem with Islam. And it was not just the liberals in India, even abroad, except for 'new atheists' such as Richard Dawkins and Sam Harris or someone like Bill Maher, liberals largely avoided commenting on Islam.

Due to such reasons, I realized that many, whom I considered to be libertarians, were actually hypocritical liberals who would take on Hinduism or Hindu beliefs aggressively for even a random statement made by some guy somewhere, but will not like to comment on Islam when people were being beheaded amidst chants of Allahu Akbar.

This was one of the major factors that made me shift away from libertarian perspectives on socio-cultural matters. I started asserting and defending my identity.

If one attacked only Hinduism and Hindu beliefs and maintained either a cowardly silence or came up with a diplomatic stand when the worst of the crimes were being committed in the name of Islam, one was creating a very unequal and unfair society. I didn't want to be part of that process. I was not someone who hated my identity. Only a special hatred for your identity could make one comfortable with such double standards.

Yet again, Modi wasn't doing or saying anything, but I was becoming more and more Sanghi. It was becoming very clear that liberals were not ready to extend the same courtesy or the same benefit of doubt to Hinduism, which they were ever ready to offer to Islam.

If Hinduism can be reduced to just caste atrocities, why not reduce Islam to just violence? If the Holy Quran can be misinterpreted and misused by extremists, why not grant that Manusmriti is no evil text either and it was also misused by a few? If Manusmriti can be burnt to protest against casteism, why can't the Quran be burnt to protest against Islamist terror attacks (as the US pastor had tried in 2010, triggering riots in several places, including India)? If Islamic traditions and texts should be seen in the context of time and through moral relativism—this, even though most Muslims insist that the Holy Quran is timeless and perfect—why should one apply modern standards of liberty and feminism to Hindu tradition and texts?

Nothing but a special hatred for Hinduism explains such blatant double standards. And such hatred for Hinduism was betrayed when Teesta Setalvad, the great secular icon and supposedly brave lady who fought against Modi, posted a picture on Twitter in August 2014, where she compared goddess Kali with an ISIS terrorist.[90]

The way I saw it—Setalvad was getting uncomfortable with some aspects of Islam being criticized by 'Right-wingers' in the wake of what ISIS was doing, so she decided to 'show them the mirror' by 'proving' that if an ISIS terrorist beheaded people, their goddess Kali, too, beheaded. Because obviously, only Right-wingers believe in Hindu gods and goddesses, liberal and seculars are supposed to mock them.

In my view, there was absolutely no other intention, even though she soon deleted the tweet and posted an apology. It was a Pavlovian response from the likes of Setalvad, who must defend anything Islamic and must attack anything Hindu. Their basic instincts tell them to compare ISIS with Hinduism, and since they can't do that openly yet, they settle for comparing ISIS with RSS.

Almost invariably 'Sangh' and 'Sanghis' are the proxy words they use in order to say things that they otherwise can't say openly about Hinduism and Hindus. They don't attack Hinduism that viciously, yet, because they can fall on the wrong side of the law. Police complaints were filed against Setalvad too. But owing to my libertarian principles, back then I had said on Twitter that Setalvad's deeds didn't warrant police action, as it fell under the wider ambit of free speech.

Setalvad had to face absolutely no consequences for her deeds. After all, she drew a Hindu goddess and not the Islamic Prophet, so she was safe. Five years later in August 2019, two FIRs against her were quashed by the Gujarat High Court, which concluded that 'there was no malafide or deliberate intention and she had not intended to hurt anyone.'[91] Well, all I can say is that I don't want to go to jail for contempt of court.

It was not just ISIS clips or news of Indian youth joining ISIS or wanting to join ISIS that were proof of Islamic radicalization or spread of

Wahhabism or Salafism (the ideologies ISIS claimed to subscribe to) in India. Zakir Naik, who became a fugitive later, too preached Wahhabism and Salafism, and he was, and remains, very popular among a large section of Indian Muslims. The popularity of various strict Sunni Islamic ideologies was and is a reality in India.

Once, my wife and I had encountered a taxi driver who was making fun of Bohra Muslims, many of whom reside in Mumbai. Some celebration or march by Bohra Muslims was being taken out on the roads and our taxi was passing by. Out of curiosity, we asked the driver what the occasion was. Since he was wearing a skullcap, we thought that as a Muslim he would know. He informed us about the occasion—an annual gathering from where the Bohras were returning—but immediately followed it up with criticism of the Bohras for not being faithful enough in following some basic tenets of Islam.

'These guys put business interests before religion,' he said. 'Instead of offering namaaz five times, they do it at one go, so that they save time for business dealings and meetings during the day. We can never do that. "Deen" (faith) is more important than "daam" (money). You only tell, does it make sense? Will you have your breakfast, lunch and dinner all in one go to save time?'

We were rather amused, but didn't say anything. It was a radical Sunni belief, present in an ordinary man in Mumbai. I'm not saying that the man was a potential ISIS recruit, but the issue of radical Islamic beliefs was not at all irrelevant to India. The liberals just pretended that it didn't exist, or they didn't want to talk about it, even though it had been playing a role since the 1980s itself, as I have earlier written in this book.

It was impossible to believe that the liberals were unable to see such signs. One expected that they would show some spine and speak against Muslim radicalism and fundamentalism too, if in principle they were against all sorts of religious fundamentalism. Obviously, they didn't.

I realized that this is how they were most of the time, even before the advent of Modi. But, with the rise of Modi, their double standards were coming to the fore more often.

In January 2013 itself, even someone like Javed Akhtar, who does have a secular outlook I would admit, demanded the sacking of a lady police officer of the Mumbai Police, terming her poem against the rioting mob of 2012 Azad Maidan riots 'communal.'[92] Then in May, an MP named Shafiqur Rahman Barq walked out of the Lok Sabha when Vande Mataram was being played, claiming that it was against his religious beliefs. Instead of condemning him, the liberals went on to debate how Vande Mataram was the 'wrong song.'[93] Poems and songs had become criminal for people who swore by principles of free speech!

The liberals just couldn't get to condemn Islamic fundamentalism. They would either resort to whitewashing or monkey-balancing. When they didn't speak up against Islamic radicalization during 'normal times', just how would have they spoken during the 'dark years' of the Modi government? Consequently, they ended up collaborating with people with outright Islamist and jihadist mentalities, such as during the protests against the CAA.

Would the direction, or at least the acceleration, of my ideological shift have been different if the liberals, and the libertarians too, had showed the same sting in criticizing Islam as they show while criticizing Hinduism? Absolutely. By that time, that is, a few months following Modi winning the 2014 Lok Sabha elections, my sense of belonging or my sense of a Hindu identity was rather inadequate and surely inerudite— and I am still trying to learn—and it would have been easier for me to stick to a wider identity as a libertarian. I was yet to read writings of Hindutva ideologues in all seriousness. So yes, I think I'd have continued to associate myself with libertarianism, with a layer of 'only culturally Hindu' to my identity.

When you look for a social identity, you need a community, or at least a crowd to identify yourself with. I needed at least a bunch of liberals or libertarians, or a small crowd, who showed that a set of principles was most important for them, and that they were willing to apply those principles equally on different sets of religious people. That didn't happen. They started being apologists of Islamism and continue to be so. On more than one occasion, they proved that they don't practice what they preach, and their declared principles don't really represent their true self.

Actually, it appeared that they had no bare principles at all, except for opposing and disparaging anything that appears or sounds Hindu. For example, many claimed that they didn't like the Sangh or the RSS, as its leaders apparently never openly and actively participated in the freedom movement. They would throw various claims about how the RSS did not support the pre-Independence Congress on this or that occasion. Without going into the veracity of these claims, by corollary, at least they should be respecting the most senior leaders of the pre-Independence Congress, because the party is their benchmark for patriotism and freedom struggle, right?

Wrong. They didn't stick to that principle. In December 2014, after Modi had spent over six months as prime minister, it was announced that Madan Mohan Malaviya and Atal Bihari Vajpayee would be honoured with the Bharat Ratna. Rather revealingly, more than the award to Vajpayee, it was the award to Madan Mohan Malaviya that triggered and frustrated a few liberals.

Well-known author and historian Ramachandra Guha tweeted: 'The more I think of it, the more the award of the Bharat Ratna to MM Malaviya strikes me as parochial and indefensible.'[94] I was taken aback, but it reaffirmed my belief that the secular-liberal ecosystem didn't dislike 'communal Hindus', they simply disliked any Hindu who was assertive of his identity and protective of the community's interests. It didn't matter that Malaviya was a respected freedom fighter and also the president of the Indian National Congress, the organization they otherwise would use to belittle the RSS.

Malaviya was one of those Congress leaders who had opposed the Congress when it had supported the Khilafat movement. He founded the BHU, which in a way was counterpoise to Sir Syed's AMU—the same Sir Syed Ahmed Khan whose beliefs and deeds became the founding principles for Pakistan.

Malaviya was a Hindu leader who was aware of Islamic challenges, and thus he was a 'Sanghi'—it did not matter that he was the president of the Indian National Congress thrice or that he was called the 'Maker of Modern India' by Mahatma Gandhi, another Congress icon the secular-liberal ecosystem pretends to respect. In the case of Malaviya, they dropped the pretence as soon as the Modi government decided to honour him posthumously.

That was another instance when liberals appeared to betray that their outward behaviour and purported principles were not representative of their true self. They proved the purported reason for opposing the RSS—the alleged non-cooperation of the RSS with the Congress in the freedom struggle—wrong themselves, by showing no respect for a Congress leader who took part in the freedom struggle.

The claim by liberals that they don't like the RSS as it didn't take part in the independence movement—an inaccurate accusation thrown at it anyway—is nevertheless a sham. As I had written earlier in the section explaining this secular-liberal ecosystem, many of them themselves see the British Raj as a 'liberating force' and have no issues with various other non-Congress leaders who collaborated with the British on multiple occasions.

The pattern was obvious. They simply opposed any Hindu who was aware of the challenges to the community and assertive of his identity, while shielding any Muslim who was not just assertive but insular and supremacist about his identity. Not My Liberalism.

Around the same time, that is, in December 2014, ahead of Christmas, many media reports suddenly started talking about 'ghar-wapsi' programmes by organizations such as the VHP and the Bajrang Dal. These programmes aimed to re-covert those Hindus who had accepted Islam or Christianity, but primarily Christianity. These programmes and events attracted more outrage from the liberals than news reports about support for ISIS in India.

And what exactly was wrong in those events? If Christian missionaries have the right to convert people—and they indeed have, for the Constitution gives the right to 'propagate' one's religion—why shouldn't the same right be extended to Hindu groups too? Why should one assume that these ghar-wapsi programmes are 'forced conversions', even though nothing in the reports suggested so? Why did they never suspect that conversions carried out by Christian missionaries could have elements such as allurement, coercion or deception? Yet again, blatant double standards were employed.

Not just that, the liberal crowd claimed that these ghar-wapsi programmes could be held because the Hindu groups were feeling 'empowered' due to a BJP government at the Centre. That again was a lie. On Twitter, I put newspaper clippings from the year 2012 and 2013, when in the same areas, the same organizations had carried out the ghar-wapsi programmes, and around the same time, that is, around Christmas, when the Congress led-UPA ruled India.[95]

When I pointed these out to some of my outraging liberal friends—and I had a few before I gave up on trying to have a rational discussion with them sometime in 2016—they sheepishly changed the goal post to 'Two wrongs don't make it a right'. They averred that it was wrong even if it happened when Congress was ruling at the Centre.

First of all, I could never understand how was it wrong if Christian missionaries were free to hold similar events to carry out conversions, but even if it was 'wrong' for argument's sake, why was the outrage missing just a year back? Why could people not spot the ghar-wapsi events when it was held during the Congress rule?

You know why? Because during the Congress rule, such news reports were published only in local Hindi newspapers, which our city-dwelling online outraging social justice warriors never read. Perhaps, they didn't even know such newspapers existed.

But once Modi became the prime minister, the Delhi-based English-language media, or the 'Lutyens media', started covering such stories prominently, while giving it their own spin. All the things that were 'wrong' in the hinterlands, which somehow used to escape the radar of the Lutyens media, was now all set to become the focus of primetime debates on English news channels. Ghar-wapsi stories are how it started, and I spotted pretty early how farcical the entire outrage was.

What issues to outrage upon, what group to support, what causes to further and many more such decisions were not taken by employing some universal set of principles or by taking into account facts and logic. They settled these questions based on their own framework, where some set of ideas and people were 'wrong' by default.

Their framework was similar to Marxism, where class struggle or class conflict is assumed to be the ultimate truth and is used to analyse every social phenomenon. In the liberal framework, the class identities were replaced with social identities. Just like the bourgeoisie-proletariat can only have an exploiter-exploited relationship, a Hindu-Muslim, Brahmin-Dalit, man-woman or a Hindi-Tamil can only have an oppressor-oppressed relationship.[96] This is the prism through which they would see any event in any part of the country, regardless of the

ground realities or facts of the individual cases. Not My Liberalism again.
I had these observations during the first few months of Modi coming
to power, and there were many more in the coming months and years.
It progressively convinced me that liberalism in India was all a sham; it
was virtually anti-Hinduism.

It can be argued that just because the bulk of self-declared liberals
in India were behaving in the most hypocritical way, it doesn't mean
that liberalism itself was a bad idea. I would still have no problem if
classical liberal positions or libertarian positions were applied without
prejudice and hypocrisy, but that rarely happened. And now we are in
an era where wokes 'cancel' classical liberals if they try to do so.

As a Hindu—and that identity only grew stronger with liberals
targeting only Hinduism—I had nothing to gain by maintaining a
libertarian position in public. It would have meant maintaining the status
quo of the prevalent hypocrisy, where I would add the weight of my
voice when Hinduism or Hindus are criticized, but remain a lone voice
when Islam or other religions are criticized.

Say, I supported Setalvad's free speech even when she drew an
offensive cartoon comparing goddess Kali with an ISIS terrorist, and
obviously she had the support of liberals, but Indian liberals were busy
criticizing Charlie Hebdo cartoons a few months later, after Islamic
terrorists attacked and murdered the cartoonists in Paris. Hardly any
of the liberals supported the cartoonists' freedom of expression. When
things are so lopsided, choosing to be neutral means choosing to
maintain the status quo.

The liberals were not doing anything that incentivized Hindus like
me to continue being accommodative and broad-minded. Muslims could
behave in the most extremist ways, including killing people, and liberals
would start talking about 'nuances', cultural differences, neo-colonialism
and everything under the sun, but not criticize some aspects of Islam.
This became a worldwide phenomenon actually. After a terror attack
by any Islamist in any European city, the first reaction of the liberals
was to fight the likely Islamophobia that may follow, instead of fighting
Islamofascism, which inspired the attack in the first place.

On the other hand, forget violent acts, even if a Hindu group or
a BJP leader indulged in issuing a seemingly ridiculous statement, the

liberals would release all their scorn on all possible Hindu iconography and beliefs—from gaumutra jokes to beef taunts, from making fun of Hindu epics to caricaturing traditions of Hindus, and so on. Sometimes one wondered what exactly have Hindus gained by not behaving like Muslims?

Not that I concluded that I should start behaving like perennially outraged Muslims, though some of my public posturing, especially on Twitter, could be like that. But I concluded that things were just too blatantly biased and lopsided to remain non-partisan, and that one needed to drop the political correctness and ask such questions that might sound communal, parochial and juvenile.

The need was not to be neutral and balanced, but to 'balance' this lopsided narrative by bringing in counter-arguments. The need was not to respect the boundaries of political correctness, but to push the boundaries to show why political correctness was hiding the truth. The need was not to aspire to become moderate, but to become 'extreme' and shift the Overton window, so that people could discover the true centre, the true neutrality.

The need was to truly be anti-establishment, by not being party to a system that continues to further the same old narrative. The need was to truly be a dissenter, by not joining the liberal bandwagon. The need was to stand up for my identity, by not surrendering and seeking liberal validation.

The need was to adopt the Sanghi label.

9

The sore losers 2.0

If you can't fight them, shame them

Towards the end of 2014 and for almost the entire 2015, the secular-liberal ecosystem was working on the 'growing intolerance' narrative. It was funny because the first group to become really intolerant were the liberals themselves, who refused to engage in cordial debates.

The initial victims of this 'growing intolerance' were presented as Christians, due to events like ghar-wapsi and some incidents of theft and vandalism in church premises. These episodes were claimed to be deliberate acts of mischief and communal violence by Hindu groups. Many such incidents were reported from Delhi, incidentally before the assembly elections of 2015, which were swept by AAP.

Over time, it came to knowledge that most of these alleged attacks on churches were not at all communally motivated or carried out by Hindu groups. Some were simple accidents, such as kids playing cricket nearby and a ball hitting the church window, or a fire caused by an electric short-circuit, while incidents of vandalism were discovered to be the handiwork of drunken men, and at least in one case a disgruntled church employee was involved.[97]

But facts didn't matter and a narrative of 'Christians under attack' was built. Various Christian groups in India and abroad made a noise about it. Prime Minister Modi himself had to come up with assuring words at a conference organized by Christian groups in February 2015, though he didn't explicitly mention Christians under attack. Modi said that his government will not allow any religious group, majority or minority, to incite hatred against others, but headlines were about Modi 'breaking silence' about 'attack on Christians'.

Traditionally, hard cold facts have not really mattered when one has a good story to tell. Emotions always trump numbers, and that's how the ecosystem had been successful in building varied sets of narratives without caring for facts. But times were changing. Narratives based on hard facts and cold-hearted logic too had discovered a market and a shelf life.

Soon it became a recurrent theme, where various narratives were built around emotions and stories by the anti-Modi camp, while they were countered relentlessly with hard facts and cold-hearted logic from the pro-Modi camp.

In March 2015, a 71-year-old nun was raped in a convent in the Nadia district of West Bengal. Coming close on the heels of 'Christians under attack' narrative, it was immediately blamed on Hindu groups. Just a couple of weeks before this incident, the Government of India had denied permission to air a documentary by BBC over Delhi's 2012 gang rape and murder case. As a protest, NDTV had kept its screen black for an hour. Both the issues were conflated, and a narrative around 'India being the rape capital of the world' was launched.

However, facts didn't back the narrative in either case. BBC's documentary was 'banned' not because it showed India in poor light—and thus the government could be accused of trying to hide the 'ugly' realities—but because the producer had not taken proper permissions and broken rules related to interviewing undertrials.[98] And in the second case, a couple of Bangladeshi infiltrators were arrested for raping the nun, not members of some 'Hindu groups'.[99]

Once the 'Attack on Christians' narrative didn't appear to work, a narrative around 'Attack on rationalists' was built. Many 'intellectuals' and 'artists' decided to return awards that were given to them years ago in recognition of their work. It was called the 'award-wapsi' campaign. Yet again, there was no data to back the claim. The award-wapsi was triggered after the murders of Govind Pansare, a communist leader from Maharashtra in February 2015, and M.M. Kalburgi, an author-activist from Karnataka in August 2015. Till date, the police have not been able to prove who the murderers were in either cases, but 'Hindu groups' were immediately blamed, and they continue to be blamed.

'Lynchistan' was another narrative sans any data or facts that was built, where the usual suspects tried to prove that incidents of mobs beating someone to death had become a regular feature under the Modi government, and it was only Muslims who were being lynched. Both these claims again failed the test of data and logic. Author and JNU professor Anand Ranganathan came out with a detailed rebuttal to this narrative, showing various news reports that proved that not only were the cases of lynching happening with the same frequency as during the UPA rule, but that in many cases Muslims were actually the perpetrators.[100]

And many more such narratives were tried. Hyper-nationalism or toxic nationalism was one such narrative, where it was wished that India should not win the 2015 Cricket World Cup, for the victory will only increase 'hyper-nationalism'. Fortunately, such narratives didn't even need data to show why they were ridiculous.

The role of the mainstream media, especially the Delhi-based English-language media, was very crucial in trying to propagate these narratives that were rarely based on data or facts. For instance, after Modi became the prime minister, one fine day the Lutyens media discovered the ghar-wapsi programme. Similarly, in a couple of years they started discovering events like lynching and cow vigilantism.

Anyone keeping a track on vernacular media would have known that these were unfortunately routine incidents. The Delhi-based English media was discovering 'lynching' as shocking headlines while the local Hindi media had become immune to 'Bheed ne peet peet kar maar daala' (mob beats someone to death) headlines years ago. The lynching incidents were reflective of the problem of local law enforcement as well as a lack of trust in the justice system. But instead of highlighting these problems, the incidents were used to peddle the narrative against the central government.

However, what was more worrisome was not the media coming up with sensationalist and selective headlines, but its active manipulation of facts to suit the narrative. One such example was of a fight over a train seat, which took place in a running train in June 2017, where a boy named Junaid was killed, at a place that was not very far away from Delhi. Somehow the media inserted a 'beef' angle to the entire incident and the crime case immediately became a communal case.

It was reported that Junaid was killed because the killers (Hindus) suspected that he was carrying beef. That was plain lie, and the same was confirmed by the Punjab and Haryana High Court during a hearing of the case in April 2018.[101] But by then, the 'lynched over beef' phrase had made international headlines. Further, fights over seats in that train route, including violent fights, was found to be a rather common phenomenon.[102]

It is not just the High Court's observation due to which I'm saying that the beef angle was inserted by the media. An email was received in OpIndia's inbox in early July 2017, where a journalist working in a leading Delhi-based news channel had sent screenshots of internal communication systems of a channel. The email claimed that the raw report filed by the local reporter on Junaid's death had no mention of 'beef' at all; the beef angle was invented and inserted by a reporter sitting in the Delhi office of the channel. Once the news with the beef angle was flashed as breaking news on this leading TV channel, other media houses too carried the story with the same angle.

This wasn't even 'responsible journalism' owing to any ideology that a reporter could genuinely believe in. It was purely an unethical propaganda. This is what the media was doing. And to top it all, another narrative was tried, where the TV media was branded as 'Godi media'. Thus, you had a media that was inventing stuff to show Hindutva and Modi in bad light, and the same media was also painted pro-Modi, basically signalling to the common man that 'reality' could be even worse. Quite potent a plan I must say.

But, perhaps the most sinister of all the narratives that were built with this modus operandi was the narrative of 'hate crimes'. This time, the secular-liberal ecosystem was armed with 'data', which was absent in its earlier attempts at pushing various narratives.

An organization called IndiaSpend had created a database of hate crimes, which was presented as the truest representative and repository of such crimes in India. Based on that database, literally hundreds of news reports were published nationally and internationally, 'proving' how Muslims were almost exclusively the target of hate crimes in India after the Modi government came to power. Apart from rise in hate crimes, it also threw fantastical percentages about 'cow-related violence' in the

Modi era. It was a fraud of the highest order.

The database created by this organization was based on news reports published in various English-language media outlets and not based on any database of police complaints or other official records. The same English-language media that didn't bother to report about ghar-wapsi, lynching or cow vigilantism with the same vigour and alacrity before 2014, thinking that such cases were insignificant local incidents fit only to be carried by the vernacular media. Suddenly, the same incidents were now found fit to be national headlines and representative of how India had 'changed.'

There were multiple serious issues with this approach. The English media was always Delhi centric, and the choice of what they may and may not report was never going to be representative of what was actually happening in India. Then you had the issue of 'responsible journalism', where hate crimes involving a Muslim as the perpetrator may not be reported at all to 'maintain communal harmony', or if at all it is reported, the facts could be diluted. And obviously, the media could report entirely manipulated fabricated reports too, such as inserting the beef angle in the fight over a train seat.

Essentially, the primary source of the database itself was biased and couldn't have been called objective by any stretch of imagination.

But IndiaSpend went a step further. It added its own bias and discretion and made special efforts not to recognize any report on crimes that involved a Hindu victim and Muslim perpetrator as hate crimes (that is, if it was somehow reported by the English-language media). It started giving specious justifications for not identifying certain crimes as hate crimes, even if similar crimes with religious identities reversed were listed as hate crimes in its database. Their double standards were exposed relentlessly on social media, and eventually they had to take down their so-called 'hate tracker.'[103]

And there were many more narratives around that time. A common objective behind most of these narratives appeared to make Hindus feel ashamed about what was happening in the name of Hinduism. The idea was to make them feel guilty for having elected Modi, whose government was supposedly responsible for emboldening and empowering bad men, who did bad things to Muslims and 'marginalized' communities in the name of Hinduism. Thus, the grand project was 'designed' to send the Hindus on a guilt trip.

There was a reason why there was this hurry to guilt-trip the Hindus. It was related to the 2014 verdict. Again, I am not saying it was a plan or conspiracy hatched by the entire ecosystem in some meeting to analyse the electoral defeat, but it does have a link to the ecosystem. Let me explain.

In May 2014, the Congress had suffered its worst-ever electoral defeat. Reduced to 44 seats, it was staring at the risk of being pushed to the margins if immediate corrective steps were not taken.

The reasons for its defeat appeared to be pretty obvious—massive corruption charges, anti-incumbency, lackadaisical leadership of Rahul Gandhi and the Modi wave. However, if one analysed them as a pragmatist, these reasons didn't warrant any 'corrective' step. They were transient in nature.

Take for example, the corruption charges. By 2019, they would have been forgotten because the Indian electorate is notorious for having a short memory. And not just that, the Congress-friendly ecosystem, after having realized that they erred by fighting with the Congress earlier, would have tried to prove that there was no real corruption. An article published in December 2017 on NDTV was headlined 'There Was No 2G Scam. So Modi Has Little Over Manmohan Now.'[104] Not so subtle, eh?

Anti-incumbency would not be a factor at all in 2019, as that was something the BJP would have to battle.

The Congress wouldn't have given up on the leadership of Rahul Gandhi so soon. They would have posed faith in the ecosystem to help them re-brand and re-launch him for the fiftieth time if required, and just in time before the next elections.

While on the matter of Modi wave, almost everyone was convinced that it was a black swan event, and won't be repeated in 2019.

However, that didn't mean that the Congress didn't need to introspect or analyse. There were reports that the Congress had formed a panel chaired by A.K. Antony, which was to submit its report on the reasons for the massive defeat.

Although that report is an internal document of the Congress and I have no idea what the party concluded, there are some incidents that point to what it could be. For example, in June 2014, barely three weeks after the Lok Sabha results, Antony had said that the Congress was seen as 'pro-minority' by an average Hindu. Some other leaders, including even Digvijay Singh, were reported as admitting that the Congress was not only seen as a party that practised minority appeasement, but even as an 'anti-Hindu' party by many.

Soon after that, in August 2014 there were reports that the Congress had decided to go for an image makeover. The party decided to celebrate all religious festivals in their offices. Up until then, the only religious festival they celebrated was Iftaar, during the Muslim holy month of Ramzan.[105] In December of the same year, it was reported that the party had decided to seek feedback from its cadre to gauge whether it was perceived as anti-Hindu.

All these reports hinted that the Congress did realize that it had a problem of image, and that it was seen as 'pro-minority' and even 'anti-Hindu' by some.

So, what should have the Congress done? The party couldn't have become less pro-minority, because 'minorities' comprise a substantial chunk of population in India and their support was critical for the Congress.

They would have needed to look at the problem statement finely to arrive at a better solution.

In essence, the problem was that an average Hindu thought that the Congress preferred minorities, especially Muslims, at the cost of the welfare of Hindus, and that the party was unfairly and unreasonably obsessed with minority issues.

Keywords being 'unfairly' and 'unreasonably', and that's where the solution lay. The party didn't need to shed its pro-minority or pro-Muslim image, but all it needed to do was to convince the average Hindu that its obsession with minority issues was not 'unfair' and 'unreasonable'.

That would have happened only if an average Hindu was convinced that the minorities in India were being unfairly and unreasonably targeted. He needed to be told that minorities were not safe, and that as a member of the majority community, he had to do something.

'Lynchistan: Hindus silent as a wave of violence against Muslims sweeps India' was the title of an article published in June 2017.[106] It couldn't have been more obvious that the idea was to send the average Hindu on a guilt trip, and to fill him with remorse for having voted for Modi, who had turned Hindustan into 'Lynchistan'.

This shaming and guilt-tripping of Hindus happened in the Kathua murder case too, where an 8-year-old girl was found dead in the Rasana village of Kathua district in Jammu & Kashmir. It was alleged that she was raped and then murdered in a local temple in January 2018. Almost on cue, many Bollywood celebrities posted their pictures on social media, while holding placards with the word 'devisthan', that is, the temple of a goddess, highlighted. Temple was made the motif while talking about rape and murder.

While these were powerful stories involving tragic deaths, and they certainly troubled many Hindus, they couldn't successfully fill an ordinary Hindu with guilt and remorse, because the liberals went too far.

Almost every time, these attempts to shame Hindus were joined by elements who were openly Hinduphobic. The Lynchistan protests saw 'Hindu terrorism' posters, and the Kathua protests went even a step further, where posters such as a condom on the trishul—a divine symbol for Hindus associated with Lord Shiva—were used.[107]

The protests stopped appearing organic and genuine to an ordinary Hindu, thanks to the participation of such elements. Also, thanks to social media and WhatsApp, these images circulated as fast as the narrative and stories to guilt-trip the Hindus.

The liberals, who thought hyper-nationalism was a problem, perhaps didn't realize that their hyper-activism and hyper-liberalism was actually the problem.

At least in one incident they were able to guilt-trip Hindus to a good extent, as they had not become too extreme at that time—it was the killing of a Muslim man in Dadri, Uttar Pradesh, in September 2015. A mob in Bisada village in Dadri had killed 52-year-old Mohammad Akhlaq for stealing and slaughtering a calf. The incident had attracted wide outrage and condemnation from all quarters. There were protests too, but I can't recall any openly Hinduphobic statements or signs in such protests. Those were early days and liberals were playing their cards smartly.

But the liberals overdid this card and became brazen with time. They ignored all incidents where Muslims were the perpetrators of any hate crime. Or worse, they started giving 'context', such as the case of Chandan Gupta who was killed on Republic Day in 2018 for taking out a 'tiranga yatra' in Kasganj, Uttar Pradesh. When he shouted Vande Mataram in 'Muslim lanes', it was insinuated as provocative enough to warrant a deadly attack on him by the same lot who rejected the idea that cow slaughter can be provocative for those who consider cows to be holy.

The usual hypocrisy, coupled with the visible presence of openly anti-Hindu elements during campaigns to guilt-trip the Hindus, had the opposite effect.

By 2019, they couldn't find this sense of guilt even in the Bisada village. 'Four years after Mohammad Akhlaq's lynching, Bisada in Dadri shows no signs of remorse' read the summary of a report on a far-Left website,[108] just a couple of days before India went to polls for the 2019 Lok Sabha elections. Forget remorse, most of the local residents were angry with the media for 'giving a bad name' to their village. They had accused the then SP government of Uttar Pradesh of wrongly arresting many Hindu men from their village to please the protesting Muslims,[109] and asked why the media never cared for those who were 'wrongly arrested.'

If it was giving a bad name to a village in Bisada, on the national level it was about trying to give a bad name to the country, and to the Hindu identity. I am not referring to the Dadri incident here, but the cumulative effect of the continuous attempts to shame Hindus on various occasions during the first term of Modi, and especially between 2015 and 2018. It didn't work.

It wasn't just around Hindu–Muslim incidents where attempts were being made to shame the Hindus. The caste card was also played, especially around Dalits.

One such incident was the suicide by a PhD student named Rohith Vemula at the University of Hyderabad in January 2016. The cause of suicide was declared to be his various clashes with the members of the pro-RSS student organization ABVP (Akhil Bharatiya Vidyarthi Parishad). Rohith had been suspended for assaulting one ABVP member earlier, and his suspension was also offered as the reason why he took the extreme step of killing himself. Since it was a central university, the Modi government was held responsible.

However, while the opposition political parties tried to target the BJP and the Modi government, especially the then HRD Minister Smriti Irani, the liberals centered it around how Dalits get a raw deal in India, especially when Hindutva becomes strong. Yet again, that was just a story sans facts, because Dalits were not really living in better conditions when the BJP was not in power.

Furthermore, a glance at the Facebook timeline of Vemula showed how he was just another guy interested in 'ordinary' things before his tone became more and more political and radical as he joined far-Left student organizations. He was brainwashed to such an extent that he had started hating everything Hindu and everything saffron. He was heard saying in a viral clip that he hated the saffron colour so much that he would tear down saffron clothes, even saris, at his house.[110]

The far-Left ideology had radically changed him, and in all probability he had stopped identifying himself with what he was. His suicide letter gave the same hint—on how he missed his original self, where he wanted to study about stars and science. He rued that 'the value of a man was reduced to his immediate identity'.[111] He further wrote in his suicide note that he blamed no one for his suicide. Yet liberals used his death, and continue to use his death till date, to peddle their agenda.

The Dalit card was played again in January 2018 when violence broke out during the celebrations to mark the victory of 'Dalit soldiers' in the battle of Bhima-Koregaon, an event that took place 200 years ago. At least one person was killed and dozens were injured, apart from widespread damage to property.

In their zeal to shame the people, the liberals practically justified the violence by asking people why should they be so outraged over just one death and violence, when Dalits go through a far worse fate regularly in many parts of India? This was the worst form of 'whataboutery' that one could witness. In their minds, the liberals might have been making a very thought-provoking argument that would immediately fill a person with remorse and guilt for being complicit in the oppression of Dalits, but they appeared to be a bunch of hypocrites who had no principles, and who would even justify violence because it suited their political agenda.

One can keep lamenting and blaming the people for becoming

remorseless and heartless, but all one needed to do was to indulge in dispassionate analysis, without applying any moral absolutism. Thus, one would realize that the same reasons due to which many became comfortable with Hindutva in the run-up to the 2014 elections, were now proving to be the reasons why they were likely to stick with Hindutva as the 2019 elections approached.

The liberals thought that the newly gained fans of Modi would realize their mistake and change their choice, while Modi fans thought that the liberals would realize their mistake and change their behaviour. Perhaps that's why nothing changed, in terms of ideologies, and in terms of election results, in 2019.

But one thing had changed since the 2014 elections; the Congress–Left ecosystem had realized the importance of the new media, and was using social media platforms far more effectively than earlier. Perhaps, they realized that their earlier disdainful approach towards the new medium didn't help them, neither in terms of electoral victories nor in terms of furthering their narrative.

If pro-Hindutva blogs or Twitter handles gained prominence before 2014, the other side created YouTube stars and stand-up comedians post 2014 as the new digital icons. Relatively new platforms, such as Instagram, too were used very effectively by them to target Modi and Hindutva. Within a couple of years, the Congress–Left ecosystem appeared to have not only bridged the gap, but rushed far ahead of the Sanghis on the new media platforms.

While the mainstream media still formed the backbone and rock basis for the narratives that were built to prove how post-2014 times were not 'normal times' and why people should be deeply disturbed and even 'ashamed as a society', the internet was used brilliantly to amplify these messages. The entire campaign around the Kathua incident, for example, was primarily launched on social media, where 'devisthan' was deliberately highlighted in various placards and posts to make Hindus ashamed of their religious identity.

But things were happening on the other side too. OpIndia, a website aimed at providing a counter-narrative to the usual liberal narrative, was launched and started gaining traction in 2015. A Twitter handle named 'True Indology' became quite popular around 2016, as it exposed way too many wrong historical information that Hindus were fed by the secular-liberal ecosystem as indisputable facts. This handle got under the liberal skin, so much so that a national newspaper devoted an entire article trying to discredit it. They kept targeting it relentlessly and got the Twitter handle suspended. However, a different account could keep the mantle on the account is active on Facebook too.

The Right wing or the Sanghis were mostly catching up and reacting in most part of Modi's first term—throwing data to prove why the 'mahaul' built with fabricated stories was wrong, or proving how the narrative being pushed was one-sided. While they appeared to be laggards, they didn't prove to be losers.

The responses and rebuttals made sure that a sense of balance, a sense of a level-playing field, at least in the virtual world, prevailed, so far as narrative building was concerned.

Slogans like 'Afzal hum sharminda hain, tere qaatil zinda hain' and 'Bharat tere tukde honge, inshallah inshallah' (India will break into pieces) that were shouted on the JNU campus in January 2016[112] were made viral primarily due to the internet, which were then picked up by the mainstream media and the other side, the Sanghi side, could also build a narrative around anti-nationalism and the 'Tukde tukde gang'.

When terrorist Burhan Wani was killed in July 2016, the 'poor headmaster's son' qualifier used for him by Barkha Dutt was made into a meme, and was used to offer criticism on how terrorists are humanized by the liberal media while the RSS workers or Hindu groups are dehumanized.

There was another incident related to Wani's killing. Violent protests had erupted in Kashmir in the aftermath of the killing, and many were left injured and dead. International headlines were made about the 'inhuman' use of pellet guns against the protestors by the Indian police. Interviews of 'civilians' injured in protests or due to pellet guns were carried by the Indian media too. One such viral clip was that of Barkha Dutt talking to an injured protestor.

'Burhan Wani was fighting for Islam,' the protestor on the hospital bed, with bandages on his face, declared why Wani was so important for them. 'He was fighting for Islam or for Kashmir?' Dutt immediately asked him, to which the protestor stuck to the 'fighting for Islam' cause but appended the Kashmir rhetoric too.[113]

Dutt was accused of putting words in the mouth of an Islamist to help him come up with a 'correction', a charge she summarily denied. For me personally, it didn't really expose Dutt but betrayed the mindset of an average Kashmiri protester. The man pelting stone in the street was absolutely clear in his mind—it was a fight for Islam, it was a fight for 'Nizam-e-mustafa', it was a fight to create an Islamic state.

In essence, it was the good old two-nation theory that divides the people and geography on the basis of existing status and extensiveness of application of Islamic laws. Kashmiri terrorists were inspired by it since its inception, but the liberals had whitewashed this mentality and hid the reality by dressing up Kashmir as some 'political problem', where the root causes were secular reasons, such as unemployment and rigging of elections. Yes, indeed it was a political problem, and the problem was political Islam. The stone-pelters were at least honest to admit it and declare the same. That clip had gone viral.

The internet also helped in highlighting some aspects that were forgotten. For example, the NDTV interview where Sharad Pawar admits to have invented an extra bomb blast during the 1993 Mumbai bomb blasts in order to show that Muslims too were victims of terrorism, was originally aired in the year 2006, but that part of the video became viral almost 10 years later.

Something that was seen as normal and responsible behaviour earlier—in fact, Pawar disclosed it with a sense of pride in that interview, saying that he was even praised by a judge for lying; and neither of these claims could attract even a fleeting sense of disbelief from the interviewer Shekhar Gupta—was seen as a shockingly craven behaviour in the time of Modi.

Well, liberals surely were right in one aspect when they claimed that the post-2014 years were not 'normal times'—yes, because what liberals had normalized over decades was now being questioned with impunity by the Sanghis.

And this is where, despite using the internet and the new media far better than earlier, the liberals failed to convince or even shame people into rejecting Hindutva. Not only their arguments could be countered, many of their arguments made an average Hindu feel that their beliefs and identity were under attack—a sentiment that invariably helped the growth of Hindutva.

This is why, of late, the liberal attempt has increasingly been to not only use the internet and the new media in a far more effective way, but also to make sure that the other side can't use it effectively. The liberals are lobbying for curbs that disallow the Right wing or the conservatives or the Sanghis to use it as effectively and freely.

Big-tech companies are being asked to de-platform or de-monetize people and entities to fight 'hate speech'. Basically, there's an attempt to have the same level of censorship and control on the new media platforms as they have had over the mainstream media platforms. And they have been successful to a large extent, especially on Twitter.

The 2019 Lok Sabha elections

While in retrospect, I'm saying that the liberal approach to create narratives to shame the Hindus worked only the other way—certainly in my case—where people decided to stick to Hindutva even more vigorously than being shamed or shocked into rejecting it, to be honest, I again had doubts on whether what I felt and experienced could only be limited to people like me or whether there were indeed many who were successfully shamed.

I was not sure whether my story and sentiments could be shared by millions of others. There was always a fear—what if I was just living in a digital echo chamber? By 2019, I had long given up on trying to communicate or debate with liberals, and that's how one creates an echo chamber for oneself. I couldn't have lied to myself that I was not living in one.

But I was sure of one thing: That the 2019 Lok Sabha elections were going to be a much more polarized election than 2014, at least in those constituencies—and I'm using the term in a figurative sense—that were directly or indirectly impacted by the digital medium.

The liberals love to blame the Pulwama terror attack in Kashmir and the subsequent airstrikes on Pakistan in Balakot as an incident that 'polarized' the elections around nationalist sentiments, but the 2019 elections were always going to be polarized because of the way liberals had been behaving ever since Modi became the prime minister in 2014.

They had owned the label 'anti-national' as a mark of 'dissent', way back in 2016 itself.[114] Then they actively tried to find fault with every aspect of the country—from the growing intolerance to being the 'rape capital of the world' to hypernationalism. They topped this up with their attempts to specifically guilt-trip the Hindus over various incidents, such as lynching and 'cow-related violence'.

Cultural identity and ideology were made points of polarization by liberals long before any Pulwama or Balakot happened. They kept attacking every symbol of identity and opposing any attempt to feel proud about that identity. They made the word 'bhakt' a pejorative, which was a quintessential word for the devotee of any Hindu god or goddess. Imagine how liberals will cry 'Islamophobia' in unison if words such as 'haaji' or 'namaazi' are used as terms of insults. They might pretend to or be mistaken about fighting Hindutva politics, but they were fighting the Hindu identity for all practical purposes.

There were a few people, writing columns in Indian and foreign publications, who turned anti-BJP or anti-Modi around 2017, especially after Modi chose Yogi Adityanath to be the chief minister of Uttar Pradesh. The BJP had swept the state assembly elections in a way that was almost as magnificent as the victory of the 2014 Lok Sabha elections. These people declared Yogi to be a polarizing figure. There was blind opposition to everything he did—from action against illegal slaughterhouses to forming a special squad to deal with the harassment that women face every day. They declared that they were fighting Hindutva politics because that is not what they had praised Modi for.

Those handful of 'Lutyens columnist' obviously didn't represent the Indian voters in general, and if they really believed in 'Hindutva bad, but Modi good'—and thus ditched Modi because he chose Hindutva in the form of Yogi—it only meant that either they were pure idiots to believe in this inherently paradoxical idea or they were opportunists who needed an alibi to join the Modi bandwagon of 2014, possibly in the hope of reaping some personal benefits, while retaining their liberal credentials.

The blind opposition to Yogi also appeared as opposition to the Hindu identity. They hated his saffron clothes, nothing else—that was the message, and that added to the polarization as 2019 approached.

I'm not at all suggesting that elections are fought and won entirely on such issues and aspects. In 2019 too, there were various reasons why people voted for Modi or the BJP, which were not directly related to the kind of ideological elements I have been talking about. For example, the various welfare schemes the NDA government had championed. These had nothing to do with the Hindu identity and many beneficiaries were non-Hindus too. However, I'm limiting myself to only those people who understood the ideological matters or divides, at least to some extent, and the bulk of them were totally unimpressed with the liberal narrative.

I was most amused to see my grandfather—who was a Congress supporter all his life—become a Modi fan in his last years. He passed away on 15 August 2019, after having seen Modi win again to his satisfaction. He was in his 90s and he hardly ever cared for the BJP earlier. But, he had started seeing Modi as someone who was the right man for the country. Not just nationalism, he had become interested in issues such as the Ram Temple at Ayodhya, even though he was not really a religious man unlike my grandmother. He was so smitten by Modi that if someone in TV debates—and he used to watch those regularly to the irritation of others in the family—said anything against Modi, he would blurt out a few words in anger.

And not just my grandfather, there were many viral clips of really old men and women from the Hindi belt signing praises of Modi and even abusing his opponents. Many of them were from the rural areas, and I often wondered—though couldn't convince myself—if a big ideological churn was happening in the rural areas too. How come these people, who voted in favour of other parties for the most of their lives, suddenly becoming Modi fans?

My father too had given up on the usual secularism and liberalism, even though he had given us a Congressi Hindu upbringing. His reasons were similar to mine though—mostly in reaction to the liberals, after having figured out how they were a bunch of hypocritical Hinduphobes. Plus, his stint in the Middle Eastern countries as a professor also had an impact, where he discovered that this whole concept of respecting all religions was one-sided love that Hindus had decided to shower the world with. Many students in those Middle Eastern countries would come up to him and tell him, 'Duktur (professor), you are a very good human being, but why are you a Hindu?'

Those guys didn't really say those words to deliberately insult the religious beliefs of my father, but because they genuinely believed that a good person should follow Islam and Islam only. They wanted to save my father from the fire and torture in hell in the afterlife. While initially my father found that amusing and even 'cute', soon it started to rankle him.

As a typical Congressi Hindu, he used to think that people should respect each other's religious choices and identities. That was not working. The Hindu idea of mutual respect appeared to be a one-way street, where you could walk a considerable distance, before realizing that something is oddly off.

I have heard similar stories from people who have spent a significant time in the US or the European countries. Many of them were shocked at the brazenness of evangelists trying to convert them. As I had earlier recounted in this book, I myself had such an experience when one man tried to convert me right in the centre of a shopping mall in Hungary.

Due to such experiences, people lose faith in the 'All religions are the same' or 'Every religion teaches the same virtues' platitudes that many Hindus genuinely believe in. They wake up to the rude realization that it's actually only the Hindus who believe so. And when you point such things to a liberal, spouting the 'All religions are the same' nonsense, they would try to prove you wrong rather than accepting that Abrahamic religions indeed are insular and supremacist in nature. In fact, the latest fad is to prove that Hinduism fares worse on these counts and it is even more supremacist and insular. Then why was this pretence of 'All religions are the same' adopted in the first place if you believe that Hinduism is worse or inferior?

These aspects were not only being noticed but debated too, and I was convinced that a bulk of the people, who might have been just 'slightly' comfortable with Hindutva and yet voted for the BJP during the 2014 Lok Sabha elections, primarily due to the 'vikas' pitch of Modi, could be far more comfortable or even committed to Hindutva in the run-up to the 2019 elections. I definitely was. I knew that if the elections were to be fought around ideological issues only, the BJP would cross 300 seats or even more. However, I still had the same fear—what if this belief is the result of living in an echo chamber?

After the BJP lost the assembly elections of Madhya Pradesh, Rajasthan and Chhattisgarh in November 2018, there surely was a scare regarding whether the narrative was slipping and if people like me—for whom ideological matters had taken centre stage—were only limited to a few urban cities and a few digital colonies.

Apart from issues with the local governments, a sense of resentment also existed among the middle-class in 2018 at the national level, because they had not got the expected tax reliefs. You couldn't have told an ordinary person to keep voting for the BJP just because the liberals hated Hinduism—this binary wouldn't have cut ice with normal people. I myself took over ten years to even conclude that liberalism in India was anti-Hinduism in practice, regardless of what it was in theory.

The middle-class resentment was addressed in the interim budget of 2019, which was presented on 1 February 2019 by the then acting Finance Minister Piyush Goyal, with income tax relief going up to ₹5 lakh annual income. The ongoing focus on rural India and the economically weaker sections was maintained too, with various welfare schemes already in action by then, be it the Ujjwala scheme to provide LPG connections to poor families, or Ayushman Bharat to provide them free healthcare, or the mission to electrify every village or schemes providing for affordable housing.

And then Pulwama happened on 14 February 2019. It was a tragedy. But it also united people as Indians. At so many places—in housing societies, in public places, in offices—various gatherings were organized to pay tributes to the soldiers who were killed by the suicide bomber in Kashmir. Some even used these gatherings to protest and shout slogans against Pakistan. Perhaps, liberals thought that all such events were organized by pro-BJP guys. And if they thought so, they were totally wrong.

It was not the first time that soldiers had been murdered in Kashmir, but this was especially horrific. Elements like the video message recorded by the suicide bomber, where he gave out threats before carrying out the attack, and the pictures of the mayhem had a wide impact.

I would argue that the public reaction to Pulwama was similar to the reaction one saw in 2012 to the Delhi gang rape incident. That was also not the first time a shocking incident of rape and murder had taken place in the country, but somehow it shook the conscience of the nation on that occasion. The same was the case with the Pulwama incident, somehow it triggered very strong emotions and united people on patriotic lines.

It was the liberals who lost their marbles and turned a rather unifying event into a 'polarizing' one. Perhaps they totally misread those small protests and events, suspecting the BJP to be behind those, just like the ruling Congress had misread the anti-rape protests in 2012, thinking it was organized by the newly formed AAP. The Congress government had lathicharged the anti-rape protestors while AAP and Kejriwal were seen with the protesting crowd. In my opinion, half of Delhi was lost by the Congress and won by AAP then itself.

The liberals obviously couldn't have lathicharged anyone, but their rhetoric was totally out of tune for the occasion. It was bound to be, for they had proudly adopted the 'anti-national' tag earlier. They just didn't know how to be part of the crowd, just like the Congress didn't know how to do that in 2012. The BJP could become part of that crowd easily, as there is a thin line between patriotism and nationalism.

Primarily, it was a crowd of ordinary patriotic Indians, not really of 'Hindu nationalist' Indians, who were paying voluntary tributes to the martyrs in their residential societies, offices and parks. It was the liberals who turned a patriotic outpouring of emotions into a nationalism vs rationalism debate, and thus polarized the environment.

The preachy messages against war, and some out and out abusive messages blaming Modi for having carried out Pulwama and later the Balakot strikes to win the elections, were bound to put off many.

When Wing Commander Abhinandan Varthaman of the Indian Air Force was briefly captured by Pakistan in February 2019, as he had crossed the border while chasing and shooting down Pakistani fighter planes, there were messages ridiculing the government for 'losing a pilot' to Pakistan. For the liberals, it was an occasion to humiliate Modi, but for an ordinary Indian, it was an occasion to be concerned about an Indian who was in Pakistani captivity.

Let there be no confusion—if Pulwama polarized the 2019 elections, the 'credit' entirely goes to the liberals, not to Modi.

Anyway, by April, the Pulwama sentiments had subsided a little and other issues were being talked about. The Congress declared that they will give ₹72,000 cash every year to poor families, which on paper appeared to be a big draw. The party, especially Rahul Gandhi, kept raising the topic of the Rafale scam, surrounding the purchase of Rafale fighter planes, even though there was no proof. Many opposition leaders also held joint rallies, where aggressive speeches were made, such as 'Modi will not allow another election in this country if he wins 2019'.[115]

Even though the leaders sounded desperate, and a little scared too, as Rahul Gandhi had to choose a second seat in Kerala to fight the Lok Sabha elections, I think many in the Congress–Left ecosystem—the motley of journalists, writers, activists, lawyers and artists—genuinely believed that Modi will lose 2019, just like Vajpayee had lost 2004 despite opinion polls showing that he had an edge over the others. Incidentally, they had been applying similar tricks against Modi as they had applied against Vajpayee.

Even during the Vajpayee era, the same lot had created a similar narrative—that it was not 'normal times' with the BJP in power. When the BJP lost the 2004 Lok Sabha elections, Arundhati Roy had written an article for a British daily newspaper that was titled 'Let us hope the darkness has passed', which referred to the Vajpayee era as 'pretty hellish six years'.[116]

If a scam in Rafale fighter jets purchase was being claimed during the Modi era, scams in purchase of arms and even coffins were claimed during the Vajpayee era; the Congress questioned claims during the Balakot airstrikes by Modi, while questions were raised about Kargil victory during Vajpayee; 'Achchhe din' of Modi was declared fake, similar to the 'India Shining' of Vajpayee; Modi was supposedly working only for a few industrialists, while Vajpayee was asked 'Aam aadmi ko kya mila' (What did the common man gain?) by Congress in 2004.

The 2004 scars were still fresh. Even though back in 2004 I didn't care for the fact that Vajpayee was voted out, I dreaded the thought of Modi losing 2019. It would be the death knell for Hindutva, as the ecosystem would be back with a resolve to purge Hindutva once and for all. It would be hellish in the truest sense of the term.

I couldn't care less what specifics Modi as the prime minister had done for Hindutva. There were many critics within the Right wing too, who thought that Modi was just too focused on the issue of development. In fact, they even blamed him for Muslim appeasement, to the extent that you can find 'Maulana Modi' taunts against him on social media.

I could have tried to reason with such people, arguing how it was a very myopic view, but I didn't have the time or patience for that. I just knew that it was only because of this person that I shifted my allegiance to Hindutva. It was because of Modi's rise that I could see how hypocritical the liberals were and how liberalism in India was a joke.

This man has to be back. What he does or doesn't do is not my concern. He should be back, because the other side is just too vile and they shouldn't be back.

It was given that if the Congress returned to power in 2019, they would have doubled down on their toxic secularism, further pushing Hindus to a stinking corner. Communal Violence Bill, which officially makes sure that a Hindu is never seen as a victim of communal violence, would have become a law. New laws to punish 'hate speech', which essentially would mean you can't talk about your grievances as Hindus, would have been created. Private companies too would have been pressurized to get rid of anyone who had an influential social media account that furthered anti-establishment views. The great purge would have begun.

Let me disclose, with much shame, that I had not exercised my right to vote in the 2014 Lok Sabha elections. I was 34 years old then, and yet to vote in a single parliamentary or assembly elections. I wanted to vote in 2014, and I made efforts to get my voter ID card made too, but the process was not entirely digital at that time. I couldn't arrange the required documents in time and submit it to the designated local office to get my voter ID card made, and thus I couldn't vote.

But in 2019, I was determined to vote. Every vote counted and everything had to be done to stop the Congress–Left ecosystem from getting back to power. Fortunately, this time the process of application was easy and online. I filled up the required forms online and uploaded the supporting documents. However, yet again, I did it dangerously close to the last date of submitting the forms.

And I thought I had messed up again. The Election Commission website was not giving me any updates on the status of my application, though it showed that all steps had been completed. When I tried to call on the numbers listed as electoral officers in Gurgaon, either they were not working or the officers just asked me to wait for the voter ID card to arrive.

I had moved back to Gurgaon from Mumbai in July 2018, after I could raise some modest funding for OpIndia from Delhi-based investors. I had resigned from Network18 much earlier, in October 2016, after having waited long enough for new investments decisions to be made, so that I could start the new initiatives for the digital division of the company, or at least for *Faking News*. I finally gave up and resigned. However, I decided to stay back in Mumbai, a city where I had relocated to due to Network18.

I had spent around five years in Mumbai before I moved back to Gurgaon, with less than a year to go for the 2019 Lok Sabha elections. Fortunately, I had spent the minimum time required at a place to be eligible for being listed in the electoral roll of that place. Back in 2014 too, Mumbai was a new place where I had moved to, and my attempts to get a voter ID card at a new place had failed then.

It was déjà vu, and a terrible one, when my voter card didn't arrive, even as voting in other parts of the country had begun.

Voting for the 2019 elections took place in seven phases, and Gurgaon was to vote in the sixth phase, on 12 May. Four phases of polling were over and the month of May arrived, but my voter ID card was yet to arrive. I couldn't even find my name in the electoral roll that was uploaded online. Yet again, I thought I had messed up, and I was really disappointed and cross with myself this time.

But as if gods wanted me to vote, I could get the voter ID card just a couple of days before the scheduled polling. In fact the card lay downstairs, in the drawer of the security guard of the building, who had forgotten to inform me to collect it after the local postman left it with him. Once political parties started distributing voter slips, he suddenly recalled that a 'small item' lay in the drawer and handed it over to me, along with the voter slip.

I was really happy and excited. And why not, I was going to be a first-time voter!

My excitement can be gauged from the fact that I was only the second person at my polling booth on the morning of the voting day. I could well have been the first, but I took some time figuring out which polling booth I should proceed to. Once there, I realized why my name was not found on the voter list that was uploaded on the election commission website. I was among a dozen or so guys whose names were in some supplementary electoral roll. Perhaps, all of them were lazy like me, and submitted the applications on the last day.

For the first time in my life I voted. I pressed the button on the EVM (electronic voting machine) hard, as if I didn't want to take any chances, and had a fine contented look when I saw the slip falling into the VVPAT (Voter Verifiable Paper Audit Trial) box. When I came out of the polling booth, I took a selfie and uploaded it on Twitter. I was so happy and proud that I had to show off! It was similar to the excitement felt by a teenager, ironically triggered by the anxieties of an aged man.

A week later, after the last phase was over, almost all exit polls predicted that the NDA government was set to return, with some even predicting that the BJP would get a majority of its own. However, the ghosts of 2004 were still lurking around in the minds of a BJP supporter. It was prudent to wait for a few days before celebrating.

And the day came—23 May 2019, when the ghosts of 2004 were finally buried. The BJP once again won a majority of its own. And not just that, it even bettered its 2014 record, both in terms of the total number of seats won as well as the percentage of popular votes it attracted. It was a tsunami again.

The defining moment was Rahul Gandhi losing his Lok Sabha seat in Amethi, which was held by the Nehru-Gandhi family for decades. This was for the first time since 1977—the elections held after the Emergency was lifted—when someone from the family had lost his or her own seat. Smriti Irani, who had given Rahul Gandhi a tough fight in 2014 but couldn't defeat him then, won in style this time.

Even after losing in 2014, Irani had decided to serve the people of Amethi. She virtually camped there all these years and helped with various things—from unplanned issues such as dousing a fire in some village to planned projects such as getting roads and factories built in the constituency. It was she who was more regularly visible, and was approachable to people, in Amethi than their MP Rahul Gandhi. No wonder Gandhi had to look for a second seat in Wayanad, in Kerala, as the party in all probability knew that there was a real risk of him losing from Amethi.

In a way Irani epitomized how the BJP had become a different organization since 2004. It was a party that believed that it can win, a party that took on the challenges head on and a party that concluded that it needs to work even harder when defeated, instead of blaming the EVMs or the people.

Modi 2.0 and liberals 2.0

Back in 2014, the liberals tried to convince themselves that Modi's victory was an aberration. They thought that Modi won due to the 'false hope' of 'achchhe din' he gave to people, who in turn had hoped for less corruption, less inflation, more jobs and more development, after having 'ignored' the liberal warning on Hindutva politics. Voters ignored it not because they had started seeing merits in Hindutva politics, but because they couldn't see the 'real threat' it posed. Essentially, the liberals concluded that the voters were fooled by Modi.

So the solution was simple in the liberals' minds—show these 'fools' the 'real threat' of Hindutva (every single narrative, from growing intolerance to cow-related violence) and talk about how there was more corruption (Rafale allegations), more inflation (occasional rise in fuel prices), less jobs (cite a 'leaked' report, incidentally just two months before the 2019 elections, claiming unemployment levels were at their worst in the last 45 years), less development (why no double digit GDP growth? What about farmers?) and taunts about 'jumla' and '₹15 lakhs'.

It appeared to be a perfect plan in their minds to defeat Modi in 2019.

But Modi won again, wining more seats and popular vote share. One would have expected them to introspect where they went wrong, but the conclusion they derived remained the same—voters were fooled again.

Perhaps, they don't realize that implicit in such assumptions is a contempt for the common people, who may not agree with them. And this has manifested in many ways in their behaviour. The contempt has actually morphed into abhorrence for people, and thus they are not really fighting a political party or a government but a set of people.

This is the significant difference between the approach of the 'Left' and the 'Right' when they are not in power. When the Right, or let's say the BJP was in opposition, they too attacked the UPA government, mocked the prime minister and fought with the Congress supporters, but they never treated a set of people as enemies. But when the Congress became the opposition party after 2014, they not only treated the BJP and the prime minister as sworn enemies, they declared a set of people—the 'bhakts'—as persona non grata, as enemies who were not welcome and whose arguments or beliefs didn't matter.

The Congress-Left ecosystem not only exposed their contempt for a set of people, but also their contempt for Hindu traditions, when they started using the term 'bhakt' as a pejorative. You can't find a parallel to this label when the BJP was in opposition.

Yes, labels like 'anti-national' and 'Urban Naxals' have been used by the BJP supporters of late, and primarily as a reaction to the frequent use of labels such as 'fascist' and 'bigot' by the other camp, but you won't be able recall a term like 'bhakt' being used by the BJP supporters during the UPA rule, where they declared a set of people as enemies. Forget treating ordinary people as enemies, even Congress leaders were not treated as 'enemies' by the people on the Right when they were in opposition.

For example, in September 2013, a US Court sent summons to Sonia Gandhi for 'shielding and protecting' Congress party leaders involved in the anti-Sikh riots of 1984.[117] Gandhi was in the US at that time for a medical check-up. No BJP leader or even any well-known supporter of the party celebrated this news. No one wished to see Gandhi being humiliated in the US. This is in sharp contrast to how the Left has been soliciting help from every foreign power to oppose and humiliate Modi after he became the prime minister. In fact, back in 2013 itself, 64 MPs had written to the then US President Barack Obama to continue the visa ban on Modi.[118]

The liberals don't realize that in their extreme hatred for Modi and Hindutva politics, they have started hating the people, and even the state on occasions. Interestingly, the liberals are indeed liberal in treating the political leadership, the state and the people as distinct entities when it comes to Pakistan, but they fail to employ the same yardstick for Modi's India.

For example, they will argue that the state of Pakistan, often controlled directly or indirectly by the army, is evil but the ordinary people—who support the same army and politicians amenable to the army—are good. This distinction is offered as reasons why there should be track-II diplomacy and efforts like 'Aman ki Asha' to 'bring peace between the two countries.'

All this is fine, but why don't the liberals extend the same courtesy to people back in India, who support the army or vote for a government they don't like? How come nationalism becomes such a dirty word back home? Why is there no pejorative term, such as 'bhakt', for any set of people in Pakistan? How come they love the Muslim Pakistan but keep crying hoarse about an imaginary 'Hindu Pakistan' that they accuse Hindutva activists of turning India into?

The truth is that there is no place for 'bhakts' in their 'idea of India.' It is virtually the new two-nation theory that they seem to be toying with, where bhakts are a different nation—an enemy nation. That's how they have been behaving, and they simply don't appear to introspect their behaviour.

On a couple of occasions, they did appear to introspect, such as some journalists reluctantly admitting that they could have deliberately overlooked the positive impacts of Modi's welfare policies,[119] but on most occasions their anguish was that people were fooled. They broadly concluded that voters had been blinded by the charisma of Modi and thus were unable to see how the NDA government was supposedly destroying democratic principles and institutions.

The former 'introspection' was more about admitting their bias, not about admitting that their beliefs were based on some wrong or outdated principles that needed to be discarded. The latter reaction, obviously, was not at all about admitting that their beliefs could be wrong, but that their efforts to prove themselves right were not good enough. The only thing they were lamenting was that they couldn't convince the common voters that they were the saviours while Modi was the villain.

Introspection is a process through which you psychoanalyse yourself. When you psychoanalyse others—imagining them as fools who were lured by a sweet talker—you are not introspecting, you are judging. That's the only thing the liberals do anyway—to judge others and to pronounce verdicts (about who is tolerant and who is fascist).

In short, after the 2019 loss, the conclusion was the same—people needed to be educated and saved from the fascists.

The messiah complex was intact.

As a result, as I write this, the behaviour of the liberals after 23 May 2019 has been a repeat of everything they did after 16 May 2014.

Every action by them has been about trying to prove, again, how we are not living in normal times and how everything is wrong. They have continued to shame people for their Hindu identity and guilt-tripped them for oppressing the minorities, especially Muslims. And, they have become more and more shrill and fanatical, celebrating 'cancel culture' and 'wokeness'.

If 'beef' and 'cow vigilantism' were inserted in any incident of crime or violence after 2014, 'Jai Shri Ram' was inserted in such incidents after 2019.

Barely a few weeks after Modi was sworn in as the prime minister of India for the second time, there were a string of news reports claiming that Muslim men were beaten up for refusing to chant 'Jai Shri Ram', and many of them were found to be either downright lies or claims that were not backed by any evidence or witness.[120]

The most brazen was perhaps what the Wall Street Journal (WSJ) did, when it claimed that the brother of Ankit Sharma, an IB (Intelligence Bureau) staffer who was killed by rioting Islamist mobs in Delhi in February 2020, had actually blamed a mob shouting 'Jai Shri Ram' for his brother's death. The brother rubbished the charges and a police complaint was filed against the WSJ.[121]

If JNU was 'under attack' in early 2016 due to police entering the campus and arresting some student leaders for having organized an event where anti-India slogans were shouted, in early 2020 JNU was under attack again as violence erupted over fee-hike protests.[122] Not just JNU, liberals wanted to portray that every university and students in general were under attack, which was exactly the same narrative that was tried in 2016 too, using Rohith Vemula's suicide.

So desperate they have been to find young leaders who would supposedly overthrow the Modi government, that they even dressed up someone like Hardik Patel—who is now the head of the Gujarat unit of the Congress party—as a 'student leader' in his initial days. The same was repeated in 2020, when they dressed up some out and out Islamists, such as Sharjeel Imam who had written articles supporting Jinnah's outlook in The Wire,[123] and two Jamia Millia Islamia students, Aysha and Ladeeda, who had eulogized the architects of the Moplah massacre and glorified the concept of jihad in many of their public posts on social media,[124] as 'sheroes' and student activists who were supposed to bring a new dawn.

In the run-up to the 2014 elections, the book contract of Tamil writer Joe D'Cruz was cancelled, while in 2020 another book contract was cancelled,[125] this time of author Monika Arora, a Supreme Court advocate, who had written a book about the Delhi riots 2020, which were triggered after the protests against the CAA.

With the liberals repeating themselves after 2019, they have continued to appear hypocritical, with double standards against Hinduism. It is far easier to talk about 'Hinduphobia' today than say in 2014, when people didn't even understand the term despite 'Islamophobia' being already in vogue by then.

Hinduphobia, which is now ingrained in the minds of the liberals, was especially visible when they joined the Islamists to protest against the CAA, which was passed in December 2019. All that the bill did was to fast-track the citizenship of religiously persecuted minorities from the three neighbouring Islamic countries (Afghanistan, Pakistan and Bangladesh), especially of those who were already living in India as refugees. But the secular-liberal ecosystem painted it as some grand conspiracy to kick out Muslims from India.

During the anti-CAA protests, there were posters where the sacred Om symbol (ॐ) of Hinduism was distorted to look like the hooked cross of the Nazis. It was a visual presentation of their oft-repeated lie that Hindutva politics and Hitler's fascism were similar. Apart from Om being distorted, the Hindu Swastika symbol was used to further this propaganda, as the hooked cross of the Nazis resembles the Swastika.[126]

While they attempted to hide their Hinduphobia by claiming that the Swastika they were using in their pictures was actually the Nazi hooked cross and not the Hindu Swastika, the distortion and denigration of the Om symbol betrayed their real feelings and attitude towards Hinduism. The only term that they could have used to justify the distortion of

Om was 'creative freedom'. Some even tried that. But when liberals try to be too smart, they only end up exposing themselves more.

The creative freedom claim fell flat as they themselves cried 'Islamophobia' when the India Today media group used a Muslim skullcap in an infographic to show the spread of coronavirus due to a single event organized by the Tablighi Jamaat.[127]

The infographic by India Today, which the media house eventually changed by making the skullcap 'less Muslim' after the liberal outrage, was just a statement of fact and figures. It didn't say that Muslims were spreading coronavirus deliberately or they were the only ones spreading the virus. It was just referring to a particular event that was in the news at that point of time. Yet, a bunch of liberals argued that such an imagery was 'bigoted' because it associated a Muslim religious symbol with the spread of coronavirus.

Then how come associating the Om symbol with fascism is just creative expression? Do liberals believe that a Muslim skullcap is more sacred than the Om symbol of Hindus? Do they believe that a Muslim skullcap must not be used flippantly in any artwork but the Hindu Om symbol can be distorted and disfigured to peddle all kinds of propaganda?

It was not an isolated attempt. Ever since the anti-CAA protests, use of any Muslim identifier—a beard, a skullcap, a hijab, even a lungi—in any cartoon has been being termed as Islamophobia by the same set of liberals who have been taking 'creative freedom' with every Hindu symbol and tradition. A janeu-wearing Brahmin with a 'choti' can be caricatured to be casteist, obscurantist, stupid and what not, but dare you draw a man with a skullcap pelting stones!

In April 2020, a team of Islamists and liberals targeted dozens of Hindus working in the Middle Eastern countries for supporting the CAA. This team complained to the employers of these Hindus about alleged Islamophobic messages posted by them on social media. That not only put the livelihoods of Hindus in danger, but their lives too, as any charge of Islamophobia can quickly be turned into charges of blasphemy in Islamic countries. In many of these cases, the Hindus had barely shared some pro-CAA cartoons that showed characters with Muslim identifiers opposing the CAA violently or offering inconsistent arguments against it.

Such cartoons were enough for the same liberal jamaat to pronounce a set of people guilty and deserving to be sacked from their jobs. This, after they had denigrated every Hindu symbol by associating those with fascism and felony, and justified the denigrations as 'creative freedom' and 'protest art'. Remember the condom over trishul during the protests over the Kathua case?

If in 2015, the Indian liberals were censoring cartoons, such as those made by Charlie Hebdo, which were supposedly offensive at it drew Prophet Mohammad, by 2020, they had graduated to censoring cartoons that depicted anti-CAA rioters or Tablighi Jamaat members. And then they wonder why they are seen as Hinduphobic, who are hand in glove with Islamists, and why people are warming up to Hindutva.

It was not just posters and cartoons that brought to the fore the hypocrisy and double standards of the liberals during the anti-CAA protests, but virtually everything they did and said either exposed their hypocrisy or betrayed their Hinduphobia.

A small controversy around the use of a nazm (poem) 'Hum Dekhenge' by the protestors had also erupted,[128] which again revealed the ingrained biases.

The nazm was written by Pakistani poet Faiz Ahmed Faiz, and is widely acknowledged and celebrated as a 'revolutionary poem' that was penned to oppose the then Pakistani military ruler Zia-ul-Haq. Since Zia is often accused of pushing Pakistan more and more towards Islamic fundamentalism—which I think is a copout, like blaming only the British for Partition; Pakistan was destined to be this way—the nazm is argued by some to be against religious bigotry too, though there is nothing in the poem that suggests so.

A couple of lines in the 'Hum Dekhenge' poem glorify and pine for a time when all idols will be removed ('Sab but uthwaaye jaayenge') and only the name of the Islamic god will prevail ('Bas naam rahega Allah ka') in the world. Some folks opposed the poem due to these lines, saying it was offensive to Hindu beliefs as they believe in idol worship. Wishing that only the name of the Islamic god prevails meant wishing for the destruction of Hinduism, they argued.

The liberal reaction, and even my initial reaction, to such objections was to laugh it off as 'illiterate' reactions, where the meaning and context of the nazm was lost on angry minds. Hindus were nowhere on the mind of Faiz when he penned it. The lines refer to the time when Islam prevailed under the leadership of Prophet Mohammad in Arabia and the pagan idols were removed from Kaaba, the holiest site of Islam. The lines were thus metaphors for injustice being removed, and justice prevailing in the country.

However, the outraged people had a point. At the end of the day, the literal meaning of the poem, at least of those lines, was about the supremacy of Islam over pagan religions. The primacy of Islam was being equated with a revolution as far as the literal meaning of the poem was concerned, and someone celebrating and singing the poem could indeed be singing it for that very reason.

And well, this guy named Sharjeel Imam, who was later arrested for his role in inciting the crowds to riot in the name of protesting against the CAA, had written an article in 2017 itself, claiming that Faiz was a not an atheist and that 'Hum Dekhenge' was a poem that was inspired from the Quran. Incidentally, the article was published by a website that was run and edited by Teesta Setalvad and her husband.

The article by Imam at one place says:

> Faiz famously taught Quran and Hadees to the prisoners in the Hyderabad jail. Faiz himself mentions that a colonel explicitly asked him why he was teaching [the] Quran when he was an atheist. When Faiz clarifies that he is a Muslim, the colonel starts appreciating his Quranic lessons. His support for the Palestinian cause, his praise for the Iranian students who were bleeding for an Islamic revolution, and his ode to Prophet Muhammad, which is his only Persian poem, his grand elegy for Hussain: all stand witness to the centrality of Islamic thought in Faiz's poetry and his revolutionary spirit.[129]

So you see, 'educated Muslims' like Imam, who attracted unqualified support from the liberal crowd, were dreaming of an Islamic revolution and drawing inspiration about the supremacy of Islam from Faiz's nazm, while the liberals were arguing with some 'illiterate Hindus' that the nazm was not about the prevalence of Islam but about the prevalence of justice and equality.

Further, it was clear that the literal meaning of the nazm was indeed about Islam prevailing over pagan religions in Arabia, though the figurative meaning as widely acknowledged was different. If liberals don't like literal interpretations—and they indeed are bad—then they should have also mocked those Muslims as 'illiterate' who opposed Vande Mataram.

Some Muslims oppose Vande Mataram because it literally means worshipping the motherland. They say they can't worship anyone but Allah, so Vande Mataram shouldn't be played in common gatherings. The liberals turn very understanding to see that point of view. They never mocked these Muslims and asked them not to go with the literal meaning but understand the context and the history of the song, which was used by many freedom fighters, including Congress leaders, to oppose the British. Why is such preaching reserved for Hindus only?

Almost every aspect of the anti-CAA protests was full of such double standards, as the liberals joined a movement that was triggered by an out and out Islamist mindset. In their minds, the liberals were saving the Constitution and humanity, while in reality they were siding with a mindset that later rioted in Delhi and had earlier destroyed a Hanuman temple in Bihar.

Even after the protestors bared their fangs and shouted slogans like 'Jamia se rishta kya, La ilahi illal-lah' (What's our relationship with Jamia? There's no god but Allah.) that were modelled on slogans used by Kashmiri separatists (just replace Jamia with Pakistan), the liberals couldn't see what they were supporting. A few like Shashi Tharoor indulged in monkey-balancing, saying that such slogans were not helpful, but he was asked to shut up. He obliged.

For me, the anti-CAA protests were the tipping point where I snapped even personal friendships with some people who supported it. Championed by Jinnah-loving folks, it was nothing but a living proof of how the two-nation theory was alive and kicking in the streets of India. Ironically, it received support from the liberals who thought they were opposing the two-nation theory.

The protests couldn't be seen independent of the narrative around it, as well as the events that preceded it. There are eerie similarities to what had happened before the Partition of India.

'Khilafat 2.0' posters and slogans were seen during protests earlier at the AMU—the same Khilafat, which sees Muslims around the world as being part of one nation, and which received support from Mahatma Gandhi in the hope of Hindu–Muslim unity, only to see the birth of the Pakistan movement.

The original Khilafat movement had started in 1919 and lasted around 1924, while Khilafat 2.0 had started getting support from the liberals 2.0 in 2019, and the Modi 2.0 term is slated to be until 2024. What next? Pakistan 2.0 movement? I won't be surprised at all.

Another incident that reminded me of the times before Partition was the murder of Kamlesh Tiwari, a local Hindu leader based in Lucknow. He was killed by Islamists in October 2019 as 'punishment' for blasphemy. In 2015, Tiwari had allegedly called Prophet Mohammad a homosexual, which was in reaction to SP leader Azam Khan terming every Hindutva leader a homosexual.[130]

In the coming months, thousands of Muslims had protested in different parts of the country, asking for Tiwari to be given capital punishment for blasphemy, even though Indian laws have no such provision. Slogans to punish him were raised even in the state assembly of Uttar Pradesh, after which he was arrested and sent to jail. Islamists felt that such a punishment was not adequate, and finally they killed him.

This incident bore similarity to the killing of Mahashe Rajpal, a book publisher who had published a book named *Rangila Rasul* in 1924. The book, which was deemed blasphemous by Muslims, was also supposed to have been published as 'revenge', just like Tiwari had used the 'homosexual insult' as revenge. *Rangila Rasul* is believed to be have been published in retaliation to a pamphlet containing offensive comments against Hindu goddesses. Rajpal was killed in 1929 by a person named Ilm-ud-din, who felt that punishment given to Rajpal as per the laws existing in British India was not adequate.

Both the incidents involve a supposedly blasphemous act against the Prophet of Islam by individuals who acted in retaliation to avenge some offensive comments, and in both the cases, the individuals were murdered years after their original act, because the laws of the land failed to punish them in line with the demands of some radical Muslims.

Ilm-ud-din is today lionized and glorified in Pakistan for his act of murdering Rajpal. Even back then, in British India, after he was executed following the death penalty awarded to him for committing a murder, he was eulogized by Allama Iqbal and Mohammad Ali Jinnah.

The liberals maintained a stoic silence over the murder of Kamlesh Tiwari. Fine that he was no 'intellectual' like their Govind Pansare or M.M. Kalburgi, but the liberals had spoken out even for criminals like Sohrabuddin. Why did this extrajudicial killing, the demand for which was supported even by MLAs in a state assembly, not found worthy of their concern? Couldn't they see how radical Islamism was a clear and present danger?

The reason was the same, because the liberals have just been repeating themselves after 23 May 2019. Earlier during Modi 1.0, they didn't bother to condemn the murders of RSS workers—in fact, some of them gave 'political context' to the murders, while T.M. Krishna, a Carnatic vocalist, admitted that 'we are unable to empathize when an RSS member is killed'[131]—so it was futile to expect that any of them could have condemned the murder of Tiwari.

Liberals have been repeating themselves and reinforcing their prejudice against Hindus and Hinduism. When Hindus won the case for the Ram Temple at Ayodhya in November 2019, the entire secular-liberal ecosystem was busy shaming the Hindus. They repeated the lies about no temple originally existing at the place, despite historical and archaeological evidences to the contrary, which were earlier highlighted by the former ASI (Archaeological Survey of India) official and archaeologist K.K. Muhammed.[132] They shamed the Hindus for getting back a piece of land that rightfully belonged to them.

The same was later done on 5 August 2020, when the bhoomi pujan for the Ram Temple was performed at Ayodhya. The temple was painted as a 'symbol of hatred' as it was being built after demolishing a mosque. They vowed never to visit this temple, as if otherwise they visit temples every other day.

Even if one agrees, for argument's sake, that no temple originally existed at the site, and the new Ram Temple at Ayodhya would effectively be a temple built after demolishing a mosque, and thus qualifying to be a symbol of hate, why didn't the liberals term the mosques at Kashi and Mathura—that were clearly built after demolishing temples—as symbols of hate? Those excrescences and excesses heaped upon the Hindu faith are rather celebrated as 'syncretic culture' by the same lot.

More than half of 2020 has passed, and as I move towards writing the last chapter of this book, the Congress and the associated ecosystem are trying to attack the Yogi Adityanath government of Uttar Pradesh over the issue of 'injustice to Brahmins.' They are cherry-picking data showing Brahmins being killed, including those with criminal history who were killed in police encounters, after Yogi became the chief minister. This is the classic mistake that I had talked about earlier—the ecosystem promoting caste politics in the hope that it will checkmate Hindutva politics, which I believe boomeranged.

While in the short term, it may help in a few elections—and we will soon know what happens in the 2022 Uttar Pradesh assembly elections, where I feel this 'Brahmin card' by the opposition will not really work—in the long term, it's only going to strengthen the Hindu identity. At least the last time they had picked an identity that could have been painted as non-Brahmin (the OBC identity) and finally non-Hindu, and this time they are trying to play up the Brahmin identity itself. What could go wrong?

But as Napoleon Bonaparte had said, 'Never interrupt your enemy when he is making a mistake.' Perhaps, that is why Modi rarely bothers to react or respond to various outrages and narratives that are being pushed by the liberals. In fact, half of his poll campaign seems to be carried out by his haters!

And the way the liberals have been behaving under Modi 2.0 until now (August 2020), the BJP may even win more than 350 Lok Sabha seats in 2024, if the election is fought only on ideological issues and Rahul Gandhi continues to extend support to liberal activism just to win some brownie points.

Yes. I mean it.

While I might sound supremely confident about more and more Indians thinking themselves as Sanghis who never went to any shakha, and the BJP reaping electoral benefits due to it, I have a rather conservative (pun intended) view to it.

A big chunk of my apparent confidence is based on—and it should be pretty obvious by now—the way leftists and the liberals behave, and the way they don't appear to be ready to re-assess their own beliefs and actions. They have increasingly been contradicting their own principles, and they appear more ready to 'correct' the principles—by turning woke—than correcting the contradictions.

Such conduct reveals them as intolerant folks with a bunch of inconsistent ideas, thus making their ideology less and less appealing to people who otherwise might not have any issues with general principles of liberalism.

This is something the non-Left should also be wary of. It is not really a winning strategy of the Left that should be copied, even though in general I support employing Left's own designs and tools to fight them. Fortunately, the non-Left broadly has shown more willingness to learn and change. Even the RSS, for example, has re-assessed its position on issues such as homosexuality or capitalism.

However, when you associate yourself with a 'conservative' ideology, by definition itself you are supposed to be resistant to change. You are supposed to protect and uphold some values and institutions, and resist attempts to weaken or distort them. That is also one of the reasons why conservative ideologies may not appeal to a young person, for the young by nature are rebellious and want to change things.

Now, that is where the paradox lies in our current times. The conservative-liberal framework has become inverted over time. It is actually the liberals who are resisting change and fighting to maintain the status quo—fighting to uphold 'woke' values, fighting to keep control on institutions (on the media, academia, judiciary), fighting to uphold censorship and gatekeeping of information and narrative, fighting to uphold what they see as liberalism and 'cancelling' even classical liberals. They have been resisting every attempt to bring change by branding every contrarian opinion or person as 'fascist'.

And perhaps that is also one of the reasons why the supposedly conservative ideologies are winning not only adherents but even elections. Not only are the liberals fighting to conserve their bastions—which at one point of time conservatives used to do—even their respective constituencies seem to have been swapped.

The liberals, often carrying leftist ideas and beliefs, were at one point of time supposedly championing causes that appealed to a large section of the common masses—be it poverty reduction, women's rights, equality or justice, and many such values where conservatives had appeared to fail. The average man in the street, surely the average poor woman from a marginalized social group in the street, saw merits in those ideas. The leftists anyway claimed to speak for the proletariat, the working class.

Today, the liberals are most of the time championing causes that frankly make no sense to the working or the poor class, or rather to the 'unwashed masses'. Even if it may make a bit of sense to some of them, those causes don't directly impact them. In fact, on many occasions, the causes are in conflict with their observed and acquired wisdom.

For example, how does championing ideas like 'Gender is a social construct' going to impress a teenager in places like Darbhanga and Deoria? When a man with a bushy moustache and braided hair wears a bra and applies lipstick while holding a placard that reads 'F**k Hindutva', I am not really sure an Amit or even an Abdul from Alwar would get inspired to fight Hindutva. Not yet.

Similarly, take for example the Dalit-Muslim unity politics. Unlike gender politics that may not make sense or be a priority for the unwashed masses, this, on paper at least, appears to be a potent idea that should appeal to the proletariat. But the observed and acquired experiences of most of the Dalits living next to a Muslim area is quite different—where they are victims of aggression and oppression by the Muslims—thus it remains a good idea only on paper and only in a few media houses, which could invent or spin certain events to push the Jai-Bhim-Jai-Meem propaganda.

As of today, these factors are working in favour of conservativism, and for so-called Hindutva politics. Hindutva groups have shown more pragmatism in their approach and have not tried to ignore the ground realities to push an idea that makes sense only on paper. The primary example is of the conflicting caste identities, where Hindutva groups have tried to find solutions keeping these realities in mind, even though ideally they would want a common Hindu identity beyond castes.

Another matter where the liberals of today are going totally in the opposite direction of their assumed beliefs and principles, is the subject of free speech. The modern liberals, rather the wokes, are increasingly in favour of putting restrictions on free speech. They have come up with excuses creating 'safe spaces', where a person's speech can be curbed because someone else claiming to be less privileged 'felt' threatened by that speech.

It doesn't matter if the speech itself had any direct call for violence that could threaten or make someone feel unsafe, but if a supposedly 'marginalized' and 'less privileged' person is 'feeling unsafe', the speech must be curbed and punished so that a 'safe space' is secured. This actually is the latest stand on free speech by the liberals.

In old days, 'safe spaces' meant spaces where people could speak whatever they want without feeling scared that they could be punished for it. Those safe spaces, often being universities and academic institutions, were supposed to allow all kinds of speech, including offensive and counterfactual, so that new ideas could germinate and bad ideas could be successfully countered.

Essentially, safe spaces meant spaces that were safe for the speakers, now safe spaces mean spaces that are safe for the listeners. Yet another inversion.

This inversion of the conservative-liberal context and the swapping of respective constituencies have made the Hindutva ideology appealing too, though not to everyone. Hindutva or the non-Left crowd is still very poor with ideas when it comes to impressing a section of the young urban crowd, and thus many of them do not find Hindutva to be appealing enough despite the aforesaid inversion.

This crowd has a totally different frame of reference due to the way our education system, and virtually every other system, is designed. They lack some of the most basic information that could help them appreciate some of the points being made by the Hindutva camp. They need to know how Hindutva is trying to change the status quo and fighting the real establishment (the secular-liberal ecosystem). They need to realize how their sweet-talking artist-activist could be more intolerant and vindictive than that impractical dull-witted man who stopped a Valentine's Day celebration on their college campus.

And coming back to where I started, the Hindutva camp will do good by not becoming intolerant like the 'wokes' and copy their 'cancel culture'. They should also make sure that they don't become the caricature of what the Left projects them to be—inherently supremacist and violent with no regard for personal liberty.

Unfortunately, I too, owing to my short temper, have made some mistakes, especially on Twitter, and I realize that it was wrong. My Twitter persona is aggressive and I'd continue to be aggressive towards the Hinduphobic elements and constituents of the real establishment, with whom I've absolutely no interest in having a conversation, but it is important not to shut doors or windows of communication with others.

Let there be no one who writes 'Memoirs of a Libtard Who Never Went to JNU.'

A short note on the RSS

Since I have self-identified myself as a 'Sanghi' and even titled this book as such, I thought I should specifically clarify that I hold no brief for the RSS, and my views or commentary in this book may or may not match with the worldview of an average RSS swayamsevak (volunteer) or ideologue.

Even though I had put this disclaimer in the beginning of the book itself, let me expound it a little more and also share my views on the RSS.

First of all, I am yet (till the point of finishing this book in August 2020) to attend any shakha even though I've been vocal about my ideological beliefs for a few years now. I still have no idea about the daily or even weekly activities an RSS member undertakes inside or outside a shakha.

Yes, I've been to a couple of gatherings of RSS members and sympathizers to understand the RSS and their beliefs, and to be honest, I can't say that I agree with all of them. And surely, even the RSS doesn't expect everyone to agree with them on everything.

From my limited interactions, I have come to the conclusion that the RSS is not 'Sanghi' enough! Obviously, I am using the term 'Sanghi' as understood or imagined by people in the popular narrative—both by those who like the term as well as those who hate it.

The aggression and belligerence that one may imagine or desire in a Sanghi was hardly there in any senior RSS member whom I met. Most of them preferred an unhurried and persuasive approach towards problem-solving.

I could be wrong in my assessment, but I don't think the RSS believes in bringing 'radical' changes, either in the society or polity. They want things to change at their own pace, without disturbing too many things or people.

If someone brands the RSS as a group of Hindu 'radicals', that will be as inaccurate as it can get. Unfortunately, that's how the RSS is often branded. I actually know a couple of former RSS members who left the organization in frustration, as they found the RSS to be just 'too soft' and slow to their liking.

It's true that there are organizations like the VHP or the Bajrang Dal—they have members who could also be RSS members, but they are not technically 'RSS-affiliated' organizations—which are aggressive in comparison, but the RSS in itself talks about 'vyakti nirmaan' (development of an individual's character) and 'samajik samrasta' (social harmony, which includes all Indians). It doesn't really talk exclusively about the Hindu society as such.

And this is where the Sangh often comes under attack by those Sanghis who have never been to any shakha. Not that I agree with all such criticism, but one of the most common criticisms of the Sangh, especially of its leadership, is that it has got its priorities all wrong, and can't see the existentialist threats the Hindu society faces. When an RSS member is killed in Kerala or Bengal, such Sanghis get angry and start attacking the leadership for not doing enough to protect their own.

The statements and thoughts that tend to include everyone born in India, regardless of his religion, as a Hindu—and such statements have come from no less than the RSS chief himself on occasion—are cited as proof of ideological confusion within the RSS, which makes it blind to the existentialist threats.

For example, during his 2019 Dussehra address, RSS Chief Mohan Bhagwat said, 'Those who belong to Bharat, those who are descendants of Bharatiya ancestors, those who are working for the ultimate glory of [the] nation & joining hands in enhancing peace, respecting and welcoming all diversities; all those Bharatiyas are Hindus.'[133]

Ironically, such statements should have impressed me in my pre-2012 days, but then I thought that being branded a Sanghi is similar to 'character assassination'. I am a pragmatist and not an idealist, so I don't really know what purpose it serves by having such an inclusive and conciliatory approach when no one is really willing to trust or embrace you.

Under no stretch of imagination could everyone born or living in India be seen as a Hindu, even culturally. I personally would categorize

Indians in five broad different categories, based on their approach towards Hindutva, that is, Hinduness. These are:

Hostile: Those who are hostile towards it and openly talk about annihilating Hindutva or Hinduism—they are honest enough to not create a fake distinction between the two terms—such as the Periyarites, neo-Ambedkarites, Islamists or Evangelists. They simply want to eradicate this identity. They see Hinduism either as oppressive or a fundamentally inferior idea, and thus worthy of being eliminated.

Condescending: Those who are prejudiced against Hindutva or Hinduism, but are willing to 'tolerate' this identity for various reasons. Most of the so-called liberals fall in this category, who would tolerate Hinduism only when it's deracinated to their heart's content. For instance, when all Hindu festivals are either heavily regulated or secularized, such as Onam—which is 'a festival of harvest and has nothing to do with Hinduism'.

Indifferent: Those who are indifferent towards Hindutva or Hinduism, primarily because they are not aware of the challenges or they are just too busy or motivated by mundane things in life—mostly the 'Congressi Hindus', whom I have mentioned earlier in the book. Their thinking is influenced more by the above two groups than the below two groups. Many non-Hindus can also fall in this category.

Supportive: Those who are conscious of their Hindu identity and also support the Hindu causes. They may or may not be vocal, but they are definitely not indifferent. Many self-identifying Sanghis—not the actual Sanghis—fall in this or the next category. Statements such as those by the RSS chief that I pointed to earlier suggest many non-Hindus fall in this category too, which I hope is true, but I'm not really sure.

Assertive: Those who are not only conscious of the identity, but are willing to take that extra step, including some risks, to celebrate, propagate and defend this identity. However, it's a not a homogenous group. How they defend it, and what exactly they aim to propagate and defend may vary from one sub-group to another.

In my opinion, the RSS should provide clarity and leadership to the last two groups (*Supportive* and *Assertive*) and try to convert the middle group (*Indifferent*). One may have a conversation with the second group (*Condescending*), but on its own terms (i.e., on the *Assertive* group's terms), and defeat the first one (*Hostile*) without any attempt at reconciliation.

I personally am almost paranoid about the future of Hindus. I think that the *Hostile* and *Condescending* groups together account for at least 30% of the Indian population; this can turn into a tipping point quite soon. Furthermore, as I have mentioned at one place in this book, I see eerie similarities between what's happening now and what had happened in the few decades leading to the Partition of India. I see history repeating itself unless Hindus wake up.

Further, Hinduphobia has been normalized and intellectualized to frightening levels, where a Hindu talking about any injustice against him is branded a bigot. Anything that celebrates or propagates Hinduism will increasingly be argued as being detrimental to creating 'safe spaces'. This has already started happening both in India and abroad, aided with the rhetoric around 'Brahminism'.

I feel that Hindus are nicely being fed and fattened for the ceremonial slaughter—that's how paranoid I am right now. Any attempt to wake them up and show them the civilizational dangers is ironically termed as 'attempts to distract from the real issues'.

My paranoia may or may not be justified, but owing to that, I feel that Hindus need community leadership that can lucidly and logically explain the threats the community faces. It should be done quickly, before more people turn paranoid like me. I am not really happy being this way!

And I feel that the RSS is best placed to provide such a leadership to the community, owing to its size and legacy. But, the organization itself wants to continue being a 'nationalist' outfit, focused on character-building, rather than a Hindu outfit focused on community-building. That's where I am not too happy.

Actually what I'm suggesting is not at all different from what Dr. Keshav Baliram Hedgewar, the founder of RSS, had said. The following quote of Dr Hedgewar is mentioned as the vision and mission of the RSS on their own website:

The Hindu culture is the life-breath of Hindusthan. It is therefore clear that if Hindusthan is to be protected, we should first nourish the Hindu culture. If the Hindu culture perishes in Hindusthan itself, and if the Hindu society ceases to exist, it will hardly be appropriate to refer to the mere geographical entity that remains as Hindusthan. Mere geographical lumps do not make a nation. The entire society should be in such a vigilant and organized condition that no one would dare to cast an evil eye on any of our points of honour. Strength, it should be remembered, comes only through organization. It is therefore the duty of every Hindu to do his best to consolidate the Hindu society.[134]

Then, has the RSS lost its way or self-declared Sanghis like me can't see how the organization is still on track and following their founder's vision? I need answers there.

Another thing that I find a little strange about the RSS is the way it approaches the problem of perception. They don't seem to have a media strategy due to which they almost 'allowed' the media to distort their image. For the most part, I think they didn't lose too much of sleep over how they were perceived, and instead chose to focus on the groundwork, which is not a bad strategy in itself. Hard work pays at some point of time.

However, on the other hand, they also appear too bothered about not coming across as too exclusivist or aggressive. They shy away from criticizing Islam, for example. They try their best to 'take everyone along' when everyone else appears to wish the worst for them. There is an element of inconsistency here, I feel.

Another usual criticism thrown at the RSS is that it has not valued attempts to create intellectuals and institutions, and that it has failed to take along thinkers like Sita Ram Goel and others in its fold. In fact, it is often accused that the RSS has internalized anti-intellectualism.

The RSS is not really new to such criticism, and it's not just the 'neo Sanghis' from whom they receive such criticism. Even authors like Sita Ram Goel have criticized the RSS on similar lines. On occasion, he had been pretty unsparing, to the extent of saying that the Hindu society is doomed unless the RSS–BJP movement perishes.

While I could have a few concerns about the way RSS functions or the way they look at developments, I am certain that the organization's existence and success is very critical for every Hindu, no matter how they are defined. Despite having deep respect for Sita Ram Goel, whose almost every book I recommend as suggested reading, I don't really think that the Hindu society can progress if the RSS perishes. Perhaps, there is no time left to create a new organization that can take up this mission.

The RSS is one of the oldest organizations in India and also selfless in many ways. It is an organization that has constantly tried to learn and adapt to changing times. And it is pretty resilient. Hardly any organization can survive after constant vilification and attacks, which include murderous physical attacks. The RSS has been banned thrice in the history of Independent India, but the respective governments had to lift the ban as they couldn't find any concrete evidence or reasons to keep the ban in place. It only shows the strength of character and strong will that it possesses. Instead of wishing that such an organization perishes, perhaps the better approach would be to collaborate with it, or even 'capture' it!

Funnily, in reality the RSS appears to be very different from the way its haters imagine it to be or the way its supporters, especially like me, desire it to be. This is not an enviable position to be in, and is in fact a double-edged sword. The advantage is that it signifies that the liberals have been fighting an RSS that doesn't really exist, so they will continue to lose because they are fighting a shadow of the RSS that has been created by their own illuminated illusions.

However, the disadvantage is that there are hordes of 'neo Sanghis', who want to associate themselves with the RSS and strengthen it, but they fail to do so, as they find the organization to be very different from the way they would want it to be. They could get disillusioned and disheartened as a result.

Hopefully, the Sangh and the Sanghis will get to understand each other better in the future. It is crucial for the continued existence of both.

Acknowledgements

Finally! Writing a book has been a long-pending desire, and I can't put in words how elated I was when I concluded the last chapter. I don't know how it will be received by the readers, but that's not something on my mind right now. As Lord Krishna said in the Bhagawad Gita—'We don't have control or rights over outcomes, but only over our actions.' And right now, I feel good, in fact, awesome, to have acted and have finally completed this book, my first book.

I had zeroed upon this idea of penning down my ideological journey back in August 2018. The aim was to share my thoughts, my observations, my feelings, because I had 'changed' a lot in the previous 3–4 years. Many of my old acquaintances would ask me what brought about this change. Barkha Dutt, the celebrity journalist (she used to follow me on Twitter as *Faking News*), once tweeted to me, rather unapprovingly, saying 'You used to be funny', that is, I used to be someone else but I had changed.

I indeed had. And there was a story behind this change. However, I was not a celebrity like Barkha, so there was no point in writing just about myself; hence, I decided to write about this 'change'—the change that not just me, but many in India were going through. So, the first note of thanks and acknowledgement actually goes to all those 'liberals' who brought about this change in me.

But, much before the liberals gave me the idea and the reason to write this book, I had always wanted to write a book—something that I've recounted in this book, too. I was approached by a couple of people back in 2013, when *Faking News* was at its peak, to write a book. But thanks to a lack of discipline—and to be fair to myself, I also had a business to run, so there was a genuine lack of time—I could never come around to writing a book. Kanishka Gupta, a literary agent, kept pursuing me for long, saying I must write. Thank you Kanishka for not letting me forget that I should write a book.

I got back in touch with Kanishka once I had written half of what is now the first chapter of this book, and asked him if he thought any publisher would be interested in an idea like this. He approached a few publishing houses with the proposal and came back to me saying three had shown initial interest. One of those was Rupa Publications. I interacted with my editor from Rupa Publications and in a matter of few email exchanges, I decided to go with Rupa Publications and was no longer interested in what 'offer' other publishers may come up with.

A few others, too, had faith in me, and kept telling me that I must write. I want to thank two people from Twitter in particular, whom I have not met in person—Aditya Kuvalekar and Vaibhav Chandruva. Not only did they keep egging me, they also gave me valuable feedback when I sent them the draft of the first chapter.

While these two get the first mention, I sincerely thank everyone on Twitter who interacted with me and talked to me about my book, even if in jest or to tease/troll me when I was taking too long to finish. Even if they didn't talk to me about the book, the online conversations helped me understand the phenomenon I was writing on.

Interactions and discussions with Twitter friends (many of them are also real-life friends), such as Sandeep Kadian (Gappistan Radio on Twitter), Rajiv Jain (YearOfRat), CoolFunnyTshirt (sorry my friend, a little tired to recollect your original name), Ashish Chandorkar, Abhinav Prakash, Kushal Mehra, Harsh Gupta, Ashish Dhar, Swati Goel Sharma, Shefali Vaidya, Smita Barooah, Sharanya Shetty, Ullas, 'Spammy' and many others (hey guys, please don't unfollow me if I didn't mention your name. This is just an indicative list!), also helped me understand the factors that were common in bringing about this change.

There are others too. Hari Kiran, the founder of Indic Academy, who kept encouraging me to write, and now wants me to write more books. Madhu Kishwar, a quintessential 'liberal activist' who too changed and started seeing merits in many things (but not all) that Hindutva ideologues said. I had met her and talked with her for hours to understand her story and perspective. Nitin Gupta, a stand-up comedian and good friend, who would often call me up to discuss political and ideological issues, and in the process I would learn from his insights and sharp analysis.

I have to thank Team OpIndia for taking good care of the website, so that I could have the peace of mind outside my working hours to focus on the book. Nupur J. Sharma, you work really hard and I hope you too write a book someday, and Nirwa Mehta, yes, you could have been an awesome 'beta reader' of the book but I was in a hurry. I would also like to thank Ajeet Bharti and team, who kept the show running.

And finally, I have to thank my family, not because everyone does but because I really owe it to them. To my parents, for giving me a cultured upbringing and for exposing me to books early. To my in-laws, for being so caring and understanding, even though I am socially awkward and irresponsible at times. To my brother, for having helped me with so many things and making my life easy, to the extent of making me lazy. And to my wife and my little daughter, for being my bundle of happiness, for being my insurance against failures.

References

1   'Facebook's failure: Did fake news and polarized politics get Trump elected?' by Olivia Solon, The Guardian (10 November 2016); https://www.theguardian.com/technology/2016/nov/10/facebook-fake-news-election-conspiracy-theories

2   Past Election Results—Election Commission of India; https://eci.gov.in/past-elections-statistics/

3   'The truth about Tipu Sultan' by Vivek Gumaste, Rediff (14 November 2018); https://www.rediff.com/news/column/the-truth-about-tipu-sultan/20181114.htm

4   'How history was made up at Nalanda' by Arun Shourie, The Indian Express (28 June 2014); https://indianexpress.com/article/opinion/columns/how-history-was-made-up-at-nalanda/

5   'I felt reduced to a vagina: Swara Bhasker slams Sanjay Leela Bhansali's Padmaavat', India Today (28 January 2018); https://www.indiatoday.in/movies/celebrities/story/padmaavat-sanjay-leela-bhansali-swara-bhasker-1155805-2018-01-28

6   The concept of 'Moral Relativism' is often applied to argue that actions of many Islamic rulers were not barbaric or bigoted. It puts forth the view that there are no universal or absolute set of moral principles, and thus one should refrain from passing moral judgments; https://iep.utm.edu/moral-re/

7   Venkat Dhulipala, *Creating a New Medina*, Cambridge University Press, New Delhi, 2015, p. 87

8   'Walk The Talk with Sharad Pawar' by NDTV (22 November 2013); https://www.ndtv.com/video/shows/walk-the-talk/walk-the-talk-with-sharad-pawar-aired-august-2006-298887

9   'Why "Sufism" is not what it is made out to be' by Zahra Sabri, Herald (28 May 2018); https://herald.dawn.com/news/1398514/why-sufism-is-not-what-it-is-made-out-to-be

10 'Pariahs turn priests in temples' by Arun Kumar, The Times of India (8 July 2007); http://timesofindia.indiatimes.com/articleshow/2185567.cms

11 'Lawyer for Muslim parties in Ayodhya case tears up map of Lord Ram's birthplace in court', by PTI, ThePrint (16 October 2019); https://theprint.in/judiciary/lawyer-tears-lord-ram-birthplace-map-in-court/306637/

12 Santosh C. Saha (Ed.), *Fundamentalism in the Contemporary World: Critical*

Social and Political Issues, Lexington Books, Maryland, US, 2004, p. 273

13   Muḥammad ibn Aḥmad Bīrūnī, *Alberuni's India* (v. 1), Kegan Paul, Trench, Trübner & Co., London, UK, 1910, p. 22

14   'After Caravan article stamps 'caste' on martyr's coffins, CRPF says 'we identify ourselves as Indians', Times Now (22 February 2019); https://www. timesnownews.com/india/article/caravan-crpf-pulwama-terror-attack-moses-dhinakaran-mehbooba-mufti-asif-ghafoor-jammu-kashmir-india-pakistan/370887

15   'Customer buys Bhagwat Purana, Amazon seller also sends a book on why the Hindu scripture is "irrelevant" as a "special gift"', OpIndia (8 June 2020); https:// www.opindia.com/2020/06/amazon-e-commerce-hindus-bhagwat-purana-irrelevant-order-free-gift/

16   'Whistleblower says Cambridge Analytica "worked extensively" in India, names Congress as client', by Devika Bhattacharya, The Times of India (27 March 2018); http://timesofindia.indiatimes.com/articleshow/63491689.cms

17   Jawaharlal Nehru's address as Congress President (29 December 1929), *Congress Presidential Addresses, 1911–1934,* G.A. Natesan & Co., Madras, 1934, p. 884; http://cw.routledge.com/textbooks/9780415485432/42.asp

18   'In Nehru vs Patel-Prasad on Somnath, a context of Partition, nation building' by Uma Vishnu, The Indian Express (9 December 2017); https://indianexpress.com/ article/explained/somnath-temple-rahul-gandhi-babri-demolition-ram-rath-yatra-ram-mandir-ayodhya-verdict-hindutvain-nehru-sardar-patel-4971403/

19   'Soviets paid Congress, CPI, CPI-M members even in Rajiv Gandhi era: CIA' by PTI, The Economic Times (30 January 2017); https://economictimes.indiatimes. com/news/politics-and-nation/soviets-paid-congress-cpi-cpi-m-members-even-in-rajiv-gandhi-era-cia/articleshow/56874849.cms

20   'Holy men stir up riots in Delhi' (archive), by Inder Malhotra, The Guardian (8 November 1966) ; https://www.theguardian.com/world/2016/nov/08/india-holy-men-sacred-cows-riots-delhi

21   'Those Unshod Hooves' by Omair Ahmad, Outlook India (3 March 2008); https:// www.outlookindia.com/magazine/story/those-unshod-hooves/236859

22   'Cong workers used to loot poll booths for dad, me: Kirti Azad' by Piyush Tripathi, The Times of India (21 February 2019); http://timesofindia.indiatimes.com/ articleshow/68088223.cms

23   'Bihar makes mockery of election' by Tara Shankar Sahay, Rediff (16 February 1998); https://www.rediff.com/news/1998/feb/16bihar.htm

24   More about the rise and fall of Lalu Yadav can be read in books such as *The Brothers Bihari* by Sankarshan Thakur, Harper Collins, New Delhi, 2015

25   Private caste armies in Bihar, South Asia Terrorism Portal; https://www.satp. org/satporgtp/countries/india/terroristoutfits/Private_armies.htm

26   'Gujral and allies did not protest "Saraswati Vandana" when he was PM, says Joshi', Rediff (23 October 1998); https://www.rediff.com/news/1998/ oct/23hindu.htm

27   'How True Is The Wire's Claim That Sadhus Lynched In Palghar Were Tribals and
     Non-Hindus?' by Swati Goel Sharma, Swarajya magazine (24 April 2020); https://
     swarajyamag.com/politics/how-true-is-the-claim-that-sadhus-lynched-in-
     palghar-were-tribals-and-non-hindus
28   'Narendra Modi on Islamic Terrorism on The Big Fight after 9/11,' YouTube;
     https://www.youtube.com/watch?v=tRCqsK5u264
29   Professor R.P. Misra (Ed.), *Rediscovering Gandhi: Hind Swaraj*, Volume 1,
     Concept Publishing Company, New Delhi, 2007, p. 175
30   Karl Marx in New York Herald Tribune, 1854; https://www.marxists.org/archive/
     marx/works/1854/03/28.htm
31   'Shahbaz gives details of SIMI training camps' by Apurva, The Indian Express (30
     August 2008); http://archive.indianexpress.com/news/shahbaz-gives-details-
     of-simi-training-camps/355034/0
32   'Rajdeep says sorry for calling Parliament attack a "great day", but then, it WAS a
     great day for vultures' by Nupur J. Sharma, OpIndia (5 December 2018); https://
     www.opindia.com/2018/12/rajdeep-says-sorry-for-calling-parliament-attack-
     great-day-but-then-it-was-a-great-day-for-vultures/
33   'Doc's testimony nails lie in Naroda Patia fetus story,' The Times of India (18
     March 2010); http://timesofindia.indiatimes.com/articleshow/5696161.cms
34   'They wanted hope but got hype,' by Sanjay Pandey, The Times of India (17 April
     2002); http://timesofindia.indiatimes.com/articleshow/7106775.cms
35   Self-written account by reporter Damayantee Dhar recalling her ordeal,
     Facebook (11 January 2018); https://www.facebook.com/damayantee.dhar/
     posts/10214975886580344
36   'The full story from Hauz Qazi: A vandalised temple, a missing Hindu boy, and a
     community losing faith' by Nupur J. Sharma, OpIndia (3 July 2019); https://www.
     opindia.com/2019/07/ground-report-durga-mandir-vandalisation-communal-
     hindu-muslim-tension-hauz-qazi-chandni-chowk-17-year-old-missing-hindu-
     boy/
37   'Aligarh, Unnao, Kanpur violence was not communal, UP DGP busts lies about Jai
     Shri Ram attacks' by Kumar Abhishek, India Today (18 July 2019); https://www.
     indiatoday.in/india/story/aligarh-unnao-kanpur-violence-was-not-communal-
     up-dgp-busts-lies-about-jai-shri-ram-attacks-1570828-2019-07-18
38   'Junaid Khan lynching: Punjab and Haryana HC says dispute was over seat
     sharing, rules out communal angle,' DNA (17 April 2018); https://www.
     dnaindia.com/india/report-junaid-khan-lynching-punjab-and-haryana-hc-
     says-dispute-was-over-seat-sharing-rules-out-communl-angle-2605862
39   'A Woman Claimed She Did Not Get A House Because She Was A Muslim.
     Turned Out To Be A Lie!' by Kunal Anand, indiatimes.com (5 March 2016);
     https://www.indiatimes.com/news/india/this-woman-claimed-she-did-not-
     get-a-house-because-she-was-a-muslim-turned-out-to-be-a-lie-233078.html
40   'Don't want police probe: Muslim boy who was forced to say "Jai Mata Di",
     Hindustan Times (30 March 2016); https://www.hindustantimes.com/delhi/

don-t-want-police-probe-muslim-boy-who-was-forced-to-say-jai-mata-di/
story-HuB4EflZPBgQnZ8k2mmR6O.html

41   'I hate Hindus, wanted to spark communal tensions', by Munish Pandey,
     Mumbai Mirror (13 October 2016); https://mumbaimirror.indiatimes.
     com/mumbai/other/i-hate-hindus-wanted-to-spark-communal-tensions/
     articleshow/54822535.cms

42   'Wendy Doniger: Partition may have been averted had Gandhi been less
     reverential toward cows' by Amitava Kumar, scroll.in (20 November 2015);
     https://scroll.in/article/768559/wendy-doniger-partition-may-have-been-
     averted-had-gandhi-been-less-reverential-toward-cows

43   'Latif was state BJP's first whipping boy', The Times of India (12 June 2008);
     http://timesofindia.indiatimes.com/articleshow/3121443.cms

44   'Advani salutes "secular" Jinnah', by Radhika Ramaseshan, The Telegraph (4 June
     2005);   https://www.telegraphindia.com/india/advani-salutes-secular-jinnah/
     cid/873488

45   'Antulay raises doubts over Karkare's killing', by PTI, The Economic Times
     (17 December 2008); https://economictimes.indiatimes.com/antulay-raises-
     doubts-over-karkares-killing/articleshow/3852711.cms

46   'RSS & 26/11: Digvijaya flags it off again, this time in Mumbai', The Indian Express
     (28 December 2010); https://indianexpress.com/article/news-archive/web/rss-
     26-11-digvijaya-flags-it-off-again-this-time-in-mumbai/

47   'Reckless TV coverage of 26/11 operation put national security in jeopardy:
     Supreme Court', The Times of India (30 August 2012); http://timesofindia.
     indiatimes.com/articleshow/15969434.cms

48   'Live TV coverage put national security in jeopardy, says Bench', The Hindu (29
     August 2012); https://www.thehindu.com/news/national/live-tv-coverage-put-
     national-security-in-jeopardy-says-bench/article3836676.ece

49   Archived homepage of Chyetanya Kunte's blog that displays the apology as his
     latest post (1 February 2009); https://web.archive.org/web/20090201045757/
     http://ckunte.com/

50   'Cash-for-vote: BJP to boycott CNN-IBN', Hindustan Times (1 August 2008);
     https://www.hindustantimes.com/delhi/cash-for-vote-bjp-to-boycott-cnn-
     ibn/story-ATDw0h741lPPx190gQdA6K.html

51   Number of internet users by country, 1990 to 2016 (Our World in Data); https://
     ourworldindata.org/grapher/number-of-internet-users-by-country?tab=
     chart&country=~IND

52   'I'll be very unhappy if Commonwealth Games are successful: Aiyar', The Times of
     India (28 July 2010); http://timesofindia.indiatimes.com/articleshow/6224739.
     cms

53   '"Paid News": The Buried Report', by Paranjoy Guha Thakurta and K. Sreenivas
     Reddy, Outlook India (6 August 2010); https://www.outlookindia.com/website/
     story/paid-news-the-buried-report/266542

54   Archived version of 'TAPPED and TRAPPED' by J. Gopikrishnan, The Pioneer

(28 April 2010); https://web.archive.org/web/20100501084941/http://www.dailypioneer.com/252253/TAPPED-and-TRAPPED.html

55   'Who's Afraid of MediaCrooks' by Anand Ranganathan, Newslaundry (28 January 2013); https://www.newslaundry.com/2013/01/28/spanker-anonymous

56   'Tell me what should I tell them?', Open magazine (18 November 2010); https://openthemagazine.com/features/india/tell-me-what-should-i-tell-them/

57   'Pitched battle over "people's war" at JNU' by Manash Pratim Gohain, The Times of India (11 April 2010); https://timesofindia.indiatimes.com/india/Pitched-battle-over-peoples-war-at-JNU/articleshow/5783093.cms

58   'Kashmir riots over Qur'an "burning" leave 13 dead' by Maseeh Rahman, The Guardian (13 September 2010); https://www.theguardian.com/world/2010/sep/13/kashmir-protesters-killed-quran-row

59   'Team Anna removes Bharat Mata backdrop from Ramlila Maidan over alleged links with RSS' by IANS, India Today (21 August 2011); https://www.indiatoday.in/india/north/story/anna-hazare-rss-links-ramlila-maidan-139651-2011-08-21

60   'Swami Agnivesh web clips spark row', The New Indian Express (28 August 2011); https://www.newindianexpress.com/nation/2011/aug/28/swami-agnivesh-web-clips-spark-row-285464.html

61   Rajdeep Sardesai has confirmed the veracity of this video clip by repeating the same in his book 2014: The Election that Changed India, Penguin Books, New Delhi, 2014

62   'Minute by the Hon'ble T. B. Macaulay, dated the 2nd February 1835' (published on site maintained by Prof. Emerita Frances W. Pritchett, Columbia University) http://www.columbia.edu/itc/mealac/pritchett/00generallinks/macaulay/txt_minute_education_1835.html

63   H.Y. Sharada Prasad, Madhavan K. Palat, Ravinder Kumar and Sarvepalli Gopal (eds.), Selected Works of Jawaharlal Nehru, Second Series, Volume 24, Jawaharlal Nehru Memorial Fund, New Delhi, 1984, p. 283

64   'Justice Katju: Whatever his motives, Periyar helped the British' by Markandey Katju, The Week (18 September 2018); https://www.theweek.in/leisure/society/2018/09/18/justice-katju-whatever-his-motives-periyar-helped-british.html

65   'The brown man's counter-apartheid' by Chandra Bhan Prasad, Seminar magazine (February 2006); https://www.india-seminar.com/2006/558/558%20chandra%20bhan%20prasad.htm

66   'The British Empire is "something to be proud of"' by Will Dahlgreen, YouGov (26 July 2014); https://yougov.co.uk/topics/politics/articles-reports/2014/07/26/britain-proud-its-empire

67   'Remembering Babuji' by Sanjay Paswan, The Indian Express (9 July 2016); https://indianexpress.com/article/opinion/columns/babu-jagjivan-ram-dali-leader-babuji-2902184/

68   Sita Ram Goel, Hindus and Hinduism—Manipulations of Meanings, Voice of India, New Delhi, 1993, p. 18

69 'Tyranny of distance' by Rajdeep Sardesai, Hindustan Times (9 August, 2012); https://www.hindustantimes.com/columns/tyranny-of-distance/story-qEp6LlUm2CF0O82ROGE5WO.html

70 'Soldier memorial desecrated, police guns stolen, women cops molested, during Mumbai violence' by Rashmi Rajput, NDTV (13 August 2012); https://www.ndtv.com/cheat-sheet/soldier-memorial-desecrated-police-guns-stolen-women-cops-molested-during-mumbai-violence-496381

71 'Making history, not repeating it' by Javed Anand and Teesta Setalvad, The Indian Express (17 August 2012); http://archive.indianexpress.com/news/making-history-not-repeating-it/989242/0

72 'Bending over backwards' by Madhu Trehan, The Indian Express (22 August 2012); http://archive.indianexpress.com/news/bending-over-backwards/991200/0

73 'Prayers for Ajmal Kasab at mosque: Police launch probe', by PTI, The Times of India (31 December 2012); http://timesofindia.indiatimes.com/articleshow/17832691.cms

74 Number of internet users by country, 1990 to 2016 (Our World in Data); https://ourworldindata.org/grapher/number-of-internet-users-by-country?tab=chart&country=~IND

75 'Pro-Modi stand stops D'Cruz book release' by B. Kolappan, The Hindu (14 April 2014); https://www.thehindu.com/news/national/tamil-nadu/promodi-stand-stops-dcruz-book-release/article5909141.ece

76 'Chandan Gupta murder in Kasganj violence: Prime accused arrested, a day after Yogi Adityanath promised action', Financial Express (31 January 2018); https://www.financialexpress.com/india-news/chandan-gupta-murder-in-kasganj-violence-prime-accused-arrested-a-day-after-yogi-adityanath-promised-action/1037652/

77 'Hindu Leader Kamlesh Tiwari Killed Over Remark Against Prophet, 5 Arrested: Police', Outlook India (19 October 2019); https://www.outlookindia.com/website/story/india-news-hindu-leader-kamlesh-tiwari-killed-for-remark-against-prophet-3-arrested-police/340751

78 'Mika Singh slams Sonu Nigam for his Azaan remark, suggests him to change his house', India TV News (19 April 2017); https://www.indiatvnews.com/entertainment/bollywood-mika-singh-slams-sonu-nigam-for-his-azaan-remark-377713

79 'Uttar Pradesh: 2 boys beaten to death in communal clashes in Muzaffarnagar' by Preeti Panwar, OneIndia (6 September 2013); https://www.oneindia.com/india/two-boys-killed-in-communal-clashes-in-western-uttar-pradesh-1301009.html

80 'For the Nation's Sake—The Congress deserves to give itself a second chance' by A.M., The Telegraph (5 December 2013); https://web.archive.org/web/20131208142744/https://www.telegraphindia.com/1131205/jsp/opinion/story_17642341.jsp#.UqSCD577Q2w

81 'India crosses the moral line of no return if Narendra Modi becomes prime minister' by Thane Richard, Quartz (10 March 2014); https://qz.com/178362/

india-crosses-the-moral-line-of-no-return-if-narendra-modi-becomes-prime-minister/

82 'Shashi Tharoor says all fine after Sunanda's Twitter outburst' by Adam Plowright, LiveMint (16 January 2014); https://www.livemint.com/Politics/ DK3DkJPW59h4P6ej2xnttN/Angry-Sunanda-outs-Shashi-Tharoors-affair-on-Twitter.html

83 Rajdeep Sardesai, *2014: The Election That Changed India*, Penguin Books, New Delhi, 2014, p. 182

84 'Now, Arun Jaitley too endorses Modi as PM candidate after Advani' by PTI, Mumbai Mirror (26 April 2009); https://mumbaimirror.indiatimes.com/news/ india/now-arun-jaitley-too-endorses-modi-as-pm-candidate-after-advani/ articleshow/15920313.cms

85 'Shri Modi's exclusive interview with India TV' (uploaded on 21 April 2014); https://www.youtube.com/watch?v=PKl1-V0lm_0

86 'Interview with BJP leader Narendra Modi' by Ross Colvin and Sruthi Gottipati, Reuters (12 July 2013); http://blogs.reuters.com/india/2013/07/12/interview-with-bjp-leader-narendra-modi/

87 'Seventy years after Jogendra Nath Mandal decided to return from Pakistan over atrocities on Hindus, his prophecies have come true', OpIndia (15 August 2020); https://www.opindia.com/2020/08/pakistani-minister-jogendra-nath-mandal-prophecies-come-true-hindu-atrocities-letter/

88 'How Sushma Swaraj "Effectively" Intervened for Evacuation of Kerala Nurses from Islamic State Captivity' by PTI, News18 (7 August 2019); https://www. news18.com/news/india/how-sushma-swaraj-effectively-intervened-for-evacuation-of-kerala-nurses-from-islamic-state-captivity-2262067.html

89 'Over 103 Indian Arrested For Having Links With ISIS, UP Tops The List', Outlook India (27 December 2017); https://www.outlookindia.com/website/story/over-103-indian-arrested-for-having-links-with-isis-up-tops-the-list/306045

90 'Teesta Setalvad apologizes for controversial tweet on goddess Kali with ISIS terrorist', Daily Bhaskar (22 August 2014); https://daily.bhaskar.com/news/NAT-TOP-teesta-setalvad-apologizes-over-controversial-twitter-picture-4721115-NOR.html

91 'Ahmedabad: HC quashes two FIRs against activist Teesta Setalvad for tweet on Hindu goddess', The Indian Express (8 August 2019); https://indianexpress.com/ article/cities/ahmedabad/ahmedabad-hc-quashes-two-firs-against-activist-teesta-setalvad-for-tweet-on-hindu-goddess/

92 'The female police officer who has written an outrageously communal poem has to be sacked. This kind of mind set should not be tolerated.' Javed Akhtar's tweet, posted on 15 January 2013; https://twitter.com/Javedakhtarjadu/ status/291030480810303488

93 'The wrong song' by Mihir S. Sharma, Business Standard (10 May 2013); https://www.business-standard.com/article/opinion/the-wrong-song-113051000980_1.html

94 Ramachandra Guha's tweet, posted on 24 December 2014; https://twitter.com/Ram_Guha/status/547703136714899459

95 Rahul Roushan's tweet, posted on 19 December 2014; https://twitter.com/rahulroushan/status/545892101683048452

96 Such belief system has been termed as 'Postmodernist neo-Marxism' by the likes of Jordan Peterson, Canada-based academician and author; https://www.theepochtimes.com/jordan-peterson-explains-how-communism-came-under-the-guise-of-identity-politics_2259668.html

97 'Crying wolf: The narrative of the "Delhi church attacks" flies in the face of facts' by Rupa Subramanya, Firstpost (17 February 2015); https://www.firstpost.com/india/crying-wolf-the-narrative-of-the-delhi-church-attacks-flies-in-the-face-of-facts-2101105.html

98 'Delhi gang rapist interview: Court blocks Leslee Udwin film', BBC (3 March 2015); https://www.bbc.com/news/world-asia-india-31710244

99 'Two "Bangladeshi nationals" held, one in Mumbai, for West Bengal nun's rape', The Indian Express (27 March 2015); https://indianexpress.com/article/india/crime/bengal-nun-gangrape-first-arrest-made-by-cid-from-mumbai/

100 'Data vs Data—is India really "Lynchistan"?', OpIndia (2 July 2017); https://www.opindia.com/2017/07/data-vs-data-is-india-really-lynchistan/

101 'Junaid Khan lynching: Punjab and Haryana HC says dispute was over seat sharing, rules out communal angle', DNA (17 April 2018); https://www.dnaindia.com/india/report-junaid-khan-lynching-punjab-and-haryana-hc-says-dispute-was-over-seat-sharing-rules-out-communl-angle-2605862

102 'Bickering, mass fights for space on packed train took Junaid's life' by Paras Singh, The Times of India (4 July 2017); http://timesofindia.indiatimes.com/articleshow/59432987.cms

103 'IndiaSpend Pulls Down Its Hate Tracker; Swarajya Showed It Was Strongly Biased Against Hindu Victims' by Swati Goel Sharma, Swarajya magazine (13 September 2019); https://swarajyamag.com/ideas/indiaspend-pulls-down-its-hate-tracker-swarajya-showed-it-was-strongly-biased-against-hindu-victims

104 'There Was No 2G Scam. So Modi Has Little Over Manmohan Now' by Mihir Swarup Sharma, NDTV (21 December 2017); https://www.ndtv.com/opinion/there-was-no-2g-scam-so-modi-has-little-over-manmohan-now-1790602

105 'Congress goes for image makeover; to celebrate all religious festivals' by Vishal Kant, The Hindu (14 August 2014); https://www.thehindu.com/news/cities/Delhi/congress-goes-for-image-makeover-to-celebrate-all-religious-festivals/article6315441.ece

106 'Lynchistan: Hindus silent as a wave of violence against Muslims sweeps India' by Samar Halarnkar, Quartz (26 June 2017); https://qz.com/india/1014162/lynchistan-muslims-die-hindus-watch-in-silence-as-india-descends-into-primeval-bloodletting/

107 'Kathua Ground Report: Why Villagers Are Not Convinced On Fairness Of Probe' by Swati Goel Sharma and Arihant Pawariya, Swarajya magazine (27 April 2018);

https://swarajyamag.com/politics/kathua-ground-report-why-villagers-are-not-convinced-on-fairness-of-probe

108 'With Its Distrust, Alienation and Fear, Akhlaq's Village Provides Glimpse of "Hindu Rashtra"' by Arfa Khanum Sherwani, The Wire (9 April 2019); https://thewire.in/politics/bisada-dadri-akhlaq-hindu-rashtra

109 'Death of accused in Dadri lynching case triggers protests in his village; effigy's of Akhilesh burned' by PTI, Firstpost (6 October 2016); https://www.firstpost.com/india/death-of-accused-in-dadri-lynching-case-triggers-protests-in-his-village-effigys-of-akhilesh-burned-3036780.html

110 'Video of Rohith, ABVP leaders spat goes viral', Deccan Herald (20 January 2016); https://www.deccanherald.com/content/524051/video-rohith-abvp-leaders-spat.html

111 'Full text: Dalit scholar Rohith Vemula's suicide note', The Times of India (19 January 2016); http://timesofindia.indiatimes.com/articleshow/50634646.cms

112 'JNU event footage authentic, says report' by Shubhomoy Sikdar, The Hindu (11 June 2016); https://www.thehindu.com/news/cities/Delhi/JNU-event-footage-authentic-says-report/article14414770.ece

113 YouTube clip of Barkha Dutt interviewing an injured Kashmiri stone-pelter for NDTV; https://www.youtube.com/watch?v=6lzevdBRWAU

114 'I am proud to be "anti-national", says Rajdeep Sardesai', by Rajdeep Sardesai, Hindustan Times (20 February 2016); https://www.hindustantimes.com/columns/yes-i-too-am-anti-national-rajdeep-sardesai/story-OzLD58Idvt8Z7XbMxP5peI.html

115 'No more polls in future if Modi comes to power again: Kejriwal', The Hindu (25 March 2019); https://www.thehindu.com/news/cities/Delhi/no-more-polls-in-future-if-modi-comes-to-power-again-kejriwal/article26628373.ece

116 'Let us hope the darkness has passed' by Arundhati Roy, The Guardian (14 May 2004); https://www.theguardian.com/world/2004/may/14/india.comment

117 '1984 riots: US court issues summons to Sonia Gandhi for "shielding" Congress leaders' by PTI, The Indian Express (4 September 2013); http://archive.indianexpress.com/news/1984-riots-us-court-issues-summons-to-sonia-gandhi-for-shielding-congress-leaders/1164527/

118 '64 MPs urged Obama to keep visa ban for Modi' by Narayan Lakshman, The Hindu (23 July 2013); https://www.thehindu.com/news/national/64-mps-urged-obama-to-keep-visa-ban-for-modi/article4945209.ece

119 'Shekhar Gupta admits that journalists chose to ignore the positive effects of Modi government's welfare schemes', OpIndia (31 May 2019); https://www.opindia.com/2019/05/we-journalists-chose-to-ignore-the-positive-effects-of-modi-governments-welfare-schemes-admits-shekhar-gupta/

120 'False Cases Of Harassment In The Name Of "Jai Shri Ram" Multiply' by Sumanti Sen, The Logical Indian (29 July 2019) https://thelogicalindian.com/story-feed/awareness/jai-shri-ram-false-cases/

121 'Delhi riots: Police complaint against Wall Street Journal for spreading

"communal tension"' by IANS, The New Indian Express (29 February 2020); https://www.newindianexpress.com/cities/delhi/2020/feb/29/delhi-riots%E2%80%8B-police-complaint-against-wall-street-journal-for-spreading-communal-tension-2109987.html

122 'Students protesting fee hike behind campus violence, JNU admin tells HRD Ministry' by Sumi Sukanaya Dutta, The New Indian Express (7 January 2020); https://www.newindianexpress.com/cities/delhi/2020/jan/07/students-protesting-fee-hike-behind-campus-violence-jnu-admin-tells-hrd-ministry-2086160.html

123 'It's Time We Absolve Jinnah' by Sharjeel Imam, The Wire (7 May 2018); https://thewire.in/history/aligarh-muslim-university-jinnah-portrait

124 'Jamia "shero" hailed by Barkha Dutt celebrates Moplah massacre, when Muslims massacred thousands of Hindus in 1921 in the name of Islam', OpIndia (17 December 2019); https://www.opindia.com/2019/12/jamia-amu-protests-violent-radical-islamists-jihad-simi-kerala-moplah-massacre-hindus-citizenship/

125 '"This is fascism"—Flak for Bloomsbury on social media as it withdraws book on Delhi riots' by Soniya Agrawal, ThePrint (23 August 2020); https://theprint.in/india/this-is-fascism-flak-for-bloomsbury-on-social-media-as-it-withdraws-book-on-delhi-riots/487655/

126 'From Devi In Hijab, Om As Nazi Symbol To "Kaafiro Se Azadi": Recent Protests Show Hindutva-Hate Is Hindu-Hate' by Yaajnaseni, Swarajya magazine (8 January 2020); https://swarajyamag.com/news-brief/from-devi-in-hijab-om-as-nazi-symbol-to-kaafiro-se-azadi-recent-protests-show-hindutva-hate-is-hindu-hate

127 'India Today accused of sharing "Islamophobic" graphic on coronavirus and Tablighi Jamaat event', The Free Press Journal (4 April 2020); https://www.freepressjournal.in/india/india-today-deletes-islamophobic-graphic-on-coronavirus-and-tablighi-jamaat-event

128 '"Attacks Hindu Belief": IIT Kanpur Complainant On Faiz's "Hum Dekhenge"' by Mirza Arif Beg, Outlook India (2 January 2020); https://www.outlookindia.com/website/story/hum-dekhenge-faizs-poem-that-went-from-rallying-cry-against-caa-to-attack-on-hindu-belief/345029

129 'Faiz Ahmad Faiz and the de-Islamisation of a Muslim revolutionary' by Sharjeel Imam and Saquib Salim, Sabrang (4 February 2017); https://www.sabrangindia.in/article/faiz-ahmad-faiz-and-de-islamisation-muslim-revolutionary

130 'Here's why 1 lakh Muslims are demanding death penalty for Kamlesh Tiwari', DNA (12 December 2015); https://www.dnaindia.com/india/report-here-s-why-1-lakh-muslims-are-demanding-death-penalty-for-kamlesh-tiwari-2154898

131 'T M Krishna: The Musical Urban Naxal' by Sandeep Balakrishna, The Dharma Dispatch (3 October 2018); https://www.dharmadispatch.in/culture/t-m-krishna-the-musical-urban-naxal

132 'Ram temple existed before Babri mosque in Ayodhya: Archaeologist KK

Muhammed' by Kumar Shakti Shekhar, The Times of India (1 October 2019); http://timesofindia.indiatimes.com/articleshow/71391712.cms

133 RSS's tweet, posted on 8 October 2019; https://twitter.com/RSSorg/status/1181435661930450945

134 'Vision and Mission', Rashtriya Swayamsevak Sangh (22 October 2012); https://www.rss.org//Encyc/2012/10/22/rss-vision-and-mission.html

Index

India is in a deep churn as the masses render the classes irrelevant and a more rooted, more confident, more nationalist new India takes shape and form. To understand the churn that is happening, read this book.

—**Kanchan Gupta**, senior journalist and Distinguished Fellow, ORF (Observer Research Foundation)

I was born into a deeply traditional and religious household. So my worldview began from a different space, compared to those who were born into less religious households. And yet, many of those born in less religious households have rediscovered their ancient Hindu and Indian roots over the last few decades. I will not comment on the politics of this, but the social movement fascinates me. And there's nobody better to learn this from than Rahul Roushan, who speaks of this journey from his own personal experience. Rahul is a great communicator, but he also possesses deep perceptive intelligence, which he hides behind a wicked sense of humour.

Read this book, and get a microcosmic understanding of the massive social changes taking place in India over the last few decades.

—**Amish Tripathi**, bestselling author and Director, Nehru Centre, London

A book on politics and ideology is often expected to be dry and serious, but this one blends elements of storytelling and political commentary seamlessly. The topic is very interesting and quite relevant to our times, and definitely worth a read. I wish the best to Rahul for his debut book, and hope it is one among many to come.

—**Anupam Kher**, award-winning actor, author and motivational speaker

Why should anyone be interested in Pagal Patrakar's story? Because this is not faking news, but real, and the story of an entire generation that questions shibboleths such as socialism, secularism and liberalism (defined in a certain way), which were unquestioningly accepted as axiomatic.

It is this questioning that junked the former ecosystem and brought Narendra Modi and the BJP to power in 2014, and again in 2019. Though junked, the former empire still tries to strike back, and instead of disowning the winds of change, it would benefit from learning how and why Rahul Roushan became a Sanghi who has never been to a shakha.

The book is evocatively written and portrays India's metamorphosis beautifully, with the underbelly of the former ecosystem also thrown in.

—**Bibek Debroy**, author and Chairman, Prime Minister's Economic Advisory Council

Many of us have been perplexed by the narrative of India being created by certain interests after 2014. Suddenly, India has become intolerant, hyper-nationalist, communal, anti-minority and what not!

In this book, Rahul explores this narrative creation and exposes the forces behind such fake narratives. The book is an eye-opener for all of us on how some vested interests aligned with the ancient regime are trying to create social unrest to suit their need for power.

—**T.V. Mohandas Pai**, leading entrepreneur and investor

A wonderfully whimsical telling of how India's ideological Right emerged from obscurity to push aside the dominance of the Nehruvian Left, the Marxist Left, the Khan Market Left and every other kind of Left that dominated India's political economy for decades.

Part personal story and part eye-witness account, Rahul writes in a unique 'stream-of-consciousness' style that gives you the feeling of living the times. Many a newly minted 'Sanghis' will identify with this journey.

—**Sanjeev Sanyal**, bestselling author and economist

At long last a searing personal account that brings to life a journey many have travelled, or have been forced to, but not had the courage to share. Ruthless in its honesty, politically incorrect to its core, this is a book that has to be read by all Indians—young or old, haters or admirers, Left or Right, Sanghis or seculars. Roushan has written something that is unputdownable.

—**Anand Ranganathan**, political commentator, author and scientist

The first social media handle that had attracted my attention was that of Pagal Patrakar, that is, *Faking News*—for his understanding of politics. I can guarantee that most people missed the nuances of his narrative, but got a macro idea of where he was trying to lead them—a shakha. But this shakha wasn't what one would want to believe. This was the shakha of modern info-war.

The swayamsevaks were 'mad' social media activists. This was a modern war of identity, narrative and Bharat. And Rahul displayed enough pagalpan to be a successful patrakar in this info-war and battle of narrative building. In fact, I have learnt a lot from his political acumen during the many conversations and collaborations I had with him.

This is one of the most important books for the students of politics, media and modern narrative builders. But, above all, this is a very important book for the Left-wingers and Right-wingers to learn what Rahul could see and they couldn't.

This is not just the story of Rahul, it's the story of modern India and it is about you. Leave everything aside and read it now, for it will take you to a shakha where even shakha people need to go—to learn, and to get inspired.

—**Vivek Agnihotri**, author and filmmaker